PENGUIN BOOKS

# Coffee, Tea or Me?

Trudy Baker and Rachel Jones met, and became fast friends, while stewardesses for the now defunct Eastern Airlines. Although different in style and appearance–Rachel tall, blonde, and breezy; Trudy shorter, brunette, and more demure–they shared an appreciation of the humorous experiences and people they encountered on their flights. One day, a passenger with publishing connections, who'd found their stories funny, introduced them to a top New York editor, launching the saga of *Coffee, Tea or Me?* Trudy and Rachel appeared on myriad radio and TV shows across the country, their winsome personalities endearing them to millions of listeners and viewers.

Donald Bain is the ghostwriter or author of more than eighty books, including *Coffee, Tea or Me?,* and the bestselling *Murder, She Wrote* series of original murder mystery novels based upon the popular TV show. His writing career spans biographies, comedies, crime novels, historical romances, investigative journalism, and business books. He was recently designated 2003 Distinguished Alumni by his alma mater, Purdue University. (A more detailed look at his career can be found at donaldbain.com.)

D0110822

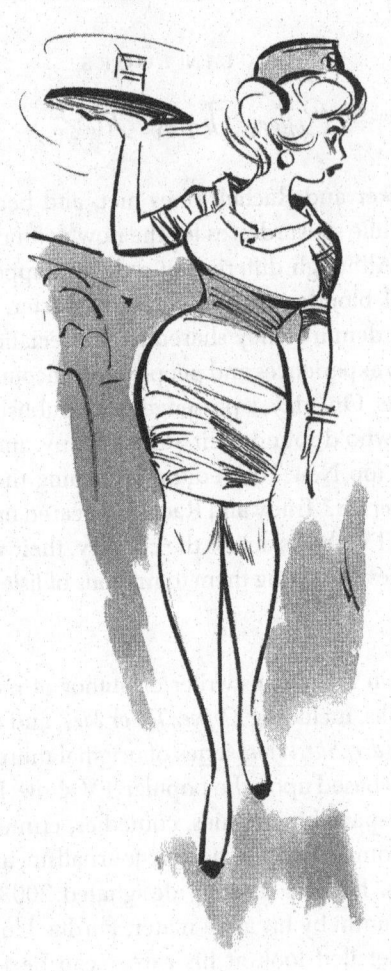

# COFFEE TEA or ME?

### The UNINHIBITED MEMOIRS of TWO AIRLINE STEWARDESSES

*Trudy Baker* and *Rachel Jones*

with Donald Bain

Illustrated by Bill Wenzel

Penguin Books

PENGUIN BOOKS

Published by the Penguin Group

Penguin Group (USA) Inc., 375 Hudson Street, New York, New York 10014, U.S.A.
Penguin Group (Canada), 90 Eglinton Avenue East, Suite 700, Toronto, Ontario,
Canada M4P 2Y3 (a division of Pearson Penguin Canada Inc.)
Penguin Books Ltd, 80 Strand, London WC2R 0RL, England
Penguin Ireland, 25 St Stephen's Green, Dublin 2, Ireland
(a division of Penguin Books Ltd)
Penguin Group (Australia), 250 Camberwell Road, Camberwell, Victoria 3124,
Australia (a division of Pearson Australia Group Pty Ltd)
Penguin Books India Pvt Ltd, 11 Community Centre, Panchsheel Park,
New Delhi – 110 017, India
Penguin Group (NZ), 67 Apollo Drive, Rosedale, North Shore 0632, New Zealand
(a division of Pearson New Zealand Ltd)
Penguin Books (South Africa) (Pty) Ltd, 24 Sturdee Avenue, Rosebank,
Johannesburg 2196, South Africa

Penguin Books Ltd, Registered Offices: 80 Strand, London WC2R 0RL, England

First published in the United States of America by Bartholomew House Ltd. 1967
Published by Bantam Book, a subsidiary of Grosset & Dunlap, Inc. 1968
Published with a new introduction in Penguin Books 2003

9  10

LIBRARY OF CONGRESS CATALOGING-IN-PUBLICATION DATA

Baker, Trudy.
Coffee, tea or me? : the uninhibited memoirs of two airline stewardesses /
Trudy Baker and Rachel Jones ; illustrated by Bill Wenzel.
p.  cm.
Originally published: New York : Bartholomew House, 1967.
ISBN 978-0-14-200351-0
1. Flight attendants—Biography.  2. Air travel.  I. Jones, Rachel.  II. Title.
HD6073.A43B34 2003
387.7'42'0922—dc2l    2003044462

PRINTED IN THE UNITED STATES OF AMERICA

# Contents

vi        *Coffee, Tea or Me?*

XVII    "Have a Merry Mistress" ........................ 203

XVIII    "The Saga of Sandy" ........................... 219

XIX    "What's a Nice Girl Like You Doing in a Plane
Like This?" ................................... 229

XX    "Should We Strike?" ........................... 259

XXI    "A Layover Is Not What You Think" ............. 271

XXII    "An Unhappy Landing" ........................ 279

XXIII    "We'll Give It One More Year, Okay?" ........... 293

# Acknowledgment

So many thanks to Don Bain, writer and friend, who's flown enough to know how funny it really can be. Without him, *Coffee, Tea or Me?* would still be nothing more than the punch line of an old airline joke.

# Introduction

$\mathcal{S}$o this stewardess enters the cockpit and asks the captain, "Coffee, tea or me?"

He displays his best leer and answers, "Whichever is easier to make."

Little did I know in 1967 that the book I was writing with a title lifted from a lame old joke would go on, along with its three sequels, to sell more than five million copies, be translated into a dozen languages, cause anxious mothers to forbid their daughters from becoming stewardesses, spawn airline protest groups, have its title inducted into the public vocabulary, and be republished thirty-six years later, branding me the world's oldest, tallest, bearded airline stewardess.

I've loved every minute of it.

Anyone reading *Coffee, Tea or Me?* today, who's flown recently on a commercial airline, will wonder whether air travel could ever have been as much fun—even glamorous—as depicted by Rachel and Trudy. I assure you it was. And like most people who traveled by air during the sixties and seventies, I miss those carefree, alluring days. Taking a flight was something special. You dressed up before boarding a plane and never had to worry about being stuck next to a seat companion wearing rubber thongs on bare feet, a sleeveless undershirt, and a baseball cap on backward. Back then, everyone was a jet-setter. Sinatra's "Come Fly with Me" was written for and sung especially to you. Smokers had their own section on the planes, and a cold, dry martini was de rigueur while cruising the skies. Although it became hip to criticize airline food, it was actually pretty good back then. (The jaded "gourmets" of the era who found fault with being served caviar, smoked salmon, Chateaubriand carved to order at seatside, and chocolate mousse while winging across the globe at 30,000 feet in an elongated aluminum cigar tube sadly missed the point.)

The early 747 jumbo jets had a pianist and singer in the upstairs lounge (Frank Sinatra Jr. headlined one of the inaugural flights). It was all first class no matter where you sat, baby, primo, top-notch, top-drawer, and topflight.

And, oh, those stewardesses. They were the crème de la crème of young womanhood, classy and cool, every hair in place, and with smiles as wide as a runway. The airlines set the bar high, and these lovely, bright, pleasant young women made sure they were up to the challenge on every flight—uniforms perfectly fitted and without a wrinkle, white gloves spotless, hats worn jauntily on their perfectly coiffed heads, confident as they strode through airports around the world, aware that admiring eyes were on them every minute and basking in the adoration. Dating an airline stewardess was like dating a nubile Hollywood starlet or lithesome runway model: "I'm dating a stewardess!" It was a credential men wore proudly, like driving a Ferrari or eating at "21."

And why not? These were special women, not only because they looked great, but because they were adventuresome, spending their working lives racing through the air high above where we mortals played out our mundane days, laying over in exotic places, bringing clothes back from Paris or Singapore to their small apartments at home base, conversing comfortably with on-board celebrities, and worldly-wise to every game any man has ever tried to play with a woman.

Today, they're called flight attendants, a change in nomenclature brought about by the influx of male cabin attendants. But back when I wrote *Coffee, Tea or Me?* they were stewardesses, and the airlines were quick to market their obvious appeal to the traveling public. They were known as "stews," and they lived together in "stew zoos." The hordes of men pursuing their affections were known as "stew-bums."

*Coffee, Tea or Me?* is about them, these objects of male adoration back when flying was fun—and yes, even glamorous.

# HOW THE BOOK CAME ABOUT

One day during a three-year stint with American Airlines as exec in charge of public relations for the three New York metro airports, I received a call from Ed Brown, an editor at Pocket Books, a division of Simon & Schuster. The first book in my writing career, *The Racing Flag,* a history of stock car racing, had been ghosted for Brown. He told me that Chet Huntley's producer (Remember *The Huntley-Brinkley Report* on NBC?) had introduced him to two former Eastern Airline stewardesses, who had funny stories to tell. Was I interested in working with them?

I met with the two young ladies at Toots Shor's watering hole in midtown Manhattan. They did have some funny stories, but hardly enough to sustain a book. I knew I'd have to use my own airline experiences—and imagination—to get the job done.

I wrote a proposal for an untitled memoir of two airline stewardesses, which sat with Brown for a month. Simultaneously, I'd found my first agent who pitched the project to Sam Post, then editor-in-chief at Bartholomew House, a hardcover start-up at MacFadden-Bartell, a large magazine publishing company. Post bought, and the project was taken away from Brown and Pocket Books.

The title *Coffee, Tea or Me?* came to me halfway through the writing of the book after hearing someone recite the old airline joke. Bingo! Boffo! How could it miss?

Well, it didn't miss. The hardcover was published to considerable fanfare on November 21, 1967. A savvy, fast-talking publicity pro, Anita Helen Brooks, was brought on board to hype it, and she booked my two former stewardesses, using the names I'd chosen for them, Rachel Jones and Trudy Baker, on dozens of radio and TV talk shows around the country and for myriad print interviews. The book took off like an SST and showed up on many bestseller lists, including the hallowed one at *The New York Times.* For the most part, reviews were good, some even calling the book "a comedy classic," and "a wickedly funny spoof of the airline industry and its stewardesses."

Alan Barnard of Bantam Books put up $75,000 for paperback rights, and Hollywood came a-calling. One after another, major film studios optioned the property, only to allow their options to lapse, which opened the door for the next option to be taken. (Eventually, CBS made a TV movie based loosely on the book, starring Karen Valentine and John Davidson. As bad a film as it was, it became one of the highest-rated made-for-TV movies in history.)

The most intriguing performing rights proposal came from Broadway legends Anita Loos and Julie Stein. They thought it would make a wonderful musical comedy and offered to option it for that purpose. But the Hollywood money up front was a lot bigger and too enticing to ignore. If I have any regrets about the intoxicating days of *Coffee, Tea or Me?* it was turning down the chance to see it emblazoned on a Broadway marquee. But it's never too late. It would still make a great retro-musical.

Bantam's paperback edition was even more successful; at one point there were more than 3 million copies in print. Aprons, coffee mugs, and hats with COFFEE, TEA OR ME? on them sold briskly in stores across America, and readers in a dozen foreign countries read the book in their native languages. We were flying high in the friendly skies.

Another publisher, Grosset & Dunlap, wanting in on the action, signed me to write three sequels: *The Coffee Tea or Me Girls' 'Round-the-World Diary,* published in 1969; *The Coffee Tea or Me Girls Lay It on the Line* in 1972; and *The Coffee Tea or Me Girls Get Away from It All* in 1974.

## ALL GOOD THINGS MUST COME TO AN END . . . OR MUST THEY?

Eventually, Rachel, Trudy, and I moved on with our separate lives. Since *Coffee, Tea or Me?* I've written another eighty-plus books, including my recently published autobiography, *Every Midget Has an Uncle Sam Costume: Writing for a Living,* in which I tell the entire story of *Coffee, Tea or Me?* along with other tales of the writing life.

*Coffee, Tea or Me?* became a pleasant memory, just as those sanguine days of air travel faded into today's decidedly less pleasant experience, marked by cramped seats, shoe bombers, long security lines, chaotic hubs, brown-bag meals (if you're lucky), and unfathomable fare structures.

The *Coffee, Tea or Me?* era was over.

Until . . . my agent of thirty-five years, Ted Chichak, received a call in late 2002 from Stephen Morrison, a bright young editor at Penguin. Was *Coffee, Tea or Me?* available for reissue? It was and it wasn't. Shortly before that call, I'd committed the book to publisher and longtime friend Lyle Stuart, who intended to bring out a new edition in 2003. Eventually, all parties concerned, including a magnanimous and gracious Stuart, decided that Penguin was the right house to publish a fresh edition of *Coffee, Tea or Me?*–the edition you're now reading. It's my hope that it will bring back fond memories of a gentler time in air travel, or introduce a new generation of air travelers to the way flying used to be. However, there was much stereotyping of certain groups in the sixties, and offensive language used to describe those sterotypes. The book reflects that era, warts and all, and reading it now makes us cringe. But it also makes us realize how far we've come in thirty-five years.

A final word to today's flight attendants, once known as stewardesses. Thanks for being on the front lines of air travel security, putting up with air rage, sloppily dressed passengers hauling steamer trunks aboard to put in the overhead bins, complainers, whiners, drunks, dunderheads who consider security measures a personal affront, and, most important, terrorists whose goal is to bring down the planes on which you serve. You have my undying gratitude for the tough job you do so admirably, and for allowing me to have had fun writing about an earlier era in air travel, and your role in it.

**Donald Bain**
**New York, 2003**
**donaldbain.com**

# Foreword

$\mathcal{R}$achel and I think alike. That's both a blessing and a curse.

You'd never know it by looking at us. Rachel is a tall, rangy blonde with a wide-open face, brown eyes, and a breezy personality. She's a go-getter, the one in the crowd who's always ready with the prod for action.

I'm a couple of inches shorter than Rachel. My eyes are black, my hair a dark brown, and I was first in line at the dimple factory. I also smile a lot, even when the news is bad.

We met at stewardess school, roomed together, and immediately felt that rare and wonderful rapport that lights up when two people get along beautifully. We fly together, live together, hold each other's hands through blighted romances, tell each other of newfound loves, laugh together at today's mad, mod world, and, from time to time, get in trouble together.

In many ways, all stewardesses have a common bond. Rachel and I were both from small towns and anxious to take a fling at the big, bad world. That's true of most girls flying today.

Stewardessing is the ideal job for girls looking to travel and see other places, make many new and varied friends, feel at home in hundreds of strange cities, and get paid for these things to boot.

Yes, it is true that a stewardess is a built-in baby-sitter, flying waitress, and congenial hostess, no matter what troubles befall her. The troubles can be endless: a mixup on meals, a shortage of liquor, engine difficulties, other mechanical quirks, male pinchers, female whiners, vomiting children, two-timing stewardesses who steal your man, and, once in a while, a plane that takes a good friend to a fiery death.

But we accept all this. The bitter with the sweet, and there's so much that is sweet about being an airline stewardess.

Our lives are different. Airline crews are a close group of people. We work together. We live together. Airline crews stay at the same hotels and layovers. But that doesn't mean it's sex, sex, sex all the time. It can be if you want it that way, and some do. We all like a little of it. But most of us are also discreet about our private lives, which simply puts us in a class with almost every other young girl tasting life and what it can offer.

One last defensive word before we spring you loose on *Coffee, Tea or Me?* A stewardess is a girl. She wears a uniform and works at thirty-thousand feet. But above all she is a girl, female and subject to all the whims and desires of all females.

One of our desires is that you know more about us, our lives, loves, and laughter. That's why we put together our similar minds and wrote this book. Smoking is permitted, and seat belts are at your discretion.

Welcome!

# CHAPTER I

## "Is This Your First Flight, Too?"

$\mathcal{I}$t rained very hard the day we made our first flight as stewardesses. We should have recognized it as an omen of things to come. At the time, it just seemed wet. We should have realized that our first flight couldn't be like anyone else's first flight.

Our brand-new, custom-tailored, form-fitting, wrinkle-proof, Paris-inspired uniforms became soaked in the dash from our apartment house lobby in the east Seventies of Manhattan to the cab at the corner. The doorman, a portly fellow known for his red face and his ever-present brown paper bag, had taken over twenty minutes to get us that cab, which cut drastically into the hour we'd allowed ourselves to reach Kennedy Airport.

"Damn, damn, damn," Rachel muttered loudly as she settled in the far corner of the backseat and surveyed her light blue skirt, now blotched dark blue. "Damn!"

"You goils ain't gonna be flyin' today." Our cabdriver was Maxwell Solomon, Hack Number 30756M.

We looked at each other briefly before crowing back at Mr. Solomon in unison. "Why?"

"You kiddin'? You wouldn't get me up in no airplane in this here weather. No, sir. Not me."

We told him we'd checked with operations before leaving and they'd told us flights were departing, although incoming flights had been canceled. We told him a big airliner never takes off unless everything is very safe and sure. We told him the weather was only local, probably, and that once you're off the ground, you fly far above the rain and wind.

"No, sir, not me. Anybody flies in this here weather is nuts or sick or somethin'."

We *were* sick. It started right then and there and never left us for the rest of the day. Mr. Solomon was right. Mr. Solomon also asked us for our telephone numbers because he'd kind of heard stewardesses were a real fun-loving bunch of girls and he knew a great place in Coney Island where there was this sensational rock-and-roll band.

"Whatta ya say, goils? I'll take the botha ya, only later, like, well, you know, like later onea ya can split and go home."

The natural inclination to tell him off was tempered by memories of recent lectures at stewardess school where we were told (a) everyone is a potential customer of the airline and (b) courtesy always pays off in sound public relations and future revenue.

"Drop dead," Rachel said with a smile.

"OK, goils, just askin'. Can't blame a guy for that. Right? Especially not witha coupla stews." He clicked his tongue against his teeth, winked at us in the rearview mirror, and drove a little faster. The large overhead sign indicating one mile to Kennedy Airport passed at 12:01 P.M. We were already late reporting in for our first flight.

We paid the big tab, tipped small, smiled graciously, and entered our terminal at JFK through the pneumatic doors. Inside the lobby was a mob of people milling around the ticket counters. Valiantly dragging our blue suitcases and handbags, we stumbled through the door leading to Flight Operations. There were as many people in ops as in the lobby. Or maybe it just seemed as many because of the solid wall of blue uniforms. We dropped our luggage and were heading for the sign-in book at Crew Scheduling when a female voice stopped us in our tracks.

"Rachel! Trudy!" There was no doubt about that voice. We turned to see the flashing white teeth, flaming red hair, and remarkable upthrust bosom of Betty O'Riley, better known to her classmates at stewardess college as Betty Big Boobs. Betty bounced and jiggled over to us, her smile as programmed and precise as a roadway neon sign. Suddenly she frowned and pouted her lips. "Y'all look so scared and lost, honeys."

Then she smiled. "Nothin' to be scared of."

Then she frowned. "They probably canceled your flight, anyway."

Then she smiled bigger than ever, "Mine's been canceled 'causa weather in Atlanta." She kept smiling this time and whispered, looking around to ensure privacy, "But ah'm goin' to dinner with the captain. He models for cigarette commercials, sometimes."

She giggled furiously, the bosom in violent action. "Ah'm gonna love it to death here."

She turned and hurried through the crowd toward a gray-templed pilot lounging against the wall, a cigarette professionally held between his lips. Her bosom made contact with at least a dozen male elbows on her short trip through the crowd, and her fanny, sufficiently oversize to counterbalance the excess weight in front, waved like a storm-tossed rudder.

We signed in hurriedly with the stewardess dispatcher, a thin, quiet fellow with large glasses and eyes that never made contact with ours. He looked down at our trip number and said, "You girls are awful late. Better hurry down to the gate."

We took his advice and pushed back through the crowd toward the door. Betty O'Riley was leaning against the wall with her captain, both of them right off the back cover of *Life*. I don't think he ever smoked that cigarette. He remained in perpetual rehearsal should J. Walter Thompson call. Betty, smiling at us, sort of flexed everything at once. We just passed by.

Our flight was to depart from Gate 16. We hurried under the signs directing passengers to the higher numbered gates. Suddenly, Rachel stopped, beat her fists against her thighs: "Damn, damn, damn." In our rush we'd left our luggage and purses back at operations. We spun around in formation and ran back up the endless corridor, people turning to watch as we passed. We grabbed the forgotten items, received another automatic smile from Betty, noticed her captain was now trying it with a cigar, and ran back through the door and up the corridor. It was now 12:30, just a half hour to flight time. We were twenty minutes late.

The departure lounge at Gate 16 was from a De Mille epic. Two ramp agents stood firmly behind their fortress of the ticket counter, their faces mirroring their determination to keep things in order according to the book. (Why would all these people want to go to Cleveland, we wondered?)

We walked up to the ramp agents and announced we were the stewardesses for the flight. One of them never bothered to look at us. The other, a chubby redhead with acne, just glanced, curled his lip, and went back to checking in the passengers. It was obvious we weren't supposed to check in with the ramp agents. We remembered our keys, one of which was supposed to fit the steel door leading from the gate's lounge area to the aircraft's parking ramp. Unfortunately, the confusion at the terminal that day necessitated parking the 727 at a gate without the enclosed jetway tunnel. After some fumbling, we opened the door and went down the stairway. We reached the door at the bottom, threw it open, and were greeted with a blast of blowing rain.

"Damn, damn, *damn.*"

We ran across the parking ramp and tripped up the portable stairs to the front entrance of the airplane. At the top, safely inside from the rain, stood another stewardess. She partially blocked the entrance, and we had to push past her to reach the dry cabin. We splattered her pretty good.

"Sorry about that," I said with a friendly smile.

"Where have you been?" she countered.

Both of us began chattering about our cabdriver, the rain, the baggage in operations, and any other reason we could think of.

She cut us off in mid-sentence. "Forget it. Just do a fast job of picking up this cruddy bird. The passengers will be boarding any minute."

We followed her orders without hesitation. After a minute of picking up cigarette butts, paper cups, magazines, and Kleenex, I made the mistake of asking, "How come the cabin cleaners didn't work on this airplane?"

I was glad I asked. It brought forth from our senior stew an actual chuckle.

"Boy, oh boy, oh boy," she said with a resigned shaking of her head. "Cabin cleaners? They *have* worked on this bird. Don't you know you've always got to clean up after the cleaners? What they don't teach you in school these days."

We *were* taught about the cabin cleaners in stewardess school. We were taught that this dedicated group of men worked hard to provide our passengers with the cleanest, neatest, and most pleasant airplanes anywhere in the free world.

"Buncha pigs," Rachel muttered under her breath as she retracted a crushed cigarette package from between the cushions of a seat. "Damn pigs."

And then the passengers started coming aboard. First came two ramp agents carrying a wheelchair between them. In the chair was a little old lady covered with a large sheet of plastic to keep the rain off. When the chair was safely inside, we removed the plastic and helped her into a seat by the window.

"I don't want to be by the window," she said.

We moved her to the aisle seat.

"I think it would be safer in the front," she said.

We moved her to the front.

"Is this a really safe place?" she asked.

"Yes, ma'am."

"Good." Always treat a first-class passenger right.

Next was a disheveled young mother with four children, the youngest about one and the oldest about four. She carried two of the kids, a ramp agent carried another, and the eldest ran ahead of everyone and jumped into a seat by the window in the first-class section.

"Billy," the mother bellowed. "Back here."

He didn't move. She deposited her two human packages in seats, ran past the ramp agent who valiantly tried to ward off his parcel's attempts to tear off his glasses, and grabbed Billy by the collar.

"I told you to be good. I told you you wouldn't have ice cream, candy, toys, soda, cake, or cookies for a year if you weren't good on the airplane."

He started crying and I felt a strange face and voice, mine, might help. I leaned over the seat and said, "I'll give you a pilot's ring if you do what your mother says."

"He'll do what he's told without bribes," his mother snapped. She pulled harder on his collar and he finally capitulated, crying all the way back to the others. The ramp agent had placed his ward down in a seat, but she was now in the process of getting up for a romp down the aisle.

Rachel smiled at the mother. "They sure are cute kids," she said with a surprising note of sincerity. "I love kids."

The pre-boards in place, the rest of the passengers started filing on, each soaked despite the big black umbrellas supplied by the agents at the terminal door. Our senior stew was up front in the cockpit with the crew, and we stationed ourselves near the door to greet the passengers as they came on board. We asked to see each ticket until some man yelled from the steps that he was getting soaked. Obviously, we ought to let them come aboard before checking tickets. We finally just waved them through with a smile and cheery "hello."

We also threw in little quips like, "Welcome aboard." "Glad you could come today." "Some weather, huh?" "My, you're wet." "Watch out for that umbrella." "Please close the umbrella before entering the aircraft." "Aaaaaaaaaaah," as an umbrella spoke gouged Rachel's arm.

One young man, much too collegiate for his thirty years, came through the door with a large package under his arm. He handed it to me.

"Here, tiger, take good care of it, will you. I've got a lot of money tied up in that piece of hi-fi equipment. You should see my *rig . . .* tiger."

The next man, shaking the water from his head like a dog in from the rain, asked, "Is this the Rochester flight?"

"No, sir, it isn't. This goes to Cleveland."

"Cleveland?" he shouted with rage. "Cleveland? I don't want to go to Cleveland. I'm going to Rochester!'

"We're sorry, sir, but this is the Cleveland flight."

"Preposterous. I want to talk to your manager. Where is he?"

"Sir, please stand aside until all the passengers have boarded. We'll get you back to your Rochester flight."

"I'll raise hell with someone about this. You just see."

"Yes, sir."

Everyone finally seated, and our Rochester-bound man back in the terminal demanding the president, we closed the heavy door, looked at each other, and walked to the front of the tourist section, the section always awarded the junior stewardesses. Our senior stew came out of the cockpit and headed to the buffet situated between the tourist and first-class sections. We followed her into the tiny galley. This seemed to annoy her. She pulled the drape across and glared at us.

"Get out there and check for heavy items in the overhead racks. And check their seat belts. Make sure no one is smoking. Ask that mother if you can do something for her. And get everyone's name on the chart. And please get off my back. I'm not going to take your hand every step of the way."

We twisted around to leave the cramped quarters when she asked, "Which one of you got the razor?"

"The what?"

"The razor. The razor for the passengers to use. You're supposed to get it from operations before coming aboard. I suppose you forgot to sign the briefing book, too. And to get the en route weather. What the deuce have I ended up with today? Six years of flying for this cruddy airline and I end up with inefficient virgins. You'd better get with it, girls. Or you won't be with it . . . much longer."

We went out in the aisle and surveyed the long columns of faces. We walked to the rear section and looked again.

"I've never seen so many occiputs* in my life," I whispered to Rachel.

The three jet engines in the tail started whining as we went back up the aisle. We looked in everyone's lap to check seat belts but some passengers had coats in their laps and we couldn't be sure. It just would have been too personal to peek.

One man stopped Rachel and admitted his seat belt wasn't fastened.

"I don't know how," he confessed.

Rachel leaped at the chance to be of service.

"Let me show you," she said. She reached down under his legs to find the ends, found them, and started fumbling with the mechanism. He loved it. She began to realize that any idiot could fasten a seat belt.

---

*I once dated a medical student who told me the back of the head was called an occiput. He taught me a lot of anatomical terms.

She completed the job. "How's that, sir?"

"Beautiful," he answered. "Thank you, Miss . . . ?"

"Don't take that belt off, sir. Have a pleasant flight."

I found an attaché case in the overhead rack.

"Sorry, sir, but you'll have to take that briefcase down," I said in a friendly tone.

"Where will I put it?" he grunted.

"Under your seat, sir."

"It won't fit."

"Oh, I think it will, sir. You just try."

"All right. Get it for me."

"Yes, sir."

It was heavy. I stretched on my toes to reach it and managed to slide it over the lip of the rack. It was soaking wet, and a tiny rivulet of water ran onto the head of a soldier sitting directly beneath.

"Sorry, sir," I told the soldier. He enjoyed being called "sir."

"Careful of that," the owner of the briefcase barked.

"Yes, sir." The stretching pulled my blouse, supposedly pull-proof, from my skirt, and my bare belly stood an inch from the soldier's nose. He actually touched his nose to my belly button. It tickled.

I managed to bring the case down to safety just as the plane began pulling away from the ramp. I lost my balance and dropped the heavy case into its owner's lap.

"You idiot," he snarled. I apologized.

I apologized to the soldier, too, but he didn't seem to want one.

Rachel was beginning to take names on the other side of the cabin, and I took the second sheet and started on my side. The first man I went to sat rigidly in his seat, his knuckles white as he grasped the sides of the chair.

"Your name and destination, sir?"

He panicked. "I thought we were going to Cleveland."

"That's right, sir. Only Cleveland. Just give me your name, sir."

"Carlson. C-a-r-l-s-o-n."

"Thank you, sir." I went on to the next.

"Your name, sir."

He quickly slurred off what sounded like Icklensale.

"Would you spell that for me, sir?"

He didn't like being asked to spell his name. He just said it again, only faster.

"I-c-k-l-e-n-sale?" I tried.

"E-k-l-o-s-h-a-l-e," he corrected with a deep sigh.

"Thank you, sir." His look was mean.

We were halfway through taking names when the captain's voice came over the PA system.

"Ah, ladies and gentlemen, ah welcome aboard Flight 81 to Cleveland. Ah, due to the, ah, bad weather conditions that I guess you've all noticed (chuckle), ah, we're going to have to, ah, wait a little while in line for takeoff position . . . ah . . ."

He seemed to want to say something else but didn't . . . or couldn't. The senior stew took up where he left off from her microphone in the buffet area.

"Welcome aboard Flight 81 to Cleveland, Ohio. My name is Miss Lewis. Working with me for your comfort today will be Miss Baker and Miss Jones. We're sorry for the delay in leaving Kennedy today, but weather conditions have canceled incoming flights and slowed up the departure of other flights. Once off the ground, we expect our flying time to Cleveland to be one hour and eight minutes. We'll be cruising at an altitude of 26,000 feet. If there's anything we can do to make your flight more comfortable, please don't hesitate to call on us. Thank you, and have a pleasant flight."

We went through the oxygen mask routine and resumed taking names. I was almost finished with my side of the airplane when I felt a tap on my rear end. I turned to see Mr. George Kelman, whose name I had just taken. He was an attractive young man with neat brown hair, an expensive suit, and an outgoing smile. He beckoned me with his index finger. I leaned closer as he started to talk, the whine of the jet engines making hearing difficult. All that airline advertising talk about their super-quiet jets ran through my mind.

"Yes, sir?"

He leaned closer, too. "This is your first flight, isn't it?"

How did he know?

"Yes sir, it is."

"I know. What I wanted to ask you was whether you'd have dinner with me in Cleveland tonight?"

I was stunned. We'd been told many times, of course, that many men would ask us for dates. In fact, we *hoped* many men would ask us for dates. Why else be a flying waitress? But so soon? With the rain and all? I thought quickly, trying to remember what the manual said about dating passengers. It didn't say anything that I could remember.

"Sorry sir, but we're not allowed to accept dates with male passengers."

"How about females?" He laughed easily and with warmth.

I giggled. "Oh sir, that's silly."

"Seriously, how about it?"

"I can't. We don't even stay in Cleveland overnight. Well, unless we're weathered in there."

"Don't worry about that. I'll come back with you and we'll have dinner in New York."

Now I was totally confused.

"Well, you see, I have to go back to work now and I have my girlfriend with me and . . ."

"Great. We'll have dinner in Cleveland or New York or wherever you say. All three of us."

I began to panic.

"Well, I'll ask her. Oh, but then you'll want one of us to go home later, like in Coney Island. Right?" Now he was flustered.

"Anything you say, ma'm." He was sweet. I liked him. But I suddenly sensed that despite the noise of the engines, the other passengers in the immediate area were listening intently. I turned from him and went on with my job of getting names. I looked back at him. He had returned to reading his copy of *Forbes,* a magazine I'd never looked into but one that undoubtedly had something to do with money.

I asked Rachel if we could date passengers.

"You bet, honey," she replied. "It's called a fringe benefit."

Names taken, seat belts fastened, and mother-with-four-children relatively settled down and quiet, our captain swung the 727 onto the runway, gave it full-throttle, and we started gaining speed for take-off. Rachel and I sat together in our jump seats, tightly belted in, and thought of Maxwell Solomon and his philosophy on flying in today's weather. The more the 727 shuddered as it gained momentum, the more we thought of Maxwell Solomon, now safely in his cab headed for Coney Island with a more receptive fare. And then we felt the slight sensation of being away from the concrete runway, free from the friction of rubber on that runway, and free of that maximum moment of strain before becoming airborne. Outside, a marshmallow blanket of gray, colorless and without substance, seemed to buoy up the mass of airplane.

The captain was making his first climbing turn when our senior stew, Miss Lewis, unbuckled her seat belt and motioned for us to follow her into the galley. We stepped inside, grabbing onto anything to maintain our balance in the turbulent turns. Miss Lewis again pulled the drape across the galley entrance.

"OK, let's get moving. I ought to let you fall on your faces all alone. But I'm responsible for the flight and I don't want to see you screw up the back end." She looked at Rachel. "You . . . get back there and take drink orders. They pay in the rear, you know. We've only got to Cleveland to serve all the meals and booze. You're squared away on meal service X-17-B, aren't you?"

"Sure," we said. What meal service *was* X-17-B?

"OK. Get those drink orders, put their trays in place, and hustle."

"Right," Rachel answered and departed the galley.

"Help me get this food set up." Miss Lewis was a stern girl, I decided. In fact, she terrified me, especially when I realized I didn't remember a thing about airplanes, passengers, food, drinks, or being a stewardess in general. I watched closely and followed her every movement, taking the fruit cups from the cold storage compartments, placing the little plastic bag of salt, pepper, knives, and forks on the trays after finding them in the same cold storage compartments, taking the Salisbury steak from the hot storage compartments and the rolls from the same place.

Rachel came back with the drink orders written on a small slip of paper. "I'd better get the drinks out there fast, before dinner, huh?" she asked Miss Lewis.

"Are you kidding?" Miss Lewis snapped as she slapped a piece of butter on each roll plate. "Give them the whole mess at once—booze, food, dessert, and coffee. Put the booze bottles on the tray and get them to the right people. Come on, get with it."

"Why don't they just serve sandwiches on these short flights?" I asked.

"Ooooooh, what did I do to deserve this?" wailed Miss Lewis.

We grabbed trays and headed up the aisle, no further questions asked.

"I ordered bourbon," said the man with the attaché case under his seat.

"Where's the soda for my Scotch?" drawled the soldier.

"Could I have a rare one, please?"

"I didn't get a napkin."

"The plane sounds funny. Are we all right?" This came from the little old lady.

"How high are we?"

"How fast are we going?"

"Say, tiger, what are we flying over now?"

"It's stuffy in here. Can we open a window?"

"Where are those free packages of cigarettes?"

"Would you feed the two children in back of me," said our flying mother of four, her voice more a command than a question.

It was bedlam. Total. We eventually matched the right people with the right drinks, managed to shovel a few spoonfuls of mashed potatoes into the kids' mouths, turned down at least six requests for more than the allowed two drinks, and only spilled one glass of water on a passenger.

Everyone finally had his meal tray in front of him, and we actually inhaled our first free breath since takeoff. We hadn't quite exhaled it when the aircraft hit a pocket of severe turbulence, sending it into a sheer and rapid descent of at least two hundred feet. The aircraft went down and the meal trays stayed up where they were, at least until nature grabbed hold of them and sent them smashing against the fixed trays that were on their way back up with the airplane. Their contact was violent, the result a cabin smeared from ceiling to floor with coffee, bourbon, gravy, butter, potatoes, fruit cocktail, and apple pandowdy. The turbulence also deposited the two of us on the floor after first reaching the ceiling during the drop. There were yips of surprise, cries of disgust, and wails of panic. We just let out a solid "ommph," and picked ourselves up. Food was on everything, including the heads of many of the passengers.

The turbulence continued as we made our way up the side to help the passengers. The plane, buffeted with severe shocks, dipped and swayed in an irregular pattern. The cabin was saturated with anger and fear, and we tried our best to calm those who were frightened and sooth those who were angry. George Kelman grabbed my arm as I rushed by with a towel to help a man wipe gravy from his face. George whispered to me, but with firmness, "Relax, sweetie. Everything's going to be OK." His smile and calm voice were welcome.

"Thanks," I said.

"Dinner?"

"Let's talk when we get to Cleveland. OK?"

"OK." Again, that smile.

We went about cleaning up the passengers and the cabin the best we could, all under the watchful eye of Miss Lewis. We had to admit later that this senior stew really did know how to keep calm in the midst of chaos. But it didn't make us like her any better.

We thought we were finally about to get the best of the cleanup chore when the first passenger reached for his "barf bag." He made it in time but the second one didn't.

I was delivering my last towel to the little old lady when a middle-aged gentleman leaped from his seat and ran for the bathroom. Rachel stopped him in mid-aisle.

"You can't leave your seat, sir. The seat belt sign is on." He was carrying his little bag.

"I've got to," he mumbled, his words slurred and garbled.

"You can't," she said again, actually pushing him back toward his seat. "This turbulence is severe and you cannot leave your seat for anything."

He looked like he wanted to cry. "Please," he pleaded. "My teeth," indicating the bag clutched tightly in his hand.

"Oh, no," Rachel exclaimed.

"Yes," he lamented, his face screwed up to keep back the tears.

Rachel looked down at the bag and drew a deep breath. "Give it to me," she said quickly, grabbing the bag from his hand and running toward the lavatory. He watched her enter the lav and then sat meekly in his seat. She emerged five minutes later with his teeth wrapped in Kleenex. He took them from her and turned to the window to hide his embarrassment.

We were approaching the Cleveland area and the captain had informed the passengers of this fact when the light from one of the bathrooms flashed on the signal panel in the buffet. Rachel went to the door of the lav to see what was the problem. Neither of us knew anyone had gotten up from his seat.

"What's wrong in there?" she asked.

"I'm stuck," was the reply from within.

Rachel stood outside the lav door and smiled. I came from the buffet to join her.

"What's wrong in there?" I asked my flying partner.

"It's a woman. Says she's stuck."

"Stuck?"

"What's stuck?"

Rachel started to giggle.

"You mean her fundament?" I offered.*

"Her what?"

"Forget it."

The voice again sounded through the locked bathroom door. "Please help me. I'm stuck."

I started giggling, too. There was nothing else to do. But we knew we'd better do something.

"Can we come in?" I asked.

*Another term from my medical school ex-beau. It means buttocks.*

There was a long moment of decision.

"Yes. Alone."

I entered. She definitely was stuck, a victim of the mechanism's strong suction force. It was a freak accident, and it had to happen on our first flight.

Rachel went and told Miss Lewis, who seemed to consider the problem a ruthless and premeditated plot to make her trip even more difficult. After Rachel and I tried various techniques to free the passenger, Miss Lewis went forward to summon the flight engineer who, along with his responsibilities for the major mechanical equipment on the plane, was also responsible for all minor cabin failures. He came out of the cockpit, a long, gaunt man with excess nose, sunken eyes, and veined cheeks. He continuously sniffed. He walked right into the lav, a flashlight in his hand.

"Howdy," he drawled to the woman.

"Oh, my God," she moaned.

The flight engineer stood still in deep thought for a few minutes before speaking.

"Shucks, ma'm, I don't reckon we can do anything 'til we hit Cleveland. Reckon all we can do would be pull, and that's sure to smart a bit."

"Oh, please don't pull," she begged.

"I'll tell the captain 'bout this here predicament and see if he's got any suggestions. Meantime, you just sit tight."

He chuckled at this pun of his and snorted with great gusto. His Adam's apple bobbed up and down like a yo-yo. He swallowed hard and returned to the cockpit.

We smiled down at the woman and suggested she take his advice—sit tight—and have a drink. The idea appealed to her and she smiled back.

"Bourbon on the rocks, please," she ordered.

"Coming up." I gave her a double.

We landed at Cleveland after a bouncy and bumpy approach and taxied to the gate assigned to our flight. We suggested to the woman in the lav that she have another drink until all the passengers deplaned. The captain had radioed ahead, and a crew of mechanics were ready to perform whatever mechanical surgery would prove necessary. We brought her a second double bourbon and went about the task of telling the passengers good-bye. Some of them, their suits spotted with food stains and their hair dampened with fruit cocktail juice, were in no need for jovial farewells.

One man, who wore a shiny black suit, a white shirt with high-roll collar, and a slick white-on-white tie, asked Rachel if she'd spend the night with him in retribution for the massive food stains on his clothing. She declined.

We stayed around after all the passengers departed to see how the mechanics would handle the plight of the woman in the water closet. They managed, after much loosening of bolts and dismantling of equipment, to free her from her oval trap. When she stood up, her knees buckled under her. The mechanics figured it was from shock. Rachel and I knew it was the two double bourbons. She regained her footing and wove her way unsteadily off the plane. I think she was too bombed to know she was in Cleveland. We heard later that the airline gave her a lifetime pass. I've often wondered if she had the nerve to use it.

Later, Rachel and I marched to operations where, for some naïve reason, we expected to receive the highest decoration for valor, service, and dedication the airline could bestow on an employee. After all, our first flight had been above and beyond the ordinary; as far as we were concerned, we had performed with extraordinary skill and fortitude. But the only official word we received was from our captain. He came over to us in ops and said, "I'm reporting you both to your supervisor for discourteous attitudes and infraction of stated and long-standing rules."

We were stunned. He turned on his heel and strode away, his hat at a cocky angle on his head. Miss Lewis sat nearby filling out the procedure forms for the flight.

"Did you hear that?" we protested. "What are we being reported for?"

Miss Lewis looked up from her paperwork and chewed the inside of her cheek.

"It's very simple, girls. You never even bothered to introduce yourselves to the captain at ops in New York before the flight. And you should know that's rule number one in crew courtesy. I don't blame him at all." She turned back to her papers. "Always meet your captain, girls."

"Damn, damn, damn," Rachel chanted as we walked away. "Damn."

"I can't believe it," I moaned. "I really can't believe it."

We opened the door from operations and walked into the lobby.

"Hi girls." We turned to see George Kelman standing near the door.

"Rachel, this is George. George, Rachel."

"Dinner?"

"I told you we have to fly back to New York."

"And I told you I'd go back with you. Anyway, I've already checked and you're not flying back to anywhere tonight. Kennedy is still closed and expects to be until tomorrow. You're staying at the Sheraton-Cleveland, downtown, and they'll call you there about your next trip. In the meantime, you've got to eat and it's all on me."

We wanted to ask how he knew all these things but didn't bother to ask. We didn't even bother to look in our manuals about procedures relating to passengers and dating them. We just took his arm, one on each side, and walked toward the line of waiting cabs.

"God bless you, Mr. Kelman," Rachel said.

"My pleasure," he smiled, holding open the door of the waiting taxi. "All of Cleveland's night life awaits us."

# CHAPTER II

## "Let's Run Away and Be Stewardesses"

$\mathcal{R}$achel and I didn't know each other before meeting at stewardess school. But our backgrounds were similar, and so were our motivations for becoming stewardesses. For that matter, our motivations parallel those of most girls flying today. And the stewardess recruiters know this. They know all about us when we're young and eager for a taste of glamour and travel, especially those of us living in small towns with bright dreams of running away to the big city.

I first thought about being a stewardess after reading an occupational brief published by Chronicle Guidance Publications. This little piece of propaganda cost me a quarter for the privilege of reading about a career as an "airplane hostess (Stewardess) 2-25-37." It was published in 1958 and contains the following point:

> *In the case of the job of hostess, the main advantage is the opportunity to travel and see new places. The main disadvantage is being away from home at least a third of the time.*

And therein lies the prime motivation to become a stewardess. Amarillo, Texas, my hometown, is pleasant but small. At least it used to be. But by the time I was a senior in high school, I knew I wanted the big time—Dallas, Chicago, even New York, I simply had outgrown Waddy Week.

I was born in Amarillo in 1942. It was a nice place to grow up. But excitement did not head the visitor attractions page in the Chamber of Commerce booklet. The new feature at the biggest movie house was an event to be attended, preferably in full dress.

My beau since junior high school was Henry, a bright young man who actually did enjoy getting dressed to the teeth for the new feature and pizza. And I was always his date at these "premières." Henry was headed for state medical school and started learning all the terms of anatomy during his senior year in high school. We used to sit for hours on his front porch while he taught me the terms and quizzed me on my retention.

Every time Henry would teach me another term, such as popliteal (back of the knee), he'd leer a little and, say, "Now I'll teach you in Braille." Then he'd groan, laugh with a hint of the juvenile lecher, and touch my popliteal, or whatever was the lesson for the evening.

I thought it was funny at first. But after running through over a hundred terms and hearing him say with each one, "Now I'll teach you in Braille," I got pretty fed up with the whole deal. Except there weren't many boys I liked in Amarillo.

So, I'd giggle, fence him off just a little bit after he got in a few touches, and try to enjoy the whole thing for what it was worth.

Still, I eventually found myself hating Henry and his medical come-on. My hatred lasted until he went away for his first year of medical school and then, after looking around at what was left, I found myself missing Henry. I'd find myself saying anatomical terms over and over in my mind, each one bringing back the thought of his touch. I actually yearned to hear him say, "Now I'll teach you in Braille."

Henry and I pledged to remain true to each other for the next twelve years or so, until he became a famous doctor. My parents wanted me to wait for Henry more than anything else they could think of. They would have liked a doctor in the family. Well, I waited for a couple of months. Then one day wandering along the main street I spotted something in the window of Sison's Drug, Food and Stationery Store. It was a poster, a big one, that carried the bold, blue headline—*BE GLAMOROUS—BE A STEWARDESS!* And there she was, a chic blonde girl all decked out in a classy, form-fitting blue uniform, a smile as wide as Main Street. At the bottom of the sign was the information that a member of the stewardess corps would be at the high school gymnasium Monday afternoon at 4 P.M. Interested girls could speak with her and find out about a career as a glamorous member of this elite group of young ladies.

I didn't tell a soul I was going to talk to her. I knew my parents would be furious that I even entertained the thought. And I was equally certain that all other parents in town would take the same attitude with their daughters. In fact, I expected to be the only one to actually stop and see that glamorous blonde on the poster in Sison's. It was my chance to escape, as Carolyn Jones did, and Cyd Charisse, to become big movie stars. I wasn't reaching for stardom, as they did. I just wanted to swing a little more than I was destined to in Amarillo.

But I was wrong. Everybody wanted to swing. The whole female element of the senior class was at the gymnasium at 4 P.M. on Monday.

Seated behind a makeshift desk were two people, obviously not from Amarillo. One was a young man, about twenty-five, wearing what I considered the epitome of big city, urban male clothing. His suit was a conservative gray, with a vest, and a deep maroon-striped tie bowed out just so from his button-down collar. His hair was neat and clung closely to his head.

Beside him was a stewardess, a brunette, with a smile every bit as wide as the poster girl. She was chatting with a few of my classmates, and when she spoke, her head cocked pertly to one side and her eyes made all sorts of movements enhancing her words.

Behind them stood a portable blackboard supplied by the school. On it was a montage of posters, some to do with being a stewardess but most dealing with exotic destinations. No matter where you looked, the words *travel* and *glamour* caught your eye. It was the same with the piles of literature on the desk in front of them. I walked forward and picked up one each of the four pamphlets being offered.

The young man smiled at me. So did the brunette stewardess. And I smiled at them, a little too much of a smile, but I decided on that very spot in the gymnasium that I wanted to be a stewardess. And smiling was without a doubt more important than anything else where an airline was concerned. My mouth started hurting and I went back to a seat.

I had just sat down when Mrs. Coolie walked into the gymnasium. Mrs. Coolie, widowed for over thirty years, doubled as history teacher and guidance counselor. She did know her history. But her guidance usually directed all of us to a state college where we could learn something to bring back to Amarillo.

She didn't look at all pleased having this wild, wicked airline gang at her school corrupting her girls. She wore flat black shoes with laces. Her hair was pulled back tight in a bun and contrasted harshly with the soft, free hairdo of the stewardess.

"All right, girls. Everyone take a seat now." Mrs. Coolie never needed benefit of microphone.

We were all seated and Mrs. Coolie began pacing in front of the table. She chewed her mouth as she paced, her hands behind her back. Then, secure in some thought, she turned to us and spoke.

"You've all come here today to hear what it would be like to travel all over this nation of ours and live in many different places. I suppose this is a dream that many young, impressionable girls have once or twice in their growing up. Yes, travel does have its appeal. I've traveled, as you all know. (The only trip I knew of was a teacher's conference in Oklahoma City.) And I've found that other places never, never . . . never have what you've left behind in your own particular place of origin. But, you each will make this choice. And those few of you who may decide to leave Amarillo and . . . yes, even Texas, will at least have benefit of a firm and solid foundation in the great history of your state. I found this fact secure in my travels. Well, as part of our continuing effort to present to you people from various careers, we today feature the airlines. And these people are here to say some things about going away and working for their airline. I give them to you now."

We applauded. Mrs. Coolie liked it as she strode to the sidelines.

The young man stood up and smiled at us. We smiled back.

"Good afternoon, girls. And thank you for coming. I appreciate that warm introduction from *your* Mrs. Coolie. Actually, we almost didn't make it here as planned. We've been conducting these meetings all over the country and were in Hollywood yesterday. It looked like the weather wouldn't allow us to reach Amarillo today so . . . well, we just stayed around the pool and watched the actors and actresses stroll by."

Everyone laughed.

"But, I'm certainly glad we *did* have a chance to see and meet each of you. You all look like you'd make fine stewardesses for the airline."

I wanted to ask which actors they saw strolling by. But I thought better of it. I wanted to ask if they'd seen Marlon Brando, my favorite. And I wanted to sign up at that moment before they got away and headed back for Hollywood.

The meeting progressed for about a half hour. The young man introduced the stewardess (I never got her name), and she told us about what she did as a stewardess and where she went and what she did when she wasn't flying. It sounded like a real-live Cinderella story. She lived in Boston where, she commented casually, there were so many college men. She said she always went to Europe on her vacations because she could fly on other airlines for almost nothing. In fact, she even said she never really knew what living could be all about until she decided to become a stewardess.

"I suppose I'll never want to stop flying," she said with a reflective sigh. "Unless, of course, I decide to accept the marriage offers of those college men in Boston."

We all laughed with her. Except for Mrs. Coolie, who sat rigid in her chair, her black shoes planted firmly on the hardwood floor, her hands firmly on her knees. It was obvious she wanted the airline gang out of her gymnasium.

The meeting ended and we were invited to stay around and ask questions. The only distressing thing about the meeting was the fact you had to be at least twenty years old to become a stewardess. But these two representatives from the airline had accomplished their given task. They had successfully piqued my interest, not only in flying but in their particular airline. I came forward to pick up a preliminary application form that the young man said would simply give them basic information on us. Then, when we became of age and went to Dallas to apply and be interviewed, they'd already know certain things about us. I went forward for those forms despite the hard stare of Mrs. Coolie, grabbed them, and returned to my chair. Then, after placing them in my purse, I went back to the desk and thanked the young man for coming.

"I hope we see you in Dallas very soon," he said.

"You will," I answered.

I walked quickly from the school gymnasium and ran through the hallway to the outdoors. I burst through the doorway and, once free of the musty, institutional smell of the building, breathed deeply. I was going to be a stewardess, live in Boston, date all those college men, and lounge around a Hollywood pool watching Marlon Brando do swan dives from the high board.

"Whatta ya say, Trudy?" It was the quarterback of our football team standing with a couple of other football players.

Suddenly, he seemed like a third-grade kid wanting to carry my books home from school. I practiced my new smile on him, cocked my head pertly, and walked away with a newfound air of confidence and well-being. It was good-bye Amarillo and hello Hollywood. Or something like that.

*   *   *

Rachel grew up in Louisville very much as I did in a happy family with lots of friends and all the usual high school fun. By the time she was a senior she was getting restless. She didn't want to stay a small-town girl with a small-town job. She'd looked over all the local boys and found none exciting enough to give her the life she wanted. She watched an older sister marry and settle down into a narrow, contented groove. Rachel knew that wasn't for her. What could she do? How could she get away? Good old Eddie who would some day inherit his father's hardware store wanted to marry her. Her parents thought it would be lovely if she married good old Eddie. The young couple could build a ranch house out toward the new end of town, join the club, play golf. Wouldn't that be nice?

Ugh, was all Rachel could say to that arrangement and her dimples disappeared under a deep frown. One day she saw an ad in the local newspaper. Airline recruiters were coming to town to interview potential stewardesses. Rachel was the first girl in line when they arrived. They hired her right on the spot—a great tribute to her looks and her school record. Usually when a girl is interviewed, there follows a long screening process before she is signed.

Rachel told me once about the scene at home when she broke

the news to her folks. It was rough going for quite a while. Her parents didn't want her to leave home. They didn't want her to fly. If she must have a career, why not nursing? She could study that right at home. Well, the harder they tugged, the wilder she fought to get away. Don't underestimate Rachel. She made it.

We arrived on the same day at stewardess school to attend class number 14-45, a six-week course of basic training under the watchful guidance of "Big Momma," a stylish Mrs. Coolie in drag. It was under her wing that we became stewardesses, a fact of her life that she probably regrets to this day.

# CHAPTER III

## "Big Momma Is Watching"

$\mathcal{W}$e arrived at stewardess school on a beautiful spring day. Winter would obviously not be back, and the cool, wet air gave us an even greater expectation of good things to come.

We entered through a narrow gate manned by an elderly gentleman, obviously retired from another line of work, who looked at our letters of admission and waved us through.

The grounds were exquisite. Flowers and shrubs were beginning to show some color against the scrim of beige buildings, each in excellent repair and no taller than two stories. And surrounding the entire grounds was a high, formidable electric fence.

Our luggage was left at the gate for later delivery to Room 16, the one we'd been assigned in our letters of welcome. It was a coincidence meeting each other at the airport as we waited for the limousine from the school. The driver was a wizened old gentleman who smiled a lot, said nothing, and drove erratically. It became obvious as we walked over the grounds toward the dormitory building that the advanced ages of the gatekeeper and driver was no coincidence. The gardeners, handymen, and kitchen help were all in the Medicare class.

"Maybe they just look old," Rachel offered.

"No, they're old," I said, "and that electric thing around the grounds is an electric chastity belt."

I was right on both counts. There would be no virginity lost here if the airline had anything to say about it.

We were greeted in the dormitory lounge by a pleasant young girl who walked us to the second floor and showed us to Room 16. It was tastefully decorated and at first glance seemed large enough for the two of us. A second glanced ruined that illusion.

"Five beds?" we asked in chorus.

"Yes. Five of you will share this room," confirmed our guide.

"That'll be nice," Rachel said.

"Wonderful," I agreed dubiously.

"You'll love it," our guide said with a strong note of finality. "The bathrooms are down the hall."

Rachel and I spent the next hour lying on our beds and talking about why we wanted to become stewardesses. We talked about the glamour of flying away to strange places. We talked about being away from home and the men we'd meet because we were living away from home. We expounded on the challenge of serving a nation's traveling public . . . and about the men who made up the bulk of this public.

I started to tell my story about Henry and his Braille line when the door opened and in walked the third member of our cozy little room. She was taller than we thought you could be to become a stewardess, thin, and dressed in what had to be a $400 suit. Her hair was out of *Glamour,* and she struck one of those ridiculous, awkward go-go poses the models all love to use these days.

"Hellooooooo," she said with a nasal whine, her hand professionally on her hip.

"Hi," we chirped back. "I'm Trudy and this is Rachel."

"Delighted, I'm sure." There was no way to like this girl, with her phony voice and gestures.

She looked slowly around the room and turned to the smiling girl guide who had brought her to the door. "I'm afraid I just don't understand. I assumed a private accommodation."

"I'm sorry, Cynthia," the guide replied, "but there are no private rooms at the school. You'll share a room with four other girls. These are two of your roommates."

"Roommates? How quaint."

"Well," Rachel said with a sweep of her hand, "it's not much but we'll all manage, I guess."

"It's absolutely vulgar," was Cynthia's reaction. "I think I'll nap."

She started to unbutton her suit jacket and then suddenly realized we were in the room. It seemed difficult for her to comprehend we were still standing there as she undressed. We just ignored her and flopped back on our beds. She got down to her slip and placed her pale, skinny frame on the bed furthest from ours. She fell asleep and snored loudly.

Cynthia had been asleep about fifteen minutes when the door opened again and in walked Betty O'Riley. She was undoubtedly the sexiest girl we'd ever seen. She was made up of a series of soft, full curves, each straining to break through her shocking pink dress. We introduced ourselves over the noise of Cynthia's snoring and within minutes, Betty had stripped down to nothing and had climbed between the sheets of the fourth bed.

"Ah always sleep in the nude," she said with a naughty wink. "Hope y'all don't mind."

"She might," Rachel said, pointing to Cynthia on her bed.

"She looks like a boy sleepin' there. There's not much to her, is there?"

"I think she's very rich," I offered.

"Ah hope so," said Betty. "It's her only chance."

The fifth member of our room didn't show up until after dinner. We managed to wake Cynthia, who declined dinner, so the three of us walked to the cafeteria building. There were more than a hundred girls seated at long Formica tables. Little old men cleared away the trays and little old men served the food behind the long, spotless counter where all the food was displayed.

The food was good, very good. And there was lots of it, including a massive dessert tray at the center of each table containing a wide assortment of creamy, sweet pastry. Betty cleaned her plate and finished off three pieces of pastry. Cynthia, who eventually arrived, managed to finish two asparagus tips and a cup of tea. We were drinking our coffee when all eyes turned to the front of the cafeteria where a woman, perhaps thirty-five, stepped up on a raised platform and adjusted a microphone to her height.

"Good evening, girls," she said before a loud screech of feedback drowned her out. An old man, presumably an electrician, rushed forward and did something to get rid of the noise.

"As I was saying, good evening." Everyone scraped a chair in response.

"I'm sorry I wasn't here to personally greet each and every one of you this afternoon, but I was detained on other matters. As you know, tomorrow morning will mark the beginning of your six weeks of study here at the school. I believe your schedule indicates a meeting at 9 A.M. in the auditorium, which happens to be the cafeteria you're in right now."

It did look more like an auditorium than a cafeteria.

"I hope you've enjoyed your dinner and I look forward to seeing each of you in the morning. Until then, have a pleasant evening. Lights out at ten, you know."

Betty went "yuuuk" at the announcement of the curfew time. Cynthia just gagged on a piece of asparagus.

"Well, what'll we do until ten o'clock?" Rachel asked.

"I'm going to sleep." Cynthia walked away from us.

"Ah'd like to go to a nightclub."

"There's no time, Betty."

"There's always time, kids. Always time."

We ended up walking to the entrance gate and watching the old gatekeeper survey the strip of cleared land along the electric fence, like a scout in a frontier film. And the visions came of old war movies on TV where the POWs race for the fence and throw themselves across it as a human bridge for their fleeting buddies. Had a vote been taken at the time, there's no doubt Cynthia would have been chosen for the human sacrifice. The thought of her frail frame sprawled over the electric fence was vivid and satisfying.

"It's 9:45," Rachel warned as we strolled past an enormous swimming pool we had found behind a high hedge. "We'd better get back."

We turned to leave when the sound of a car's screeching tires brought our attention back to the front entrance. A shiny Ford convertible was visible through the dust its skidding halt had created, and a radio was going full blast with a singer lamenting a lost love. The old doorman leaped up from his chair and yelled to the car's driver.

"Hey, git that car outta here and take that damn-fool music with ya."

The door of the car opened and a young man wearing jeans and long sideburns got out and approached the door.

"Are we too late?" he asked with a twang.

"Too late for playin' that damn-fool music."

"No, too late for my girl to get in. She's supposed to start school here tomorrow."

The old man didn't believe. "Where is she? You got a letter?"

The boy turned back to the car and yelled, "Hey, Sally Lu. Come on out here."

There was a pause and then the other door of the car opened. Out of it stepped a pretty little blonde with all the obvious physical signs of a recent necking session. She came forward to her boyfriend's side.

"Sally Lu, show the man your letter."

The girl fished in the pockets of her jeans and handed the doorman a piece of paper. He studied it under the single light and shook his head at the couple.

"This ain't no way to start school, young lady. No sir. Big Momma . . . I mean, Miss Gruel sure ain't gonna like you buzzin' in here in the middle 'a night . . . 'specially not with no young fella with ya and all fulla lipstick like he is. No sir. You better git right on inside. You got one minute 'fore ten."

The young man grabbed Sally Lu and held her in a long and lingering embrace. They parted with great difficulty and he ran to the car to drag out her suitcase. He handed it to the doorman and she started to cry.

"I'll pick you up at six tomorra night, Sally Lu."

"Don't you come back here any night at six," the doorman warned. "Not for a week, anyhow." His final words were cut off in a cloud of swirling rubber and dust.

"Where do I go?" Sally Lu asked the doorman.

Rachel leaped in with the answer. "Hi. I'm Rachel Jones. And we've got to run. What room are you in?"

"I think it's sixteen."

She joined us and we ran full speed upstairs stopping only once for Sally Lu to wipe her tears with a soiled Kleenex.

We'd just reached our room when suddenly the entire building went black. Then, just as suddenly, three giant searchlights popped on and began scanning the front and sides of the dorm. We were met at the door by our guide of that afternoon. Her stewardess smile was gone. In its place was a thin, grim lip-line, and her arms were crossed over her breast.

"This is no way to start six weeks of training. Do it again and you'll never know the joy of being a stewardess."

We tried to explain about Sally Lu but our guide simply pointed to the stairs. We climbed them and entered Room 16.

Cynthia was asleep on her bed, the covers pulled tightly under her chin. She had dragged a dresser from the wall and placed it in front of her bed, a mahogany fortress never to be scaled.

"That's Cynthia," we told Sally Lu.

She cried.

"That's your bed over there."

She cried harder now, her sobs out of control. The noise of her crying brought Cynthia to a fast rise, the covers still clutched tightly under her chin.

"What is this all about?" she demanded.

"Sally Lu is our other roommate," we explained.

"Well, can you manage to control your emotions, Miss Sally Blue, or whatever your name is?" Cynthia was haughty at that moment, but also looked afraid we'd launch a full-scale attack on her fortress.

To add to Cynthia's woes, the door flew open and an old Mexican came in with Sally Lu's bag.

"Get out of here, you . . . you . . . you horrible thing," Cynthia screamed at him. He froze in his tracks and then noticed Betty O'Riley who was reaching behind for the hook on her bra. As she popped it open, the Mexican wheeled and fled the room, never bothering to close the door.

"Shut that door," Cynthia yelled at me. I was up to here at this point with Cynthia Monroe.

Betty, minus bra, walked over and closed it. She seemed to gush all over the room, and the sight of her hardened Cynthia's face into shock. She quickly turned to the wall.

The only light in the room was cast by the searchlights as they moved back and forth across the front of the dorm. We managed to get undressed, find our respective beds, and fall into them. It seemed pointless even trying to locate the bathrooms. We all fell asleep to the quiet sobbing of Sally Lu. Cynthia snored.

* * *

The bathroom was a madhouse the following morning. There were girls everywhere trying to get ready for the big meeting at nine. Cynthia must have gotten up at six because she wasn't to be found in the room or the bathroom.

Breakfast was delicious. We stuffed ourselves and then went outside to allow the staff to clean up the cafeteria and convert it to an auditorium.

At precisely nine, we were all seated at the tables again, a pile of books, papers, charts, and a large box of cosmetics in front of each chair. We were looking through the material when the speaker of the night before again stepped onto the raised platform and adjusted the microphone.

"Good morning, girls." Feedback again, only louder. The old man ran to fix it.

The problem corrected, she continued. "Whenever I hear that dreadful noise, it reminds me how quiet our new jet aircraft really are." She added a big laugh at the end.

The eleven girls seated at a long table near the platform all laughed with careful, studied laughs. We watched them for the rest of the meeting and noticed they did everything in syncopation— smile, frown, shake head up and down, etc. We played the game and laughed right along with everyone.

"Well, let me see. I saw some of you last night during the dinner hour. My name is Miss Gruel and I'm the director of the stewardess school."

"That's Big Momma, like the doorman said last night," Rachel whispered.

Gruel went on, "I welcome you on behalf of the airline, its management, and board of directors. And, of course, your sisters of the skies, your fellow stewardesses.

"You're about to begin a glorious and glamorous career as hostesses of the air. Each of you has indicated to us during preliminary interviews high aptitude for this most demanding and rewarding of careers. We begin this six-week course of instruction with the highest hope that each of you will make a definite contribution to our airline's already promising future. It will not be easy. These six weeks have been carefully prepared to demand the most of each individual. But with fortitude, desire, and hard work, you'll all be greeting friends and parents on that very special occasion—graduation! In the welcoming booklet you find on the tables, you'll see a very specific and detailed list of rules and regulations that will govern you during your stay here. I don't feel I have to say more than to state even the slightest infraction of any rule will result in your immediate dismissal from school. Work hard, girls, and the future of aviation and service will be yours to enjoy."

She obviously appreciated the thunderous ovation we gave her, much as Mrs. Coolie did back in Amarillo. She tried to appear humble as she strode off the platform, but it was no use.

Each of the eleven girls at the long table now came forward and told us about her areas of instruction. They had all been stewardesses at one time or another and hadn't lost their smiles. After an hour and a half of speeches, we were allowed to break for coffee, orange juice, and Danish pastry. I was biting into a butternut Danish when Betty O'Riley, wearing a very tight sweater and skirt, asked me, "What does infraction mean?"

"It means breaking the rules," I informed her.

"Wow. Y'all mean all those rules in the book?"

"Guess so."

"We'll be climbing the walls before six weeks are up."

"Just don't climb the electric fence," Rachel threw in.

"They must use something, huh?" Betty continued with her questions.

"What do you mean, 'use something'?"

"Y'all know," Betty explained, "some sort of chemical that makes you forget about sex . . . Y'all know what I mean . . . Something to take away that tingle when you think about boys. That kind of thing."

"Saltpeter?" Rachel asked.

"No, silly, that's for boys, Ah think. Anyway, all these places use *somethin'*. Frankly, ah hope they do. Ah never stop tingling."

We didn't doubt her for a minute.

Sally Lu hadn't said a word since we met her at the gate last night. She seemed to take a liking to Rachel and said to her, as we were returning to our seats for part two of the meeting, "It says in the book that we can't leave the grounds for a whole week. That's awful. Warren, my boyfriend, will break the door down. It's awful."

Rachel was afraid she'd cry again.

"Don't worry about it, Sally Lu. Maybe you can throw kisses from the window."

"I hope so," Sally Lu sighed, seemingly relieved by this piece of encouragement.

After lunch, another feast topped off with chocolate ice cream, whipped cream, and pecans, we had our first meeting on makeup, hairstyling, and general grooming.

The class was conducted by a faggy-looking man with long, wavy hair and a twitch in his left eye. He sketched facial outlines on the blackboard while a sharp looking girl in a stewardess uniform welcomed us to the classroom.

"Welcome to your first class in how to look more beautiful, radiant, and charming. I'm Miss Lucas and with me is Mister André, a well-known hairstylist and makeup expert. When Mister André is through with you, your own family won't know you're the same girl they knew when you left to become a stewardess."

Mister André picked on Cynthia first, much to her delight. He pointed out how nicely her hairstyle complemented her facial structure to which she replied, "It should. My stylist is very highly paid." We all felt a little waifish by comparison.

The next girl he called to the front of the room was Betty. Gay or not, he couldn't keep his eyes off her forty-inch chest. It was at this precise moment that Betty got her nickname. Rachel leaned over to me and whispered, "She's got to have the biggest set of boobs I've ever seen. And we know they're all for real." Cynthia read a book while Betty was up front.

Mister André told me my face was oblong, and Rachel was

handed the sad news she was moonfaced. Cynthia was termed classic, and Sally Lu was actually called ordinary, sort of Middle American. We decided that Mister André's face was definitely early-fag. And his long, lacquered fingernails didn't clash with this diagnosis.

They really worked us in stewardess school. The training was no joke. To graduate you have to pass the FAA test—that's the Federal Aviation Agency—and the test is a long written affair that requires you to know everything there is to know about all the planes the company flies. First we went over those planes inch by inch in classrooms, using textbooks and charts. We had to know where the emergency exits are, how to use them, how much fuel the plane carries, how the galley works, what equipment to use in emergencies, and where it is. We had to know all of this and much more for four different types of planes.

Training started every day at 8:00 in the morning. We were up at 6:30. The commotion in the bathroom was unbelievable as we all rushed to shower and fix our hair. We had to be dressed fit to kill every morning, our fingernails absolutely perfect, our faces made up. After a week of classroom work, they took us aboard the jets out back. A dozen times a day we climbed aboard and worked in one area and then another—the cockpit, the galley, the lavatories.

We had special over-water practice so that we would know all about the life vests, the rafts, and the emergency equipment. One day they took us all to a nearby lake and put us in life rafts—those big, yellow inflated rafts that bob around on the surface. There were about six of us and a supervisor on each raft and six rafts drifting around on the water. At first we paid strict attention because we knew this was important. It might someday be a matter of life and death. Naturally Rachel and I had managed to get on the same raft. By this time all the girls knew, look out for Rachel and Trudy—anything can happen. Well, we floated pretty close to the next raft and right there at arm's length I saw the little cork that you pull to let the air out of the raft. Rachel read my mind, "No!" she said. But I knew she really wanted me to do it.

I looked over at the other raft and waited for the supervisor to turn her head. Rachel, bless her, put out her hand and paddled us a little closer, all the time saying "No, no!" I reached over, pulled the cork and SWWSSHHH that raft went flat, all the girls fell into the water, spluttering and coughing, and that supervisor with her wet hair in her face shouted, "Which one of you did it—Trudy or Rachel? It had to be one of you."

* * *

Later on they took us out on actual flights and pulled all kinds of stunts on us. They cut the engines to see if we'd panic. The first time they did that to me, the captain came on the PA and said, "The right engine has cut out and so has the left one. You'll notice we're over water." Then he handed me the mike. I guess I was supposed to say something cheerful to the passengers so in my heartiest voice I said, "OK, folks, we're going to swim."

I think they had a conference that night to decide whether to expel me or not. I hung on. But many of the girls didn't make it. During the six weeks they dropped twenty-three out of the forty-five who started with our class and that is about normal. Sometimes they throw you out for breaking the rules or not studying, but mostly because you don't prove to have a stewardess personality—you don't really like people. That's the key to it. You have to like people and be willing to serve them day and night and take care of their needs and demands. When we made our trial flights, they filled the planes with the worst SOBs they could find. They were there to test us. A man on an aisle seat would say, through clenched teeth, "I did not order this damned steak rare. I want it well done." You bring it back to him well done and he says, "This is the worst airline I've ever seen. I order a cup of coffee and I get a glass of milk. Where do they find such stupid girls?"

Not only are you forbidden to blow up, but they watch even for a vexed expression on your face. They want to be real sure that you can take the worst a passenger can dish out and that you'll stay friendly and even kid him and say, "You're right—I'm with you."

About the third week the grind let up a little. We could go out at night and they raised the curfew to 11 P.M. On weekends there was a continual party around the pool. Fellows came over from an air force base nearby, and captains and officers working for the airline stopped by to look over the newest crop of stews. We made friends quickly and easily.

Of course, Sally Lu, being from the town, spent every night with Warren, her hot-rodding beau. She confided one night to Rachel that Warren had gotten her pregnant three times, but each time he took her to a friend who was going through medical school who, in turn, took care of Sally Lu. We all agreed upon hearing the story that Sally Lu could not be thought of as an exceptionally bright girl.

They would race back to the school every night just before ten, and she'd throw him kisses through the fence while he cursed at the gatekeeper. One night, as he was yelling at the old man, his arm accidentally touched the electric fence. It knocked him down but he got up again.

"Maybe it made him sterile," Rachel said hopefully as Sally Lu told the story to us that night. Sally Lu cried half the night.

"How stupid can you be?" Rachel exploded at her one night in the room. "Why don't you stay away from him until you're married, or take the pill?"

"Well, I always ask Warren to stop a little sooner but he never does. Poor Warren. I guess it's pretty hard when you're a fella." Then she cried.

On Thursday, just four days before graduation, Sally Lu burst into the room and announced, "Warren wants to treat all of you to a Coke for bein' so nice to his girl. Isn't that just so sweet of him?" Betty, Trudy, and I decided to go with them. Cynthia declined and remained slumped at her desk browsing through a copy of *Women's Wear Daily* that her mother sent her.

We piled into Warren's car for the drive to a local drive-in, where girls sit in their fathers' cars while boys cruise around the parking lot in their fathers' cars. Usually they never hook up. But the parade is always fun to watch. The place was called Ma's Root Beer Stand, a fifteen-minute drive from the school but accomplished in ten by Warren. We sat sipping our drinks while Sally Lu shared a big orangeade in the front seat with Warren, their two straws sucking up the syrupy soda in between kisses on the ear and light touches of the thigh.

"Why don't you two get married?" Rachel asked, the root beer going to her head.

"Soon's I git my own gas station," Warren proudly answered as he gunned the running motor for emphasis.

"That's why I decided to be a stewardess," Sally Lu said giddily as she played with the hair coming through Warren's shirt front. "Soon as he has his own station, I'll stop flyin' and we'll get married. Right, hon?"

"You betcha," he grunted. "Unless she goes and meets some fancy dude on one a' them airplanes." He laughed off the comment but his look indicated he would slit her throat if she did.

Sally Lu nudged him and kissed his ear.

We left Ma's at 10:15, in plenty of time to get back before curfew, especially with Warren driving. He shot away from the parking lot and headed along a dirt road that was a new shortcut he'd found. Totally desolate, it wound around the perimeter of the school grounds. We were directly behind the campus when Warren's drive shaft popped or broke or snapped or did something that brought us to a rattling halt.

After much swearing by Warren, we decided to try to walk back in hope of beating the curfew. We were sure losers because it looked as though a car hadn't been over that road for a year, but anything was better than sitting there all night.

"Come on," we prodded as Warren held Sally Lu tight against the front fender and smothered her with kisses.

They broke and we took off at a slight trot. We soon slowed to a walk and had progressed about fifteen minutes when we spotted a car ahead, parked under an oak tree. The sight of it gave us a momentary feeling of glee. But that feeling lasted only six seconds. Then, the car took on a menacing shape. Maybe a madman was there waiting for the girls he saw walking down the road. Maybe there was a dead body.

"I wish Warren was with us," Sally Lu moaned as we gathered behind a tree perhaps seventy feet from the car.

"Look, maybe it's just somebody necking, or admiring the moon, or something." Good old Rachel, steady as a rock in all situations.

Silence reigned until Rachel again spoke up. "Look, we're late already. And we have to pass that car to get back to the gate. I'll slip up quietly and see what's up. If everything is OK, we'll pass. If it looks like a nut or something, you can all weep over the great sacrifice I made for you."

"If he's good lookin', yell." That was Betty.

Rachel stalked the car like someone out of a James Bond movie. She stooped low as she came up behind the vehicle and then raised her head to look in the rear window. She stayed there looking for over a minute. Then, she turned and came back in a low run.

"You'll never believe it," she panted. "Never!"

"What's up?"

"You'll never believe it," she repeated. "It's Big Momma. Gruel. With a man."

"You're putting us on."

"No, I'm not. And you know who I think it is? I think it's that man who delivers meat to the cafeteria."

"Gruel with the meatman?"

"I think so."

"He's kinda good lookin'," Betty recalled.

"He's not," I said.

"Ah wanna see," Betty insisted.

"I don't think we should," Sally Lu protested.

"Come on. You've got to see it to believe it."

It was a ridiculous thing to do. All Gruel had to do was catch us and we could kiss our wings good-bye. But then again, and the thought ran through all our minds, Gruel would be hard-pressed to make any fuss. We were within ten feet when we heard Gruel's voice. It had taken on a little girl quality, a far cry from the studied tones she used in the classroom.

"Alan," she squealed, "don't do that."

"Shhhhhhhhh, Louisa," a gravel voice replied. "It's dark and I'm reading your lovely figure in . . . whatta ya call it? Braille."

I wanted to throw up. The whole world must use that cornball line. And I almost spent a lifetime hearing it.

"Ah wonder if he's wearing his apron," Betty muttered.

We stood there in the darkness, barely breathing. Then we circled the car and reached the front door. When the doorman called in our late arrival we received a stern scolding from the dorm adviser.

"You'll have to answer to Gruel in the morning."

The thought was almost appealing. We got into bed and Betty said, "Ah was last in line when we sneaked past the car. Ah saw them climbin' into the backseat."

Miss Gruel looked tired the next morning as she lectured us on the terrible thing we'd done in breaking curfew. Our broken car story didn't hold much weight with her, but it probably did save us from being kicked out of school.

We didn't see Gruel again until the final class on conduct and personal habits. This was, by reputation, Big Momma's favorite class. She always taught it herself.

Her lecture was brutal. It ran on for an hour in wall-to-wall words about the importance of living a life worthy of the stewardess image.

"Perhaps you take offense at what you might construe as meddling into your personal lives. But your personal lives will be mirrored in your conduct as a stewardess. It is my wish that each of you always give deep thought before giving yourself . . . how shall I say it . . . giving yourself to other than the man you marry, if marriage shall be your wish. It was stated so nicely years ago by some unknown scholar who said, 'Is an hour of pleasure worth a lifetime of hell?'"

We sat there trying to look deep in thought at this profound message. Betty Big Boobs broke the silence. "Mah only question is, how do y'all make it last an hour?"

Gruel didn't understand the question at first. Then she did. Class was over and Betty became a stewardess against the better judgment of everyone.

The next to the last night before graduation I couldn't take it any longer and I said, "Rachel, let's go. Let's get out of here and go into town."

"Oh, no," she said. "It's only a couple of days more—let's not get into any big trouble."

"You're not going to let me go alone?"

"Of course not."

We sneaked out the balcony window at the end of the corridor, right next to our room, and got down by hanging onto a downspout and some heavy grapevines. Before we left we fixed our beds to look as if they had bodies in them—we knew there was a bed check at midnight. Well, it worked fine. We went to the bar where the airline people hung out and we danced and kidded and had a fine time and I met Chuck.

Chuck was a first officer and had already been with the airline for a year. He was very tall with a marvelous smile, a great blond crew cut and crazy blue eyes under huge eyebrows. I'd never seen such blue eyes in a man. He started getting me drinks and paying attention to me and finally I said, "Come on, handsome, we're going to dance."

He said, "You've got to be unreal. You must be from the South."

I said, "You've got it—I'm from Texas and we love everybody."

He was from way up in Minnesota where it's so cold you can practically ice-skate in the summer. We talked and kidded as if we'd known each other forever. I hated to leave, but Rachel's saner head prevailed. We got a lift back to school about midnight. We scampered across the front yard, crouching low to escape the beam of the searchlight and scrambled up our vine and pipe to safety.

The next night, the eve of graduation, there was no holding me. I had to see Chuck again. Rachel and I would be leaving for New York over the weekend. I wanted to find out where he was going to be. He looked too good for me to let him disappear just like that and leave it to chance that we might meet someday on a flight. Or maybe our paths would never again cross. I couldn't bear that thought.

Rachel protested—it was too dangerous to take a chance only hours before graduation. Word had gotten around that any last-minute infraction would bring last-minute expulsion. Then the whole six weeks would go for nothing. But there was no holding me. So Rachel took super precautions. I don't know how that kid did it, but she had someone smuggle in two department store mannequins. We tucked them into our beds and pulled the covers up to their shiny chins. We swore our roommates to secrecy. Much as we bickered with them from time to time, we knew none of them would turn us in, not even the lofty Cynthia.

We got down our vine and reached the bar and did we have a ball. We had the greatest time of our lives. Chuck and I danced for hours, all those crazy wild dances where you never touch, but even at arm's length you get on the same beam and move with the frantic beat as intimately as if you were twined together. All the fellows from the airline knew Rachel and I were about to be graduated and they insisted on toasting us, so of course we had to toast back. They really shouldn't have let us do all that drinking, but we were flying and no one could stop us.

"He's going to be based in California for the next three months," I told Rachel sadly during a lull in the racket from the jukebox. "I won't be able to see him unless I get a California flight."

"My money's on you, kid," Rachel said. "I bet you'll make it in a week."

Then the party closed in on us again, the drinking and the dancing and suddenly it was 3 A.M. and we were bombed. Well, they got us back to the school grounds and we made it to the wall of our dormitory and I looked up and said, "God, how am I ever going to get up there?" I went first and I kept calling to Rachel, "Come on honey, you can do it."

Rachel just stood there at the bottom and said, "I want to die. I want to die." The next thing I knew, she got sick.

I tapped on the window and called Betty and Sally Lu to help us. I slid down again and tried to pass Rachel up to the others. She was completely limp by then. I shoved her up and they almost had her and then she twisted her foot in that blasted vine and there she was back on the ground with an aching ankle.

Now we've had it, I thought. We'll never get her back up and how'll we explain it and we'll be busted in the morning. And this time *I* wanted to die. But I wasn't going to give up without a fight. Somehow the three of us tugged and hauled Rachel up, pulled her clothes off and stood her up in the shower.

"I want to die," she wailed.

"Listen to me," I told her. "You're going to die if you don't listen. You can yell now. Yell all you want. And when the supervisor comes, tell her you slipped in the shower and twisted your ankle. Got it?"

I guess she got it because the supervisor came running and Rachel was bawling and the rest of us were shrieking.

"How did this happen?" she demanded.

"Well, it's graduation day," I explained, "and we just couldn't sleep we were so excited, so Rachel decided to take a shower and I guess she slipped."

Rachel graduated with a cast on her ankle. "I could just kill you," she hissed to me when they pinned her wings on.

Graduation was very solemn and impressive. Our parents came for the occasion and everyone cried a little as we marched down the main stairs in the dorm in uniform singing our class song, a silly set of words put to the melody of *Liza*. The vice president of sales, who we later discovered was having an affair of long standing with Miss Gruel, pinned our wings on us after making a little speech. Miss Gruel told us we were the best class the school had ever had. We knew she told that to all the classes. But we liked hearing it anyway because we all felt the past six weeks had been a turning point in our lives. Even the giddiest of us had gained assurance and knowledge. We were ready for the outside world and all the challenges it would bring. We were stewardesses.

There was a parting benediction from Miss Gruel. She sent a memo to the airline brass: "Don't let Trudy and Rachel fly together." I guess it got filed in a wastebasket.

# CHAPTER IV

## "You're Nothing but a Stew-Bum, George"

$O$ur first flight together, as already chronicled, was less than perfect. But despite its many hazards, we did take away something of tangible worth–George Kelman.

George represented our first experience in accepting dates with passengers. Like every other girl seeking a career as a stewardess, we were fully aware of the reputation the corps had acquired. Our last days at home in Amarillo and Louisville had been filled with stern parental warnings. You had to be promiscuous to want to be a stewardess, was the consensus of family and friends. We would have to spend our days and nights warding off rape attempts of captains, passengers, and all those love-'em-and-leave-'em guys. Our folks harped on the dangers so much we almost found them appealing.

But George Kelman, our first passenger date, proved everyone wrong. He was, if there is such a thing, the perfect gentleman.

That night in Cleveland George took us to one of the city's better restaurants. The more we ate and drank, the more George seemed to enjoy himself. We worried, of course, about sitting there drinking when we probably would have to work a trip back to New York in the morning. Stewardesses aren't allowed to drink within twenty-four hours of a flight, and although our return schedule was unknown, it would most likely fall within the next twenty-four. But George was very convincing on this subject.

"Don't worry about that drinking rule, girls," he said as he poured us another glass of Beaujolais. "I've got plenty of Clorets. No one will ever know alcohol has passed your pretty lips. The only thing you have to worry about is a stew-spy. I've looked around the place and I'm sure there isn't one here."

"Stew-spy?" The thought was incredible, too much so to be believed.

"Yes. Stew-spy," he confirmed. "You'll find out all about them when you go to your first union meeting. In the meantime, just take my word for it and watch your step. You can't trust any girl you fly with, unless you really know her. Even then, don't be too sure."

Rachel and I looked at each other with suspicion. Then we laughed and drank more wine.

We checked back at the hotel before leaving the restaurant and there had been no calls. We then proceeded to a nightclub on Cleveland's outskirts, a barnlike place with a rock-and-roll band on a raised platform over the bar and two go-go dancers on the bar itself (much to the discomfort of a few hardfisted drinkers). It looked like a pick-up joint.

The music was terrible, its din jarring the brain with every rimshot and twang. We ordered drinks from a mousy little girl in a sequined bunny costume, and settled back to watch the action. Stray fellows and girls were everywhere, each trying to outguess the other. One of the girls, a muscular blonde with smeared eye shadow and dirty fingernails, leaned against the wall next to our table. Every so often, a young man with long sideburns and starched dungarees would come over to her, offer to buy a drink, and ask, "How's about makin' it outta here with me?"

She always replied, "Git me a Wild Turkey 'n Seven-Up and I'll think 'bout it." He'd trudge off to the bar and she'd wait, nursing the previous drink and scratching her nose.

One hulk of a guy, obviously not heavy in the mental department, came over to her and said, "Hey, sweets, whatta ya say we run 'cross town and do a couple lines a' bowlin'?"

"Bowlin'?" the girl repeated. "Git me a Wild Turkey 'n Seven-Up and I'll see."

"OK, sweets," the hulk replied and went back to the bar to fight the crowd for his order.

"I wonder if she'd go with me if I suggested weight lifting?" George kidded.

"Give her a try," we suggested.

He did.

"Maybe," she answered him with a straight face. Then she realized what he'd said. "You say weight liftin'?"

"Yup."

"Buy me a Wild Turkey 'n Seven-Up and I'll see."

"Let *me* think about *that*," George countered, keeping a straight face as he sat down.

The girl muttered, "Weight liftin'?" again, and called to the hulk who had offered bowling. "Hey Billy, come on over here."

He gave up his spot at the bar and came back growling, "Now I lost my place in line."

"This here guy wants to take me weight liftin'," she told him.

He wasn't sure he understood. But he felt safe in saying, "You some kinda wise guy?" George flinched.

The hulk became bolder. "Come on, fella, you bein' a wise guy to this here girl?"

George looked gravely concerned. He fished a ten-dollar bill from his pocket and threw it on the table, and with firm pressure on our elbows made us stand up. He got up with us.

The hulk came close to George, their proximity emphasizing the difference in height and brawn.

"Look, no trouble intended," George said weakly as he tried to slide past his adversary. "Just a little joke, you know. El joke-o, huh?"

"Where was you gonna go weight liftin'?"

"Nowhere, nowhere. Honest. Just a simple jest."

"You don't look like no weight lifter to me."

"And you sure do. Look, I'm sorry. Buy yourselves drinks out of the ten on the table. OK?"

George's generosity stymied the hulk for a moment, enough time for us to take large strides for the door. We heard him muttering, "Weight liftin'?" as we pushed past the bar crowd and onto the exit. A sweaty go-go girl waved good-bye without breaking stride in her jerking and frugging.

The air outside, and the quiet it offered, was welcome. "Someday I'll learn to keep my mouth shut in these joints," George sighed. "I should have known every guy in there was probably a weight lifter. Bad news, these places. Come on, we'll go back to the hotel and have a nightcap. Better yet, we'll find a bar near the hotel."

We found a cocktail lounge near the hotel and went in. We were barely inside when a table of girls, definitely stewardess types, spotted George and gave him a big Hello.

"Hi, girls," he beamed. We wondered how he knew them but didn't ask. Why shouldn't he know girls? But why stewardesses? Spies? Silly!

We each had a stinger, weak ones, and George insisted he walk us back to our room in the hotel. We expected the inevitable pitch to come in for a drink or, considering there were two of us, an invitation for one of us to go back to his room. But nothing like that happened.

"Girls, I really enjoyed it." He fished in his pocket and came out with a half-used roll of Clorets. "Here, for the morning. Your supervisor will never know you've had a drop. Sleep tight."

"Good night."

"See you tomorrow on the flight, girls."

"You're going back with us?"

"Sure. I'm anxious to see how you do with your second flight. Should be interesting."

"But we don't even know what flight we're working,"

"They'll probably call you sometime tonight. They always manage to call when you're asleep. They'll call you and I'll know, too. See you then." He turned and walked back to the bank of elevators. We went into our room, very much up in the air about this whole George Kelman thing.

"He knows so much about being a stewardess," Rachel mused as she struggled out of her girdle. Neither of us had been girdle-wearers until becoming stewardesses. The manual said you always had to wear one while working, and slipping into one had become habit.

"Maybe he's some kind of spy," I suggested.

"I don't think so, Trudy, but maybe he's with the airline in another capacity. No, that doesn't seem logical. But he's rich. That's for sure. Imagine flying back with us just to see how we do."

"I think it's a big line."

"Probably, but he's kind of cute, though."

"Uh huh. I wonder what he does for a living."

"Me too. What about those other girls in the bar? They all seemed to know him."

"Well, I suppose he meets a lot of stewardesses with all his travel and everything. He really is cute."

Rachel had her pajama bottoms on and was slipping into her top when she noticed her bare bosom in a full-length mirror on the wall. Rachel was nicely built although on the small side.

"I wonder if he knows Betty Big Boobs," she asked her mirror image.

"Who knows?" I answered. "He wouldn't like her anyway. He doesn't look like he has a breast fixation."

We climbed under the covers.

"I like him," Rachel giggled. "I really do."

"I think he likes you, Rachel."

"I don't think so, Trudy. It's you he likes."

"Anyway, I'm glad we went out with him. He's up for grabs. OK? No hard feelings when one of us runs off and marries him."

"You don't need him, you have Chuck."

"Sure—in California. Good night."

Everything was silent for a minute.

"Gee, Trudy, I hope he isn't a spy."

"Don't be silly. Good night."

"Good night." (pause) "Trudy?"

"What, Rachel?"

"You don't think he's queer, do you? I mean, he didn't even try a thing."

"How could he with the two of us?"

"Well, he could have asked one of us down to his room."

"Would you have gone?"

"Of course not."

"Then why do you think he's queer? He knew neither of us would have gone with him."

"I guess you're right, Trudy." (Two minutes of silence this time.) "Have you ever gone to bed with a man?"

"Rachel, what is this? I've told you about Henry."

"I don't mean in a car, silly. I mean in bed. A hotel."

"Of course not!"

"I was just wondering."

"Well stop wondering and shut up. I'm tired."

"Me too. Good night."

"Good night."

We'd been asleep about a half hour when the telephone woke us both up. Rachel picked it up.

"Howdy. Miss Baker?" a nasal voice asked.

"No, this is Rachel Jones."

"Miss Baker with you?"

"Who is this?"

"This here's Rob at crew scheduling. You two gals are gonna fly tomorra at noon. Reckon all the soup in New York'll be gone by then."

Rachel sighed and laid back on her pillow. "Have you told Mr. Kelman about the flight?"

"Mister . . . who?"

"Forget it. Thanks for the warning on the flight tomorrow. Good night."

"'Night . . . Say, what are you gals doin'?"

"We're sleeping. Good night."

"You're both brand spankin' new, ain't you?"

"Right. Good night."

"You ain't been breakin' any rules, have ya?"

"If it's against the rules to hang up on you, yes. Good night." She banged the receiver back in its cradle and rolled over. "Creep."

We slept a solid hour when a door slamming next door brought us both up to a sitting position. A man's voice in the next room said, "Hurry up. I don't have a lot of time." The walls were paper thin.

"Afraid your wife will scold you?" a female voice answered.

"Don't be smart," he said, a little annoyed.

The next noise was a bed creaking. A few giggles, some scuffling, three minutes of silence, and then he said, "Good night, hon. Sleep tight. See you next time you're in town." The door closed quietly and his footsteps padded past our door.

"Who's in the next room?" Rachel whispered.

"How should I know?"

"Is it a stewardess?"

"I haven't the foggiest."

"Let's check in the morning."

"OK. Good night, Rachel."

"Good night, Trudy."

The next sound was the telephone. It was 9:30 the following morning. I answered it. "Hello."

"Hi. George Kelman, here. How about some breakfast?"

"When?"

"Right now. You've got to be at the airport at eleven. Noon flight, right?"

"That's right. We'll be a half hour."

"Fine. Meet me in the dining room and we'll cab it out to the airport. See you at ten."

"OK." I hung up and pushed Rachel out of her bed and onto the floor. I wake up when a pin drops, but Rachel can sleep through a machine gun duel in the next room. "Come on. George is buying us breakfast and picking up the cab tab to the airport." Rachel just curled up on the floor and started to go back to sleep.

"Come on, Rachel, we haven't got much time."

It took a playful kick in the ribs to bring her to her feet. We managed to get ready, pack, and out the door by ten, and met George in the dining room. He was sipping orange juice and reading *The Cleveland Plain Dealer*.

"Good morning, Mr. Kelman."

"Hi, girls. I already ordered eggs, bacon, juice, and coffee for you. Have a seat."

We raced through breakfast, hardly talking to each other, until Rachel responded to his question about how we slept.

"Great," she told him, "if we hadn't been party to a little scene next door. These walls are like cardboard. Some married man and his girlfriend. Kind of interesting."

"Which room on which side of you?" George asked, never looking up from his reading.

"The one on the right," I said. "I mean on the left. On the side furthest from the elevators."

He laughed a little. "Lewis's room, huh?"

"Who's Lewis?" I asked.

He seemed annoyed at my slowness. "Lewis. Your senior stew on yesterday's flight."

We were shocked. "Miss Lewis?"

He was still annoyed, this time at our naïveté. "Yes. Miss Lewis. So she was swinging a little, huh? Interesting."

Miss Lewis was already on board when we arrived to work our noon flight. Her face was as stern and unyielding as ever. The temptation was great to let something slip to show our knowledge of her extracurricular activities. Perhaps another few months on the line we would have that kind of boldness. But it was not prudent for two novice stewardesses.

George was quiet throughout the trip. He posed another temptation for us. Should we ask the obvious: how he knew where Miss Lewis was staying? That seemed unwise, too. But the more we thought of George Kelman, the more we became convinced there was something wrong with him. He either had to be officially connected with the airline, a spy for the stewardess union, a bring-'em-back-alive agent for The Amarillo or Louisville Chamber of Commerce, or maybe just a raving idiot who always wanted to be a stewardess.

The flight this time was uneventful. We felt a little more confident about our chores, although we still managed to spill a few drinks and to misplace a passenger's raincoat. (We finally found it on the floor of the coatrack under Rachel's overnight case.) George didn't say anything as we left the airplane. But he did wink at Miss Lewis, who stood by the cabin door as he passed. She just looked away and bid farewell to the man behind him.

We went through the sign-out procedures in operations and headed for the taxi line. We were exhausted. The trip, the weather, Miss Lewis, and George Kelman had proven too much to handle in such a short span of time. We should have conserved money and taken the Carey bus back into Manhattan, but a cab was faster, easier, and more comfortable. And comfort was highest on the immediate list of priorities.

We collapsed once we hit the apartment. If we didn't have to buy our own uniforms, we wouldn't have even bothered to take them off. Our apartment was furnished with only a couch, two beds, a director's chair, and a camel saddle from Arabia. I never got past the couch. Rachel fell instantly asleep on her bed. Then the telephone rang.

"Hi. This is George."

"Please, no," Rachel pleaded. "Call tomorrow, when we've had twenty hours sleep. Not now."

"Sorry to bother you, Rachel, but you've got to eat dinner. Right? It's on me. You name the place."

"George Kelman, whoever you may be, dinner is the last thing on our minds at this moment."

"By midnight you'll be hungry. How about a few pizzas? At your place. Or mine. Or the pizza place. You name it and I'll be there with the mushrooms. That's my favorite kind of pizza. What's yours?"

The fatigue had brought out an unusual testiness in Rachel. "No! No pizza, no eggs, no steak, no oysters, no soup, not even a candy bar. We're tired and we're going to sleep without George Kelman. I mean we're . . . Oh, the hell with it." She hung up with a bang.

We slept until ten the next morning and made it out to JFK for a one o'clock Cleveland trip. Yes, George Kelman was standing there when we arrived, just outside operations. It was beginning to take on a nightmarish quality, this whole George Kelman thing. Or shades of sophomoric romance with the jilted suitor spending seven days and nights following you around.

When we saw him standing there, we started giggling.

"Hi," he said happily.

"Are you going to Cleveland again?" we asked.

"Nope. Not today."

"Why?" Rachel pressed our sudden good luck.

"I'm going to Los Angeles."

"Just what business are you in that takes you to all these places?"

He thought that over for a moment. "Well, none, really. I'm what you could call independently wealthy."

"Sure," I said with sarcasm, "and I'm Doris Duke."

"I knew you didn't look like a stewardess," he quipped.

We looked around for any snooping eyes and ears and put what we felt was the crusher on him. "Look, just what is it with you?"

He was hurt. "Well, I'll be damned. Here I am, a regular guy who's sorry he woke you up last night and comes all the way out to the airport to apologize. Do I have to take a loyalty oath, too?"

"We're sorry, George. Guess we're a little on edge after the first flight and all. How long will you be in LA?"

"Overnight. Be back tomorrow."

"Oh. Well, have a great trip. See you again."

"Gee, I hope so. How about dinner tomorrow night?"

"Can't. Besides, just which one of us are you asking?"

"Both of you. Honest. I'll call you."

"OK. Bye."

"Bye."

We had dinner with George four more times during the following six weeks. He flew with us again to Cleveland, once to Cincinnati, and treated us twice in New York. It was all weird; totally weird. In fact, it was downright frustrating that he never asked one of us out. It always was the two of us together. There was never a pass, never a pinch, or subtle brush of the hand—nothing. Just a free-spending guy with good manners and a happy way about him. We actually came to the point of no longer wondering about George and what he was. To be candid, he had become a great meal ticket, one without the usual strings attached.

We did find out a little more about George a week after our fourth dinner date. We had gone to the theater the night before, sixth-row center seats, compliments of Mr. Kelman, who couldn't join us because of an out-of-town trip. Rachel, who was flying reserve that month, had pulled a Seattle trip for the following day, and it was on that flight that some of the mystery was solved.

Rachel was surprised when she saw him board the 707 for Seattle. He seemed a little taken back at seeing her, but recovered quickly and gave her a hearty greeting. The other three stewardesses didn't seem to know him, or notice him.

The flight was an hour out of New York when Rachel, doing a

head count against the one the senior stew had performed, discovered there was one too many heads. She mentioned it to the senior stew, a chesty little California girl with bangs, and a hustle-bustle way of doing everything.

"I know, I know," she said when Rachel mentioned the problem. "I've got a dummy aboard."

"A what?"

"A dummy. Dummy. A friend. Forget it. Just drop it."

"I don't understand," Rachel persisted out of sheer curiosity. "What's a dummy?"

"Look, sweetie, there's a guy on board I happen to do a few favors for once in a while. That's all there is to it. It's done all the time. You know when a flight is going to be light so you slip him on board. Just cool it and start serving the food."

Rachel went about her chores, looking into every male passenger's face for a sign, a clue. Which one was the dummy? George Kelman was an obvious choice, with his stewardess connections and all, but that didn't seem to make any sense to Rachel. George was wealthy. Or at least he said he was. Besides, if a stewardess wanted to do him a favor, why risk her job slipping him on the airplane? Why not sleep with him? Then she remembered the possibility of his being gay. Or maybe he was a gigolo, his trips were his payoff. She looked at him again. No. Impossible. Too sweet.

It had to be another man, a boyfriend of the senior stew. And which one that was certainly wasn't any of Rachel's business. She tried to forget about it, content with her new knowledge that it was possible to sneak a friend on board an airplane.

Rachel was the first stewardess off the plane in Seattle. She hurried across the lobby, did her checking out quickly, and stationed herself behind a concrete pillar by the hack stand. "I ought to have my head examined," she muttered to herself as she tried not to look too much like a private eye behind the proverbial potted palm.

What she was waiting for soon materialized. The little senior stew with the bangs came from the terminal with George Kelman. They entered a cab and headed for downtown.

Rachel, devil that she can be at times, thought quickly. She raced for a phone booth and dialed the hotel where the crews stayed.

"Hello. This is Rachel Jones, a stewardess. I just got in on Flight 61 with Miss Crowly and Miss Ramkin, and Miss Ramkin and I would like a room adjacent to Miss Crowly's. We have homework to do together."

"Yes, ma'm. I'll put you and Miss Ramkin in Room 1131."

"Thank you."

That night, Rachel stayed close to the room. Miss Ramkin had a date, and Rachel sat alone, her ear straining for signs of activity next door.

She dozed off about midnight and was awakened at two by laughter in the hall. It was George's laugh.

Rachel got mad at herself for being such a busybody, but that didn't deter her from pressing a water glass against the wall. "This is terrible," she scolded herself.

All she'd heard about a water glass being a good conductor of sound was proven wrong that night. Only snatches of the conversation could be heard, a tribute, we suppose, to the hotel's substantial walls.

But she did hear the senior stewardess say, "You can stay if you'd like to, George."

And he answered, "No, thanks. Got to run."

And that's exactly what he did.

Was George Kelman really queer? Or was he simply a pleasant guy with a fetish for stewardesses? We were baffled.

I was the one who found out about George, quite by accident through a friend of his. I started dating Bill, a New York psychology student, about a month after Rachel's ear-to-the-wall report from Seattle. Bill was an interesting type of young man; bright, moody, subject to long lapses into introverted discussions on matters that concerned him deeply. He went into one of these spells one night in his fourth-floor walk-up apartment in Greenwich Village. He lit a cigarette and started talking about sex, how everyone has an individual need for specific sexual satisfaction, and about some cases he knew that were unusual.

"I know this guy, George. Really strange. He has an unbelievable fixation on stewardesses. It's so strong, he'll spend every dime he has just to hang around them. It's lucky he's loaded."

I was all attention. I accepted Bill's romantic gesture of lighting another cigarette for me, and asked, "This wouldn't be a George named Kelman, would it? You don't have to answer, if you don't want to. But you'd better."

"Oh, you've joined Kelman Airlines, have you? I didn't know you were one of the flock George can claim victory over."

"No, Bill, honest, he's never even tried to touch me. Or Rachel. But he's always asking us to dinner and even used to fly with us. Frankly, we just wrote him off as a good-natured queer."

Bill laughed and lit another cigarette.

"I don't doubt he never tried to touch you. But, George Kelman is no fag. He's just different. He only makes it with pros. Hustlers. Call girls. Plenty of money for any girl he wants, anytime. But the stewardess thing is another matter entirely. He loves being thought of as a big brother to the girls. Of course, he gives the guys the impression that he's in bed with every one. But he's never even tried. He likes to be the trusted guy with the girls. He actually considers stewardesses the ultimate in chaste, sweet American womanhood."

"We are."

"You're not."

"They told us we were at stewardess school."

"They must all be sick down there."

"But it all sounds so ridiculous about George. Why?"

"Who knows? Maybe I should, being a psych student and everything. It's just that some guys need this kind of relationship with clean-cut girls. Maybe it's his personal retribution for always sleeping with prostitutes. But one thing is for sure. Every stewardess who's given him a chance to hang around has found him to be a charming and delightful guy. No strain, no fuss. No passes after every date. Just good company. Funny."

I tried to digest it all for a minute and then asked, "Why does he sneak on board airplanes? If he's got so much money, why doesn't he just pay for his trips?"

"He usually does. But getting an occasional free ride is sort of a game. It's like stepping on the grass when the sign says you shouldn't. Some of the girls just do it because they feel a large debt to him for all the dinners, gifts, and even loans. You girls are strange. You don't want to *have* to sleep with a guy who spent something on you, but after a while, you start to feel guilty. He should be getting *something*. Right? So, they give George a free trip."

"I can't wait to tell Rachel. We've been avoiding him lately. Now we'll be more tolerant."

"Marvelous. Another poor soul saved by my expert analysis."

"What would you call George, then. A stew-bum?"

"Good a term as any. Don't push me away." I had been exerting counterpressure on Bill's straying hand.

I got back to the apartment very late and told Rachel the whole story. She was fascinated, disbelieving, but bowed to Bill's academic credentials. I was going over it with her again when the phone rang. Rachel answered.

"Hello? George Kelman. How are you?"

"Great, Rachel. How about some dinner tonight? The two of you."

"George, you have a date, even if you are nothing but a stew-bum."

"Ahhhhh, where did you hear that?"

"It makes no difference. It's just our little term of affection for you. Pick us up at seven."

"Right."

We see George Kelman often. His stable of stewardesses has grown, and he has less time for us old-timers. We've met other stew-bums besides George, but he remains unique among the airport Johnnies or hostess hoppers—other terms used to designate the type. The others, while having a similar fixation on stewardesses, also take normal male actions with the girls they go out with. George remains to this day a paragon of virtue with the stewardess corps. His place in aviation history as big-brother-in-residence seems secure.

# CHAPTER V

# "Can We Fit Eight in This Apartment?"

$\mathcal{T}$ake eight girls—one alcoholic, one dieter, one borrower, one compulsive liar, one pet lover, one overall bitch with a nervous curl of her lip, and the two of us—mix them together in a $750 a month penthouse apartment in Manhattan, and you have the makings of a chapter in this book. Lacking a nymphomaniac, we make no pretense at trying to outdo *The Group*. We simply present our own.

Pulling New York City as a duty station is easy. With so many flights originating from the city, the need for stewardesses is great. Also, many girls who try New York for the first year of their flying career decide to transfer to other cities. As they say, it's a great place to visit but . . .

We did as most new stewardesses to the city tend to do. We moved into the stew zoo, a large apartment building in the east Sixties. But we did try first to find our own apartment, one in which we wouldn't feel back in the atmosphere of the stewardess school. We followed the ads in *The New York Times,* and made every attempt to be the first ones answering any advertisement that looked appealing. We should have saved our energy. New York landlords just don't want stewardesses living in their buildings. We rank only behind racial minority groups in feeling the vise of housing prejudice.

We first applied at a pretty brownstone in the upper Eighties where, according to the newspaper ad and the sign outside, there was an apartment available. We rang the downstairs apartment bell, marked super. He came to the door, some mustard from lunch remaining on his triple chin.

"It's taken," he said after looking at us for no more than two seconds. There was mustard on his summer undershirt, too.

"What's taken?" we asked.

"The apartment. It's taken."

"How could it be taken so soon?" Rachel asked, shaking her head back and forth in disbelief.

"Look, goils, take my advice, huh? Go on over on sixty-fifth where all the other stewardesses live." He started back into his apartment.

"Wait a minute. How do you know we're stewardesses?"

"Ain't you?"

"Yes, we are. But how did you know?"

He shrugged his shoulders modestly. "I don't know. It's a funny thing. All you stews look alike."

Rachel wasn't about to take this lying down. "If the apartment's taken, why haven't you taken down the sign?" she demanded.

The super was impatient now. He rubbed the back of his thick neck and screwed his face up in frustration. "Look, goils. Don't make a fuss. The place is taken. That's it. I leave the sign up because I git lonely and like to have people knockin' on my door. OK? Try the stew zoo."

He slammed the door in our face. We'd never heard of any place called the stew zoo. And his reference to it seemed a deliberate attempt to label us animals. At least that's the way Rachel took his comment. She stood there banging her fist on his door. He responded by turning up a recording of Maria Callas at the Met. Rachel banged louder, screaming as she banged, "Call me an animal, will you? You're the animal. A . . . a pig animal."

I pulled her away. "Come on, Rachel. Forget it."

We tried five other places and were rebuffed in each case. At only one of these places was the landlord open about not wanting to rent to stewardesses.

"Look, girls," he sniveled, "nothing personal. But every time we let stewardesses in the building, it's trouble. You break the lease and hop on an airplane for God knows where. You have parties all hours of the day and night and it bugs everybody else in the building. You get behind on your rent. Or you load the place with other girls and pretty soon there's ten of you in a one-bedroom place. Please. Go away. Go over to the stew zoo. It's fun there. Companionship and all that. You know?"

We asked the obvious question. "What is and where is the stew zoo?"

He told us. And we went.

The stewardess population in the stew zoo seldom goes below two hundred. Aside from being a home away from home for so many stewardesses, it's pretty typical of most of the large apartment buildings in New York. We made a lot of good friends there. The halls were never without a uniformed girl of one airline or another. Girls ran in and out of each other's apartments, borrowing stockings and gloves. Evening dresses came and went on loan. It was fun and crazy. There were the stew-bums, George Kelman included, who could be seen coming and going from various apartments, always on a first-name basis with the doorman. The supply of bottles to keep his brown paper bag full usually came from the stew-bums.

We became friendly with Joan Livingston, a stewardess for another airline, who shared the apartment next to us with Jane Baldwin, another stewardess. We got into the habit of dropping into each other's apartment at any hour. Joan and Jane were pleasant enough, although Joan could be snippy and short, her upper lip taking on a strange curl when these moods came to the surface. Her roommate, Jane, we both agreed, seemed to drink too much for her own good.

"Jane always looks a little drunk," we kidded with Joan one day as we walked down the hall together.

"I've never noticed," was Joan's cool answer, her lip curling.

We were having coffee one morning, a day off, in Joan and Jane's apartment, when Joan asked, "How would you two like to move out of this place?"

"Do you have anything better?" Rachel asked.

"I sure do," Joan said. "Here's what we're thinking. I've been going with a fellow who's loaded. I mean really loaded. He lives in a penthouse on the West Side that cost him $750 a month."

"Marry him," I suggested.

"That comes later," Joan said with a smile. "But listen to this. He's moving out of there for a new apartment on this side of town.

And he's offered to sublet his penthouse to me. There's over a year to go on his lease."

"That's great," I said. "But how are you and Jane going to pay that much rent?"

"By getting other girls to share it with us. You two are the first we've asked."

I did some quick figuring in my head.

"That's over $180 a month. Impossible. We couldn't afford that kind of rent."

"Of course not." She was annoyed at my comment, and her lip started to curl. "That's only four of us. But add four more and it makes eight to share the rent. That comes to $93.75 for each person. That's no problem, is it?"

"Eight people!" Rachel banged her knee into the coffee table as she got up from the couch. "Eight people! Can we fit eight into this apartment? It'll be a dormitory."

"Wait'll you see it," was Joan's reply.

We saw it that night. Her boyfriend, a fortyish bachelor, let us in with an overzealous welcome. He gave Joan a long kiss and then proceeded to show us the penthouse. It was splendid. And the problem of fitting eight girls vanished after we looked at each of the four huge bedrooms.

"What have you been doing up here all by yourself?" Rachel asked Richard, as he poured us all a drink.

"I just love room," was his reply. "I can't stand to be cooped up like you usually are in New York. I hate to leave this place but I've found something even better. I can't pass it up."

We sat there and took in the living room as we sipped our Scotch and water. Jane drained her glass with one long, continuous swallow. It was refilled by Richard. The room was magnificent. Every inch of the floor was covered with deep, rich red carpeting, accented in front of the grand piano, the fireplace and the ceiling-high bookcases by white animal skins. The furniture was sort of early Chinese, primarily black, with various dragon designs and rising suns in appropriate places. Jane was on her third drink when I asked, "How can we ever furnish this place?"

Richard laughed a rich man's laugh when asked a silly question about money. He looked at Joan and said, "I love this girlfriend of yours and I'm giving her all the furniture. Besides, I need a change. I'm buying all new for my next apartment. Everything you see here is staying."

"But what's the landlord going to say about eight girls moving in here?" Rachel was always the practical one.

Richard smiled a rich man's smile. "He can't say a thing. I've loaned him money at various times, and you might even say I own part of this building. I own part of him, too. You just move in and enjoy it."

Jane walked a little unsteadily as we left. Joan stayed behind with Richard.

"Jane, I don't understand something," I said as we walked out of the building. "If this guy loves Joan so much, why doesn't he just hand over the apartment to her? Why does she have to share it with seven other girls?"

Jane shrugged for a long time in preparation for her answer. She laughed a couple of times, too, at something only she was thinking. She never did answer the question.

Rachel and I had reservations about moving into the penthouse. The thought of living together with that many others was pretty scary. But the stew zoo paled in comparison to the elegance of that penthouse. And the experience of living in such splendor even for a short period of time would be worthwhile. We decided to go ahead with the move.

Joan naturally assumed a position of power. After all, it was her boyfriend who made the move possible. It was now *her* elegant furniture that we would be enjoying. It was her deal, and she knew it. Her lip took on a grand twist now, and she tended to speak with disdain. But we really didn't care.

Joan brought the other four girls into the picture. There were Sally, Marie, Helen, and Sarah. We accomplished the assault on the penthouse in one day and soon settled into a routine that seemed to work very nicely. That is until we got to know each other.

Jane seldom left her room. We'd never met a girl who said less and drank more. It was kind of funny to see her weave into the kitchen or across the living room. How she managed to keep sober when flying the line was something we discussed frequently, but the fact that she continued to fly was proof enough of her success.

We seldom saw the other girls. Everyone seemed to be on a different shift, a fact of stewardess life that makes living together more easily accomplished. For the first month we were never all in the penthouse together. But on the first day of the second month, we did happen to find ourselves together. And Joan acted on the occasion.

She beckoned all of us to the living room and announced she had something to talk about. We straggled in, each in her own particular costume of relaxation. I was in my usual Levi's and sweatshirt. That's the only way I can relax, in Texas pants and a shapeless, baggy top. Not glamorous, but the most comfortable clothes in the world. Rachel, on the other hand, relaxes in regular street clothes. She always has on a nice dress and stockings. She looks so ladylike I sometimes can't stand it. Joan was wearing a sleek Japanese kimono, a real one she had picked up in Tokyo. Jane was in an ancient muumuu. Sally had on tight orange stretch pants with a poison green turtleneck pullover. We all suspected that Sally was color-blind; nothing she wore ever matched. The poncho outfit and boots belonged to Sarah. The granny dress with high collar and long sleeves was Helen's idea of what to idle around the house in.

Marie sported her usual Bermuda-length shorts and button-down oxford shirt. An outsider would have thought we were quite a sight. We hardly looked at each other as we flopped around on the floor waiting for Joan to start the meeting.

"Well, here we are. I hope you're enjoying what Richard did for us."

"Who's Richard?" asked Helen.

"He's the one who made all this possible," Joan answered with a haughty rise to her voice. "Anyway, I think with all of us living so close together, we should have some sort of rules. I think we need them."

"She sounds just like Big Momma," I whispered to Rachel who had taken off her shoes and was polishing her toenails.

"Shhh," Rachel cautioned.

Joan went on.

"I've written up a list of rules, simple rules, and had them run off on a duplicating machine. I'll pass them out now and you can read them."

Jane excused herself and disappeared into her room. She came out a few minutes later looking more relaxed.

Joan passed out the white paper with the purple printing on it. We each took one and began to read.

*TO: Residents of the penthouse*
*FROM: The rules committee*
*SUBJECT: General operating rules*
*1. Each pair of girls will clean up their own bedrooms.*
*2. Bedrooms are privileged areas. Do not enter anyone's bedroom without prior permission.*
*3. Label all food stored in the refrigerator or kitchen closets.*
*4. Men may be entertained in any general area of the apartment or in your own bedroom. Work out any conflicts with your roommate. Try to encourage men to use their own dwellings for certain intimate activity.*
*5. Arguments will be settled by the rules committee.*
*6. No loud noise at any time.*
*7. 2% late charge will be levied for late rent payments for the first three days. 5% after that.*
*8. Each set of roommates will have their own telephone installed in their bedroom and will use only that phone.*

"Who's the rules committee?" Helen asked.

"Jane and I," was Joan's answer.

"Why you two?" was Helen's next question. It seemed a logical one, except to Joan.

"That was decided when Richard allowed me to ask you girls in to the penthouse."

"Who's Richard?" Helen didn't give up easily.

Joan simply ignored the question. Jane went back to her room for another moment's worth of relaxation.

"Are the rules clear?" Joan asked in a loud voice.

No one answered.

"Good. That's all for this meeting."

We all went back to our rooms.

"I think the power is going to her head, don't you?" I asked Rachel when we were safely alone.

"She is a little overbearing," she agreed.

"The others are a good bunch."

"Yeh. They seem great. Gee, I wish there were some way to help Jane out. All that drinking, I mean."

"She sure puts it away. I like her, though. And underneath all Joan's veneer, she does seem to stick by Jane. That's pretty nice."

Another month went by in the penthouse without serious incident. We were spared any more meetings, too. And we began to know our roommates in this housing venture.

Sally, a pretty but shy little brunette, was as sweet as could be. The delightful thing about her was her habit of telling little white lies. She couldn't help embellishing the stories she told, usually with the story improved by her embroidery.

Helen, tending to be overweight, was on a perpetual diet. She'd been on one for six years in a never-ending battle to satisfy the airline's rigid weight checks that came often and unannounced. Yogurt was her staple food, her portion of the refrigerator a virtual supermarket display of the world's yogurt varieties.

Marie was a darling, in her own way. She loved animals. Any animals. In her room, which she shared with Sally, were six birds of varying origins and species, a live mink in a cage and a baby alligator in a large fish tank. His name was Nelson. He was frightening even in his infancy.

Helen roomed with Sarah. Sarah loved to borrow things. Sometimes she returned them. Most of the time she didn't.

That was our group. The diversity of interests and problems seldom posed any serious threat to the penthouse's tranquillity. Not until the fourth month of residence when all the individual quirks meshed together to create a night from *The Twilight Zone.*

That night Rachel and I watched Johnny Carson until we'd fallen asleep. We'd been asleep for maybe an hour when the sound of our bedroom door being thrown open brought us both up to a sitting position.

Standing in the open doorway was Jane. She was drunk. Stoned. Her head was going from side to side as if getting up steam to say something. She finally did.

"Where is it?" she muttered, her voice with that slurred quality whiskey in abundance will bring about.

"What in the name of . . ." I was cut off.

"Where is it, I said?" She stepped into the room now, almost falling over the threshold.

"Where is what?" Rachel yelled.

Jane flipped on the overhead light.

"My bottle. My bottle. Where is it? You stole it."

Rachel laid back on her pillow. "Will you please go to bed, Jane," she requested softly.

Jane let out an ear-piercing scream. Then, she leaped on Rachel's bed and pulled the blanket off. "Gimme my bottle," she yelled, trying to punch Rachel as she said it. Rachel rolled out of bed quickly and ran around in back.

Jane's scream had awakened the entire apartment. Joan was the first to arrive, closely followed by Helen.

"What's going on in here?" Joan snapped.

Jane was leaping up and down on Rachel's bed.

"She stole my bottle," she said.

"Who stole your bottle?" was Joan's reaction.

"She did," Jane yelled, pointing to the both of us.

"We didn't steal anything," I protested.

"Yes, you did," Jane continued. "Sally said you did."

"Sally?" we said in unison.

Marie now came rushing into the scene.

"Shhhhhhhhh," she said with exaggerated facial and hand gestures, "you've woken up the animals. The birds are all chirping and Nelson is restless."

Once the visions of Marie's menagerie in flight passed, thoughts came back to the original problem: Who took Jane's bottle? Did someone take Jane's bottle? Did Sally say we took her bottle?

"Where's Sally?"

"Sleeping."

"How can she sleep when an alligator can't sleep?"

"She's always been a sound sleeper."

Jane had tolerated this aimless chitchat for as long as she could. She went to Rachel's dresser and began digging through lingerie for the elusive bottle.

Marie left the room and reappeared with a sleepy Sally.

"What's the matter?" she mumbled, rubbing her eyes and stretching.

"They woke up Nelson," Marie told her.

"Oh." (Yawn)

"Nelson is not the problem," Joan said sternly.

"The birds, too?" Sally asked. (Yawn)

"Everybody, except you, Sally."

"Oh." (Yawn)

"Did you tell Jane that Rachel and Trudy stole her bottle. Did you, Sally?" Joan could be a hard quizmaster.

Sally performed two quick yawns and scratched her stomach.

"No, I didn't say that."

That set Jane off. "You did, you did, you did," she yelled at Sally.

"No I didn't. I just said maybe they did. Jane said her bottle was missing and I said maybe Rachel and Trudy took it." (Yawn)

Rachel and I smiled smugly. "See?" we said. "It's simply a case of mistaken identity."

"Do you know anything about this, Sarah?" Joan asked her. Sarah was sitting on the floor in the corner. She jumped up when Joan spoke.

"Not me. Not me. No, sir. Not me."

"Well, *somebody* took my bottle, that's for sure," Jane lamented.

"Sarah?" I said with a strong upward inflection. Sarah avoided our eyes. She did one of those little toe-in-the-sand movements and cleared her throat.

"Sarah?"

"Why would I take someone's Scotch?"

I stood there feeling like Sherlock Holmes in the last reel of *The Late Show*.

"Ah hah," I said pouncing. "No one ever said it was Scotch that was stolen."

"Oh," was Sarah's reply.

"Is that all you can say, Sarah? *Oh?* After we've caught you with a slip of the tongue that proves you took Jane's bottle? You're always borrowing things. You must have borrowed Jane's bottle." I was pressing my discovery to the hilt.

Sarah stifled a yawn and said calmly, "Well, Jane always drinks Scotch. That's how I knew."

Jane tottered unsteadily in the corner while all the cross-examining was going on. "That's not at all true," she said with a strange annoyed tone to her voice. "I'm especially fond of bourbon."

"What did you do with the bottle?" Joan asked Sarah.

Sarah stood firm. "I didn't take any bottle."

Everyone seemed to accept Sarah's finality. They turned to us again.

I started to giggle. Rachel joined me. Joan got mad.

"This is a very serious matter," she intoned with all the piety of a lay reader on Christmas. Joan could do this quite nicely. She seemed forever preaching about something, her actions seldom matching her words.

"We know it is." But we couldn't stop laughing.

The night ended with nothing solved and everyone mad at everyone else. Rachel and I chuckled ourselves to sleep.

We were about to leave the penthouse the next morning for our flight when Marie came flying out of her bedroom, tears running down her cheeks. In her hand was the lifeless form of Nelson, the alligator. It's hard to tell when an alligator is dead, especially from a distance. But Marie confirmed it.

"He's dead," she shouted.

"How?"

"I don't know." She was heartbroken. The little reptile didn't move in her hands.

We went into Marie's room. Sally sat sleepily on her bed. The birds were all chirping happily, a thing birds probably always do when an alligator dies.

We went over to the fish tank where Nelson drew his last breath and looked into the water. The water was never especially clean, but that morning it had a definite bronze tone to it.

"What's in the water?" Rachel asked Marie, now calmed down just a little.

"I don't know. Is anything in the water?"

"Sure." Rachel dipped her finger into the tank and sniffed it. "Smells like Scotch."

"Scotch?" Marie said with horror.

"Yeh, Scotch. Take a sniff."

Marie did.

Then she dipped her own finger into the tank and licked the water on its tip. "It *is* Scotch," she moaned.

"Maybe he died of cirrhosis," Sally said from the bed.

"Who did this?" Marie shrieked at the top of her voice.

That scream did it. Everyone came running into the room.

Everyone chattered away at once.

"A little respect for the deceased, please." Rachel suggested.

The chattering was still going on when we left for our flight. We returned that night to a grim penthouse. Jane was drunk, bless her heart.

"Well, who did Nelson in?" I asked Joan, who sat quietly reading a book.

"Sally said maybe you two did."

"Here we go again."

"Did you?"

"No."

"I didn't think so. Jane and I have solved the problem, though." (The rules committee, remember?)

"How did you do that?"

"Marie will be leaving in the morning."

"Marie? Did she poison Nelson, her own alligator?"

"No, of course not. But those animals all over the place were just too much for anyone to bear. She's leaving with her zoo." Joan went back to reading.

Marie did leave the penthouse. The mysteries of the missing bottle and the dead alligator were never solved, although Rachel and I came up with a solution we felt was plausible. We figured Sarah borrowed the bottle and Sally knew it. She accused us to protect Sarah. Then, Sarah got scared and dumped the bottle in Nelson's tank to get rid of the evidence. We gave up trying to figure out what she did with the actual bottle. You can't solve everything.

So Marie moved out and Libby moved in. Libby was a friend of Helen's, their particular closeness bonded by a mutual need to diet constantly. Libby was a discothèque dancer in Greenwich Village. Sally moved in with Sarah, and Helen roomed with Libby. Together, they cornered the market on yogurt. They also turned the penthouse into a gymnasium for their numerous exercises for figure improvement. Things went along for a month until Libby, or Helen, we're not sure which, accused somebody of eating her yogurt.

Sarah admitted borrowing "a little teeny bit," but Sally said she thought Sarah had borrowed a lot. The only one in the clear was Jane who often said yogurt and whiskey just didn't mix.

And so it went. Our chic, glamorous penthouse soon fell into a long shadow of bickering, a human inevitability where girls are concerned, especially eight of them. Rachel and I departed for an apartment in Greenwich Village where we stayed in relative bliss.

It's true that our experience in New York is probably not at all typical of most stewardesses. Those who remain seem to find some sort of fun out of living there. Certainly the penthouse hadn't contributed a great fondness for fun city. But it's also true that New York is a tough place to live for any stewardess.

For instance: The telephone company, that great symbol of everything bad about a monopoly, is very reluctant to give a telephone to a stewardess. We understand they're reluctant to give a telephone to anyone, but the fact that a stewardess works for an airline, and, by virtue of that simple employment circumstances, has easy access to airplanes, thrusts a dagger of deep mistrust into the hearts of the telephone company's employees.

It's the same with department stores. These moneymaking giants of commerce seem certain we'll spend a day in their store with our new charge card, buy at least fifty thousand dollars worth of goods, and immediately wing off to Saudi Arabia to avoid payment of the bill. What amazes you is when you receive one of those form letters stating you are a preferred customer and a credit card is waiting for you at the Preferred Customer, Gold Plated, A-1 First Class, Chosen-by-God credit desk. Just try and get it.

We've since found these problems to be common to other cities besides New York. But it just doesn't seem as bad. Everything is magnified in New York.

If you, stymied in becoming the world's greatest Wall Street broker, concert pianist, or most famous actor on Broadway, should decide to pursue the career of a stew-bum, knowing where we live in the cities of this nation will be helpful. The following listing is published for your use.

**New York**
>    The East Sixties and Seventies of Manhattan
>    Forest Hills
>    Jackson Heights
>    Kew Gardens

**Chicago**
>    Aurora
>    Near North Side
>    Apartments near airport

**Miami**
>    Coral Gables
>    Villa Springs
>    Miami Springs
>    Coconut Grove

**San Francisco**
>    San Mateo
>    Belmont
>    Redwood City
>    Sausalito
>    Downtown

**Los Angeles**
    Westchester
    Inglewood
    Gardena
    Long Beach
    Manhattan Beach
    Van Nuys

**Denver**
    Aurora
    Downtown

**Houston**
    Downtown

**Dallas**
    Apartments near airport
    Downtown

**Atlanta**
    N.E. side of town
    Chamblee
    East Point
    Buckhead
    South side of town

**Boston**
    Back Bay
    Beacon Hill
    Brookline

**Washington, D.C.**
    Georgetown
    Arlington (Virginia)

Also, there are definite places where we have fun. As a stewardess working a flight, we aren't able to serve more than two drinks per person. But that doesn't mean we can't have more than two drinks when off-duty and in any one of our favorite bars. If you ever feel in the mood to have more than two drinks with a stewardess, give these places a try, each a known hangout for sisters of the skies.

## St. Louis

Any bar up and down Gaslight Square

## New York

Sullivan's
Friday's
P. J. Clarke's (or any P.J. joint)
Wagon Wheel
The Baron Steak House
Sammy's
York
Clos Normand
La Popotte
Le Marmiton
Rattazzi's
Hawaii Kai Club
Dawson's Pub

## San Diego

Mickey Finn's
Coronado Island

## Atlanta

Mr. Brother's Place
Sans Souci
Kitten's Korner
Ruby Red's
Al's Corral
The Red Barn
The Lion's Head
Top of the Peachtree

Fan & Bill's
Yohannan's
The Malibu Room
The Round Table
The Falcon Lounge

## New Orleans

Al Hirt's Place
Pat O'Brien's
Pete Fountain's
Whisk-A-Go-Go

## Miami

Tie One On
The Eden Rock
600 Lounge
The Villas
The Dream Bar

## Washington, D.C.

Beef Treat
Blackie's
Junkanoo
Palladian Room
O'Donnell's

## Mobile

Quarter Note

## Hawaii

Duke Kahanamoku
Don Ho's

## Las Vegas

Stardust
Silver Slipper

**San Francisco**
    The Crown Room
    Chuck's Place
    The Two Turtles
    Basin Street South
    hungry i
    Big Al's
    Playboy Club
    Gay Nineties
    Alioto's
    Whisk-A-Go-Go
    Doros
    Red Garter

**Los Angeles**
    Manhattan Beach
    The Chatter Box
    Shakey's Pizza Parlor
    Disneyland Bar

**Toronto**
    Skyline Motel Bar

**Chicago**
    The bars of Old Town
    The bars of Rush Street

# CHAPTER VI

# "This Is Your Captain Speaking"

$\mathcal{Y}$ou can always recognize a captain from the calluses on his finger from pushing the call button for coffee. Sometimes we think that's all the captain does up there—summon us for coffee. Most captains are great guys. They have a sense of humor, they know how to treat a girl, they take care of their girls. Good captains are extremely protective of their stewardesses. They don't permit any funny business, by anyone, where their girls are concerned.

I'll always bless the captain of one of my early flights. The two senior stews were stiff, unfriendly girls, and I was decidedly ill at ease. Just before dinner a passenger toward the rear of the plane signaled. I went back. A man sat there. His pants were unzipped and he was fully exposed. He grinned up at me with a nasty expression that froze my blood. I panicked and ran to tell the senior stew. She coldly suggested that I inform the passenger of his condition in case it was an accident. I approached him gingerly and said, "Sir, I'm sorry, but would you please zip your zipper."

He leered at me and said, "Why don't you let me put a tiger in your tank, young lady?"

I was completely flustered. The other stews were clearly not going to be any help. I went forward and told the captain. Without a word the captain turned the controls over to the first officer, put his hand on my shoulder an instant to reassure me and strode to the rear to deal with the situation. He got the man closed up all right. Two policemen met the passenger at the next stop and hauled him away. The captain rang for me immediately after the incident. "You all right, honey? You OK?" He sensed how distressed I was.

"I'm shook, but I'll make it."

"That's a good girl. Don't let the goons get you. Wait for me in Toledo. I'll take you to dinner."

That captain was a born big brother. At dinner he kept me laughing steadily with stories of his boyhood in North Dakota. He showed me pictures of his seven-year-old twins and his Great Dane puppies. His easy chatter crowded all thoughts of the distasteful encounter from my mind. At my hotel door, he tilted my head back, kissed me on the forehead and said, "You're a good girl, Trudy. You'll be OK now. Sleep well." Now that's my idea of a captain. I only hope his wife is good enough for him.

On the other hand, there are some captains, not many of them, who think the whole point of taking a plane from one city to another is to make a lunge for a stewardess two minutes after landing. Sister stews have told us some pretty horrendous tales about captains. You could begin to think that some of the most oversexed males in the country are right up front in the cockpit of your super-powered, fan-jet, dyna-lift, whisper-quiet airplane. Waiting for only one thing—to paw their way into your chaste chamber at the hotel.

What never ceases to amaze us is the stamina and staying power of these pilots, most of whom are over fifty years old. They're not old for the same reasons old men are selected at the stewardess school. It's taken a pilot a long time to gain the necessary hours and experience to command a multimillion-dollar jet aircraft. There's been a lot of talk recently about the upsetting effect jet travel has on the bodily functions of crew members. Maybe there is a physiological reason for captains' retaining their sexual drive, even after the age when most men find it necessary to develop another hobby. Maybe the key to potency is more jet travel. (We now lay claim to any airline advertising campaign based on this assumption.)

Of course, a few months on the line and you soon develop your own code of conduct with the cockpit crew. Either you Do or you Don't. And you try not to tell your roommate or your hairdresser. You make up your own mind whether your captain really does have the right to all your services. Captains realize that the longer a girl flies the line, the harder she'll be to conquer. Stewardesses who've been around will generally have latched onto one particular captain or have acquired other interests. So those on the make stalk the new girls, fresh from school where Big Momma made virtue sound dull and walls were for climbing.

It was on Rachel's third flight that she was introduced to the "manual flush" routine so popular with cockpit crews where a new girl is concerned. It was a light flight and dinner had been served when the little light flashed in the galley indicating that service was needed in the cockpit. It's an unwritten rule that the junior girl handles the cockpit chores, unless a senior girl has something going up front. This day, Rachel was the one. The other girls had evidently sworn off crew members for the week and simply pointed to Rachel.

She nervously pranced up the aisle, fluffing her dark hair and straightening her skirt. The flight engineer patted her fanny as she slid by him, a gesture Rachel assumed was normal cockpit procedure. Besides, she wasn't about to be labeled a square so early in the game. She stood silently, in back of the captain's right ear, his head just reaching her chest.

"Rachel," the captain said with a smile as he turned to show his wrinkled profile, a must for all captains, "we seem to be having trouble with the flushing apparatus in the lavs."

What could she say.

"Yes, sir."

"It looks as though we'll have to go to manual flushing techniques this trip," he continued, frowning to indicate the gravity of the situation.

Rachel quickly flipped back through her mental file of procedures and could remember nothing of a manual flushing problem. But that didn't prove a thing. Would a captain lie about something like this?

"We're very busy up forward here, as you can well imagine, Rachel. I'm placing you in complete charge of the manual flushing procedure. That little button in front of me, the one farthest away, activates the manual flushing operation. Every twenty minutes, I want you to come forward to the cockpit and flip that button. You'll flip it and hold it for forty-five seconds. Got it?"

"Yes, sir."

"Better give it a try now, Rachel."

The only way Rachel could reach the button was to lean over the top of the captain's head. She strained to get her finger to the switch, her breasts melting comfortably around the captain's ears. Finally, after much squirming, she managed to reach the button and flip it.

"Hold it steady for forty-five seconds," the captain commanded, his head rigid back against her bosom.

Rachel started to sweat as she kept her finger on the switch. She kept shifting her weight from foot to foot, each movement rearranging her breasts on the captain's head and neck.

"Manual flushing completed," snapped the copilot in crisp military tones.

"Roger," the captain confirmed.

"Whew," Rachel sighed.

"See you in twenty minutes, Rachel."

Most new stewardesses are put through the manual flushing routine. Some come back to the galley cursing the captain. Some, embarrassed, say nothing. Some can't wait for the twenty minutes to pass. Good thing all Rachel's attitude was that it could have been worse.

Another favorite trick is to hoist a new stewardess up into the overhead coatrack before passengers have begun to come aboard. The crew then sits and watches the girl try valiantly to get down, tight skirt and all.

We give it back at times to the cockpit crew. A copilot (commonly called a first officer on most airlines) or flight engineer making his first flight as a crew member with the airline can look forward to having his sleeves sewn shut, his cap insignia turned upside down, and his coffee served in one of those dime-store dribble cups.

Captain Smyth was a fine pilot, one of the airlines best. He was also a religious fanatic. When he wasn't pushing a 707 around at thirty thousand feet, he was guiding his own congregation of six hundred people in a church he founded about ten years ago. It had no affiliation with any recognized religious order.

Captain Smyth was a nice guy to fly with. He was always polite to his stewardesses and would tolerate no dirty talk in his cockpit. Many cockpit crew members refused to fly with him. They took offense at his pious approach to flying. But there were always a few first officers and flight engineers who held similarly strong religious beliefs, and when they'd get together on a particular flight, we'd term the cockpit "Boeing's Basilica."

If you flew often enough with Smyth, you soon found yourself turning to him for fatherly advice. In effect, he'd set up his own flying confessional. And it's amazing how many girls took advantage of his religious leanings.

One night in the crew motel in New Orleans, a pretty brunette took her tale of woe to Captain Smyth's room. It seems she'd become deeply involved with a married passenger and his marriage was threatened as a result. She told our self-ordained captain the entire story and waited for his words of wisdom.

"I want you to take off your clothing and lie on the floor," were his initial words of advice. "You must lie there awake all night and pray to the spiritual bodies of the universe that they may wipe you clean of this sin."

"You're joking?"

"Joking? Hardly. Do as I say and I'll remain at your side for the entire night, if need be. You can gain through my strength."

Naturally, the story got around. And that ended any evangelism as far as Captain Smyth and his girls were concerned. He's still a fine pilot, but the stewardesses working his flights now confine their problem-telling to a psychiatrist boyfriend or roommate.

At times captains can be trouble for a stewardess, even though their intentions are honorable.

Marge Bascom was a striking blonde girl who had been with the airline for over two years. She had a particular friendship with a veteran captain that, she claimed, never went beyond the platonic stage. She was a pretty open gal, and there was no reason to disbelieve her.

Her trouble with this captain came after a delayed flight into Kennedy from El Paso. They finally arrived in New York at 1:30 A.M., and the captain offered to see Marge home to her apartment in Manhattan. His wife was away and he thought he'd stay in town rather than trek home to Westchester.

They took a cab into the city and went up to Marge's apartment. Her roommates were out of town on layovers. When she offered to make him a drink, he accepted, and settled down on the couch as she prepared martinis in the kitchen.

"Mind if I change into civies?" he yelled through the archway.

"Be my guest," she answered.

"Give me a minute out here before you pop out," he warned. (It *was* platonic.)

"Take your time."

This captain, with the honorable intentions, was down to his shorts and T-shirt when a key turned in the front door and a tall, young man stepped into the foyer.

"What the hell?" he gasped.

"Who are you?" the captain asked, a little dismayed by his state of undress.

"Marge," the young man shouted, storming past the captain into the kitchen.

*Zap, smack, whop* came from the kitchen and the young man tore out of the room.

"You bastard," he hissed at the captain who was racing to get dressed. "You dirty bastard." With that, the young man made his exit with a flair of slammed doors and profanity.

Marge emerged from the kitchen holding her mouth. A thin line of blood trickled from its corner and her eye was beginning to puff.

"What is this?" the captain asked as he went to help her.

"That *was* my fiancé," she said. They never did make up, and Marge is still flying the line looking for another intended.

There was a time when a crew could stay together as a working unit. The airline allowed the captain, first officer, flight engineer, navigator, and stewardesses to bid as a unit for various trips, and it wasn't uncommon to find a congenial group flying together for a year or more.

But those days are over. And ironically, the change was brought about by ex-stewardesses who married captains as the result of this cozy situation.

Every airline has an organization of ex-stewardesses who band together to rehash old stories and aid their former airline in matters of policy and publicity. In reality, the girls primarily use the organization to maintain the illusion of still being glamorous stewardesses. It's an organization Rachel and I have pledged to each other to avoid at all costs when our flying days are over.

But they're an influential group of women, and when they decide to put the pressure on a given airline, their collective voices are listened to. That's what happened to the permanent crew situation. Many, or perhaps most, of these ex-stewardesses married crew members whom they got to know quite well when they were flying as a team. Many of them managed to steal captains from spouses of long standing.

Once they won their Flash Gordon from the other gal, they were put in her shoes. And they didn't like it. So, using the power they had, they convinced their airline that crews should not be allowed to fly together for any extended period of time. They won. Their victory spread to other airlines and pretty soon you couldn't fly with that great crew any longer. The silly thing is that this maneuver didn't really accomplish a thing. If a husband is going to stray, he'll do it no matter how new his crew is to him. But the girls feel more certain in their own hearts that they've ensured a long and happy marriage. Maybe we'll react the same way when we're married, grounded, and scared of losing our hero. We hope not.

Of course, even with the breakup of permanent crews, it's still possible to fly with a particular favorite pilot. Every crew member works on a bid system when it comes to receiving monthly assignments. The stewardess bid results come out before the cockpit crew results. If a captain has something going with you, he can usually, if he has the needed years of seniority, bid for those trips you've been awarded. But this situation can lead to great sadness.

A stewardess with another airline was madly in love with a handsome captain. They'd carried on an affair for six months, and he'd always bid for and receive most of her trips.

The sadness came one day in flight operations. She hurried up to him with the glad news, "I got San Francisco again, Harry. You'll have no trouble getting it, too."

"Gee, I'm sorry, Lucia, but I got stuck with Buffalo and Toronto. What a rotten break."

"Buffalo and Toronto? You've got enough seniority to get any trip you want. I can't believe you'd lose out and end up with those dog runs."

"I tried, Lucia, I really tried. I'm sorry." With those words of apology, Harry walked away to the hellish fate of a Buffalo non-stop.

But Lucia wasn't about to take this turn of events without a little checking. She slithered down to the departure gate and watched Harry climb on board with a new stewardess, who was sort of a cross between Sophia Loren and Gidget. It was obvious that Harry decided to fly the milk runs because they were the only ones the new gal could bid and win. Lucia learned there and then that a sure tip-off of a dying romance between senior captain and stew is when he suddenly becomes junior again, both in seniority and outlook.

Most crews will get together after a flight for a dip in the motel pool. It makes no difference what the hour is, and 2 or 3 A.M. swims are common. We all splashed into the pool this particular night in Miami with the exception of our captain, who begged off without any specific reason. We were having a wonderful time in the cool water when he finally did appear and ran up on the edge of the high board. He perched there, minus blue serge uniform and wings, and sprang up and down in readiness for a swan dive. Oh, yes—he was also minus his swim trunks.

There he was, our leader, posed proudly like an out-of-shape statue in all his natural glory. Occasional spotlights around the pool perimeter reflected off the water to illuminate his splendor. Then, with a healthy Tarzan scream, he leaped into the water to join us.

We all paddled around for an hour. Our captain wasn't drunk from all we could ascertain. It was a simple matter of flying fatigue.

"Roll me in the clover and do it again," he sang as he lazily paddled back and forth across the pool. His singing brought a few complaints from sleeping guests at the motel, and the manager, as understanding as he was with airline crews, came out and asked us to leave the pool. We did, forming a circle around our nude captain.

We asked him about it the next morning at breakfast and he mumbled something about the threat of the H-bomb and starving children and other vague references. We didn't press the issue, and his subsequent dips in the many pools we frequent were always with trunks.

There are so many stories about captains. Some are true, some are almost true. Many are simply too grotesque and sordid to write about. In their professional role of commander of a giant commercial aircraft, they're fine, expert professionals performing a very responsible job. Passengers seldom have to worry about their captain. Stewardesses are the ones who sometimes worry.

Rachel has a favorite captain story. One wintry night there were about ten stews sitting on the floor in our apartment drinking red wine, listening to Oscar Peterson records, and swapping girl talk. We went through quite a bit of wine that night and the competitive spirit became keen. Each girl tried to top the others. The stories became more and more personal and, I suspect now as I look back, less and less truthful. After a while there was a kind of lull. I turned to Rachel, "You've been very quiet over there. Haven't you been raped lately or anything?"

"Well, now that you mention it . . ."

All Rachel needs is one prod and there's no guessing what'll come next.

"C'mon, tell us. What happened?" the girls begged

"I never told you about Louis Lamb, did I?" Rachel settled herself against a pile of cushions. "You know, the big-deal captain who thinks he's God's gift? I wasn't going to tell anybody, I mean, it's kind of sick. Pour me another glass." I did.

"Well, I was working some trips with him couple of months ago and we laid over in Detroit. I kind of liked him. He's a good-looking guy, you have to admit that. So he took me out and we drank a lot and pretty soon he had me talked into staying with him. We went back to his room and after a while he went into the john and I got undressed and waited under the sheets. It took him forever to do whatever he was doing. And then . . . Oh, pour me another wine, huh?"

"C'mon, get to the point," I said.

"Yeah, let's hear it," the others chorused.

"OK. So I'm in bed and all of a sudden the john door opens and out he comes, not a stitch on, and he's got his arms out at his side, like wings on an airplane. And he starts running around the room and dipping from side to side and making motor sounds, like *Rrrrrrrrrrrr*. I swear he was nuts, really nuts. All over that damn room and I sat up and boy, I was scared. Then all of a sudden he zoomed at the bed, *Rrrrrrrrrrrr*, and he said, 'OK, baby! Maybe you've had it from the best. But you've never been screwed by a 707.' I'm not kidding, girls. That's what he said. Boy, did I get out of there fast. I hate to look like a kid, but I'd just as soon have it like I've always had it. I guess I'm just a country girl at heart."

We all laughed for at least twenty minutes. There were girls sprawled all over the floor, laughing like crazy. The next morning I said to Rachel, "Come clean. That Louis Lamb story. Did it really happen?"

Rachel looked at me, her brown eyes round as searchlights. "Why, Trudy, would I lie to you? Ever?"

"I don't think you'd lie to me. But you could have been putting those girls on last night. Did it happen?"

"Like I said." She put her arms out and went, *"Rrrrrrrrrr."*

I started laughing all over again. There's no telling with Rachel. But this I do know: captains can be a strange breed.

# CHAPTER VII

## "You Must See So Many Interesting Places, My Dear"

$\mathcal{M}$y visits back to Amarillo always take a particularly pleasant turn when I stop to see my Aunt Laconia, a fascinating person, and the only family member pleased with my stewardess career. Aunt Laconia is a librarian and naturally reads a lot, mostly about places she's never been. Aunt Laconia should have been a stewardess. She was a beautiful girl in her youth.

When I visit her, we usually pass the first ten minutes with general chitchat about Amarillo, the family, and local gossip. Then, when it's time for tales of my travels, Aunt Laconia begins with, "You must see so many interesting places, my dear."

Before I begin my travelogues for Aunt Laconia I have to give her a careful rundown of a day in the life of a stewardess. Otherwise, she'd think we're fresh as a daisy and raring to go the minute we hit a new town. We like to go all right. Stewardesses are young and swingers and we'll have plenty of time to catch up on our sleep when we're older and grounded. But even with all the enthusiasm in the world on our side, there are times when we're simply too bushed to do the hot spots.

You, the carefree passenger, may snooze your way from New York to San Francisco or dip into a light novel or watch a shoot-'em-up movie. Meanwhile, here are a couple of things that we're doing:

Our flight leaves at two in the afternoon. We check in at operations at one and hustle down to the airplane. We go through all the setting up and you, our paying customers, come on board. There are one hundred thirty of you.

Flight time is about five hours. And here's how we spend it.

. . . We prepare and serve two hundred sixty diverse drinks, all from the liquor cart that was designed to fit in the aisle, not to function as an effective bar-on-wheels. One of you becomes irate because we don't serve mint juleps. It's not our fault. Nor is it when the premixed martini isn't dry enough. And we're sorry we hit that turbulence that caused us to spill ginger ale on your only suit.

. . . Now come one hundred thirty hot towels. We explain to eighty passengers what to do with them. And our hands become TV-rough and red from handling them.

. . . Collect the towels. Set up one hundred thirty trays. No, we don't have special trays for children. No, we don't have peanut butter and jelly on board. No, you don't have to eat. Yes, if you're going to eat, you have to do it now. No, you can't have another drink. No, we do not have *Playboy* on board (men always ask that and wait for our reaction. It's our least favorite line and we wish they'd stop).

. . . Serve one hundred thirty meals. You ordered a kosher meal? Gee, the caterer didn't put one on board. (Should we tell the next passenger who ordered a special meal that the airline never delivers on those orders? Should we simply make up our own kosher meal for the next passenger? We've done both.) We're sorry the steak isn't rare enough. It's a shame you don't like bacon crumbs on the salad. We're sorry, we're sorry, we're sorry. Our legs are beginning to feel it now, the running up and down, the bending, the apologizing, the rat race.

. . . Coming up are one hundred thirty desserts. Don't yell at us because the ice cream is too frozen to push your spoon through. I'll bet your mother did make better apple pie.

. . . After-dinner drinks now. We're still pouring wine from dinner. Some are getting drunk now. And some of those are getting obnoxious.

. . . You're too cold? We'll make you warmer. Too warm, now? We'll make you cooler. Sorry, but we don't carry *Downbeat*. No, I won't go to bed with you. Yes, I will go to bed with you. We're really tired now. We've run up and down getting you water, matches, cigarettes, magazines, Kleenex, pillows, blankets, writing paper, telegram blanks, postcards, the typewriter, the razor, and anything else you might want—within reason. No, even outside of reason.

. . . There's San Francisco below us. And we know what you're all thinking as you file off the airplane past us. Who, what, why, when, where are we going to swing tonight? Yes, sir, here we are, those swingers of the sky, about to tear up hilly old San Fran and have an orgy on a houseboat in Sausalito and drink ourselves silly and still show up tomorrow morning with our smiles, hair, and uniforms in place, sans wrinkles and ready to serve you in the best tradition of our airline.

Well, you know, you're not altogether wrong.

We check out of the airport about five, reach downtown San Francisco at six, take a shower, put our hair up, think, boy, this is one night I'm going to do nothing but sleep. It's shut-eye from now until I'm called for the 8:30 A.M. flight back tomorrow. Nothing will get me out of bed. Nothing.

The only trouble is that in about ten minutes the phone rings. It's Susie or Grace or Mark or Phil—one of our pals from this flight or other flights. "Hi, Trudy, hi Rachel! C'mon, there's a party in room 1026 and then we're going down to the wharf." I say I'm too tired. Rachel says she's too tired. We're both too tired. But while we're protesting, we're already pulling the rollers out of our hair and reaching for our shoes. "Come on, Rachel," I say, "let's go!" And we're off to a big night in San Francisco.

Most of our layovers now are only eighteen to twenty-four hours. In the past when planes were slower we often stayed in a place for forty-eight hours or more. Then we have more time to sightsee and get to know a city. But even with lots of time, stewardesses aren't much for visiting museums and trotting around to historic sights. The museum stuff that I tell Aunt Laconia I usually get from travel booklets. She likes so much to hear me talk about culture. I always play down the nightspots; she isn't very big in that department. But stewardesses are.

Here, then, is a stew's-eye view of some of the livelier towns in the U.S.A.

*San Francisco:* Just the simple act of taking a walk can be an enjoyable experience in San Francisco, with its hills and white buildings and cool-wet bay breeze. The night life is the best, although all the topless craze of late seems to have caused some confusion in the minds of San Fran's eligible dates. We love dating there. We love a drink at the Top of the Mark. We love listening to jazz at the Matador or Jazz Workshop. But we *don't* love going to watch some Iowa farm girl flop her silicone breasts around on the top of the bar. As they say at county fair girlie shows, "Ladies free 'cause there's nothin' inside you ain't seen before." But, topless or not, San Francisco will always reign supreme.

*Boston:* Boston is a nice city. And it has so many nice, eligible college men. It does help your cause if you're at all conversant with urban renewal and local politics, two apparent running manias with Bostonians. We always manage to find time for a ride on the swan boats on the Common; beer, beans, and sandwiches in Harvard Square; and maybe even a little sailing on the Charles. Most stewardesses try for at least a year's duty in Boston. All those educated, potential lifelong mates are a pretty potent motivation.

*Miami:* Never a dull moment in Miami, unless you're looking for lazy, dull moments under the sun. The beach in Miami is relaxing, and you can squander away your time watching the beach boys flex or the bar girls outflex the beach boys. All that crystal-blue water and towering white cloud formations can make you wish you didn't have to leave. You might even bump into Jackie Gleason on the golf course, which can be a massive experience.

*Dallas:* We'll include Houston, too. That's because this Texas haven for humidity holds a special spot in my heart. We were flying a Miami–New York trip when I started feeling stomach pains. They got worse, and pretty soon I was doubled over in the aisle, passengers and fellow stew hovering around me. It was my appendix–burst. We detoured quickly to Houston where an ambulance whisked me away to the hospital. Once the pain was gone, I began to wonder how mad all those passengers were about having to go to New York via Houston. But then the get-well cards started to pour in from over half the passengers and I stopped worrying. The traveling public does have a heart.

In Dallas, the stewardess sport is to cruise the streets in search of young oil tycoons. Once you've exhausted that possibility, you go after old oil tycoons. Failing all chance at an oil windfall, you can daydream over the Chinese junks or "his 'n' her" bathtubs at

Neiman Marcus and wish there was an oil tycoon to . . . Well, you know.

*Chicago:* The local gals seem unusually jealous of all the laying-over stewardesses in their windy city, and manage to keep prize males out of sight and reach. This is a shame because Chicago is such a ball to visit with all the pub crawling, especially in the winter when it's too cold to do much else but pub crawl. Maybe our union can negotiate a truce with Chicago's female population. On second thought, our union doesn't seem to have any negotiator that hardfisted to pull off that trick. We'll just have to keep pub crawling in search of some escaped males. Luck to us.

*St. Louis:* For some natural reason, winters are colder and summers hotter in St. Louis than anywhere else. But in the spring and fall, St. Louis offers a great deal to do and see. In your plaintive moments, you can sit and wait for some hotshot pilot to fly a 707 under the newly completed Gateway to the West arch.

*Atlanta:* Once you've found the inner circle, you can find a swinging time in Atlanta. For some reason, Atlanta likes stewardesses. A lot of bars cater to us, and one little favorite spot, Kitten's Korner, is fast to put it on the house for us. It's definitely *our* favorite house in Atlanta.

*Cleveland:* For all that smoke and water pollution, Cleveland has its charms. Besides, with a good crew, we can have fun anywhere, even in a steel mill.

*Detroit:* They make cars in Detroit, and men make cars. Detroit has an ample male population who know where the action is and who are willing to spend money to make it happen. We like Detroit.

*Los Angeles:* Los Angeles is a thing all to itself. It's great and it's horrible. Some of the greatest times we've had occurred in Los Angeles. When those memorable times weren't happening, we hated LA. It's just one of those places, we guess.

*Memphis and Nashville:* If you like Dixieland Jazz, and we do, you'll like these two Southern cities.

*Montreal:* We date mounties in Montreal and have parties in cabins on the river. Sometimes our dates take us for rides in their canoes, which is fun and, due to the structural design of a canoe, provides relative protection from too vigorous advances. It's also a drag if you're looking for vigorous advances. Or wet.

Although we work for a domestic airline, we have plenty of chances to see the world. Through exchanges with other airlines, we can spend a weekend in London for $39. We can go to Paris for less than $50. Everywhere we get 75 percent off at hotels and we pick up all kinds of free passes. I spent four days in Paris that I'll never forget. I adore Hawaii. The stews there spend a lot of time in Don Ho's famous nightclub. I once flew from Miami to Lima, Peru, for a weekend and still had change from a $20 bill when I returned.

Aunt Laconia doesn't believe me when I tell her that I once took off from Atlanta, went to Chicago and on to Los Angeles to have a drink with some friends. I came back the same way, took a quick shower and was off on a working flight to New York. A couple of days later a friend called and said, "I was trying to get you Tuesday night. Where were you?"

"Tuesday . . . Tuesday," I said, "let me think a moment. Was that the night I went to the movies? Oh, no. Tuesday I was having a drink in LA."

# CHAPTER VIII

# "You Must Meet So Many Interesting Men, My Dear"

$\mathcal{M}$y same Aunt Laconia will occasionally interrupt my tales of travel to say, "You must meet so many interesting men, my dear." This is her shy, sly way of prying into the sex in my life. I do not try to let her down when it comes to my romantic interests. But naturally, I don't mention *all* the men in my life. I don't think Aunt Laconia really wants to hear the gory details. Then again, maybe she does. Still I never take a chance with the whole truth. Even when I confine my tales to storybook young college men who share ice-cream sodas with me through two straws, she asks with a sweet and hopeful smile on her face, "Is he the one?"

"I don't think so, Aunt Laconia, maybe next year."

I've debated often whether to tell Aunt Laconia about Chuck. She's a pretty shrewd old gal and if I started talking I'm sure she'd sense that this one is more serious than all the others. She's bound then, one way or another, to tell my parents. And after that on every visit home they'd all be staring at the fourth finger on my left hand and making not-so-gentle hints. I've decided to leave that part of my life a closed book as far as my family is concerned.

I didn't see Chuck for about four months after I got to New York. I thought about him a lot. A million different nights I said to Rachel, "What do you think? Will I hear from him?"

She had unshakable confidence that Chuck would reappear on the scene in a big way. "Give him time," she assured me. "He'll turn up."

Several times I spotted his name on crew lists, so I knew he'd been in and out of New York. It was a crisp early fall day and I was alone in the apartment when the phone rang. "Are you wearing your jeans?" a man's voice asked.

"Sure. Who is this?" I asked.

"Good. I'll pick you up in half an hour. On my motorbike. We'll go for a ride."

"Who is it?"

"Why, Trudy, I'm surprised. I thought you Texans were friendlier. It's Chuck." And he hung up.

He must have called from around the corner because he was at the door in a couple of minutes. He was wearing boots, dungarees, an old orange flight jacket, and a crash helmet. He swept me into an enormous kiss that lasted nearly forever, but wasn't half long enough, and then he dropped down onto the sofa. "Where've you been?" he demanded. "Pin a pair of wings on a girl like you and you disappear. Did you miss me?"

You must know by now that I'm not often at a loss for words, but I was tongue-tied. "Yes, I mean I was here . . . in New York . . . Where . . ."

"Forget it," he said. "Let's go."

His motorbike was parked just outside our building. He handed me his helmet and showed me how to strap it on. "We'll have to get you one of these things," he said. "This time you'll have to wear mine. You sit there." He pointed to the small rear saddle. "And hold on here." He arranged my hands around his waist. "Hold tight. We're blasting off." It wasn't a very big scooter, but it made a takeoff sound like a 707.

"Where're we going?" I shouted into his ear as the wind rushed by. The automobiles on both sides of us were much too close for comfort. We missed pedestrians by mere inches. But I could sense his sure command of the vehicle and a great feeling of exhilaration began to take hold of me. We sped up to Radio City, wove in and out of the shopping crowds on Fifth Avenue, zoomed over to the East River Drive, hurtled along the river to an ancient, decaying wooden wharf, way downtown among the skyscrapers where old men were fishing in the afternoon sun. We parked the bike, sat on a splintery log, and talked. That is to say Chuck talked. I was still too dazzled to find my tongue and every time I looked into those blue eyes of his I fell apart all over again.

He talked about his special assignment in California. He'd been on loan from the airline to a plane designer working on experimental new planes. That had been exciting but his real love was flying and he was happy now to be back on the line. He wanted to know everything that had happened to me since my first day as stewardess. I told him about that crazy first flight and the lady stuck in the john. I told him about other flights and about people I'd met, about Rachel and Betty and the others in our class. Once I got started talking, I could hardly stop. The words just poured out. We jabbered away on that dock until the wind rose and it turned cold.

"C'mon, I'll take you home," he said. "You can change your clothes and we'll do the town tonight."

Rachel was in the apartment when we got there. "Hi," she said to Chuck, as casually as if she'd seen him the day before. "What'll you drink?" She fed him bourbon while I went to dress. When I came out of the shower, Chuck was gone and Rachel was packing her overnight bag. "What's up?" I asked.

"Chuck's gone to change. He's staying with a friend a couple of blocks away. He'll be right back."

"What are you doing with that bag?"

"Didn't I tell you?" Rachel asked, all innocence. "I'm going to Great Neck for a couple of days to visit the Morales'." Rachel had an admirer who was a metallurgist from Colombia, South America. Through him she'd met a whole crowd of wealthy Latin Americans. She hadn't said a word about going to see the Morales'. I was sure she didn't really have a date with them.

Well, I didn't tell Aunt Laconia about the next two days. Not that she wouldn't have liked to hear. But there are some things a girl can't tell—even to her best friend. I didn't tell Rachel much either. Not when it's so real and important, you don't go yakking away.

"Is it the real thing?" Rachel asked two days later when Chuck had collected the last of his socks and shirts and Rachel had unpacked her overnight bag.

"Well, yes and no."

"What does that mean?"

"It's big with us all right, but . . ."

"But what?"

"But we're not going to do anything about it. Not now, anyway."

"What do you mean? You meet Mr. Right. Then you kiss him good-bye. Why? He isn't married or anything, is he?"

"No, but he's been married and that's the problem."

It was kind of hard to explain because it wasn't altogether clear in my mind. But one thing was sure. Chuck believed in marriage more fully and intensely than any man I'd ever met. He had a kind of holy feeling about marriage. It had to be right and it had to be forever. He'd married several years earlier a girl from his hometown who couldn't take the life of a flyer's wife. Marian couldn't stand the separations and the worry. After six months she'd given him an ultimatum. He'd have to give up flying or she'd leave. He couldn't stop flying. It was all the world to him. Marian got a divorce.

Chuck wasn't going to let that happen to him again, ever. For a couple of years, ever since his divorce, he'd avoided entanglements, refused to get serious with any girl. He was still avoiding entanglements. "Trudy," he'd said, "I have a feeling it may be us someday, you and me. But if it is, it has to last as long as we do. I won't settle for anything less. You're just beginning. You've got a million places to go and a zillion guys to meet before you're ready to settle down. You may not be ready for years. I'm not going to hurry you. Take your time. Get all your living done. I'll be around. You'll be hearing from me." He ruffled my hair once more. Kissed me again, picked up his bag, and a few minutes later I heard the zoom of his bike.

So I didn't tell Aunt Laconia about Chuck.

Instead I told her about handcuffed prisoners we've had on board, political bigwigs, Don Juans, men who say funny things. There was the Catholic priest and the Seventh-Day Adventist minister sitting together on one flight. The priest ordered a Scotch and water. The minister said, "I'd rather commit adultery than drink."

The priest looked up at me and said, "I didn't know I had a choice today." That was a fun trip.

With some hesitation I told about the stewardess who dated a photographer and began posing in the nude for him. On one of her flights the captain buzzed for her. He pointed to the centerfold photograph in a cheap men's magazine where she saw herself displayed in all her natural skin. "Anyone you know?" the captain asked jovially. The poor girl gave the photographer the gate.

I gave Aunt Laconia an edited version of my encounter with Mr. Relick. I met him during my one and only flight to Mexico City. I was on reserve and pulled this flight when one of the regular girls became ill. I was pleased with the prospect; I hadn't the needed seniority to bid successfully for the Mexico City run, and Rachel's envy enhanced the windfall.

It was a wonderful trip down. The airline created a Mexican fiesta mood for the passengers, and everyone seemed exceptionally cheerful. We spent the night in Mexico City. The thrill of being in a foreign country buoyed me after the long flight. The crew, regulars on the Mexico run, took me everywhere, showed me everything, and I fell into bed at three in the morning with a head full of *magnifico, bueno si-si,* and *buenas noches.* The first officer made a mild overture about spending the night, but took my polite negative response calmly.

The next morning we departed Mexico City with a full load, mostly wealthy businessmen, a few with their families. One of the men, a Mr. Relick, was particularly charming. He was courteous to the girls, never asked for anything without prefacing it with Please. Besides, he was handsome, about forty, with that attractive graying at the temples. We found time to talk a bit toward the end of the trip, and he asked me to join him for coffee in New York. I accepted. I was pleased to be asked, and frankly hoped it would prove interesting.

We had our coffee at the terminal, and I found out a few things about Mr. Relick. He was divorced, maintained a home in Mexico City, apartments in Paris and New York, and was successfully engaged in international import and export. I proved a good listener and he asked me for a date.

I bubbled all about him to Rachel as I showered and prepared for the evening. I evidently went overboard because she asked, "Isn't there anything wrong with him?"

"I don't think so, hon. Come to think of it, there is one flaw. With all his charm and sophistication, he has a little rough edge to the way he talks. I like that though. Know what I mean?"

"No."

"Oh, you do so know, stupid. Like Anthony Quinn or Jack Palance or Harry Guardino. A little bit of dem and dose. But manly, like he's lived."

"That ruins the whole thing. He sounds awful."

"Oh shut up. You're just jealous because I came up with a winner."

"Where are you going to dinner?"

"I don't know, but I bet it'll be nice."

"I hope so."

"Should I wear a girdle?"

"Definitely not. Bill Harris says girdles are the curse of American women. He says unless you really need one, you shouldn't wear it. And you don't need it, Trudy." Bill Harris was a flight engineer Rachel was seeing.

"But Big Momma said we all need it."

"Big Momma's a thing of the past. No girdle. Go loose tonight."

"What do you think he'd like me to wear?"

"Well, Trudy, if he really talks like you say he does, he'd probably like to see you in sequined slacks and gold high heels. No girdle. Guys never like girdles."

I wasn't wearing a girdle when Mr. Relick picked me up. We took a cab to an elegant Italian restaurant with "21" prices. Mr. Relick's charm became even more pronounced as the evening wore on. The most interesting thing was that his tendency to fall into a Brooklyn speech pattern also increased. He knew all the right things to say, but had trouble maintaining what was obviously a forced urbanity. Strange but delightful.

We continued the evening at Basin Street East where we enjoyed Duke Ellington and his band, a favorite of Mr. Relick's. The Ellington magic swept me up as it did the rest of the crowd, especially when the band played a medley of Ellington evergreens.

"All the guys in the band—Carney, Hodges, Brown, Anderson, Gonzales—they all hate to play the medley, Trudy. They've played those tunes at least eighteen thousand times, and it gets old. But that's what has to be played. He plays a lot of new stuff, but the crowd always wants to hear 'Indigo' and 'A-Train' and those things. Great band, isn't it?"

"Wonderful," I responded. "I love it." I did notice the bored expression on some of the musician's faces, now understandable in light of my escort's explanation.

"What a marvelous evening," I said as we climbed into a cab.

"I bet you can't wait to get home and out of your girdle, huh?" It wasn't a particularly charming thing to say, but humorous in light of my earlier conversation with Rachel.

"I'm not wearing one," I answered, realizing the answer wasn't any more charming than the question.

"I wasn't prying," he said quickly.

"I know."

"Well, since you don't have a girdle to get out of, how about making it to another place? I know a great coffeehouse in the Village. I'll buy you an espresso."

"Great. I'm off tomorrow. The night is young, Mr. Relick."

I can't remember the name of the coffeehouse, but it was what I supposed such a place should be. All around were dirty-looking young men and women, each trying very hard to conform to the nonconformist image. Mr. Relick and I sipped our espresso and he reached across the table and took my hand.

"Trudy, being out with you is great. Really great. I'm truly enjoying myself and I've got something to repay you with."

What a switch. He wasn't asking me to repay him, the usual feeling on the part of the fellow who's paid for dinner and expensive entertainment.

"Oh, Jim," I said with complete sincerity, "I don't deserve a thing. The fun has been all mine."

"No, no, Trudy. I insist."

He was drunker than I had realized, and his speech was now quite slurred and heavy, a great deal of the charm gone from it.

He lowered his voice, glanced around, and looked me straight in the eye. With the secrecy came a hardness, a businesslike look, but more ruthless than that. He suddenly looked like Bruce Gordon, the actor who always played Frank Nitti, the enforcer on *The Untouchables*. He sounded like him, too.

"How would you like a grand a month, Trudy? Tax free."

"A grand? That's a thousand dollars, isn't it?"

He chuckled. "That's right. A thousand bucks. How would you like that?"

"Do I have to blow up an airplane?"

"No, no. Nothin' like that. Very easy loot. You're not against money, are you?"

"This sounds too easy, the way you tell it."

"Well, you interested?"

I sat there pondering his question very carefully. The evening had been fun, and I had a sinking feeling whatever was going to come next would in some way ruin that fun. But maybe I was wrong. I had to appear interested.

"Sure I'm interested in money. Everyone is."

"OK, Trudy. Here's the deal. And I'm trusting you a hell of a lot to even offer it to you. You know I'm in the import business. Well, one of the things I import is marijuana."

There wasn't another soul in the world at that moment. Everything ceased—all sound, movement, color. I felt a sickness creep up into my stomach, and my hand started shaking on the table.

"I don't feel very well," I said and started to rise. "I'm sorry. Please excuse me."

"Wait a minute," he said shaking his head back and forth and grabbing my arm. "Sit down."

I sat, but said, "Please, Mr. Relick, I want to leave. I don't like any of this," I wanted to hit him, or scream for the police, but he was frightening, sitting across from me. I just wanted to forget there was ever a Mr. Relick, a Duke Ellington, or a Mexico City. I wanted this whole day and night to disappear.

"Don't get shook, Trudy. I'm not askin' you to use dope or anything like that. Hell, I don't use the stuff. I just want you to help me out when you come up from Mexico now and then. Not all the time. Just sometimes. There's no trouble. You girls come in and out without anybody botherin' with you. Just carry some stuff once in a while. That's all."

The coffeehouse was full, and I was afraid someone would hear us. I leaned across the table and whispered to him, "Look, let's just forget about this. OK? I never heard what you said and that's it. Please. I can't do anything like that."

"Don't be stupid. Do you think you'll be the only stewardess who's smuggled stuff across lines? Trudy, some of the international girls make a fortune doin' it. And there's no risk. If anybody did find some stuff on you, you just say some crook must have put it there. Some crook like me. No sweat. Besides, I've already got a girl, one of your buddies probably, working with me. It's easy out of Mexico. How about it?"

"No. Please don't ask me again. I enjoyed tonight and want to forget it ended this way. Please!"

I grabbed a cab by myself and went back to the apartment, looking behind at every corner to see if he was following me. Once inside, I bolted the door and leaned heavily against it. My sobs came in heaves, their intensity bringing Rachel from the bedroom on the run.

"Trudy, baby, what's the matter?" she asked as she put her arms around me. "So he likes girls who wear girdles. So what?"

We stayed up the rest of the night as I told her of my evening. I finally stopped shaking long after the sun had risen, and Rachel persuaded me to lie down and sleep. I woke up a little after noon and there was Rachel, my good friend Rachel, sitting reading in a chair.

"Feel better?" she asked.

"I guess so."

"Want to call the police?"

"I'm afraid, Rachel, to do anything like that. I just want it to never have happened."

"I know how you feel. But you should call them, I guess."

I didn't. As wrong as that may be, I didn't do anything. I wanted only to obliterate the entire affair from my life.

Six months later I picked up a copy of the *Daily News* and read that Mr. Relick had been picked up along with other mobsters in a raid. They had been meeting someplace when the police interrupted their assembly. His picture was there, that same handsome face I first encountered on my Mexico City flight. I've never heard of him again.

Getting involved with the gangster element as a stewardess isn't too difficult. Rachel and I know a girl who dated a mobster in Detroit. He was a nice-looking young man, maybe a little too slick, but attractive. He told her he was a troubleshooter for a finance company.

They dated every time she had a layover in Detroit, and her first inkling of his true occupation came one night at his apartment. They had been to bed, gone out for dinner, and were back in bed when he asked, "Do you love me?"

"I don't know," she answered in all fairness. "Maybe I do. I don't know yet."

"I was just wondering. I was just wondering if you liked me enough to do me a favor."

The stewardess sat up and sipped from a brandy snifter at the bedside. "Well sure I'll do you a favor. I don't have to love you to do that."

"Maybe not. But it would help. I might as well level with you. There's this guy coming in town soon and he means a hell of a lot to me financially. What I wanted to ask you to do was . . . well, sleep with him for a couple of nights."

"Wait a minute," she snapped in natural indignation at his request. "If you think I'm going to be a whore for a buddy of yours, you're crazy."

The Detroit hood got up from the bed and slipped into his shorts. "Look, I just asked. It's not like I want you to do it for nothing. You'll get paid . . . by my company. You'll be doing me a favor and makin' fifty bucks besides."

She was furious. "Pay me?" she yelled. "It's bad enough being asked to do it as a favor. But pay me?"

He was almost dressed now. "That's right, baby. And there'd be lots more where that came from."

She quickly got out of bed and dressed. She was on her way to the door when he grabbed her by the arm and swung her around.

"You broads make me sick. You screw anybody who buys you a decent dinner and holds your hand, but taking hard cash for it makes you vomit. I told you I was in the finance business. Sure I am. But a different kind. I make finance out of broads like you. Only they ain't all like you, and that's a big break for me. I'll level with you. I run a string of call girls. Hustlers. And you could make a bundle just workin' a little on the side when you're in town. Big bread, baby. And all you gotta do is lay on your back like you've been doin' with me and enjoy it."

She swung at him but he was faster. He slapped her back against the wall and threw the door open. "Get outta here."

We heard the story fourthhand, but had it confirmed later by the girl herself. You can be sure this is a story I didn't tell Aunt Laconia.

Pimps and dope pushers aside, Rachel and I both agree that Lucius Dumbarton was the craziest man we've met in our flying career.

Lucius was a happening director.

"What's that?" Rachel asked as she brought him his second drink. It was a quiet night flight in a nearly empty plane.

"I direct happenings." Lucius formed his fingers into a rectangular hole through which he peered out the plane's window.

"What are you doing?" was her second question.

"It's like a movie, baby, a movie. You know? Andy Warhol does wild things like this. Really beautiful. Like, try it. Make a lens with your fingers."

Rachel tried. The rectangle kept becoming a circle, and when she looked all she saw was fingers.

"You still didn't tell me what a happening director is," she tried again.

"You know, happenings. You've never seen a happening?"

"Afraid not, Mr. Dumbarton."

"I'll take you to one of mine. You'll dig it."

"I see." She didn't.

"I'll bet you didn't dig what I was doing a minute ago, when I was looking out the window."

"You're very right. I didn't."

"See. I knew it."

"You're very perceptive, Mr. Dumbarton."

"Call me Lucius."

"Fine, Lucius."

"I'll tell you what I was doing before, Rachel. That was your name, wasn't it? Rachel?"

"You're right again."

"I knew it."

"I'm impressed."

"Good. You'll be more impressed when you dig my happenings. Oh, yeh. Before. What I was doing was being a camera. A motion picture camera. You just set up the frame with your fingers and let it roll. Like Andy, only he uses a real camera. He just lets the camera roll on one thing. Like the Empire State Building. Or a banana. Or a Ping-Pong ball. And things happen. Like, no one plays Ping-Pong while Andy is filming. Oh, no. That ball, or that big building just sits there. Maybe for a half hour or more. Just that thing doing nothing. Beautiful. Power, baby. Insight. Inner conflict between the man and the machine. War and peace and the womb and plaid stamps. Beautiful. So beautiful. I do it myself all the time. With my fingers. Nothing moves, like. I set up on the sky, maybe. Just that plain, blue sky. Better gray. More power. And you know what? One time a bird, a big damn bird, flew right into my picture and that isn't all. He actually came back again, from the other side, and came right through again. Oh, if I only had film in my fingers that time. Tooooooo much."

Rachel was quick to display her ignorance of such beauty. "That's all these movies ever do? Nothing moves? Nothing?"

"Of course nothing moves." He was scornful. "If the building moved it would blow the whole thing. It's like you take a guy and sit him on a chair and let the camera roll. No movement. Just maybe a twitch in his eye. And he can blink. Or maybe you do it with a cat who's asleep. That's been done already. A whole hour of this sleeping cat. Wow!"

"Did a bird fly across his face?" Rachel was kidding, but maybe she wasn't.

"You're putting me on, right? How could a bird fly across his face? I mean, like, he's asleep in his bed. Dig? A bird . . . his face. Oh, man, am I gonna have to hip you."

"I'm afraid so, Lucius. It'll take a lot of hipping, too."

"Beautiful. Tell you what. I'm running two happenings next week. Classics. You'll understand better when you see them. One is called *Miscegenation.* It's like one guy and a watermelon. There'll be a lot of social significance with this happening. Wait and see. The other happening is called *Meat Meet.* You'll absolutely die with this one."

Rachel accepted his offer, despite his advance billing of the events, and met him at a small Spanish restaurant in the Village the night of the happenings. He was wearing exactly the same unwashed clothing, his hair was one week longer, and no soap company could boast of increased profits on his account.

He remained silent and morose throughout the meal, so much so that Rachel asked, "Are you having a happening now?"

Lucius just shook his head back and forth and never took his eyes from the tabletop. "No, baby, no. But dig this tablecloth."

Rachel looked down. It was a red and white check, and contained large, permanent grease stains.

"Are you going to make a movie of the tablecloth, Lucius?"

"Oh stop talking, baby, stop talking. Like, things were happening on that cloth. Did you see that fly? I mean you didn't even see the fly, did you?" Lucius flailed his arms around in the air. "Oh man, that fly was making it right into the scene. Right into it."

Rachel was sorry she'd interrupted such a monumental event. "Maybe the grease on the tablecloth attracted him. Maybe he'll come back."

"Ah, screw the fly," Lucius said with great authority. He motioned for the check.

They walked many blocks until Lucius turned off into the dark doorway of a loft building. Rachel scurried in after him and followed him up pitch-black stairs until they reached a large, metal door that admitted a shaft of light underneath from inside. Lucius pushed it open and she followed him in.

Rachel described the happening scene two days later. It went this way:

"Trudy, you wouldn't believe it . . . never in a million years . . . It looked like a big warehouse and there were all these weird people sprawled out on the floor . . . One guy was actually making love in the corner with a girl . . . and there were guys holding hands with guys and . . . oh, my . . . Well, the only light was from some purple bulbs hanging from the ceiling . . . They were like floodlights . . . Lucius told me they were ultraviolet lights and they're important to a happening . . . (I evidently shook my head at this point) . . . You don't know why either, huh? . . . Anyway, in the middle of the floor was a big blanket . . . He told somebody to change the direction of the lights . . . He told the couple in the corner to stop it . . . They did stop . . . Pretty soon music started playing . . . It was Southern music . . . Like *Dixie* and *Stars Fell on Alabama* . . . Out came this skinny fella with a loincloth around him . . . It really didn't cover him at all, especially when he sat down on the blanket like an Indian . . . You could see everything . . . This same boy was painted black all the way down one side and white all the way down the other side . . . Split right in half . . . A girl in a mink coat and nude underneath carried out a whole half a watermelon and patted the skinny guy with the loincloth on the head and laid the watermelon down in front of him . . . He picked it up and started chomping away . . . He chomped and he chomped and that couple started making love in the corner again and Lucius was making little groaning sounds and everyone watched this nut eating watermelon with the juice and seeds all over him . . . Trudy, he ate that damn watermelon for forty-five minutes . . . I kid you not . . . forty-five minutes . . . The couple in the corner just kept going at it . . . Everyone else seemed to be getting their kicks from the watermelon man . . . Finally, he got up, rubbed the juice and seeds all over himself, hugged himself tight, rubbed some black makeup on the white side and white makeup on the black side and then do you know what he did? . . . He cried . . . He bawled and ran out of there . . . Everyone was cheering and applauding . . . It was awful . . . awful . . ."

Rachel was too tired to go into detail about the second happening, *Meat Meet*. It consisted of five men and five women, each wearing only a loincloth, getting on the blanket and rolling all over each other. It was a great big tangle of arms and legs and other things. Lucius was one of them. Pretty soon the spectators started getting up from the floor, dipping paintbrushes in cans of paint, and dabbing the colors on everyone on the blanket.

The bodies on the blanket were in a constant state of motion while Muddy Waters' records played in the background. Soon, everyone was covered with the multicolors of the paint. Then, out came the nude girl in the mink coat carrying a big bucket full of ketchup. She dumped it on the mass of bodies. They spent a half hour rubbing it into each other. Finally, the happening was over.

The bodies then disappeared into corners where they wiped each other off with burlap bags. Lucius came back to where Rachel was sitting on the floor and plopped down beside her. He was still covered with paint and ketchup. All around were couples—men with women, men with men, women with women.

"Oh, you were really in luck tonight, Rachel baby," Lucius informed her proudly. "Things really happened, didn't they?"

"It was . . . wonderful, Lucius. Just great." She felt horribly uncomfortable in her woolen dress and heels.

With those words of encouragement, Lucius grabbed Rachel, pushed her onto her back, and climbed on top of her. He kissed her and ran his hand up her leg.

Rachel is no lightweight, and she pushed him off. "Stop that, Lucius. Don't touch me again." She looked down at herself and gasped when she saw the paint and ketchup smeared on her dress.

"Look what you've done to my clothes," she shrieked. "Just look, you . . . you . . . you happening director."

"Shhhhh, baby. No scene. Don't sweat the color. And don't ruin the total happening. Oh, don't do that. I mean, the happening's happened, and now's the time for the big impact. We've got to fulfill the magnetic cosmos of two forms, two human elements, two sweaty, salty bodies. You and me. Now!"

"You're nuts," Rachel yelled. Everyone was watching.

"Beautiful," one tall, slender Negro parted from underneath his white companion. "Beautiful happening."

A girl whistled her approval. "Oh yes, girl-girl. That's the way it is. Tell it that way. Make it happen."

Rachel fled the room to a thunderous ovation.

"It was the best happening they'd ever seen," she told me as she finished her tale.

"I'll bet Betty Big Boobs would have been a better happening," I teased.

"I was going to say she was there but didn't think you'd believe me."

"Or Cynthia," I further suggested.

"You know, Trudy, that's what that damned stewardess school needs. A happening. A Lucius Dumbarton happening. Let's put it in the suggestion box."

We didn't, of course. But visions of Big Momma, the meat man, Cynthia, Betty, and the faggy hairstylist being painted as they rolled together on a blanket provided a whole day of inner grins.

Yes, we've had them all on board—wealthy men, poor men, imaginative men, dull men, men who offer jobs, men who give lavish gifts just for the fun of it, and men who give little gifts with many strings attached. Yes, we meet interesting men. And good or bad, meeting men is the name of the stewardess game.

# CHAPTER IX

## "The Radar Is Built In"

As we've mentioned, captains rate highest on the list of stewardess dangers. Second on that list are married male passengers.

We have, out of necessity, developed an inner radar system that is part of the game we play among ourselves. To keep long flights from becoming boring, we use the radar to guess the marital status of each male passenger, his nationality and profession, on the basis of the kind of approach he makes to us. The nationality and profession portions of the game are described in Chapter XIX. This chapter deals only with the "Is he married?" sequence.

As the men come aboard, we make snap judgments as to their state of freedom. Then, as the flight progresses, we have the opportunity to verify our initial opinions. The most obvious tip-off is that common and widely used banner of matrimony: the wedding band. Not that we accept credit for correctly identifying a married man who's wearing one. Men who wear a wedding band are automatically disqualified from competition.

We're referring to the man who removes his wedding band just prior to boarding the airplane. He's kissed his wife good-bye in the departure lounge and, as he walks up the loading ramp, he slips his ring off and places it in his pocket. He boards the airplane secure that he's removed all traces of his spouse and the restrictions she places on him.

But he underestimates the ingenuity of his stewardess. We've trained our eyes to detect the slightest trace of pale flesh on his ring finger. And in 99 percent of cases, that ring in his pocket has left just such a pale mark. Of course, the more he's out in the sun, the more pronounced the mark is likely to be. But even men who only see the sun on their walk to the train will fall victim to this giveaway.

I suppose he doffs the ring when his mind begins to reflect back on all those stewardess stories he's heard. He remembers hearing from Joe, a guy in his office, how he made a stewardess in the backseat of the airplane on his last business trip. He recalls the office boy telling how he is pulled into strange stewardesses' apartments and raped nightly. He pictures the stewardesses who will be working his flight as busy, lusty, quivering mounds of flesh just waiting for him to come aboard so the bacchanal can begin. He figures he'll have a better chance if these sexpots of the sky don't know about his wife and seven kids. So, off comes the ring, exposing maybe a year of lily-white skin. He might as well wear a sign.

When he comes on with a big wave of the hand, we automatically check him off as married, on the make, and devious to boot. But let's give him credit for being imaginative. Let's assume he's gone so far as to carry a small tube of flesh-colored makeup. Or maybe he wears gloves all the way. Or never takes his hands out of his pockets.

That brings into action our second method of determination. We ask a simple question when he's off guard.

"Do you live right in Manhattan, sir?"

"No, I live in Smithtown. Out on the island."

That's it right there. A bachelor will generally live in the city. Only a married man with grass-loving kids would live so far out and put up with the rigors of commuting. Sure there are exceptions. And many times this married man from Smithtown, realizing he's come up with the wrong answer to our question, will try to make himself one of those exceptions.

"Yes, I decided to leave the city and all its dirt and noise. I love nature and the outdoors, the horses I keep, the dogs, the tranquillity. I love the country."

But we don't buy that rationalization. He's had it as far as we're concerned, unless we're looking for a married man to date.

Now let's assume we've still not been able to make a positive classification of this unidentified flying object—the male passenger with the leer in his eye.

Go to stage number three. How does he make his approach? Is he aggressive or cool? Does he force the issue or make it casual?

Married men don't have a great deal of time to wine and dine a girl they're after. They can't afford to pursue her casually over a long period of time. They want her *now.* And their approach reflects this pressure of time.

But a single guy will take his time. He'll make it sound interesting, fun, and exert little or no pressure. There's an amazing difference between these two species of men, and the differences are quite pronounced.

Now, we've ascertained their marital state. Or maybe they've freely admitted they're married, and even owned up to a couple of children. At this point they begin their talk campaign, hoping to win us over to their side. Some of their conversation goes as follows.

—"My wife just doesn't understand me." (This ancient line is only used by very out-of-touch men.)

—"My wife loves me too much. It's stifling. I'm smothered by her love. I need to be with a woman who doesn't love me, like you, someone who can face me objectively." (This is fairly enlightened and can be so refreshing in its absurdity that you might fall into the logic.)

—"Once the children came, my wife forgot I was even around." (Another old line, but valid in too many cases.)

—"We bought a dog and ever since my wife has forgotten I exist." (Come on, fella.)

—"It's the bomb. Tomorrow may never come." (That's a good reason to get a good night's sleep, as far as we're concerned.)

—"I went to Sweden once." (Is he trying to tell us he'd had an operation?)

—"It's good for a man to have different sexual experiences. Why, Doctor Joyce Brothers says . . ." (Why don't you call Dr. Brothers?)

—"This is the twentieth century." (He's fairly bright, at least.)

—"It's good for a man to stray once in a while. He appreciates his wife more." (Flattering to us, huh?)

—"My wife is so immature. I need a mature woman, someone with insight, understanding, someone to confer with on an intellectual level." (Who, me?)

—"My wife and I have an agreement. She knows I run around a

little." (It's a sure bet he's scared silly of his wife and the last thing he wants to happen is for her to find out.)

   –"If you do go out with me, promise to be very quiet about it. My wife would kill me." (At least he's honest.)

   –"We're getting a divorce soon." (Call me from Mexico.)

   –"My wife is frigid. That's not easy for me, you know." (Her either, Charlie.)

   –"I'm writing the great novel of our times and I need to live, to experience all of life." (Have you ever been to a happening?)

   –"I'm seventy and still need love." (Have you written your will yet?)

And so on.

No matter how we feel about dating married men, each of us ends up with at least one in our careers. The only time I've become really involved was when I truly didn't know he was married. My radar completely broke down and I believed everything he said, including the fact that he could only date me on Wednesday because he went to school every other night of the week, including Saturday and Sunday. I hate to tell you how I found out about his wife. It was one of the darkest experiences of my life. Thank God she was the calm, reasonable woman she was.

I was at home reading a book a captain had given me, a gripping novel about the peacetime army, *Stockade,* when the telephone rang. I picked it up, still engrossed in the book.

"Hello."

"Hello, I'd like to speak with Trudy Baker please."

"This is Trudy Baker."

"And this is Mrs. Pearl." I was elated. The book I was reading was written by Jack Pearl, and for a moment, this woman seemed connected with him. But that fantasy lasted only a fraction of a second. Then I realized I knew another man named Pearl. His name was Bob Pearl, a draftsman, the man I'd been dating every Wednesday night for the past six months.

"Bob Pearl's mother?" I asked timidly.

"No, his wife."

What do you say in such a situation? I said nothing and let her continue.

"Miss Baker, I've known all about you and Bob. Don't ask me how. It's really irrelevant. But what I do want to say is I'd like to stay married to Bob. But I won't if he'd prefer to continue seeing you. I've offered him a divorce but he's declined."

"Mrs. Pearl," I said slowly, "I'm sorry. I did not know Bob was married. He said he wasn't and I believed him. I'm sorry."

"Didn't you find it unusual that he could only take you out on Wednesday?"

"Yes. At first. But I stopped thinking about it. I was happy with Wednesday."

"Well, at any rate, I do demand that either you stop seeing him or I'll start divorce proceedings. Bob says he doesn't want that and I now leave it in your hands."

"Mrs. Pearl, I want nothing to do with your husband. Believe me, nothing."

"Thank you. I'm sorry he lied to you."

Quite a woman. That was the end of that.

Actually, there's one kind of passenger any girl will date, or at least go to dinner with, whether or not he's married. That's the man who sits there quietly, behaves himself like a gentleman, but you know that he's aware of you. You're sure that he wants to ask you for a date but doesn't know how. As he's leaving, he'll often say something like this: "That was a very nice flight. I enjoyed it and you're a nice stewardess. I'd like to have you on my flight again. The next time I'm on your flight, maybe I can buy you dinner."

That's fine. Even if he's married, most of us will go out with a guy like that, have dinner, enjoy his company and that's it. No wild time. No big sex thing. But we're both in a strange city, away from home, and we want to spend a pleasant evening. There's no harm in that. Of course, it can happen that from such a casual beginning there can develop a very deep and complicated attachment. That's a risk we take.

Yes, the radar is built in. What we do with its findings is another matter.

# CHAPTER X

# "They Looked So Normal"

There isn't a great deal you can say about homosexual men and women you meet on a flight, except maybe to comment that there are more of them than you might think. Just as we're able to size up a man's marital status, profession, and nationality, we've become quasi expert in labeling the gay guys who fly with us. It really isn't difficult when you think about it.

Some make it easy for us through their outward mannerisms. It's a fairly safe bet to say, "Here comes a fay one," when the subject of your comment floats up the loading ramp, his feet six inches off the ground, twinkle-toes past you, and lightly settles in his seat, one leg daintily crossed over the other in best feminine fashion.

Much tougher to recognize are those with big biceps bulging under their coats, rugged faces, and harsh, manly ways of speaking. They're dangerous, if only because you can fall in love with one before you know he isn't capable of returning the affection.

Certainly, there are times and conditions when a homosexual is preferable. Many girls working foreign lines testify that a good portion of the male stewards working their flights aren't as masculine as you might expect, and this very lack of drive for the opposite sex ensures these girls a relatively safe trip, especially in the close confines of the galley.

Then, too, a fay fellow can be valuable simply as an escort, when escorting is the sum and substance of what you expect on a given evening. There are many girls who maintain a warm friendship with a homosexual man, and enjoy his company on those occasions when all she wants is a pleasant fellow to take her to dinner, the theater, and to bring her home without pawing and panting. But as a steady diet, none of us wants that man around.

We've found that most effeminate men on our flights are extremely passive. They generally possess a high degree of intelligence, are witty, too polite, and offer no trouble to a stewardess. But despite these apparent advantages, their very presence is unnerving and disconcerting.

The biggest problems with a homosexual on a flight come when he's an overt one, a practicing queer with little discretion for the time and the place. We've all been involved in these cases, and they can leave you shook for days.

I remember one young man, neatly dressed and from all appearances a gentleman, on a flight from Dayton to Houston. He sat in seat 6B.

We were airborne and just leveling off at cruising altitude when a passenger signal light flashed in the galley. It was for seat 6A, occupied by an elderly businessman who had settled down to paperwork the moment he came aboard. I walked down the aisle to answer his signal, and as he saw me coming, he got up and met me in the aisle.

"May I have a word with you?" he asked, his expression one of disgust.

"Of course, sir," I answered, and led him back to the galley.

"Look, Miss, I don't want to be a complainer or prude. But I wonder if there isn't something can be done about the young man sitting next to me." He was referring to the neatly dressed young man in 6B.

"What's the problem, sir?" I expected him to say he had excessive body odor, or was playing a wooden flute, or maybe he was even reading *Playboy*. Perhaps the sight of the center foldout was bothersome to this businessman trying to work.

"I don't even want to get into a description of it with you, Miss. I think the best thing would be for you to go down the aisle and look at what he's reading. You'll understand then."

It seemed a reasonable request, and I did as he suggested. I wish I hadn't. There was the young man in his seat, his eyes focused on a magazine he had in his lap. It did have a centerfold like *Playboy,* but this one had nothing to do with girls. Folded out was a full-length photograph of a nude man posed against a tree. He was the pinup of the month. It wasn't the first time I'd seen a man in the nude, but the setting and timing left me in a slight state of shock.

I came back to the galley where the businessman stood patiently. "That's awful," I said.

"Yes, it is. The thing I want to know is what we can we do about it. I'd ask to change my seat but it's obvious there isn't a vacant seat in this airplane. But I won't spend my whole trip looking at his . . . his pinups."

"I think the captain should be advised about this."

"That probably would be a good idea, Miss."

I went to the cockpit and explained what the problem was.

"Pictures of naked men?" the captain asked with disbelief. "Come on, Trudy. You're kidding."

"I'm serious. A foldout, no less. And his seat partner, a distinguished type, isn't happy, boss. I suggest you come on back and straighten things out."

The captain, a tall Texan with droopy eyes, came back and approached the young man with the magazine. The magazine was still on his lap but turned to a different page. This page featured a large advertisement for a community shower gadget that would attach readily to any shower enclosure. The illustration showed six men standing nude in a circle as water flowed from the overhead rig. One was washing another's back.

"I'm gonna have to ask you to put that magazine away, young fella," the captain drawled. "It's . . . well, it's indecent, if you follow what I mean."

The faggy fellow raised up in his seat and surveyed the captain with great scorn and resentment, as a woman might do when confronted with someone of financial position at an Episcopal tea.

"Indecent?" the faggy fellow echoed in an annoyed whine. "You're indecent, Captain Marvel." He broke into a high-pitched giggle and blinked his eyes at the bewildered captain.

The captain pondered the man's reaction to his request and decided to take immediate action. He reached down and gave the magazine a pull. "Gimme that thing," he demanded.

The homosexual hung on tightly. "Don't you dare touch this," he screamed, "Or I'll have you demoted . . . and whipped!"

"The hell you say," the captain retaliated. He gave an extra pull and came away with most of the magazine. The homosexual was left holding the corners of a few pages.

The queer young man turned red with anger. His lips quivered, he breathed hard, and he turned around to everyone within hearing distance, which took in most of the passengers.

"This man is a sadist. He's violating my rights as an individual and a citizen. He should be whipped. That's right. Somebody help me."

No one moved. They returned to their magazines or to looking out the windows. The captain just stood there, his prize, the bulk of the magazine, tightly clenched in his fist. He turned on his heels and stalked back to the cockpit. I went in with him and asked what I should do.

"Not a damn thing, Trudy, unless he makes any more trouble. He'll probably settle down now. Let me know if you need me again."

Before I left the cockpit, I took a moment to look at the magazine. It was some sort of official publication for homosexuals. It was the sickest magazine I've ever seen.

The fellow in 6B kept quiet for the rest of the flight. The businessman returned to his seat with great reluctance and no further trouble came from that section of the airplane.

It was on arrival that the homosexual decided to raise a little hell with the captain's confiscation of his magazine. He waited in the lobby until the captain came off the airplane, and boldly walked up to him.

"You big bugger," he snarled in the captain's face, his hands waving about like Bette Davis. "I hope you get some horrible disease from the next girl you're with."

He wiggled away, his tight pants accentuating his girlish derrière.

"I'll be a son of a bitch," the captain muttered as he walked over to us. "These damn fags'll take over the whole damn world."

We still kid the captain about the incident. He says he's kept the magazine as a reminder of the experience. I don't need anything to remember it.

Occasionally, we receive a complaint from a male passenger who claims another man is making propositions to him. In these cases, we try to switch his seat. When that isn't possible, we ask him to grin and bear it, a difficult request to make of any virile man. It's bad enough for a girl to be stuck next to a guy who makes unwelcome advances, but it must awful for a man to be annoyed by a member of his own sex.

We can see only one solution. We advocate the offering of half-fare tickets to all homosexuals. Why not? They give reduced fares to everyone else. By doing it for homosexuals, we could at least pinpoint them and assign seats accordingly. Of course, this would bring up the problem of whether to seat them together and put up with a nonstop flight of male hanky-panky, or intermingle them with normal passengers and suffer the consequences. Either way, we know there'd be trouble. But you have to admit a half-fare for perverts is an interesting concept, no matter what its pitfalls.

"Please take your hands off me . . . I said *stop it!* I'll punch you . . . I really will . . . Don't do that . . . *Watch it!*"

Was this Rachel in the backseat with a boyfriend? Me in the backseat with my Braille-reading buddy?

No.

It's what you might have heard had you eavesdropped on the two occasions when Rachel and I were confronted with lesbians.

Sure, we've had those women who come aboard, their hair done up in a butch haircut, wearing no makeup, and dressed like any normal, virile man. But they're no problem. You know who they are and therein lies the safety factor. The same goes for the asexual type. They are, according to what we've read and observed, above sex of any kind. Obviously, they pose no problem to anyone.

It's the seemingly feminine, pretty, sexy girl who really throws you when she pinches your leg or makes a habit of pressing too close when there's room to avoid contact.

My particular confrontation was with an Olympic swimmer. I met her at a party while living in the stew zoo. It was a good party in that it attracted many people from outside the airline business. We get tired of talking airplanes all the time.

Gretchen was a lovely girl. She'd competed in the Olympics, was currently a swimming instructor, and was constantly surrounded by men at the party. All that swimming had given her a lean but muscular body, her shoulders larger than most girls. She had a radiant smile and short but carefully styled blonde hair. You couldn't help like her, man or woman.

She seemed to be enjoying and inviting all the male attention that was directed at her. There she stood, a drink in her hand, smiling broadly, as each guy tried harder than the other to impress her. Toward the end of the party I was in the kitchen with a few people when Gretchen came in for a drink refill. The others left the kitchen soon after she arrived.

"It must have been fun traveling to the Olympics," I said as she prepared her drink. "I'd love to hear more about it."

"Yes, it was fun," she said without looking up. "It was a marvelous experience. Do you live in this building?"

"Sure do. I call the stew zoo home."

"When do you fly again?"

"Tomorrow. A noon flight. I'm going out tonight after the party to stay with some friends in Rego Park. It's close to the airport. Besides, I always enjoy getting out of the stew zoo for a night."

She looked at me and flashed a broad smile. "It doesn't seem so bad here. Lots of friends with common interests and all that. Say, I live in Huntington. That's on the Island. I have my car in town. I'll be happy to drive you out after the party and drop you off in Rego Park. I take the expressway anyway."

"You'd still have to go out of your way."

"So what? I'd love to drive you. Count on it, OK?"

"Gee, that's fine. Thanks. Anytime you want to go."

"We'll stay another hour if that's all right with you."

"Perfect."

We left the party together and climbed into her Mustang. We were at the Midtown Tunnel in no time and, once through it, Gretchen pushed the car to about sixty-five. Long John Nebel was on the radio, and we laughed at the debate he was having with someone over whether Catholic priests should be allowed to marry.

"I don't think anyone should be allowed to marry," was Gretchen's remark, a throaty chuckle punctuating the comment.

"Why not?" I asked, laughing with her.

"It all seems so silly, really, I guess I'm just a little drunk."

She pulled off the expressway at the Rego Park exit and followed my directions. It was a gloomy night, and a few drops of rain began to pock the windshield.

We were proceeding down a dark street when she pulled to the curb, cut the engine and the car's lights.

"What's the matter?" I asked. I assumed something wrong with the car had prompted her action.

"Nothing, Trudy," she answered. She sat passively behind the wheel and watched the raindrops as they ran together into tiny rivulets on the glass.

"Don't you feel well?" I asked. I didn't sense anything to be afraid of, and was expressing normal concern.

"No, I guess I don't feel well." With that, she reached over and took my hand from my lap. "Would you understand?"

"Understand what?" I still didn't get what was happening.

"Understand someone who looks at things differently from you. I am different, Trudy." She slid across the seat, neatly sliding over the console. Then she kissed me on my cheek, letting go of my hand as she did and letting it drop back into my lap. Her free hand clamped on my breast.

Now I knew what was going on. I always feel a little silly in retrospect admitting my slowness in the situation. But once I knew, I acted quickly. I jumped out of the car and stood there in the rain.

"I'm sorry, Trudy. I'm sorry," Gretchen pleaded out the open door. "I'm sorry. Please get in. I'll drive you to your friend's house."

"You seemed so, so normal—" I stuttered at her.

I walked away from the car. Fortunately, Gretchen pursued me long enough to hand me my overnight case through the window.

The last thing she said was, "I'm sorry, Trudy. Really sorry. Please don't tell anyone."

I didn't answer. Long John's voice could be heard through the open window saying. "I don't care what a man is. If he's got needs, he's got 'em, collar or no collar." With those apropos words, she drove off. I've never seen her again.

Rachel's run-in with a lesbian was more bizarre than mine. Rachel always does things on a big scale. She infiltrated a whole den of them quite innocently.

She'd become friendly with a department store buyer on a flight from New York to Salt Lake City. The buyer, a stunning woman, invited Rachel to visit her in New York. A few weeks later Rachel received an invitation to a dinner party.

At the party were five others, including the hostess. There were two men, or, as Rachel put it, "sort of men." The other two guests were both women, "sort of women," in Rachel's words.

After dinner, during which all of New York's artists, writers, and politicians were analyzed in terms of their phallic symbolism—a train of conversation Rachel simply accepted as sophisticated—everyone retired to the living room.

An hour later, the hostess asked for silence, opened a desk drawer, and brought out a large, gray envelope. She took from it what appeared to be photographs, and without a word handed the pictures to Rachel.

There were seven, eight-by-ten pictures, each showing the hostess and the other girls in the dinner party in various poses of love-making. Everyone giggled as Rachel perused the file. Anyone else, as shocked as Rachel was, would have quit with the first one. But that's Rachel. Her philosophy dictates that once something bad has begun, you might as well take it all in before you react. She studied each picture, aware of the eyes intently studying her face for signs of a favorable reaction. After looking at all seven she put the photographs down and turned to the hostess.

"I have to leave, now," she announced flatly, "I have a lover who gets very mad when I'm late. She really gets violent."

Rachel took her coat from the closet and walked out of the apartment. Once outside she pressed her ear to the door. Inside, someone was saying, "She *is* one of us. Let's invite her again."

The hostess could be heard replying, "Don't be an ass. She made fun of us. I hate her."

"I hope she gets pregnant," one of the gay fellows threw in. They all giggled and Rachel walked away.

Passengers come in all styles and types. But as long as they buckle their seat belts, observe the No Smoking sign, and don't pinch us as we pass, we couldn't care less.

# CHAPTER XI

## "You Ought to Be in Pictures, Sweetie"

$\mathcal{N}$o matter how long a stewardess works at her job, she never becomes too jaded to feel a little twinge of excitement when a celebrity comes aboard. Meeting celebrities was something we all expected would happen when we decided to fly for a living. And we've met them, all in the confines of an airplane where there's no makeup, scriptwriter, or out-of-focus photography to cover the blemishes, both physical and personal.

Taken as a group, celebrities are usually more difficult to handle than normal, everyday passengers. Their lives are lived in expectation of attention. Why not? They usually receive the attention they look for.

Naturally, we have favorite celebrities with whom we fly. These are some of them.

*Arthur Godfrey*–A charming man, and one who knows as much about flying as the captain up front.

*Henry Fonda*–As easy to get along with as pie. Married to a former stewardess, which might provide additional understanding.

*Al Hirt*–Loads of fun and will even take out his horn and play a few notes if you've served him a few times before. He once ran that whole jam session for us on a flight.

*Bob Hope*–Funny, considerate, and easily pleased. "Why aren't you in pictures?" he asks the stew every time she goes by.

*Van Cliburn*–A very quiet gentleman.

*Lee Marvin*–One of the most regular-guy celebrities we've served.

*Eddy Arnold*–Never fails to thank us and tell us how nicely we did our job. Drinks the airline dry on every flight, but never anything stronger than milk.

*Robert Kennedy*—Nothing political in our praise. Good sense of humor and will ask for a direct line to the White House.

*Jack Jones*—Very nice, and a good cardplayer.

*Ford & Hines*—Nutty but nice. Gave a friend of ours a trip into New York City from JFK in their black limo.

*Joan Rivers*—Her routines about flying are favorites of the stewardess corps. We tried not to steal anything from her for this book. She can steal anything she'd like.

*Duke Ellington*—"We love you madly," Your Highness. We go to see and hear him play in cities all over the country. We always give him first-class service.

*Phil Harris*—Just makes us feel good.

*Jack Sterling*—A most amazing man when you think of his getting up that early for so many years and still being pleasant.

*Skitch Henderson*—A good pilot himself. His giggle can perk up many a dull trip.

*Chet Huntley*—Doesn't frown as much on an airplane as he does on TV. Delightful man. No matter how busy he is always takes time to tell the stewardess it was a great flight.

*Mike Douglas*—Never really feels secure when flying but covers it up pretty well. We've never met a star who's more sincere and easygoing.

*George Hamilton*—Sits quietly in his seat and says Thank You for everything. Always a pleasure to have on board.

*Jonathan Winters*—So funny . . . he's in character for every mile of the flight. Once did for us his episode about the oldest airline stew in the world. He hobbles down the aisle, talking about the days of the Wright Brothers when he was first a stew and complains that the jet age has knocked him out. It's hard for him to compete with the beautiful twenty-year-old stews on the new jets. We break up every time we hear him.

*Johnny Carson*—You can't get tired on a trip with him. He tells us to come up and be on his show. I bet if we showed up he'd put us on the air.

*Jack Benny*—You know he really is thirty-nine.

*Phyllis Diller*—I thought I'd see something out of a crow patch when I heard she was coming aboard. Actually, she's one of the most charming, attractive women you could meet. Love her sense of humor.

*Merv Griffin*–You can't top him. He talks to us the way we like to be talked to, understands what a tough job we have.

*Miss America* 1965–If she hadn't been crowned Miss America I think she would have wanted to become a stewardess.

*Lucille Ball*–One of the most delightful people I've ever waited on. She's just precious and I love her flaming red hair. She's got talent she's never even shown to the world.

*Elizabeth Taylor and Richard Burton*–I panicked when I heard they were to be on the flight. How would I look? How would I act? Would I please them. Please, God, don't let me ask for their autographs. Don't let me spill a drink on them. Well, I found them just wonderful. Elizabeth Taylor is probably the most beautiful woman I've ever seen in my life. You have to see her close up to realize how beautiful she is. Both of them sat there quietly, a perfect couple, never asked for anything special. I guess she sensed I wanted their autographs but didn't dare ask them. They both wrote their names on a piece of paper and handed it to me, and I nearly fainted when I saw it said, "To one of the nicest stews we've ever traveled with." I treasure that paper with my life.

Other good-guy celebrity travelers are:

| | |
|---|---|
| Steve Allen | Joe Garagiola |
| Bob Newhart | Charles Percy |
| Bob Considine | Van Heflin |
| Hubert Humphrey | Hoagy Carmichael |
| Jimmy Durante | Jimmy Breslin |
| Peggy Lee | Jackie Robinson |
| Ella Fitzgerald | William B. Williams |
| Brad Crandall | Tony Bennett |
| George C. Scott | Tony Martin |
| Ed McMahon | Tony Randall |
| Red Sutherland | Richard Nixon |
| Julie Harris | Gregory Peck |
| Truman Capote | George Burns |

| | |
|---|---|
| Charlton Heston | Herb Caen |
| Sonny Tufts | Louis Nye |
| Frank Fontaine | Peter, Paul & Mary |
| Jimmy Cannon | Alfred Hitchcock |
| Veronica Lake | Janis Paige |
| Louis Sobol | Bud Collyer |
| John Peckham | James Mason |
| Lionel Hampton | Jack Lemmon |
| Fred Robbins | Jack O'Brien |
| Edie Adams | Frederick A. Klein |

The following celebrities have also flown with us:

| | |
|---|---|
| Jack Paar | Broderick Crawford |
| Joan Crawford | Joey Adams |
| Robert Goulet | Judy Garland |
| Art Linkletter | Johnny Mathis |
| Celeste Holm | Jerry Lester |
| Susan Hayward | Julie London |
| The N.Y. Yankees | Sidney Poitier |
| Ed "Kookie" Byrnes | Hedy Lamarr |
| Jack Carter | Zsa Zsa Gabor |
| Gary Morton | Allen Funt |
| Jerry Lewis | Mort Sahl |
| George Jessel | Danny Kaye |
| Anthony Franciosa | |

# CHAPTER XII

## "Wow! We're Going to Work a Press Trip!"

*M*EMO FROM: *Supv. Carlson*
TO: *T. Baker*
ACTION: *Special assignment.*
*Report Mr. Craig, PR Dept.,*
*Main Office, 0930 8 May.*

"I got a memo, too," Rachel told me when I showed her mine. "Wow! Sounds like we're going to work a special party or something with Huntley and Brinkley and Walter Cronkite and all those people."

"Let's call Dan and see what he knows about this. He must know who Mr. Craig is."

I dialed the number of Dan Lindgren, our airline's public relations representative at Kennedy Airport. We'd met Dan one day when he was frantically trying to find two stewardesses to pose for a publicity picture. He'd dragged us out of the snack bar, only after Rachel made him show his airline ID card, and herded us over to the fountains in front of the International Arrivals Building. We took off our shoes and stockings and were wading around in the pool portion while a news photographer snapped us from every angle. It was supposed to be a cooling picture in the midst of New York's record heat wave.

Things went nicely until a Port Authority police car drove up and arrested Dan for trespassing in the pools. Dan managed to talk the cop out of confiscating the film, but was taken away from the scene to explain things at headquarters. Despite all the police nonsense, the picture made the papers, and we proudly sent many copies back home to parents and friends.

We'd run into Dan occasionally after that in the terminal. He was usually with a big, handsome fellow named Sonny Valano, the airline's official photographer. It was Sonny who answered the phone when we called.

"Sonny?" Rachel asked.

"Yeh."

"This is Rachel."

"Who?"

"Rachel Jones. Remember the pool . . . And the cops?"

"Oh, yeh. How've you been?"

"Fine."

"Good. Wait a minute."

There was a moment of silence. Then we could hear Sonny screaming profanities at a messenger who had obviously arrived late. Sonny muttered as he came back on the line. "OK, Sally," he said, "What can I do for you?"

"This isn't Sally. This is Rachel. Rachel Jones."

"Oh, yeh. How are you, Rachel?"

"Fine."

"Good."

More silence. I broke it this time.

"Sonny, this is Trudy and . . ."

"Who?"

"Trudy. Trudy Baker. I was in the pool, too."

"Oh, yeh. How are you?"

"Fine."

"Good."

"Sonny, we've gotten special assignments for some press flight. We're supposed to report to a Mr. Craig on Tuesday morning. Do you know what it's all about?"

"Sure. I requested Rachel and Trudy."

"How could you request us if you can't remember our names?"

"I keep a file."

"Oh."

Sonny excused himself again to take some prints off the dryer that were about to go through for the second time.

"Sorry, Trudy, but . . ."

"This is Rachel."

"Right."

"I was saying, Sonny, about this press trip and wondering who Mr. Craig was."

"Jeez, I left a roll of negatives in the soup. I gotta run. Here's Dan."

Dan Lindgren got on the phone and we all went through the identification process again.

"Dan, we were asking about Mr. Craig. Who is he?"

"Yuuk."

"Oh."

"But don't tell him I said that. We work for him."

"OK."

Dan explained about the trip. "It's to introduce our new 727 service to Atlanta. We fly a whole planeload of press types down there and wine 'em and dine 'em and bring them back the same night. Big drag but Sonny thought you'd like to work the trip."

"We'd love to go. Just the two of us?"

"No. Sonny got a third girl. I think her name is Betty O'Riley or something similar. Know her?"

"Yuuk."

"Oh."

"But don't tell her I said that."

"OK."

"How've you been, Dan?"

"Terrible, Sonny and I were out here until two this morning working with a gang of faggy photographers and lesbo models. They were doing a brassière ad. You know, broad in bra on wingtip under moonlight? And I've got to be here tonight to VIP a columnist's dog. It's a poodle, I think. And we've got a newscaster up in the club getting boozed up. He's flipping because his flight was delayed an hour. And Sonny has to shoot a retirement dinner for some captain. And, let's see. On, yeh. John Craig, the guy you have to see, our boss, is coming out tonight to meet his wife. They're going to LA for the weekend. And boy, do I dread seeing him. He'll smile at me and pat me on the back and ask how my family is. I'll tell him everyone is great. He figures that's all he has to do for me for the next six months. He read at Dale Carnegie or someplace that you always ask your employee how his family is. Then you can knife him for another six months. He's really bad news. But he's the fair-haired boy of the new VP and he's swimming in power. Oh, I almost forgot. An African starlet is arriving at eleven and we have to do a picture and a release. And some circus lions and tigers are being shipped to Memphis on air freight. More pictures, if they can get the model to put her head in the cat's mouth. See? That's how I am."

"It's a shame I asked."

"Anytime. Have fun with Craig. He's really not very bright, and you can put him on easily. See you on the trip."

We saw John Craig on the appointed morning. He was kind of seedy-looking in a corporate way, a refugee from the low-paying city rooms of newspapers to the higher-paying conference rooms of public relations. He liked girls and he told us so. It was disconcerting to talk with him; he seemed to go into deep thought before every sentence, even a simple one like "Hello."

"Hello," we said back.

"I saw your picture in the paper and thought you'd be perfect for this press flight. I always appreciate a good-looking couple of stewardesses."

"But Sonny said he was the one who . . ."

Craig cut Rachel short. "Yes, good old Sonny. Good boy. OK, here's what we have planned. We'll have a meeting with Mr. Looms in about ten minutes. He's our vice president for public relations. Brilliant man. I think he'll like you. It's his first press trip and he's a little on edge about it. He's never been in the aviation industry before. Lots of PR experience, though. He's been with eight different companies in the past seven years. All of them as VP. That's quite a record."

It obviously was, but we didn't know how to take it. It sounded bad to us. Anyway, we were still thrilled with the thought of serving all those big names of the press. And management was certain to notice us. What worth such notice would bring was dubious, but it seemed important nonetheless.

The meeting was held in Mr. Looms's spacious office. The carpeting was thick, and we enjoyed sinking into it with each step as we took chairs across from the massive desk. Behind it sat a head, a huge, balloonlike head with red, wavy hair. Below the hair was a large, forced smile. He looked like a clerk who issues marriage licenses.

Other people started coming in, including Dan Lindgren, Sonny Valano, John Craig, and an assortment of men and women of the PR department. Looms swiveled around so his back was to the people. When everyone became very quiet, Looms spun about in his chair and slammed his fist on the desk.

"Let's get one thing straight," he began, his tone extremely angry. It seemed a strange way to start a meeting. "I want a perfect press trip next Sunday. A perfect one. I won't tolerate any mistakes. Understand that?"

Heads went up and down.

"We're really going to sell this airplane. Atlanta is just the beginning. Pretty soon, we'll be offering it to passengers coast to coast."

A big man interrupted. He was obviously his own person as he blew his nose in a red railroad handkerchief. "Stewart," the man said, "this airplane will never fly coast to coast. It can't. It doesn't have the range. It was never meant for coast-to-coast travel."

Looms obviously didn't like this kind of factual back talk from a subordinate. He slammed his fist on the desk again and yelled, "Scotty, stop trying to destroy this project."

"But Stewart," the big man went on, "it's silly to talk about coast to coast for a 727."

"Goddamn it," Looms screamed, "you know what I mean. I need straighter thinking than that."

The big man, Scotty, sat back with a sigh, a look on his face indicating thoughts of other and better places to be at the moment.

"As I was saying," Looms drove forward, "I wont tolerate any mistakes on this trip. I want this whole project to have magic, drive, sparkle. Got that?"

Everyone wrinkled his brows in thought except Scotty, who just blew his nose in nasal defiance. Then, Mr. Craig raised his hand, a silly smile on his face.

"Mr. Looms, I've been giving this whole project a great deal of thought. Even on the weekends, when I'm with my family, I want it to go off right. I think the key to its success is to try our hardest to put some magic, some drive, you might even say sparkle into it."

Looms's face lighted up and he became excited. "That's the kind of thinking I mean," he proclaimed to everyone. "That's exactly what I mean. You do see what I mean, don't you, John?"

John Craig assumed a semi-humble pose and said through his smile, "Yes, I do, Stewart. Yes, I do."

"See," Looms said to the group. "That's the kind of thinking I'd like to feel I'm surrounded with. You're all paid enough to think that straight."

Scotty belched and said he had something to do. Looms's eyes followed his imposing form out of the room. Dan Lindgren leaned over to me and whispered, "There goes the smartest guy in this whole damn airline. Looms hates him for that."

Looms stood up for the first time. "I know what you're all thinking. You're all thinking I'm a bastard and a tough guy. Well, I am. But I know how to get the most out of my people. Always have, everyplace I've been. And we'll have a perfect press trip." His scalp was beaded at the edges of his red hair.

Craig stood up in a gesture to end the meeting. "I think I speak for everyone in this room when I say how fortunate we are to have your kind of leadership, Stewart. We'll give 'em hell on Sunday." Craig wasn't sure if it was Christian to give 'em hell on Sunday. But Looms was obviously pleased by his comment about leadership. And Craig was pleased Looms was pleased. They beamed at each other as we all left the office.

The flight was to depart Kennedy at noon the following Sunday. We arrived at ten, and after checking in with crew scheduling, went down to the lounge area. There was a crowd of people drinking from the makeshift bar set up in the corner. Sonny lounged against a wall, a Yashica-Mat camera around his neck.

"Gee, the press gets here early, don't they," Rachel said.

"What press?" he responded. "It's all PR people. The press won't arrive for another hour."

We noticed a tall, gaunt man standing talking with Mr. Looms and some other men. It looked like our airline's president, Mr.

Lincoln, at least as we remembered him from his picture. Sonny confirmed that it was. Looms spotted us, broke away from his group and bounced up to us.

"Hi there," he said. "I'm Stewart Looms, vice president of public relations. I didn't get a chance to say hello at the meeting last week. I hope you're pleased I selected you for this trip. I saw your pictures in the paper and decided right then and there you would be perfect." We looked for Sonny but he had quickly walked away.

"We're delighted," we said.

"Good. You just stay near me and everything will be all right. And don't let that tough talk of mine at the meeting scare you off. You've got to be that way with your staff. I've been very successful with it. Eight vice presidencies in the last seven years. That's really going some, wouldn't you say?"

"Oh yes, Mr. Looms."

The press arrived and headed immediately for the bar. Looms was everywhere back-slapping and chitchatting, always with an eye on Mr. Lincoln. We strained to recognize any of the press people in the lounge. There wasn't one who even looked vaguely familiar. We asked Dan Lindgren about it.

"Why should you know any of them?" he asked in return. "You don't really think Craig is capable of lining up any names, do you? This whole thing is a game. Craig ends up inviting guys from *Turtle Breeders' Quarterly,* assistant editors from makeup magazines, secretaries from NBC, CBS, and ABC so they're represented on the sign-in sheet, and maybe a guy or two from a daily paper who live off free PR food and booze. The best bet he came up with today is the managing editor of a New Jersey weekly, a personal friend. Like I said, it's all a game. Craig fills the place with bodies and Looms, silly Looms, thinks he's done a fantastic job."

"That's awful," Rachel said.

"Sure. And Mr. Lincoln thinks Looms has done a great job because of all the people. When nothing appears in print or on TV, they all chalk it up to bad breaks. It's all pretty silly, when you think about it."

"How much do they spend to be silly this way?" I asked.

"Fifty, maybe sixty thousand. But don't worry about it. Enjoy it now. Pretty soon everybody will be drunk and you'll be fighting for your life."

"What a sick way to make a living," Rachel commented as the absurdity of the thing began to sink in.

"Not really," Dan said. "It's just this bad when you have a psycho like Looms running the show. It used to be better. Lots of great people in this department. But they'll all pick up and leave soon."

"You too, Dan?"

"I've already got lines out all over town."

The lounge was bulging at the seams now. People were everywhere, drinks in their hands and a great deal to say to each other. Each received his periodic pat on the back from Mr. Looms, and there was never a PR man too far away with an instant drink.

All the chatter was brought to a halt when Looms leaped up on the table and held his hands up to the people. "Quiet, please. Quiet, please," he said, looking to Mr. Lincoln for approval of his approach. The president just scowled.

"Hey, ye gonna need coats in Atlanta?" a drunk yelled from the rear of the room.

This question seemed to fluster Looms. He asked a staff member at the side of the table about the coats, and the staff member said everyone should bring coats.

"Yes, indeed," Looms answered the drunk, "coats in Atlanta."

"Hooray," another drunk yelled from the bar.

Looms continued. "Well, ladies and gentlemen, it's time to get on down to the big bird." He chuckled at his terminology—terribly inside. He looked at Mr. Lincoln who seemed pained. "Well, as I said, we can go down to the 727 now and get in our seats for the trip to Atlanta. Everybody ready?"

No one answered Looms, which upset him. He jumped down from the table and patted Mr. Lincoln on the back. "Well, Mr. Lincoln, guess we're ready to go. Sure got a fine group of people here, didn't we?"

Mr. Lincoln took a final sip of his drink. "Who are they all, Looms?"

Looms was quick on his feet. "Oh, you know, top-echelon folks from the nets, wires, dailies . . . that caliber. We're right in there with the best today." Lincoln snorted and walked away from his PR man.

Looms spotted Craig as he was walking out with the group and grabbed his arm. "John, we've got top people here today, haven't we?"

Craig was fast on his feet, too. "You bet, Stewart. What we've done is to really dig and find the people who can produce . . . really produce for us. No sense having the managing editor of *The Times* or *Newsweek*. They can't do anything for us. We've got the do-it guys. The guys with some magic and sparkle."

"Good boy, John." They walked out together proudly. Behind them came the last member of the magical press corps, the cartoon editor of *Welfare Weekly*.

We helped the drunks into their seats, fumbled with their seat belts, gave the special PA announcement for the occasion, and sat back as the plane streaked down Runway 31-Left at Kennedy. The wheels had barely left the ground when everyone seemed to get up at once. They clustered in the aisle, first in a large group in the rear, and then moving up to the front.

Someone spotted something out the left side of the airplane and they all piled over to see, the plane taking a shuddering change in flight characteristics. It was that way the whole trip; back and forth and up and down until the pilot must have simply given up trying to maintain any sort of straight and level flight.

Dan Lindgren was right. The entire flight was a valiant fight to keep the booze flowing and the drunks in line. Looms kept running into the galley with nasty mixed drink orders like whiskey sours and daiquiris for one guy or another, and Craig would always come in right after him to check on whether we were following orders.

The only one who seemed to be enjoying the whole affair was Betty O'Riley. She almost missed the flight, racing in at the last minute with a story about how this fantastic male model just wouldn't let her out of bed. Once we were airborne, she was right in the midst of all the elbows and hands with a tray of Scotch or bourbon and a big smile.

Sonny took lots of pictures, his strobe unit flashing all over the cabin. It wasn't until we were seated at dinner in Atlanta that he confided to Rachel and me that he had forgotten to bring any film, and was doing all his picture taking for effect only. Betty was attracted to his camera like a snake to water. She managed to be in every scene photographed, including some with Mr. Lincoln. It would be a sad day when she found out there was no film.

We landed at Atlanta and taxied up to a waiting line of black limousines. The drunks were poured into cars and off we went to a downtown hotel. At dinner the press type on Rachel's right passed out just as the main course was served. He fell headfirst into the mashed potatoes, much to the chagrin of Mr. Lincoln. Others fell by the tableside as the dinner wore on. The only saving touches were the caustic comments interjected by Sonny and Dan.

After dinner, we were all hustled to a nightclub that featured an exotic dancer, an off-key singer, and a comic who, after being encouraged by the fifty dollars Mr. Craig gave him, told some jokes about the airline and New York. More drunks fell asleep at their tables, a woman from a cosmetics magazine got sick, and Looms made a scene about bad service.

All of these misadventures didn't prevent Rachel and me from having a good time. At dinner and at the nightclub we were treated like guests, not employees. We danced with Sonny and a couple of the press fellows who could still get around. We spent a lot of time turning down drinks. It seemed a shame to say No to all that free-flowing booze. But under the friendly but stern eye of the airline's president we didn't think we should take the slightest chance. Several times I could see Rachel glancing over at Mr. Lincoln.

"What are you thinking?" I asked.

"I was wondering if he'd like to dance."

"Why don't you ask him?" I suggested.

Rachel shook her head. "I wasn't wondering that hard." For once she didn't respond to my needling. "Why don't *you* ask him?" She flung the challenge back at me.

"I think I will," I said, pushing my chair back.

Rachel was startled. "You wouldn't really, would you, Trudy?"

"Just watch me." By the time I'd walked over and tapped Mr. Lincoln on the shoulder, *everyone* was watching. I hadn't counted on such a big audience.

"Excuse me," I began, but realized my voice was too diffident. I'd have to come on much stronger if I didn't want to end up with egg on my face. I put on my heartiest Texas tone, "C'mon, president, baby, let's dance."

There was an instant of frozen silence. Then Mr. Lincoln stood up tall and serious and said, "I'd love to, Miss Baker." Now there's a man who's really a sport. We had a lovely dance—luckily it was a slow number. I don't think Mr. Lincoln would have been up to the dog or a fast twist.

Sonny patted me on the back afterward. "That was the best thing that happened this whole trip." What truly astonished me was Mr. Lincoln knew my name. I've never gotten over that.

The limos drove everyone back to the airport for an eleven o'clock departure for Kennedy. Once we were inside the airplane Dan Lindgren took a head count and came up one short. Finally, after much questioning, it was learned that the eighteen-year-old daughter of a woman on board was missing. The mother, an administrative assistant at a local New York television station, was rip-roaring drunk. She really didn't seem to care about her missing daughter.

The PR staff, those still standing, fanned out in all directions to find the missing girl. Someone vaguely remembered she was in one of the cars coming from town, so she certainly must have been at the airport. They searched under parked cars, up trees, in empty airplanes, and in the stalls of the bathrooms. Nothing.

Then, a half hour later, Sonny came down the corridor with a limp girl slung over his arm and shoulder. He had found her curled up behind the closed bar of the terminal, her head resting on a bottle of rye.

Everybody accounted for, we flew back to New York. This leg of the trip was peaceful because everyone was asleep, except Mr. Looms and a few of the PR people. Betty leaned all over Looms and he loved it. Rachel and I talked to Sonny. Dan was asleep in a seat next to the lost-and-found girl, who kept thrashing her arms around and yelling, "I hate you, Mother, you bitch." No one else seemed to hear or care.

More black limousines were waiting at Kennedy for our triumphant return. They left carrying their precious cargo of press people to various destinations. We were walking out to try and catch a cab back to the city when Mr. Looms came running up behind us. We assumed Betty had scored with him, but she was seen leaving the terminal with the captain of the flight.

"Girls," Looms said with a tired gleam in his little eyes, "I'll take you home. We can have a nightcap at your place and I can tell you about the whole concept of these trips." He was actually standing on his toes as he spoke, like an over-the-hill ballet dancer.

"No thanks," we said. "We're beat."

"Don't be silly, I'll get John Craig and we'll meet you someplace if you'd like. You know, I can see that you get a lot more of these special assignments. As the vice president, I can do that." Craig came running up to us with great relief—he'd found his leader.

"Good night," we said and turned away from them to go outside.

"I'll see you again, girls," Looms said with a nasty turn to his voice. We could hear him, just as the door closed behind us, say to Craig, "I told 'em I was too tired."

# CHAPTER XIII

## "Please, Not Another Press Trip"

*M*EMO FROM: *Supv. Carlson*
TO: *T. Baker*
ACTION: *Special assignment.*
Report *Mr. Fowler, Sales Dept.,*
Main Office, *0930 11 June.*

As with the notification of our press trip, Rachel received her second memo the same day mine arrived. We went to see Miss Carlson together.

"Congratulations, girls," Miss Carlson beamed as we walked through her office door. "You must be popular."

"The question is, with whom?"

Miss Carlson checked a file she had in front of her. "According to Sonny Valano, that press trip you two worked was the biggest success they've ever had. He suggested you for this next assignment."

"It's not another press trip, is it?"

"No, it isn't. Look, if you two don't want these assignments anymore, I'll be happy to take your names off the list. I get asked every day by at least a dozen girls how they can get to do special assignments. If you can't use the extra ten-dollar daily fee, forget it."

"Don't be hasty, Miss Carlson," I responded quickly. "We love doing these things. Anything at all."

"Not anything," Rachel said, a smile lighting her face.

"OK." Miss Carlson had had enough of this banter. "Go see Mr. Fowler in the New York sales department. We're becoming involved in a big promotion and part of it calls for stewardesses being interviewed on radio and television. Sonny says you two are pretty glib."

"Sounds like fun," I offered. "Just the two of us?"

"No. Sonny also said you two and Betty O'Riley worked beautifully together on that press trip. She'll be with you."

We didn't reply.

"What's the matter? Betty's ego getting to you? She's really a good gal down deep. She grows on you."

Rachel was about to add, "like fungus," but thought better of it. "I'm sure down deep Betty O'Riley is a lovely person," Rachel managed coolly.

We reported to Mr. Fowler at the specified time and place. He was a very pleasant man and seemed eager to see us enjoy the assignment.

"The first thing you girls are going to have to do is be interviewed on a local radio show. You've probably heard of it. The Big Wilson show?"

"Sure," we responded. "He wakes us up every time we have an early flight. Funny fellow."

"Wonderful guy, too," Mr. Fowler assured us. "The interview is set for Friday morning. They're doing the show as a remote from the skating rink at Rockefeller Plaza. You'll be on sometime between nine and ten."

"We thought Betty O'Riley was in on this also."

"She is. She couldn't make it this morning but I've arranged a briefing this evening for her. You know her?"

"Sort of."

Mr. Fowler told us all about the promotion and the interview, and impressed on us the fact that we had nothing to worry about. "Biggie is a very easygoing guy, girls. He'll lead you right along in the interview. Just be yourselves."

We could only foresee disaster for the airline if Betty O'Riley acted as she normally did. But that was Big Wilson's problem, we decided. We even resolved not to follow Rachel's suggestion that we pass a note to Big Wilson on which we told him Betty's nickname.

"We can't do that," I protested. "What if he slipped on the air and said it?"

"Don't be silly, Trudy," Rachel said in defense of her idea. "Professionals don't slip when they're on the radio."

"I don't care. As much as I don't like Betty, we have no right to do this to her. Besides, one look at her and anyone around will come up with that nickname himself."

I won out.

We arrived on time at the skating rink and were greeted by Frank Deveau, the show's director. Betty was already with Mr. Deveau, in the midst of a long, involved story about her most recent beau, when we barged in.

"Where's Big Wilson?" we asked after Mr. Deveau arranged for coffee for all of us.

"The news is on and he went for a walk. You've never seen him?"

"No. We were talking about him on the way over. We've decided he's under five feet tall and weighs about one hundred pounds."

The director smiled. "How did you know?"

We were pleased we'd envisioned Big Wilson so accurately, with only a voice to go on. "Well," I said modestly, "we figured the nickname Big was a joke. You know, one of those show-business jokes."

Frank Deveau laughed. "Good thinking. He'll be back in a minute. He gets up at 3:30 every morning to make the show at five, and I think he walks to keep awake."

Frank introduced us to the show's engineer, another very pleasant fellow named Jerry Schneyer. Betty took an immediate liking to him. She must have thought she was back in the cockpit of a 727, because she immediately blinked her eyes and asked, "What are all those li'l dials and lights and things? My, how much y'all must have to know."

Jerry Schneyer looked up from what he was doing and leaned over to Betty. "No, it's all done inside. They just put me out here for show. You know, keeps the people interested." With that, he turned back to what he was doing.

Betty turned and flashed her eyes at Frank Deveau. "My, Mr. Deveau, ah do declare ah didn't know that. Isn't that just the cutest thing?"

"Yes. The whole thing is a fraud," he concurred.

The remote broadcast was being handled within a portable three-sided room, the walls hinged together to form a back and sides of the set. A large crowd was gathered in front.

"Hi, Biggie," we heard someone in the crowd yell. Then someone else said the same thing. We looked hard into the crowd for the little fellow to come through. Instead, a very large man stepped up onto the slightly raised platform on which a small piano, desk, engineer's equipment, director's desk, clock, microphones, and other broadcasting paraphernalia stood, ready for use.

"Anybody see Big Wilson?" he asked us.

"We're waiting for him," we replied.

"Me too," he said.

All of a sudden, Frank Deveau pointed to the big man we'd just spoken with, who immediately sat down at the little piano's little bench and started to play ragtime. After a few bars, he stopped and said into the microphone suspended above him, "Good morning, good morning. This is ol' Biggie and it's good to see ya all here this morning."

"*That's* Big Wilson?" I whispered to Frank Deveau. "No," he answered. "It's Oscar Levant in disguise."

Betty giggled. "Ah jus' love show business."

Deveau ignored her.

Biggie played a few more bars on his piano, did a commercial for wine, urged listeners to listen to Mimi Benzell at noontime, and gave the time and temperature. Jerry played a recorded commercial, after which Biggie came back with, "We're about to lose our beloved director, Frank Deveau. He's over there applying for a job as a stewardess. All in favor of Frank being a stewardess? Hands. Hands down. You've got good taste, Frank. Keep it up."

Betty assumed his remark about good taste was directed at her. She wiggled in her chair and smiled broadly at the audience gathered in front of the set.

"When are we going to be interviewed?" we asked Frank.

"Few more minutes. After he interviews some of the people standing out front."

Wilson did those interviews after playing a Les Brown record.

"OK, OK," he mumbled into the mike as he got up from the piano bench. He certainly had earned his nickname. He had to be six foot five at least, and we guessed his weight to be three hundred. We were told he didn't weigh that much but we held to our belief. "Let's chat with a few of the folks out here this morning. Merry Jerry Schneyer has the traveling microphone and let's see . . . You, sir . . . what's your name?"

The audience interviews lasted maybe three or four minutes. No one said anything startling and Biggie was on his way back to the platform when a little old man grabbed him by the sleeve. He turned around and the little old-timer threw him a salute.

Wilson chuckled. "Well, hello there. What's your name?"

He held out the microphone in front of the man's face. The man took the microphone from Wilson's hand, much to Biggie's surprise, looked at it quizzically and held it to his ear.

"What say?" he asked Wilson, now secure with his newfound hearing aid.

Everyone broke up. It was a marvelous scene. Wilson came back to the platform, his large frame shaking with laughter. Frank Deveau was doubled over in his chair, and how Jerry Schneyer managed to keep from pushing all the wrong buttons in his hysterics was a tribute to his experience. The little old man saluted again and walked away.

"We'll be right back after the 9:30 news."

Big Wilson called us up to the microphone at about 9:40.

"All right, all right. We've managed to steal those three lovely young ladies away from Frank Deveau who is currently sitting in the corner sulking . . . or are you sleeping, Frank? . . . Anyway, I may begin to fly again . . . You are three beautiful hostesses . . . or do they call you stewardesses?"

Betty jumped in with an answer. "Well, Mr. Wilson, honey, some airlines call us some things an' some airlines call us other things. Actually, we're hostesses in the true sense of the word. We're taught that every li'l passenger should be treated with pipe-and-slipper courtesy an' . . . ." Betty was about to recite the entire training manual.

"I'm sorry I asked," Wilson proclaimed.

Betty laughed hard and jiggled herself for the audience.

"Well now, what are your names? I know your names but no one else does. On second thought, don't tell your names."

We were totally confused.

"Go ahead. Tell us your names."

We did.

The rest of the interview went smoothly. It was true what Mr. Fowler had said: Big Wilson was a wonderful interviewer. We managed to get in the name of our airline a few times, a fact we were sure would please the management.

"Well, girls, it was marvelous," Biggie concluded the interview. "I may even take up flying again."

We smiled. And Betty asked, "Oh, Mr. Wilson . . . May ah call you Biggie? (giggle) . . . Ah didn't know you were a pilot!"

"I'm not. But my friend, Vern Ostermeyer is. Do you ever fly with Vern?"

"Ah don't know any Captain Ostermeyer," Betty said after searching her memory.

"That's a shame. Shame. Thanks again, girls. It was real fun talking to you. And you tell your boss, whoever that is, you deserve a raise. Or I'll tell him. Or somebody'll tell him. OK?"

We asked Frank Deveau after the interview who Captain Ostermeyer was. He replied, "Famous Cleveland pilot. A lot of people flew high with Vern. Very high. You're too young, I guess. Ask your boss."

We asked Sonny later about Vern Ostermeyer. "That's the name Big Wilson has given to V.O. whiskey. V.O. Vern Ostermeyer. Got it?" We were very sorry we'd asked.

Betty wanted to stay and talk with Big Wilson some more, but reluctantly agreed to take a tour of the NBC studios. It was set up by Jim Grau, head of promotion for the WNBC radio and television stations in New York. The tour was fascinating. When it was over, Betty asked Bill Schwarz, program director for WNBC, "Ah'd love to be in television. Ah just love show business. It's in mah blood."

"I'd see a doctor," was Mr. Schwarz's reply.

She wasn't to be denied. "He really is big, isn't he?"

"Who?"

"Big Wilson."

"Not really. It's done with mirrors." With that, Jim Grau wished us well and returned to his office.

"Ah jus' love to make jokes with all those showbiz folk," Betty said as we walked back to the sales office. "Ah understand them."

"I think they understand you too, Betty," Rachel responded with a wide grin. Betty hummed "There's No Business Like Show Business" all the way to the office.

Since our unparalleled success with Big Wilson, we've worked numerous other special assignments for the airline. Of all of them, our experience at a big political convention in Atlantic City must rate as the highlight. Or low point. It depends on how you view it.

We must first explain our initial reaction to Atlantic City itself. Never having set foot on the fabled boardwalk of that resort city, we naturally assumed it was a city of rich old men and ladies who strolled the boardwalk summer after summer, retired at nine in the evening, and performed exactly six touch-your-toes each morning upon arising.

See how wrong you can be?

Atlantic City is the swingingest city we've ever seen. Certainly, as the site of such an important convention, the city had geared up its natural resources for the occasion. But all they did was amplify what is always there: An all-night, whoop-do-do, give-'em-hell honky-tonk town with wall-to-wall prostitutes and mosquitoes.

There are, of course, as you would expect in a convention city, some lovely beachfront hotels. We didn't stay at them. We were quartered at one of those pink stucco places outside of town where the number of summer insects was rivaled only by the number of hookers running in and out of most of the rooms.

Our job, along with four other girls, was to greet visitors, mostly press, at the airline's hospitality suite. It was set up in one of the public rooms at a boardwalk hotel, and the traffic was even heavier than you might expect. At first, we were told to ask for press credentials when people came to the door. But that system simply didn't work out, and we abandoned it in favor of an open-door policy. Once the word got around town that the party was for one and all, the major problem was keeping up with the demand on the liquor supply. We must commend our public relations people for their efforts in this regard.

We spent a total of two weeks in Atlantic City. By the end of the first week, we were certain neither of us would be able to make it through the second. By the end of the second week, we were equally certain neither of us would ever feel as young as we did two weeks before. It was that grueling.

Our routine at Atlantic City was simple. We arrived at the hospitality suite at 10 A.M. We helped serve doughnuts and coffee until 11 A.M. at which time the airline's bartender arrived on the scene. At 11 A.M. sharp, the doughnuts were put away for another day, and only liquor was served.

We were allowed an hour for lunch, and then acted as hostesses until 6 P.M. We were given an hour for dinner. We then went back to our positions at the door until 11 P.M. After that, our time was our own.

We tried to enjoy Atlantic City's nightlife the first few nights. But it didn't work.

First of all, the nightlife is hardly what anyone from any major U.S. city would enjoy. It's low-brow, dirty, and amateur. It's major clubs feature talent that is long on stamina and short on ability. The clubs all close from 5 A.M. to 6 A.M., a city ordinance requiring this respite for cleaning purposes.

Also, any girl in one of the clubs who doesn't have an escort on her arm is immediately labeled a hooker. She has to be, and we can understand any man thinking she would be. Even the most hardened of men who were working at the convention for the airline agreed they'd never seen so many "professional girls" in their lives.

On the few nights we did venture into town after our stint at the hospitality suite, the scene usually went like this.

**Setting:** Bar stools. Many people. Bad singer onstage. Blue and red lights whirling around and reflecting off silver spangles.

HE: Hi, baby. Drink?

ME: (SAY NOTHING. IGNORE HIM)

HE: I said hi, baby.

ME: (STILL IGNORE)

HE: Drink, baby?

ME: No!

HE: That's good. No sense wastin' the time.

ME: (IGNORE. DON'T UNDERSTAND FIRST TIME)

HE: Let's go.

ME: Where?

HE: My place. Yours? Up to you.

ME: Go away.

HE: How much?

ME: Go away.

HE: I got twenty.

ME: Listen you creep. Get Lost, I'm . . . I'm different.

HE: Whatta ya do that's different? Maybe I'll pay more.

Or,

HE: Hello there.

ME: (ASSUME HE'S NICE YOUNG MAN) Hi.

HE: Let's go.

ME: I don't even know you.

HE: (MUMBLES TO HIMSELF) What is this routine?

ME: I don't just walk off with strangers.

HE: Name's Mark. Hey, you are a hooker, right?

ME: I'm a stewardess.

HE: (GIGGLES) Great gimmick. Let's go. How much?

ME: For what?

HE: Well, how 'bout French.

ME: Irish.

HE: Irish? Never had that. That's somethin' new.

ME: Huh?

HE: Ok. Irish it is. How much?

ME: Three hundred dollars.

HE: Three hundred? For how long?

ME: Five hours. Two drinks, dinner, and a junior pilot ring. First-run movie, too.

HE: Sorry I bothered you.
ME: Me too. Bye!

There was obviously money to be made in Atlantic City during that convention. Unfortunately, we just aren't the kind to take advantage of such a situation. A few stewardesses are.

Other special assignments have found us handing out travel folders at department store promotions, checking coats at an appliance dealer's convention, and posing for pictures to be used in publicity releases. Rachel was once interviewed by a newspaper from her hometown; local-girl-makes-good kind of thing. They photographed her serving a meal to Sonny Valano, window-shopping at Bloomingdale's, reading a book in our apartment, and walking away from a BAC-111 with a captain. It appeared as promised, and they ended the piece by saying, "This vivacious local girl, now a glamorous member of the elite corps of jet-setting airline hostesses, stated her biggest problem was keeping track of her hectic social life in New York. Obviously, she's captured the hearts of New York's bachelor set, sad news for the Louisville beaus left behind."

Rachel's mother was on the telephone the night the article appeared.

"What are you doing up there?" she demanded. "Sounds like you're just flittin' away your time runnin' around with too many boys."

"Momma," Rachel said pleadingly, "I haven't had a date in three weeks. The newspaper guy was a jerk."

"Well," her mother sighed with a resigned finality, "newspapers don't lie. That's all I can say."

"Don't worry, Momma. I'll be home soon. Bye."

"Bye, Rachel. And don't you let any of them fast-talkin' boys up there get you in trouble."

"I won't, Momma. Bye."

"Bye."

The fringe benefit we liked best was working charter flights of businessmen. A big company will charter a plane to fly its sales executives to Kansas City or its brass to LA. These are men who're used to flying so they don't give you any trouble. They work hard and they like to relax hard. The liquor is poured in cascades on these flights. The usual two-drink limit is off and stewardesses can drink, too. We can also accept tips.

On one charter from New York to Houston we had all cattlemen aboard. We broke out the bourbon the minute we were off the ground and we had all those meatmen bombed before we were past Washington. When we landed in Houston I got hold of the PA and instead of making the usual announcement, I shouted, "Head 'em up and move 'em out!" Those tall Texans got off roaring. I'm not exaggerating when I say I got twelve Texas hats, a pair of souvenir boots, and $150 in tips.

That was what we call a hot flight.

# CHAPTER XIV

## "There's Another Drunk in 3A"

$\mathcal{G}$overnment regulations say that we can only serve a passenger two drinks in tourist and three in first class. We don't go along altogether with that ruling. Most passengers don't want more than their limit. But if we have a man aboard who is drinking and having a good time and holding his liquor well, we don't see a reason in the world why he shouldn't have another. He can handle it. He'll feel better for it. He'll thank you for it and remember your airline. So it's really good business. We especially enjoy seeing a passenger who climbs on the plane with a grouch at the whole human race get off at his destination purring like a kitten. Only liquor can do that.

We must confess that there've been times when we've taken the rules into our own hands. We've given extra drinks to a man we've sized up as a good drinker. We've slipped doubles to passengers when the circumstances seemed right. If you recall, on our very first flight we poured doubles into that ill-fated woman who got stuck on the john. We made her life bearable that day. I suppose that if there were many stewardesses who were alcoholics like our ex-roommate Joan, they'd be busy converting the whole flying public to unlimited liquor consumption. But we don't think that's a very big risk for the airlines.

Since most passengers don't use their full quota, there's no great problem about getting an extra little bottle for that hardfisted sales manager in 5A. But even when the whole plane is drinking to the hilt, we have ways of accounting for the extra servings. One of my favorites is to spill a few drops of Scotch or whatever on the carpet. You smear it around with water to make a big wet spot, but not enough to remove the scent. Then you report that you were walking down the aisle with two trays of six drinks when the plane lurched. Naturally you had to open twelve more bottles.

A good drinker on a plane is one thing. A drunk is altogether different. Nobody likes a drunk. This goes double and triple for stewardesses.

When a drunk comes on board, we shut the aircraft door, climb to thirty thousand feet, and there we are, a captive audience for the fellow with the bulbous red nose and ninety-proof breath.

All the drunks holding an airline ticket don't actually succeed in getting aboard. The airline and its personnel have the right to deny passage to anyone deemed too intoxicated to fly. They can exercise the same sort of restrictions on people with excessive body odor, filthy clothing, and, most recently, men wearing earrings. The problems arise when the man with earrings or smelling like a Bowery bum is president of one of the ten top Blue Chips.

You can see the problem. Tell the president of a large company that he's not wanted on your airline, and you can talk thousands of dollars of revenue out the window. The airline becomes very upset when this happens, and few ticket or ramp agents will risk incurring that kind of wrath.

When we spot a drunk staggering up the ramp toward the aircraft, we don't hesitate to go out to the passenger service person in charge of that flight and ask that he be removed. The captain can always demand that a person be taken from the plane. He's in charge of that flight, and what he says goes. But while the plane is sitting there on the ground, the captain will generally leave decisions to the ground personnel. As we said, airline employees think long and hard before denying passage to paying customers.

Sometimes people think we're just being nasty when we complain about a passenger who has had too much to drink. That isn't the case. We simply don't want to have to clean up his seat and the passenger himself after his stomach has rebelled against the whiskey he's poured down. We really don't want to spend our flight listening to his jokes, usually all bad, but hysterically funny to him. We don't want that overweight businessman, perhaps a sweet person when sober but switched into an Errol Flynn by martinis, to pinch and maul us all the way.

In short, taking care of one hundred thirty passengers is hard enough. One drunk is worth at least ten people. We can do without him or her.

You can't always recognize the drunks on your flight at boarding time. They all don't enter the plane stoned. Some can't hold their liquor, and the two drinks they're served during the flight send them into a drunken whirl. Some are on a very strict diet, or taking medication, and very little whiskey loops them. Some have been drinking for two hours at the airport bar. They seem to hold their liquor beautifully, but they're really on the verge of intoxication. The first drink on board is the one that does it. The second transforms them into a flying nightmare for us.

Then there are the people who never get drunk. They want to be drunk, but don't like to drink enough to reach that state. So, they act drunk. They think being drunk will be interpreted by us as a sign of a swinger, a devil-may-care jet-setter. Usually, these make-believe drunks are frightened about flying and use the drunk routine to explain away the shaking hands and trembling lips.

We've had some memorable drunks aboard our flights. I remember particularly Mr. Lunts, who commuted regularly between New York and Chicago. Now any regular traveler with an airline is a prized possession. He's given special membership in the airline's private club, is greeted and escorted by the airline's passenger service people, and receives general VIP treatment. Usually, when he comes aboard, we're told of his status and are asked to handle him with extra special care.

The first time I had Mr. Lunts as a passenger, I requested he be removed from the flight.

"Don't be silly," I was told by the ramp agent working the departure. "That's C. X. Lunts. He's with us every week. Take good care of him."

"He's drunk," I protested.

"So what?" was the reply.

"So what?" I came back with. "What about the other passengers?"

The ramp agent was very firm. "Mr. C. X. Lunts is always drunk when he flies. But even when he's drunk, he pays for his ticket and sends all his employees on our airline. Now if you stop and think for a minute, his money helps pay your salary. And mine too. And it helps feed my children and helps keep my wife off my back about all the new things she wants. In short, Mr. C. X. Lunts goes with us, no matter how gooned he is. That's the word."

I stood there shaking my head up and down to indicate understanding. "Message received and understood. What does the X stand for in his name?"

"I haven't the slightest idea. Why don't you ask him. But wait till after he's had his two drinks. It might be an embarrassing thing with him."

There had been no doubt in my mind that Mr. Lunts was drunk when he came aboard. He weaved happily up the loading ramp, never quite sure which way he would lean next. He was a tall, skeletal man, his angular height giving the impression he was a pole bending in a strong breeze.

"He looks like the Leaning Tower of Pizza," Rachel commented after he passed us at the door.

"More like the Leaning Tower of La Guardia," I mumbled. Rachel liked the description. She laughed.

We were waiting in line for takeoff clearance when Mr. Lunts first made his presence on the airplane known to everyone. He stood at his seat, turned to the other passengers, and announced, "This is the most wonderful airline in the whole wide world. And these are the most wonderful young ladies in every corner of this valued and im . . . im . . . impassioned land of ours and yours and mine." He sat down with authority, pleased he had set the record straight.

The next time Mr. Lunts decided to exert his individuality came when he opened his attaché case. We were airborne only a few minutes and hadn't begun serving drinks or dinner yet.

His case was filled with miniature bottles of booze, the same kind we serve on flights. He began passing them out proudly to everyone within reaching distance. They all seemed quite pleased with their gifts.

I went up to him and said, "I'm sorry, Mr. Lunts. But airline regulations allow only two drinks per passenger. I'll have to ask you to put those away until we've landed."

He looked hurt. Really hurt. He stood up, faced the cabin again, and said with great sincerity, "Ladies and gentlemen, I am truly sorry. Truly sorry. In my haste to be . . . to be . . . to be gangrenous . . . Uh, gangre . . . to give each and every one you gathered here today in this wonderful, sleek modern facility a voice . . . uh, a gift, I violated the sacrilege. . . . a sacred by-laws of this wonderful airline, and these wonderful girls here present. So, if you will be so kind and present, please put all those li'l bottles away and don't drink not even a tiny weeny drop 'til we come to our departure . . . ah, destination." He sat down to the clapping of a few hands.

He declined dinner, saying, "I never eat when I'm driving, and I hope our fair admiral up in the starboard cockport of this sleek, modern airplane feels the same way that I do now about these and other matters of ramification."

After dinner, Mr. Lunts led a few of his fellow passengers in a rousing community sing, the chief song "The Star-Spangled Banner," with a few bars of "If I Had a Hammer" thrown in for emphasis.

Upon landing, Mr. Lunts assured us he was planning to inform management about us and our superior attitude and performance toward our job. As he put it, "You are the exemplifying advantage of aviation history today, young ladies, and furthermore, your skillful laying down . . . ah, laying down . . . ah, laying down of the regulations and personal habits of every admiral will be forever in my heart . . . and hand. Good day."

We see Mr. Lunts a great deal whenever we pull New York-Chicago as a route. He's always drunk, never very unpleasant, and always promises to praise us to management. He gave us each ten dollars for Christmas and has never argued when we've reminded him of certain rules. Even with his happy way of getting drunk, he poses a problem. But all drunks should be like Mr. C. X. Lunts, if there have to be drunks on airplanes at all. By the way, the X in his name means nothing. A former business partner was also named C. Lunts, and the X was slipped in to help differentiate various aspects of their dealings. He might come up with another story when he's sober, but finding him in that state will probably never come to pass.

Unfortunately, Mr. Lunts is the exceptional drunk. In contrast, we offer Mr. Lippingdone.

We met Mr. Lippingdone only once. It was on a flight from New York to San Antonio. It was horrible. Mr. Lippingdone is at least three hundred pounds. He boarded the airplane on that particular day in our lives and proceeded to bump into Rachel as she stood in the open doorway greeting passengers. He completely lost his balance, and his bulk flattened her against the wall with a devastating thud.

He immediately turned on her and snarled, "Why don't you stand somewhere else? You're blocking the whole door." With that warning, he stumbled into the cabin, falling left and right as he made his way up the aisle.

"Either that son of a bitch flies or I do, but not both," Rachel cursed as she felt for broken bones. She stormed off the plane and grabbed the ramp agent by the arm.

"Listen," she said, "there's a two-ton drunk on the plane and I'm not flying with him."

The agent laughed. "Oh, Lippingdone? Big pain in the rear end. But he's close with the board of directors, and the word is VIP him to death. Big stockholder, too. Sorry, sweetie, but he's yours. Maybe he'll fall asleep."

"You bet he will," Rachel warned with determination in her voice. "I'll make damn sure of that if I have to slit his throat to make it come about."

Lippingdone was trouble from the minute we took off. We received numerous complaints from passengers about his foul language, foul actions, and general foul self. He spilled his dinner all over himself and screamed at me, "I want to see the captain, goddamn it. You set the tray to tip over on me. I know that for a fact (belch). I know all the people you work for on this (belch) airline, and I intend to see that you (belch) and your friend get your asses fired (belch)."

We tried to steer clear of him and succeeded until the light flashed on in the galley indicating someone wanted service in the forward bathroom. We looked at each other in despair. Lippingdone had gone in there moments before. Neither of us wanted to be in that small bathroom with him. We pointed at each other. Rachel with a sigh made the supreme sacrifice.

She knocked on the door and Lippingdone threw it open.

"There's no soap in here," he bellowed. "No soap!"

"It's right there, Mr. Lippingdone," Rachel said with all possible kindness, pointing to a pile of small bars of soap resting on top of the vanity.

"You call that soap?" he menaced, banging his hamlike fist on the counter. "That's not soap."

It was then that Rachel noticed the small, round window in the bathroom. She couldn't believe it at first. And when she finally did come around to accepting what she saw, she had to bite her tongue from laughing. Even this painful technique didn't keep some audible snickers from coming out. Lippingdone went into a rage.

"Laugh at me, will you? Laugh, huh? I'll have your ass fired." He thought she was laughing at the soap problem. Then he followed her eyes and realized she was laughing at the window. It was carefully covered with toilet paper, the edges of the paper held to the wall by Scotch tape.

Lippingdone turned a deep red. His whole body trembled with rage, his lips twitched, and his jowls shook. Rachel couldn't contain herself any longer. She broke into gales of laughter, which made Mr. Lippingdone's condition even worse.

"This is marvelous," she said between outbursts. "The other passengers will love to hear about this." She turned to leave the lavatory but Lippingdone grabbed her by the arm.

"Don't you dare. I happen to be a modest man, something you wouldn't understand."

"Oh yes, I do understand, Mr. Lippingdone."

"Damn it," he muttered to himself, furious he'd forgotten to remove the paper in his furor over the soap. "Damn it," he repeated, only louder.

Rachel pulled herself together. "Look, Mr. Lippingdone, you've been nothing but trouble for us all day. I won't say a word about the window if you promise to shut up and sit in your seat. Not a word all the way to San Antonio."

He shook again with vehemence. Rachel thought he was going to strike out and hit her. But he didn't. He said, "Oh, all right." He sulked out of the lavatory as Rachel removed the paper from the window and flushed it down the john.

It worked. Our fat Mr. Lippingdone sat silently for the rest of the flight. Rachel told me about what had happened, and we had a marvelous laugh behind the closed curtains of the galley.

We stood at the door at San Antonio as the passengers left the plane. Mr. Lippingdone was last to leave. As he came by us, head down, hands stuffed deep in his pockets, I handed him a little thing we'd made up in the galley from a napkin. It was a perfect circle, just the size of the lavatory's porthole. Written in lipstick was, "For Your Next Flight!"

Of course there are certain drunks you excuse. We've had drunken soldiers flying out of San Francisco after spending their tour of duty in Vietnam. Who can blame them? We've had people with large problems that led them to drink too much before boarding the plane. Many times they want to talk about these problems, which range from flying to claim the body of a loved one to dejection over jilting by a lover.

Of all the drunks we've known, none can compete with Mrs. Frazier, a passenger flying to New York from Los Angeles. To begin with, the general run of people boarding airplanes in Los Angeles often leaves something to be desired. Their dress, manners, and overall behavior tend on the whole to rank lower than other cities. But this particular person, Mrs. Frazier, wasn't to be believed.

She was literally carried on the airplane by a Hollywood-looking young man. He was barefooted, had hair down to his shoulders, and wore a T-shirt and chino pants.

"This is my son, Frazier," Mrs. Frazier mumbled as he lowered her into her seat. "I love that name, don't you? Frazier Frazier. Beautiful, isn't it?"

I asked him whether she was fit for the trip.

"Oh yeh, baby. She's just gettin' cool now. A very hip chick, my old lady. Very hip. Even surfs with me once in a while. Not too good, but A for effort, like."

Frazier Frazier left mommy on the plane. She fell asleep and we crossed our fingers she'd continue in that state until New York. No such luck.

She woke up an hour out of Los Angeles and it was show time. She was wearing a tight, gold dress when her son carried her on board. The first thing she did was to unzipper the back and take her bra off. Once she accomplished this maneuver, much to the delight of this man sitting next to her, she strolled up the aisle swinging the bra over her head. She also threw in a few bumps and grinds for good measure.

Next came her panties. They were slipped off in her seat and she threw them at a man across the aisle. He caught them and winked at her. We must admit that never once did her dress come off. Her stockings and shoes were discarded, but the dress maintained her decency. She insisted on helping us serve the meals, but we made it very plain that she was to stay in her seat.

"My, my, what efficient girls," she chided. "Just the kind of girls my Frazier needs."

She held hands with the man next to her, poured champagne into her shoe . . . and giggled when it ran out the open toe. She showed us an exercise she used to increase the size of her chest, implying we both could stand enlargement in that department. And she tried to frug with the flight engineer when he came back to replace a bulb in a reading light.

We got so we just couldn't take Mrs. Frazier any longer. She must have had her own secret supply of booze, because she kept getting more zonked as we got closer to New York. We watched with interest as she left the plane. On hand was another young man ready to help her up the ramp. She leaned over his back and together they managed to pass out of our sight.

"Don't ever let me get that drunk, Trudy," Rachel said as we walked together to operations.

"Do me the same favor."

# CHAPTER XV

# "Baby-Sitters of the Sky"

"...Well, Miss, the air forces acting on this aircraft are equivalent to both drag backward in the reversed direction of the motion and a lifting force at right angles to the direction of the motion. That is to say . . ."

His mother modestly termed him *precocious.* To us, he was a seven-year-old genius.

". . . To most learned people, the French Revolution is dated from the states-general convention at Versailles in May of 1789 . . ."

We'd never met a genius before and certainly never expected him to be seven.

". . . absolute monarchy reigned, of course, from the sixteenth century until the Revolution . . ."

"He's especially interested in French history," his mother said, as another would of her son's special interest in soccer.

Naturally, we catered to this little fellow with the oversize mind. It was unnerving to talk to him, especially when you tried to think of something to say that might sound reasonably intelligent. You just knew you'd fail.

Before we reached Memphis, we'd learned about frogs, physics, algebra, celestial navigation, selling short on the market, Asian customs of courtship, and the future of every major politician in the nation.

"It's the most incredible thing I've ever seen," I told his mother as she gathered up belongings just before descent. "I can't believe it."

"Yes, Craig is bright. Very bright."

We landed and I came over to the mother to say good-bye and see if I could help her with anything. She looked very sheepish.

"Do you have some paper towels?" she whispered.

"Sure. Any problem?"

"Well, it's Craig," she looked at him. His pants were soaked.

"He's been very slow to toilet train," she said with a sigh.

"Oh."

That kind of thing could be a problem for Craig in later life. I've never forgotten him.

We've never forgotten Johnny either, a six-year-old who flew with us from New Orleans to Chicago. Who said there's never been a bad boy? Meet Johnny.

He boarded the plane with his mother, and promptly whipped out a very realistic six-shooter from his belt and said, "Bang, bang," at us. That was cute, except he managed to jam the gun into Rachel's belly while pulling the trigger.

He took all the magazines off the rack before we had a chance to distribute them, and wailed when we asked that he give them back.

"I'll get them from him in a second," his mother said quietly to us, winking to indicate something. She kept her promise, but only after a half hour went by and we came back and asked again. He made an airplane out of the menu and flew it across the aisle. It made a perfect, nose-first landing in the face of a very stuffy lawyer who was trying to get some work done.

He threw up twice.

He spilled his milk all over the seat.

He ran up and down the aisle yelling, "Batman. Batman." An air force major grabbed him by the arm and whispered something in his ear. Johnny returned to his seat.

"What'd you say to him?" I asked the major.

"I told him I was the Penguin in disguise and that I was planning to throw him out of the airplane unless he sat down."

"Very effective. I'll remember that."

Johnny refused to leave the galley when we asked him to do that little thing. "I don't have to," he whined, and stuck his tongue out at us.

Rachel looked around to make sure no one else was watching. Then, she took a knife from a compartment in the buffet and pointed it at Johnny. "Oh yes you do, little boy," she said with a sinister snarl on her face. He took the hint, but not before showing us his tongue on the way out.

Ten minutes later, his mother stormed back into the galley.

"My boy said you tried to cut him with a knife."

"Not us, ma'am."

"He never lies."

"I'm sure he doesn't, ma'am."

"I'll report you."

"Yes, ma'am."

Johnny stayed in his seat for the rest of the trip. His mother glared at us all the way to Chicago. As we got close to arrival, we decided it wouldn't be such a good idea to have his mother report us. We felt it might be wise from a practical sense to make amends. We tried, as Johnny and his mother passed by us at the open cabin door.

"It sure was nice having you fly with us today, Johnny," Rachel said happily, leaning over to make sure he heard her.

Johnny answered her. He stood on his tiptoes and whispered in Rachel's ear. His mother grabbed him by the back of the neck and marched him out of the airplane. "You'll hear about this," she threatened. There was no doubt we would.

"What did he say to you?" I asked her after they'd passed out of sight.

"He said, 'I hate you, you stupid doo-doo head.'"

"Oh."

"His father made a great mistake having that boy. Someone ought to send them some birth-control literature."

"Amen," I agreed.

Of course we heard from Johnny's mother. Our supervisor called us in to answer for the mother's letter, which had gone to the president. We told her the story.

"Look, I understand," she said, "but no knives, OK?"

"OK."

We've had other little boys and girls on our flights who could have benefited from a few threats, backed up with the blade of a knife. But we'd learned our lesson. We're now more subtle, and tell them things like, "Why don't you play outside awhile?"

As we said, parents are usually to blame when a child causes trouble on a flight. We realized we were correct in this feeling after taking care of children who were flying unaccompanied. Remove them from mommy and daddy, and they behave beautifully.

If a child is even halfway good on a flight, he or she can be a delight. Children make a lot more sense than many of the adults we've flown with. In fact, not all the passengers who require baby-sitting services are children.

It was a night coach from Miami to New York and seemed like a quiet night. But when I went back for a routine check of the seats, I found I was missing two people. I remembered that an older couple had come aboard and I recalled seeing them go into the lavatory. Perhaps they were still there. I checked—they weren't. I counted passengers again. Two short. I told the other stew. She said, "Come off it, Trudy," and began counting with an air of great superiority. She came up two short. Together we checked every cranny of the plane—including the johns and the galley. Nothing.

Finally I went up to the captain "Now, look. Don't say I'm crazy, but two people are missing. They just couldn't have walked off, but we don't know where they are."

The captain walked down the aisle looking at the passengers—some asleep, some reading. Suddenly he let out a yell, "Come here, you'll never believe this."

He was looking up at the rack above the seats where pillows and blankets are kept. There curled up in the overhead rack were our two missing tourists, nicely clothed in pajamas, covered with blankets, and sound asleep. I guess they'd always traveled by train before, so they'd figured the racks were berths and just climbed up and turned in. Well, that whole plane broke up. There wasn't anyone on board who wasn't laughing hysterically.

I must remember to tell Aunt Laconia about my sleeping beauties.

# CHAPTER XVI

## "Even Your Best Friend Won't Tell You"

$\mathcal{I}$t was a great party, but hardly worth a thirty-day suspension.

The get-together, an impromptu one, was in honor of a departing stewardess. She was leaving the glamour of the sky for the altar, an event not to be questioned and most certainly to be celebrated.

The celebration began with six of us. It turned into a loud, sloppy ruck within an hour after we toasted our first glass of champagne to the bride-to-be. It ended at 3 A.M.

Rachel and I stayed until the bitter end despite having to work a 10 A.M. trip the next morning. It flashed through our minds a couple of times how tired we'd be, but it wouldn't be the first time. And we never gave a thought to the rules prohibiting a crew member from drinking twenty-four hours before a flight. That sort of regulation made sense for the men who had to fly the airplane. But it didn't make much sense for stewardesses. A good toothbrushing, breakfast, a few mints, and no one would be the wiser. Right?

We were checking in with dispatch when we were handed the note.

"What do we have to report to the supervisor for?" I mumbled as we went to her office.

"Maybe we're going to be commended," was Rachel's suggestion.

"Yeh. Like the first trip we made."

Our supervisor at this period was a pretty good gal. She seemed sincerely regretful as she said, "Sorry girls, but I've got to give you both thirty-dayers."

"What for?" We were just as sincere in our ignorance.

You could almost feel sorry for our supervisor. She hesitated, looked down at her desk and said apologetically, "Drinking within twenty-four hours of a trip."

"The party last night?"

" 'Fraid so."

"Oh, come on. Who the hell sticks that close to that twenty-four ruling? The place was crawling with stews."

"Look, I'm sorry. I didn't make this up. I've got the word to suspend you for thirty days. And I can't do a thing about it."

The real implications began to sink in at this point. How did they know about the party and the time it broke up?

"How did you know?"

Our supervisor quickly handed us the suspension notices and got up to leave. "I'm sorry." She walked out of her office.

George Kelman savored a crisp piece of sausage pizza as he thought about our tale of woe. It was the first night of our suspension and George, already aware of what happened, arrived with the pizza pies and a sympathetic shoulder.

"Well, now you'll believe me when I talk about stew-spies."

"You think that's what happened to us?" Rachel quizzed.

"No doubt about it."

"Who?"

"Never know." He started on another piece but discarded it for lack of cheese. "Wish they wouldn't skimp on cheese. Cheese is the best part."

"Who's the stew-spy who turned us in?"

"As attuned as I am to the whole stewardess scene, I have to admit ignorance in this matter. I know there are stew-spies but I don't know who they are. But this might be a good time to figure it out. Who was at that party?"

We started to think back and realized most of the people crashed the party. We didn't know 80 percent of them. We told George this.

"That's a shame. But I'll check into it further. That's a promise." He left our apartment with all the grim determination of a CIA man embarking on a highly dangerous assignment.

"Good luck, George," we yelled after him.

He completed the role he was playing by muttering grimly over his shoulder, "I'll need it."

We got jobs as salesgirls in a department store to tide us over during our suspension. George wasn't heard from again for two weeks. When he did call us, he was breathless with excitement.

"I've got to see you tonight, Rachel."

He came to the apartment at eleven that night. We'd worked late at the store, and he massaged Rachel's feet as I made drinks. When I served them, he rose from the couch and paced the room, hands behind his back, face furrowed in concentration.

"It's atrocious, girls. Abominable. A disgrace on every airline."

I know it was cruel to break his train of thought but my feet hurt, too. "George, how about rubbing my feet."

He beat his fist against his head. "Rub your feet? Really, Trudy. I'm about to unfold a story of deceit and duplicity in front of you, and you worry about your aching feet. Really!"

"I'm sorry, George. But we've been standing all night and . . ."

"Enough of this. Do you want to know about the stew-spies who were responsible for your suspension?"

"You bet," we screamed in his ear, our sore feet forgotten.

"OK. Now listen." He resumed his pacing. "Would you believe your airline has a dozen girls working as stew-spies?"

We reacted with proper surprise.

"Yes, a dozen. Maybe some are your very best friends. What do you think of that?"

"Horrible. Which one turned us in?"

"I don't know."

We were naturally disappointed. We had expected him to tell us who the culprit was who caused us our thirty-day stint at the department store.

"What are you girls disappointed about?" he snapped at us. "I can't work miracles. Anyway, I did find out how they work. Listen to this. All twelve girls are regular stews and collect their salaries just like you do. But the airline has a contract with a private detective agency in Chicago. And that agency has the twelve girls on their payroll, too. They collect double and work as spies. Nasty, huh?"

We agreed.

He went on. "Now, I'm going to Chicago and follow up on this whole thing. Maybe I can find out the names of the girls. This whole thing really has me upset. I always knew there were stew-spies but never really saw any damage they'd caused. Now I'm outraged."

George made two trips to Chicago but never found out who the girls were on the double payroll. We finished our month in the toy department of the store and resumed our flying careers. The worst part of the experience was the mistrust it implanted in us. We didn't trust anyone anymore. Every girl we worked with assumed a traitor's mask, each her own stool pigeon in this despicable plot.

However, despite George's failure to uncover the names of the girls, we came up with a prime suspect of our own. Her name was Janis Pool, and she talked too much about stew-spies and how terrible they were. She hated to be questioned about what she knew, but seemed possessed by the subject. We asked George about her.

"I ran down a dossier on Janis Pool," he told us, "and she could be a stew-spy. Very definitely could be. Too much money for just a stew with one income. Lives alone. Always bids Chicago and gets it. Keeps to herself. Loves to talk about stew-spies."

"We've noticed that, too, George. You really think she's one of them?"

"Can't say for sure. But she's a strong possibility. I'll check further."

We didn't wait for later findings by George Kelman. Janis Pool was it, we decided. She had to be.

"Was she at the party?" I asked Rachel.

"I didn't remember her. But I don't remember most of the people, do you?"

"No."

But the girl for whom the party was given did remember Janis Pool showing up. "She came in about midnight and only stayed for a drink or two."

That did it. Janis Pool was our Nathan Hale and would have to be dealt with.

We began a day-by-day harassment of the suspect. First, on an evening trip, we broke open one of the small ammonia vials used to revive fainting passengers and placed it in the oxygen mask used by us to demonstrate proper technique to passengers before take-off. Janis was all smiles as she held the mask in her hands waiting for me to read the instructions over the PA. I began reading and she placed the mask to her face in accordance with my words. She almost died. She sputtered and coughed, tears carrying makeup down her face, as she plunged into the buffet area.

"Why did you do this to me?" she cried as we stood there in gaping amazement at her condition.

"Do what?"

"Put the ammonia in the mask."

"Janis, don't look at us. Must have been one of those nasty cabin cleaners. That's who must have done it."

"I'll get his ass fired," she threatened through her weeping.

"I'll bet you can, Janis," Rachel said.

"You bet I can," Janis reiterated.

We pulled all sorts of very silly and sophomoric tricks on Janis Pool, each helping us rid ourselves of deep-seated feelings of vindictiveness. Our decision, a kangaroo-court one, was that Janis Pool was a stew-spy and had turned us in to management. We couldn't see any further. We called her at odd hours and hung up. We took messages from her box and enjoyed her problems when she didn't answer them or take the appropriate action. We even spilled things on her in the buffet, an especially nasty trick because stewardesses usually maintain only one uniform.

We're still convinced Janis Pool was the spy. It's never been proven. In retrospect, our actions against her were mean and un-called for. But we did what we did and felt better for it at the time.

Certain airlines still maintain the stew-spy system. Our union tries very hard to bring about the end of this big-sister system. So far, they've been unsuccessful.

Of course, we recognize that girls are deceitful creatures at best. There doesn't seem a day goes by without one stewardess stealing away another's boyfriend. We've seen hair-pulling matches between friends of long standing, poison-pen notes, vicious gossip, and nasty, day-by-day retaliation between the girls. We guess that's the way we are—take it or leave it!

But adopting the "all's fair in love and war" creed is acceptable when only love and war are involved. Our jobs are a different matter of much greater importance than a lost lover. We don't personally know a stew-spy. That's fortunate for them.

# CHAPTER XVII

## "Have a Merry Mistress"

$C$harlie Smagg opened the door when we knocked. His head bobbed back and forth like one of those stranger-than-fiction, real-life Christmas dolls. He was drunk. That was obvious.

"Hi, Charlie," we said happily despite the blowing snow swirling around our legs.

"'Twas the night before Christmas and all through the plane not a creature was stirring not even one li'l ol' bubble in a glass of bubbly champagne." His head bobbed faster.

"Can we come in, Charlie?"

"Why, of course. Course. Come in. Come in."

The motel room was a welcome pocket of warmth. There were maybe a dozen people in the room. A party atmosphere prevailed.

Charlie Smagg, the first officer on the flight that brought us to Rochester on this Christmas Eve, was obviously the first to arrive at the party. Besides, it was his room, a good running start for anyone.

We weren't supposed to be in Rochester on Christmas Eve. Our schedule called for a return trip to Kennedy Airport late that afternoon. But the unpredictable winter weather of upstate New York held off just long enough for us to land in Rochester at noon. Then, like an overanxious curtain puller at a bad play, the weather swooped in and shrouded the area in a white cloak of snow.

The word that we would not be getting home for Christmas brought sadness to Rachel and me. Neither of us had ever been away from home on Christmas. Our plans were to go back to Kennedy as scheduled, and look for empty seats to Texas and Kentucky. Failing that, we'd at least be able to enjoy the day together in the familiar surroundings of our apartment. But winter wasn't kind.

The whole crew checked into the motel together after a slippery car ride from the airport. The desk clerk, a wizened little man with bad breath and a runny nose, set the tone for the evening when he said to the captain, "Have yourself a merry mistress, captain." It did not instill any feeling of ho-ho-ho and glad tidings in us.

We shared our room with Rhonda, the third girl on the trip. Normally on layovers, two girls share a room. But the storm put rooms at a premium. "Well, what'll we do for the night?" Rachel asked as she pulled things out of her suitcase. "Sing Christmas carols?"

"Why not," I agreed. "We might become the Andrews Sisters of Rochester. Ted Mack might hear us and make us famous."

"Right. We could play all the best nightspots of Rochester on the same bill with a hacksaw-blade player and a Maltese Santa Claus who does bird calls."

"It makes me so mad," Rhonda said as she pouted in front of the mirror. She was very pretty, with honey hair and fair complexion and an ample figure. Her major problem was she knew it. "My boyfriend and I were going to have dinner and drive up to Connecticut and . . . Well, it was going to be fun. Damn airline. Damn snow."

The phone rang. I answered.

"All right," the voice on the other end said, "get down here." It was Charlie. "We've got some Christmas cheer here for you girls."

"No thanks, Charlie. I'm beat. I'm off to bed."

"Marvelous, Trudy. I'll join you."

"No you won't."

"Is Rachel there?"

"Yup."

"Come on down to the room, Rachel. Little drink for Saint Nick."

"Sorry, chief, but no thanks. I'm falling apart."

"Oh. Where's Rhonda?"

"Right here."

"Put her on."

Rhonda took the phone from Rachel.

"Rhonda, sweetie, how about some Yuletide cheer?"

"Love it. Be right down."

That started the Christmas Eve Party in Rochester. Rachel and I did go to bed as planned, but soon found it impossible to sleep. We got up and went to the party. It was in full swing by the time we arrived. There were four stewardesses from another line who'd met a fate similar to ours. There were three men, not airline types, who happened in on the festivities and were invited to pool their liquor supply with the crew's stock. They evidently had a large supply to offer. Everyone seemed high.

"Hey, a coupla more girlies. Yay, yay. Come on in honeys." Our greeter was one of the outsiders, a salesman of heavy construction equipment. He had big bulging eyes and his shirt collar was too tight, its cloth wilted under the folds of his neck. His nose was red and veined. It was the first year he'd missed playing Santa Claus at the office party in Pittsburgh.

The room couldn't stand thirteen people. Smoke threw up a dense screen that gave the scene the feeling of a Fellini film. The radio, one of those quarter-in-the-slot jobs, blared forth with Christmas music between hard-sell commercials, and drippy disc jockey chatter.

"Name's Sidney," the equipment salesman hollered over "White Christmas." "You from around here?"

"We fly with them," Rachel said, pointing toward the captain reclined in the bed, Rhonda snuggled warmly against him. Charlie Smagg plopped down beside them, a fifth of rye clutched to his chest.

"More stews, huh? Great. Whattaya drink?"

We ordered.

He brought the drinks, handed them to us, and promptly grabbed Rachel by the waist and whirled her around the room in step to "Rudolph the Red-Nosed Reindeer." He was surprisingly light on his feet for someone that fat. Rachel managed to get free from him and sat on the desk chair. Charlie Smagg got up and handed her his bottle. She gave it back. He tried to sit on her lap but slid off onto the floor. "Greatest stew in the world," he yelled up to everyone over the music and chatter.

Another of the outsiders came over to me. "Hello there. My

name is Scranton. Scranton Rigby. So you're a stewardess. So's my daughter."

"No kidding? Who's she fly with?"

"Well, no one right now. Got married. Got divorced. Looking for another stewardess job. Good thing she learned about the little pill before she got divorced from that idiot. Good thing. Kids get hurt, you know. Wouldn't be able to find another stewardess job either, with kids and all that. Good girl. Say, maybe you can help her."

"Gee, I don't think so."

"Well, we can talk about it later. Another drink?"

My glass was still full. "No thanks."

The four stewardesses from the other airline were clustered around the third strange male in the room. He was small, very small. His few long strands of remaining hair were carefully positioned across his head to achieve maximum coverage. His suit was double-breasted, plaid, his shirt a fine check, and his tie wide and brilliant with pink roses on a black field. I strolled over and introduced myself to the group.

"Josh is a writer," one of the girls told me after he'd mumbled an introduction to me. "Isn't that interesting?"

"Yes, it certainly is."

"Go ahead and tell us some more," the girls insisted as Josh carefully patted his hairs in place. He was pleased to be asked.

"Well, as I was saying, it's very difficult for me to convey some of the humor of the business to outsiders. You know, show business is a fraternity in itself. I mean, the Broadway crowd I pal with is something else. Something else. There are so many interesting tidbits about the stars and all. Like Sonny Tufts."

"Sonny Tufts?" I chanted with sheer wonder.

"Yes. Sonny Tufts. Did you know he was from a very wealthy family in Boston? Big banking family. And Sonny studied grand opera in Rome and was going to make his debut at the Met. You do know what the Met is, don't you?"

I nodded.

"And I might add that Sonny was quite the society band leader. Did you know that?"

"Noooo."

"See what I mean. It's such an *in* thing. You've just got to look deeper than what you read in the columns."

"Have you ever been in anyone's column?" I asked. I wasn't testing him. I was simply interested.

He chortled a little, admired his polished fingernails, and said, "That's what my press agent is for. Keep me out of the columns. Ho, ho, ho."

"Yes."

The others giggled.

"What are you doing in Rochester, of all places?" He didn't like that question either.

"Soaking up local color. I'm doing a play with an upstate setting. I want to feel it, touch it, live it, although it is dreadfully dull, dear hearts. But *being* what I write is important. It really is paramount to meaningful writing."

"What have you written?"

"I've never written for the mass media. You probably have never read or seen my works."

I walked away. Rachel came over and we mixed fresh drinks.

"Who's the little creep?" she asked.

"Playwright, he says. Name's Josh Something."

"No kidding?"

"Yes, I think he's kidding."

"What's he ever written?"

"Something to do with Sonny Tufts. With an upstate New York setting."

Rachel didn't understand. It wasn't important.

The chubby equipment salesman turned the radio up louder. The disc jockey was talking about how the holiday season touched him deeply.

". . . and to all of you out there tonight, wherever you may be and whatever you may be doing, I hope you share with me in all the warmth of this great season. Yes, it's hard to conceive of peace on earth and goodwill to all men when our boys are away fighting the jungle wars of the world, but irregardless of that . . ."

"Irregardless?" Josh screamed.

Charlie Smagg took a swig.

Then a commercial followed the disc jockey. It was for a local cesspool company with a seasonal special.

"And now here's the big one, the all-time, top-forty Christmas *favorite*—'The Christmas Song.'" The DJ's last words were punctuated with an electronic whine that lasted far into Mel Torme's version of his own song. The equipment salesman grabbed Rachel again and swung her around on the carpeted floor. He lost his balance and fell down, vainly reaching for support from Rachel. She let him fall.

There was a knock at the door. Rachel answered. It was the desk clerk. He ignored Rachel and peered past her through the smoke. There was a dirty gleam in his eye as he fixed on the captain and Rhonda. Snowflakes settled on his nose and the wind blew some on Rachel.

"It's cold. What do you want?"

"Oh, yeh. Long-distance telephone call for Mr. Josh Pierre. Figured he was here."

Josh came to the door. "Probably my agent," he threw back over his shoulder. "Be right back. I hope Merrick has come to his senses." He left with the desk clerk.

". . . Merry Christmas to you." Mel Torme sang out his tune, the final notes rudely cut off by a station promotion for the local quiz show. Then came a rock-and-roll version of "God Rest Ye Merry Gentlemen."

"Ba ba doo, ba ba doo, ba ba doo," Charlie Smagg sang as he danced across the room, his bottle clutched tightly to his bosom. "Let's dance, Trudy, my love."

We danced. You could almost feel the smoke brushing up against you as it hung heavy from the ceiling. The smoke, heat, loud noise, and drinks were getting to me. I was almost enjoying nutty Charlie Smagg and his two left feet.

". . . tidings of comfort and joy ba ba doo ba ba doo, oooh tidings of comfort and joy ba ba doo ba ba doo YEH!"

Josh came back in the room.

"Just sold another one."

"Another what?"

"Play. Option." He sneered at us.

"I bet it was his mother," I whispered to Rachel.

"Or the keeper at his funny farm," she further speculated.

"You were telling us about Sonny Tufts and that time on Sunset Strip, Josh."

"Right. Right. Now you may wonder why I know so much about Sonny Tufts. Well, it goes way back to . . ."

An hour passed.

"Did you know the Japanese actor who played King Kong was only five feet tall?" The girls, all drunk now, were still infatuated with Josh Pierre. "And they do the whole thing with mirrors."

The captain and Rhonda were kissing it up pretty good now on the bed. Scranton Rigby was telling me about the bad man his daughter had married and how the poor girl was suffering from the divorce.

"I feel great rapport with you, Trudy," Scranton said, "and I'd like to help you. Like a father. I want to keep you from falling into the pitfalls my daughter has suffered." Then he tried to kiss me and pinched my rear end.

"You're no father."

"I am. I am. Let me tell you . . ."

It was news time on the radio. To the accompaniment of staccato telegraph keys, whistlers, sirens, drums, and wind machines, all the world's gruesome headlines were given with breathless excitement.

"We'll be back in a moment with the details."

Then a message from a clothing store with "Jingle Bells" playing in the background.

"Let me have the key to the room, Trudy." Rhonda stood with her hand out. I gave her the key. She left with the captain. Charlie Smagg laid down on the bed and curled up with the pillow. "This news makes me sad," he said. He switched stations. There was Christmas music everywhere. He settled on the original station. He hummed along with "Hark the Herald Angels Sing."

"Actually, Sonny Tufts and King Kong are the kings of trivia. Did you know that?" Josh Pierre was still holding court, although one of the girls had left his circle and joined Charlie on the bed.

Every party emits its own particular sense of things to come. You could perceive upon entering Charlie's room a distinct emanation of future wildness. That's fine, in many cases. But the people in Charlie's room weren't right for some unexplainable reason. Scranton Rigby and his paternal line, the waltzing heavy-equipment salesman, little Josh Pierre, the other girls, and our own crew didn't seem to mesh. Maybe it was just the time and the place. At any rate, the end result was depressing. The room was terribly hot, the music too loud, and the overt advances of the fellows a little too overt. I wanted to get out of there. "Do you want to throw snowballs?" I asked Rachel.

"Hey, gang," Rachel announced. "I've got a great idea. How about a snowball fight?"

The suggestion was met with mixed reactions. But the lack of unanimity didn't deter us. Rachel flung open the door, the blast of cold, wet air causing her to catch her breath.

"Come on," I yelled, "let's go."

No one moved except Rachel and me.

Rachel put on her coat and ran outside. Soon, a large, wet snowball came flying through the door and splattered with a dull *squump* against Josh Pierre's lapel.

"Let's get 'em," Charlie yelped and raced outside. Others followed. Only Josh remained in the room, a sophisticated sneer on his face showing his contempt for such sophomoric conduct.

The snowball fight was fun until the heavy-equipment salesman pinned me down in the snow and used the spirit of the fight as an excuse to slip his hand under my coat. I let him have it in the face with a solidly packed snowball and slipped out from under him as he sputtered the glaze off his face. Two of the stewardesses were sitting on top of Charlie Smagg and shoving snow down his shirt.

Scranton Rigby, tottering unsteadily on a small snowbank, threw a snowball at me as I ducked behind a bush by the motel's entrance. He missed me, of course, but made a direct hit on the desk clerk who'd ventured out to watch the fight. That brought him into the fray with a great deal of zeal. He tackled Rachel and her screams indicated more than a simple snow fight. Scranton

Rigby, father image that he was, jumped on the desk clerk. The clerk got up, swore at everybody, and went back into the motel. It was only fifteen minutes before the police arrived.

They were nice about asking us to stop the fight and return to our rooms. We all went back to the party room and sat quietly as melting snow formed little puddles on the brown tweed carpet.

Cooled off by the snow and the local policemen, the party resumed with noticeably less gaiety than before the outdoor frolic. Drinking was moderate, chatter was relatively subdued, and dancing was formal to the point of stiffness. Charlie Smagg was sober. Josh Pierre was falling asleep in the chair. The heavy-equipment salesman told jokes and Scranton Rigby laughed at them.

The party started to break up at about 2 A.M. The local radio station was still filling the airwaves with Christmas music, the late hour cutting down on the frequency of commercial messages.

"Wake up, Mr. Pierre," I said, gently shaking the little fellow's shoulders.

"Momma, Momma," he babbled as he came out of his sleepy slump in the chair. "Oh, here I am. Right. Thanks."

Charlie Smagg was asleep on the bed, the bottle still clutched tightly in his arms. Scranton Rigby reminded me to keep in touch with him.

"If you're ever in Pittsburgh, drop in," were the heavy-equipment salesman's parting words.

"We sure will," we answered him.

We were outside before we thought about Rhonda and the captain.

"There isn't anything we can do," I told Rachel as we shivered against the wind. "We'll just knock and tell them we're tired and want to go to bed."

We did that. We were frozen by the time they came to unlock the door. The captain was dressed but Rhonda was in her robe.

"See you tomorrow, girls," he said as he returned to Charlie Smagg's room. Rhonda turned down the covers and climbed into bed. "Good night," was said all around and sleep came quickly.

The telephone's harsh jangle brought us out of the first hour of sleep. It was the captain.

"Sorry to bother you but I thought you ought to know we dumped one."

It took a minute for his terminology to be understood, but I finally realized he meant our airline had lost an airplane.

"Where?"

"Over Wisconsin. It was on the news just now. Not much detail."

"Any crew names?"

"Not yet. No sense losing sleep over it. We can't do anything. We'll find out all about it in the morning. Say good night to Rhonda for me."

"Sure."

Our captain, a twenty-year veteran, could go to sleep; he'd been around before when planes went down. But we hadn't. We turned the radio on and waited impatiently for the next newscast. Then the announcer broke in on the music with a bulletin.

"The plane was believed to be carrying a full load of holiday passengers, but the exact number is not known at this time. Officials of the airline have indicated no known cause for the disaster. Stay tuned to this station for further details."

We tried to stay awake but couldn't. We woke up in the morning to a newcast in which they listed the names of the crew members. We didn't know any of them, except one.

". . . and Miss Sally Lu Johnson."

"You know," Rachel said slowly, "if I had to pick someone from our class at school who would end up like this, I think I'd have picked Sally Lu."

"She was going to quit when Warren bought his own gas station. Looks like he didn't make it quick enough."

I started to cry and so did Rachel. Rhonda didn't know Sally Lu, but she wept, too.

I guess all stewardesses have a true feeling toward the other girls, whether they're close friends or not. We work together in such narrow quarters. We share our after-work lives with each other. We depend on each other. Folded away in the back of each of our heads is the knowledge that danger and death are always out there waiting. We know this. We accept it. I think each of us develops almost the same philosophy: if it's meant to be you, it will happen to you. If it's not your turn, you're OK. And this is the way we would want to go—if it must be.

Rhonda tried to comfort us by telling about her own very bad experience. She'd had a big romance going in New Orleans and wanted to stay on for a few days. When she reported in sick, her roommate took over the flight for her. The plane went down in the Rockies. Her roommate's body was never found. "My first thought was that I'd killed Gerry," Rhonda told us. "I'd sent her to her death. I was torturing myself with guilt. I didn't think I could fly anymore. But after a while I had to accept that this is the way it is. We all have a turn. Sally Lu just didn't make it."

Breakfast with the entire crew was filled with talk of the crash. Each one of us reported what we'd heard on the radio, and the cockpit boys went into their theories about what might have happened.

"Well, how do you feel girls? Ready to make the trip back?" The captain looked us straight in the eye with the question.

"I'm shook a little," I answered him.

"Well, don't be. Did you know that more people are killed at railroad crossings every year than in aircraft accidents?"

"And more people are killed on bicycles," Charlie threw in.

The statistics weren't at all comforting. "I don't think Sally Lu knew about those statistics," I answered

"Well, you'll get over it. You have to."

He was right, of course. And we did. We left the motel for our trip back to Kennedy. We finally got a break in the weather late that afternoon and were at our apartment building at seven that evening.

There was a telegram in the letterbox from Rachel's mother. It read, "CRASH TERRIBLE THING. THINK YOU MUST STOP FLYING. PLEASE. LOVE MOTHER."

"It's funny, Trudy, but I don't feel that way. I don't think I've ever felt more like flying. Know what I mean?"

"Yes, I do."

In front of our apartment door a happy surprise was waiting for us. Chuck was sitting bolt upright against the door, fast asleep. I fell into his arms. "You big goof," I cried, "what are you doing here?"

"I was in Chicago with a forty-eight-hour layover when I heard about Sally Lu. I knew you were socked in up there in Rochester. It must be a helluva Christmas for you, so I dropped by and figured I'd wait for you." He looked at his watch. "Come on, I've just got three hours. I'll buy you Christmas dinner."

Rachel suddenly started to remember an appointment with her friends in Great Neck. Chuck grabbed her arm and gave her a bright blue stare with those crazy eyes of his: "No party-pooping. It's both of you pigeons for Christmas dinner, or nothing, OK?"

"OK," Rachel said, retrieving her arm. "Do you have your bike outside?"

"This kind of weather I use reindeer," he replied.

"Come on, kids, let's go," I said. We dropped our bags in the apartment and then, each of us clinging to one of his arms, we walked Chuck around the corner to a little French restaurant. I don't know whether Chuck was in exceptionally great spirits or whether he thought he ought to be to cheer us up. Anyway, he kept us laughing during the entire meal.

"I'll never get over the things you girls do to each other," he told us at one point. "Remember your chesty friend Betty?"

"Sure, we see her all the time."

"Well, she was hot after the captain on a flight I was on to Phoenix a couple of weeks ago. The junior stew was a young kid just out of school—a fresh, on-the-make little doll. We all noticed her because she'd hitched her skirt way up to look like a mini."

"How did Betty take that?" Rachel wanted to know.

"I think she called and raised a couple of buttons on her blouse," Chuck answered. "Naturally we drank a lot of coffee that flight and got to know the kid—her name's Gwen—pretty well. By the time we reached Phoenix, Gwen was flopping all over the captain from behind, chewing at his ear and saying, 'Tell me about those li'l bitty ol' dials and buttons, honey. What's that one over there?' and she sorta hitched herself over his shoulder to point at the dial, so of course he nestled his head back between her breasts."

"I bet the captain hated that," I said.

"Not the captain—Betty. She came barging in yelling, 'Get your hot pants outta here!' I had to break up the slugfest. It's something to see two dames stage a catfight. But that isn't all."

Chuck held up his wineglass for a refill. "On the return flight Betty had Gwen demonstrate the life vest and oxygen mask and . . ."

We didn't let Chuck finish. I said, "Ammonia." Rachel said, "Pepper." The three of us burst into such wild laughter that the waiter thought we'd lost our minds. I was right. Betty put ammonia into the oxygen mask, Gwen took a deep breath to illustrate inhalation technique and the ammonia fumes all but killed her.

"You dames are something," Chuck said with a sigh. "A guy has to be an idiot to get mixed up with any of you."

That was our Christmas dinner. We forgot all about the rotten time in Rochester. For the moment we stopped thinking about Sally Lu. It was just good to be alive and able to laugh. After coffee Rachel said she had to dash. She raced off on an imaginary errand. Chuck and I went back to the apartment. We had very little time but we put it to the best possible use, the very best.

Who says there isn't a Santa Claus?

# CHAPTER XVIII

# "The Saga of Sandy"

"Where does Sandy get the money to do all the things she does Trudy?" Rachel asked one night as we were watching *Batman*.

"Beats me. Maybe she has a rich uncle."

"I don't think so."

"How do you know?"

"I just know. I sense it."

"Maybe she takes in washing on the side."

"Yeh. Maybe that's . . . Ouch!" Rachel was reacting to a strong right hand to Batman's head by the Riddler.

The Sandy in question was Sandy Sims, an attractive girl who also flew for our airline. She did seem to get a great deal from life on her stewardess pay. Sandy always vacationed in Europe, an easy feat for stewardesses with cut-rate travel fares. But Sandy stayed in the most elegant hotels while there, and came back with suitcases full of expensive goods. She lived alone in a high-rent brownstone, wore three-hundred-dollar suits, owned a Triumph which she housed in a midtown parking garage, and was never without funds.

There are rich girls working as stewardesses. But Sandy Sims wasn't one of them. People who knew her testified to that. She came from a modest family and wasn't dating any rich playboy as far as anyone knew. In fact, she wasn't known to date anyone. She was a loner, but a pleasant one, who was always ready to pitch in on a flight and lend a hand when needed.

Maybe our questioning was based on jealousy. But a lot of the girls talked about Sandy. Some even said, "Maybe she's hustling on the side." Then we'd laugh. We couldn't believe a stewardess would do that. Prostitutes were girls who came from slums and were forced into lives of vice through bad breaks and unsavory people.

We asked George Kelman about it one night.

"Don't be silly," he said with honest detestation. "What cheap novels have you been reading? There's never been a stewardess hooker and there never will be."

"Yes, sir," we said, saluting.

"Dirty minds," he added.

This made us a little angry. "OK, George, where does she get the money?"

This angered him. "What the hell business is it of yours, anyway? Maybe she just doesn't blow it like you two do. Drop the whole thing. You're just jealous as hell."

His words made sense. We forgot about Sandy Sims and her money until two months later when we received a monthly schedule that included her on most of the legs.

We were flying New York–Dallas, with a layover in the Texas city. As usual, Sandy took a room by herself, saying she had a great deal of reading to do. It cost her above her traveling allowance, but that never bothered her.

Rachel and I were in Room 356C. Sandy was in 365C. It was about eight o'clock. I was settling down for the next juicy chapter of a motion picture actress's best-selling autobiography, while Rachel was doing sitting-up exercises on the floor. The phone rang.

"I'll get it," I said. I picked up the receiver and heard, "Is this Sandy?"

"No, it's not. You have the wrong room."

"Sorry!" He hung up quickly.

"Who was that?" Rachel queried.

"Some guy for Sandy. What room is she in, anyway?"

"Forget. Hey, maybe it's some rich oil man and he's keeping Sandy. Yeh, that's it."

"Oh."

I read further in the book and Rachel turned to push-ups. "It's good for the breasts, you know," she grunted from the floor.

"Tell Betty Big Boobs."

"Up . . . down . . . up . . . down . . ."

The phone rang.

"Hello."

"Sandy?"

"This isn't Sandy's room. You've got the wrong one. Check the desk."

He hung up without another word.

Rachel was now on deep breathing exercises.

"In . . . out . . . in . . . out . . ."

"I'll get it," she said when the phone rang again. She picked the receiver up quickly. "Hello . . . No, she's taking a shower. Who's calling?"

The man's voice on the other end hesitated. "Uh, when do you think she'll be finished?"

"Pretty soon," Rachel replied, her voice a strange cooing, sexy sound.

"Oh," the guy said. "Would you tell her Larry called?"

"Sure. But can't I help you?" I was listening closely now, my book relegated to the floor.

"You help me? . . . Well, . . . I didn't know if you . . . I don't think so. Good-bye."

"He hung up," Rachel said, still holding the phone to her ear.

"What was that routine?" I asked. "She's not taking a shower."

"I know. But I wanted him to talk a little. Who are all these guys calling her?"

"Rachel, you are truly jealous. And a busybody to boot."

Rachel turned and looked me straight in the eye. "Aren't you interested, too, Trudy?"

"Yup. Let's figure out what to say to the next call. OK?"

We plotted our action. Rachel would answer and say Sandy had left for an appointment but asked that Rachel substitute for her. The phone rang ten minutes later and our plan was in effect. Only Rachel, as so often happened when I egged her on, became even bolder than we had planned.

"I'm sure you'd like me," I heard her saying and couldn't believe my ears.

"Are you a . . . a stewardess, too?" the man asked.

"Yes, I am. Sandy and I have . . . well, sort of our own private little thing going. Are you coming up?"

"Rachel, you idiot, that's our room. It's one thing to find out about Sandy, but not to have the guy come up here." I wanted to kill her.

"Why not?" Rachel hurried around the apartment picking up clothing and other personal items. "Might be fun. Ever been on call?"

"Of course not."

"Me either. But I bet we could act like one. I mean two. Now don't get upset. I don't mean we're really going to do what a prostitute does. We can just talk to him and maybe find out more about Sandy."

"But how are we going to get rid of him?" I wanted to know.

Rachel hadn't thought about that. She suddenly paled. "Gee, let's see . . ."

Now it was my turn to improvise. "Suppose we tell him we charge two hundred dollars."

"You're a genius," Rachel assured me. "That'll do it."

But the whole thing had me worried. "You know, Rachel, Sandy will find out about this. She's bound to. He'll tell her about the high price and all."

"He will not. He'll never mention a word. And if he does, we just deny anything. Don't worry about it."

Within minutes, we had our hotel room looking good enough to rival anything Sadie Thompson could have dreamed up on such short notice. One light illuminated the room. The drapes were drawn. We wore our bathrobes (with Bermuda shorts and sweaters underneath). We were beginning to feel the part, and that was a little frightening. We waited for what seemed an eternity before there came a feeble knock on the door.

"Go ahead," I whispered to Rachel.

"You," she countered.

"You started it," I retorted.

"I'm scared," she quavered.

I ran over to her. He knocked again. "Evens," I said. "OK. Odds for me."

"Once, twice, three . . . shoot." I put out one finger and she put out two. Rachel would answer the door. He was knocking louder now.

She slowly opened it and there stood our caller—our first customer. He looked awful.

"Howdy," he said with a broad grin. "Here I am."

"Hi," Rachel managed to say, her voice having obvious trouble getting past her Adam's apple.

"Can I come in? This is the place, isn't it."

Rachel hesitated for a moment. "Sure. Come in."

He walked through the door and stopped dead in his tracks when he saw me.

"Two of you?"

"Yup."

"I'll be damned. Didn't know there was two of you."

"Yup. Two of us," I said, trying to appear at home with the situation.

He rocked back and forth, from one foot to another, as he made up his mind what to say next. He seemed as nervous as we were.

"Sit down," I said to break the silence.

"Name's Bert. What's yours?"

"Roberta," I said, not knowing why that name came into my head.

"I'm Zelda," Rachel threw in.

"Zelda?"

"Zelda."

"Nice name."

"Thanks."

He fidgeted in his chair. He twirled his tie in his fingers and kept blowing his cheeks out.

"Well," he finally managed to say, "I guess we'd better iron things out right now. I mean, about the two of you and all. I mean, about the money. You know?"

Rachel took the initiative. "Sure. The money. We can get to that in a minute. Uh, why don't you take off your shoes. That's a good idea. And loosen your tie."

I was afraid she was overdoing it. Fortunately he didn't want to take his shoes off. He did loosen his tie.

"You from Dallas?" I asked.

"Yup."

"Where'd you meet Sandy?"

"Never did meet her. Another fella told me 'bout her. Didn't know there were others."

"Other what?"

"Well, you know what I mean. Gals like yourselves making a little extra in your spare time."

We evidently looked hurt, or shocked, because he came right back with, "Not that I blame you. Guess you don't make that much workin' for the airline. And guess you figure there's nothin' wrong with it 'cause you're gonna do it anyway. Am I right?"

"Well, yes."

"How'd you get started?" he asked, leaning forward to indicate sincere and deep interest in the subject. This was crazy. He wasn't supposed to interview us.

"Well, it's a long story."

He looked at his watch. "Look, I gotta get home. What do I do. Choose?"

"I guess so," I answered.

"Well, no hard feelings I hope. I'll take you." He pointed directly at me.

For once I was speechless, all my Texas bravado fled. What now?

"You got another room up here?" he asked.

"No. No other room. Just this one."

His eyes began to light up. "Boy, you gonna watch?" he asked Rachel.

"Guess so."

Bert got up and came over to me. He put his arm around me and kissed me on the neck.

"Wait a minute," I said in a panic, pushing him away at the same time.

"Oh, yeh. About that money. My friend said it was thirty-five. OK by me."

Rachel jumped into the discussion. "Thirty-five? You must be kidding."

"Well, that's what he told me. How much is it?"

"Two hundred."

"Two hundred?"

"Sure. We're clean, nice girls. Not like the others who do this. Two hundred."

"Boy, he sure was wrong."

"Sorry. You'd better leave. There are others waiting."

Bert walked out under a cloud of gloom. We'd never talked about what we'd do if our customer became violent, or if he had the two hundred. Lucky for us, Bert was just sad and poor.

"Well, how about Miss Sandy Sims?" Rachel said with pride that she'd uncovered the plot.

"We know where she gets the money but so what? What do you think we're supposed to do about it?"

"Nothing. I just feel better now that my curiosity can be put to rest."

We decided the evening had been fun. But what a strange feeling to be talking to that strange man about going to bed with him, especially when the money question came up.

"What did you do last night?" we asked Sandy the next morning on the plane.

"Not much. Had a good night's sleep. Say, by the way, the desk clerk had our room numbers mixed up. I got a couple of calls from friends of mine who said they got your room instead. At least I think it was your room. Thanks for setting them straight. I have a lot of relatives in Dallas and it was good to hear from them. You didn't get any other calls for me, did you?"

"No, no, Sandy. Not a one."

"Good. I hate to miss a phone call."

Sandy Sims is the only stewardess we've ever met who made extra money this way. There are a few others we've heard about. But we've never met them. We understand they try to work the charter flights that take a group of men to a convention. That seems sensible to us.

# CHAPTER XIX

# "What's a Nice Girl Like You Doing in a Plane Like This?"

We talked a little earlier about how a stewardess learns to recognize a married man from the moment he walks on board the aircraft. This developed perception, coupled with the aid of a telltale, pale imprint of a hastily removed wedding band, proves extremely valuable in a very practical sense.

But sizing up a male passenger's marital status isn't all we do when things are slow. We also play the game of guessing where he's from and what he does. As stewardesses on the receiving end of perhaps more direct passes than any other group of working girls, we've been able to compare notes on the pitches different men make and how these pitches relate to their nationality and profession. After long and careful study of countless stories by our fellow stewardesses, together with a normal amount of firsthand experiences, we've been able to come up with our own handbook on the subject. If a given profession or nationality isn't listed, we can only offer the probability that men in that category don't fly, or don't like girls, or both.

## GERMANS

German men always do things by the numbers. They seem to base their amorous advances on pages from a strange and misplaced book, a book that will never make the best-seller charts here in America. They try to give you the impression that to accompany them from the airplane and share their bed would be a contribution toward some better, super-world. They usually attack the larger species of stewardesses—the flight's flying Brunhildes.

It is our considered and combined judgment that Germans and

actors share honors for being the cheapest dates a stew can accept. Thus, since accepting a date with a German man isn't about to pay off in an evening in the better restaurants, clubs, or theaters, you've got to justify your acceptances as accomplishing something for the State. Very few stewardesses accept dates with German passengers.

## ITALIANS

Italian men don't pinch stewardesses. True, they use their hands a great deal when talking, but they aren't the grabby kind. What they do is look at you long and hard with eyes that catch hold of a loose thread and unravel all your clothes. They have the ability to *look* your clothes off, a state of affairs possessing almost a hypnotic effect. You *want* to take your clothes off once that spell has been cast.

Rachel was once approached by a rather famous member of Italy's motion picture industry. He cornered her in the galley on a half-empty flight to Los Angeles. He stood with his eyes riveted on the V of her blouse as she poured a cup of coffee for herself. Most of the other passengers were asleep.

"You have a lovely figure, Miss Jones," he purred, never straying his eyes from her bosom.

"I've noticed you've noticed," she answered.

"What is wrong with appreciating the lovely body of a woman?"

"Nothing, now that you mention it."

"I would like to ask you something and feel that you will not take offense, if I may?"

She looked him square in the eye. "Go ahead. I figure I've still got the right to say No." She poured cream in her coffee. "And, I've been asked a lot of silly things before."

He seemed crushed by her use of the word *silly.* "No, no, no, no, my dear young lady. There is nothing silly about what I am going to ask. My thoughts are beautiful, pure, and on the highest plane of appreciation for what is fine in life. I simply wondered if you would accompany me to my rented villa in Beverly Hills. If you will accept, and I am so confident that you will, I make a solemn oath to you on all that I hold sacred not to even touch your exquisite body with my most unworthy hands. I only wish to look at you as nature intended me to view you, without the harsh cloak of that uniform and those horrible underthings you are forced to wear. I simply wish to fill my eyes with your charm."

Rachel just looked at him. "You're putting me on."

The Italian put his hand to his brow in a supreme gesture of deep and bitter hurt. "Oh, to take such a beautiful and natural wish in so light a vein . . . To think I . . . what is it you say? . . . *put you on?* Oh, no, no, no, no . . . I am simply a lover of living sculpture . . . flesh instead of cold hard marble."

As Rachel tells it, she almost pulled his curly head to her bosom to comfort him, he looked so hurt. She didn't, and left the galley to check on the passengers. She glanced back up the aisle to see him hunched against the wall, his eyes squinting in obvious artistic appreciation of her hip movement, his hand still to his head to help the hurt she had inflicted. He never said another word the rest of the trip.

"I kept passing his seat," she told us over drinks that night. "and I swore each time I was stark naked. I mean, my clothes were *gone*."

## AMERICANS

American men always manage to include a hint of humor in their advances to a stewardess. This has to do, I suppose, with the fact that American men never really take sex seriously. They know it's fun, love the obvious pleasures it brings, but just can't make themselves romance a woman. We feel it's the fear of being rebuffed. They seem afraid of attempting too serious an advance. The humiliation of being told No would be too great a blow to their egos.

Maybe it has to do with the need to preserve that rosy-cheeked, Jack Armstrong image American men are stuck with. Whatever it stems from, they manage to come up with the most awkward, clumsy, and least effective approaches of all male passengers. It's a shame, really, because of all the potential playmates on a flight, those very same rosy-cheeked Jack Armstrongs are the most appealing. After all, we were brought up sexually with American boys. *But*–as women, we like and need a little bit of the chase, the romancing, the wooing, and the intrigue, if only to help us justify to ourselves the final surrender. Of course, we don't want to give the impression that American men never score. We love them. And most of our flings are with them. It's just that they could do a hell of a lot better.

## FRENCHMEN

Frenchmen suffer from too lofty a reputation. It's hard to be known as the world's greatest salesman and try to convince someone who's read your clippings that you're not always selling. But despite this knowledge of the French reputation, the aura created still lingers on, especially when a Frenchman can corner you long enough to slide those beautiful sounding syllables off his tongue.

What's fun about accepting an after-flight date with a Frenchman is knowing you won't be rushed. No, the French manner, according to those who have experienced it, is for a lingering, easy evening. Not that we're naïve enough to ignore the eventual goal of our French date. I suppose it's just a matter of enjoying the flight before actually reaching your destination.

We were working a flight with your friend and ours, Betty Big Boobs, when a handsome Frenchman, an architect from Bordeaux, stepped on board for the trip from New York to San Francisco. With all Betty's boasting of the legion of men hot after her body and soul, she never included a Frenchman among her conquests. Maybe she felt she *needed* a Frenchman for her lineup. Anyway, she clamped onto him from the first minute. She rubbed that chest of hers all over him when serving, managed to stretch herself in search of more damned unnamed objects in the overhead rack immediately above him, and, in general, really put on a show.

He, of course, knew it immediately. And he played it beautifully. He played hard to get. The more indifferent he became, the bigger and more overt were the advances Betty made to him.

As they left the airplane in San Francisco, Betty whispered to us, "Ah wonder if they're as good as they say—Y'all know, long fuse—short explosion."

You really can't believe anything Betty tells you where men are concerned. She did show up for the next morning's flight, exhausted and beat-looking. Her eyes drooped low and dark and her neck showed a series of blotchy, irregular marks. She told us about it in the galley.

"It was so beautiful," she sighed as she counted off the booze lockers. "We danced and he cooed in my ear all those pretty, dirty li'l French words, and he bit my neck and we drank and rubbed noses and all like that. And then when we finally ended up in his room, ah was so damned tired ah didn't know if he was French or Eskimo. Ah guess he enjoyed it, though. He made a lotta noise."

## SPANIARDS

It seems that every Spanish gentleman traveling on our flights considers us a collection of young, fighting bulls, despite the obvious conflict in gender. And, a Spaniard loves to wave a red cape of promise in our eyes every mile of the flight.

He's convinced that all women run to red, especially when the matador is dark, mysterious, and renowned in matters of love. In effect, he dangles *himself* in front of us, hoping one of his flight's bulls will tire and succumb to the inevitable thrust a bull is subject to at the end of the battle. I myself have tired and lost on one occasion. I've always been kookie over red.

Spaniards like to board the aircraft with their ties off, their shirts unbuttoned three or four from the top, and their pants indecently tight. This seems to apply to all men of Spanish origin, regardless of their financial standing. Admitting a slight amount of prejudice, I vote for Spaniards as the world's greatest lovers. I know other girls who agree. The only ones we know who were disenchanted after a fling with a Spaniard were those who took their advances seriously. Spaniards are never looking for anything that even smacks of permanence. They're like married men in that respect. They're simply after an exhilarating and challenging afternoon and evening in the ring with a new, healthy, and spirited bull. It's fun to try the sport on occasion, and unlike the case of the real bull, you don't get killed in the end.

## ENGLISHMEN

Men from England are effective simply because they ignore you. The trick is not to misread their intentions. They have on their mind what any other male passenger has on his mind. They rely on a passive technique, however, one that goes with the universal impression of the British gentleman.

We've never been able to figure out why the British are considered cold and aloof where physical love is concerned. From what we've heard, some of the gayest, hottest, and most unusual bedroom scenes have resulted from a stewardess accepting the stiff and proper advance of a Britisher. They sit in their seats, splendid in tweedy tweeds, sipping the tea you've served them, their curved pipes close by at their sides. Immediately, you project yourself into a future that finds you rubbing toes in front of a roaring fire in the drawing room of an English manor house. A shaggy Collie sleeps at your side and you listen attentively as the master relates how the downtrend on the London Sugar Exchange is playing all sorts of havoc in New York.

"Yes, sir," you answer and promptly ready yourself for the Mrs. Minniver role.

It's all so marvelous dreaming these dreams as you smile at the tweedy gentleman in seat 5A.

But after hearing stories from girls who've tried to play out that dream, you come to realize that men from England are not only as hot-blooded as their Southern counterparts, but their intentions aren't nearly as honorable as their attitude would suggest.

But you must admire their technique. They actually ward off any advances a stewardess might make, all for the sake of implanting the needed trust in the girl's mind.

## ARABS

One of our captains, a guy with at least thirty outside business interests and the money to prove their success, did business of one sort or another with an Arab firm. We were flying with him from St. Louis when he asked us about our plans for that night.

"Look, here's the situation," he said as we passed over Columbus, Ohio. "These two very wealthy Arab businessmen are in New York for a few days and I've arranged a party for them at the Waldorf. It'll be at their suite of rooms and they're pretty damned important to me. I thought you might like to come, enjoy the food and drinks, and rub elbows with all that oil money."

We arrived at 8:30 dressed in our best and were ushered into the suite by a tiny fellow with a white turban and gold teeth.

The suite was large and beautiful with many rooms off the main living room. About twenty people were chatting over drinks. There was a heavy smell of lamb in the air and this spicy fragrance, mixed with the heavy, sweet odor of some sort of pipe tobacco, brought on a strange feeling of menace.

Our captain introduced us to Elkim al Salim, a sinister-looking man with a big, pockmarked face, heavy brows, and a set of gold teeth. It was a little unnerving to see him look us up and down, turn to the captain and smile and nod his head in indication of acceptance, then look at us again. It was like being on the open slave market.

We mixed with some other people for about an hour. The captain brought us fresh drinks and we asked him about the guests, most of whom were women.

"Well, don't get shook but there are quite a few call girls here tonight. You know how it is. These big shots from other countries like to swing with something different when they get here."

"It must cost him a fortune," Rachel offered.

"It costs me a fortune," the captain answered.

"You?"

"Sure. It's good business to keep him happy. A couple of broads a night and he's good for more business with me."

We never figured our captain for a pimp. We never expected the next line either.

"Look, now don't take me wrong, but he really has his eye on you two. He said something about sweet, unspoiled girls. You both could pick up a bundle here tonight. And you wouldn't be the first stewardesses to moonlight."

Without a word, Rachel and I walked away from the captain and went into one of the other rooms to look for our coats. We had just found them on a bed when our Arabian oil mogul with the flashing mouth appeared in the doorway and closed the door behind him.

"I didn't expect you to be ready so soon," he said hoarsely. "But I'm pleased."

We started past him but he barred the way.

"There's no need to go anywhere. Right here is fine. My staff will see that we are not disturbed. I trust the two of you won't become too loud."

"Get out of the way, you pig," Rachel screamed at him. It didn't upset him. In fact, it made him smile.

"I think that's good that you want to fight a little. I like that. Warren said you might struggle a little and I told him that makes it all the more pleasurable for me. Would a little smoke of hashish help?"

"Get your ass out of our way," Rachel piped, "or you'll go back to your harem with my foot still there."

He lunged at me but I stepped aside. Rachel opened the door and I followed her out of the room. We knocked over some drinks on the way through the main room, took a second to upset our captain's drink down the front of his suit, and got out of there on the run.

We were going to report the captain but didn't. He resigned from the airline the next month to take care of his other interests.

Naturally, we've told this story many times to many people. The telling and reactions we get have given us some insight into the whole Arab thing when it comes to sex.

A friend of ours who spent six years in Arabia with the Arabian-American Oil Company explains it this way. Arab men are all sexually unhappy, no matter how large their harem. Women of Saudi Arabia are not attractive by any stretch of the imagination. So, when an Arab has the chance to get out of the world's biggest sandbox, he tries to cram as much action as possible into his sex life. It's the same with booze. He can't drink in his own country and consequently can't get enough when he's away. His sex life is actually so unsatisfactory that many Arab men prefer clean, fair-skinned boys to their own women, a problem facing every military and oil man assigned to Arabia.

## SCANDINAVIANS

Let's face it. When the women of your country are held in the highest esteem for beauty and lovemaking, you've got a tough time trying to escape their long shadow. That's the way it is with Scandinavian men. They approach you as if it's the result of maximum and directed effort, and that's a feeling that no woman has ever appreciated. Someday, when the eyes of the male world shift from the Nordic beauties to perhaps Yugoslavian or Congolese women, then Scandinavian men will have a chance. As it is now, they usually ask if you like to ski and if you answer in the affirmative, and you are a true ski nut, things might work out between you. It's also true that Scandinavian men are quiet and seldom make passes. This makes identifying them for game purposes difficult. Generally, they're blond, which is somewhere to start.

## IRISHMEN

No matter how an Irishman tries to escape it, he's bound to be heavy laden by the Cross. This makes giving a stewardess a line difficult because the Irishman, all his professed charm and wit notwithstanding, fumbles in his attempts as he looks over his shoulder for ghosts and spooks and the like. Still, despite the handicap, Irishmen try hard.

This talk of the heavy yoke of religion is not confined to the old-world Irishman. Even a member of the young, "God is dead" generation is tightly bound by ever-present fears of spending an eternity in Hell for one night with a stewardess. He usually will make the decision to act on his physical motivation, but he's rarely able to shake the feeling that he's being watched.

We know a West Coast stewardess who was quite serious about a young Irish accountant but finally gave up.

"That business of crossing yourself everytime gave me the creeps," she confesses. "I kept getting the feeling he was praying for me to perform good. Like a baseball player."

Actually, a stewardess probably would be happiest with a Unitarian. You have a clearer conscience when you know everything will be all right the next day if you find a little old lady to help across the street.

## SCOTSMEN

Never believe all that jazz about a Scotsman being cheap. We've found them to be free spenders, a finding that rates them high on our list of prospective companions. They'll spend every cent they have in pursuit of a particular girl, usually with substantial results.

A Scot is moody, proud, unpredictable, and difficult to get along with in many instances, but once he's interested enough to commit himself, you can do a pretty effective job of making things run your way.

## RUSSIANS

We seldom have any trouble with Russian men. Our requirements are such that we must keep a reasonably trim figure. Russians can't seem to see women except on the end of a plow, and it's obvious we don't have the necessary pulling power. Russian passengers usually just watch the movie or listen to Russian classics on stereo.

## JAPANESE

Miniaturization just doesn't seem to have an advantage where sex is concerned. TV sets and radios, yes—but never sex.

\* \* \*

Once the nationality of the men on our flight is established, we turn our attention, after serving drinks, dinner wine, and strawberry parfait, to an analysis of their field of work.

There are sure and certain tip-offs, of course. The style of his briefcase, a football helmet over the arm, a copy of *Method Acting* clutched to the breast, a uniform, a typewriter, a stethoscope, a storyboard, a picture of Earl Warren, or a button reading "Black Power"—all are clues to what the man does. When such obvious aids are evident, we take off three points.

We should also preface the next section by admitting that good or bad personal experiences with a certain man in a certain profession will tend to taint these comments slightly. The same holds true for the previous section on nationalities. You'll just have to accept our opinions as presented and react in your own way.

## PUBLIC RELATIONS MEN

Men engaged in this dubious profession are usually confused about their work. And it shows in their approach to us. After striking up an idle conversation about the altitude, weather, or ETA, they'll tell you about their job as image builders, management consultants, marketing executives, or community relations experts. They never will admit to being flacks unless they function in the show-business area. If they are of the theatrical type, you can count on being told, "I can make you a star, baby." And sometimes they can.

PR men rank high on our date list. They always dress nicely

and have huge expense accounts. Those with gray hair have larger expense accounts than others. A typical opening from a PR man might start with, "Say, honey, I've got an idea you might be interested in. We're opening a new bottle plant in Tempe, Arizona, and you'd make a perfect queen of the ceremony. You know, cut the ribbon and pose for the local press and that jazz. How about it?"

"Oh, are you a public relations man?"

"No, I'm a management consultant. I double in community relations."

"Gee, would I get paid?"

"Hard to tell how much at this time, but I swing a lot of weight with JB . . . He's chairman now. Good exposure for you. Never know about those things."

If you've been flying long enough and have been involved in your own airline's press activities, you'll turn him down cold.

There is a surefire way to make *your* approach to a PR man if he looks interesting to you. One of our fellow stewardesses from Los Angeles always used this line:

"Well, that's just wonderful that you're in marketing and community relations. Doesn't that involve trying to place stories in newspapers and on TV?"

"Yes. That's just part of the overall team effort of the marketing management deck. We've all got to be pretty good writers, you know."

Our friend would let enough time elapse and then throw in the clincher.

"Funny thing I should meet a marketing man. My brother is managing editor of the *Los Angeles Times*. I guess he's the one who says what goes in the paper. I really don't know too much about these things."

He's hooked. He'll spend every dime he has wining and dining you, his motives double-edged. He figures he can either take you to bed, get a story in the *LA Times*, or maybe both.

It does help if your brother really *is* in a high capacity in the news media.

# ENGINEERS

Gravely lacking any background, academic or practical, in the arts or humanities, engineers will try to make chitchat about the aircraft's performance characteristics or outer space or why the ball always comes down after it goes up. It's best to feign ignorance if you're interested; engineers hate anyone to know anything about their sphere of knowledge.

Occasionally, an engineer will have the brains to realize that a stewardess isn't interested in all that mechanical routine. This type of individual will say something like, "Have you read *Moby-Dick* lately?" You've got to give him credit for trying.

"No. I always wait for the paperback on these new best-sellers. The prices they get are ridiculous."

Now that he's impressed us with his deep love for literature, he springs the big question.

"How about *The Carpetbaggers?*" Oh, that leer, that twisted grin, and those raised eyebrows. "Pretty blue stuff, huh?"

Again, it depends on whether you want to continue the relationship. If you do, you come back with, "Well, times have changed and I think we all have a looser, more realistic view of these things. At least, I do."

I personally can't stand engineers. One actually took the dinner check in Cleveland and figured the markup of the food we ate with his slide rule right at the table. Rachel dated one who damned near gouged her chest out with a pocketful of pencils, pens, slide rule, ruler, pipe, and fingernail file.

But they make good, solid husbands, if you can stand a lifetime of excerpts from *Moby-Dick*.

# ACTORS

Actors usually try very hard to appear humble. They expect this unexpected humility to completely sweep a girl off her feet, or at least result in an autograph request or a quickie in the jump seat.

Actors will yawn frequently when they talk to you. They like to use vulgar, four-letter words in their speech, to show their non-comformity with us run-of-the-mill folk. They love to end their sentences, especially those containing many four-letter words, with an ever-so-slight lowering of the voice to indicate sophistication.

Actors are make-believe people. They usually ask you to meet them in some delightful female impersonation spot on *The Strip*, or a delicious little stretch of sandy beach where so and so film was photographed on location, or on a terrace in the Hollywood Hills where that darling old actress met with that absolutely dreadful fall.

Every stewardess accepts a date with an actor at least once in her flying career. It's a necessity if you're to go back home and answer all the questions about your newfound career of glamour and excitement.

My only intimate experience with an actor came on my eighteenth month with the airline. The girls on the flight presented me with a cupcake decorated with one and a half candles, right after we served the meal on a New York–Los Angeles trip. This little ceremony seemed to interest a fairly well known leading man who'd fallen asleep the minute he boarded the aircraft and slept all through dinner. I was naturally flattered when he called me over to his seat and wished me many years of happy flying.

"I think you ought to have a little more celebration than that cupcake," he told me in a voice that was deep and familiar. "I'd like to provide it for you when we reach Los Angeles."

I was tingling with excitement. I searched my mind for things I had read about this star's marital status. I remembered he had recently married a starlet after divorcing wife number three or four. But that didn't make one bit of difference with me. This was my big chance to go out with a movie star, a man who left millions of women drooling in their popcorn in theaters across the nation. His starlet would just have to do without him for one night.

"That sounds wonderful. I'd love to," I told him.

"Fine. Here's the address of an apartment in Beverly Hills. It belongs to a friend of mine. Come up as soon as you can and I'll have the staff prepare dinner for us. I can't stand all that nightclub rat race in Hollywood. I'll even get our own live music. After all, a girl doesn't survive a year and a half in these damn airplanes every day, does she?"

"She sure doesn't," I said breathlessly. "I'll be there."

I was the talk of the galley all the rest of the trip. And I was sworn to make a full detailed report the next morning.

I watched him leave the airport, carefully noting whether his newest wife was on hand to greet him. The only person I could see was a Chinese driver in a black uniform.

After I rushed through my postflight routine, I took a cab to the address he had given me. It was hardly to be called an apartment, at least not by my standards. It was a large house set back behind an even larger house. The long driveway was dark and I made my way carefully along exquisite shrubbery that formed a clean-cut silhouette in the moonlight.

I went to ring the bell, but the door opened before my finger reached the button. It was the same Chinese man who'd picked up the movie star—*my* movie star. (I think I'll call him Robert for the rest of the story.)

The chauffeur-butler led me up a long stairway to a massive room that spanned the entire length of the house. It was simply gorgeous. I sank ankle-deep into the white carpet. My host came across the room to join me, his hands outstretched, his eyes indicating pleasure in seeing me. I felt silly in my wrinkled uniform and cursed myself for not having changed before coming. I had a dress in my bag downstairs and wanted desperately to run down and get it.

"You look simply beautiful, my dear," he said as he took my hands.

"You're very sweet, but I have a dress in my bag downstairs and I think I ought to change."

"By all means, if that's what you'd like to do. But why a dress? Why not be comfortable?"

"I have slacks . . . and a sweater, if that would be all right."

"That would be wonderful." He laughed that same wicked laugh that always sent me to the powder room when I saw him in the movies. "I'm a nudist at heart. But I won't put you through that kind of embarrassment . . . yet. Go change while I make you a drink."

I ran downstairs, grabbed my bag, and followed the butler to a powder room. I pictured Robert upstairs swishing gin around in a crystal pitcher as I fumbled with the buttons on the uniform. The slacks I had with me were the tightest I owned, and the sweater wasn't any looser. I came out of the bathroom and went back upstairs to join Robert.

He handed me my drink, toasted me, and we both took a healthy sip. I had just brought the glass down from my lips when he grabbed me and planted the biggest, wettest kiss on my lips I'd ever experienced.

"You're very lovely, you know," he crooned. I wanted to look around for the cameras and microphones. He said it just as he'd said it to all those glamorous actresses in films. I grabbed him and returned the kiss.

"Easy, easy, my dear. The night is ours. We'll make it ours."

I know that kind of dialogue sounds corny. But who was I to argue with his scriptwriter? Besides, here I was with my reason for flying—my glamour, my excitement, my romance. Who would believe this back in Amarillo?

He kissed me again and moved away. "Now a superb dinner," he said, "the perfect wine and music for the soul and for the two of us." I was totally under his spell as he spoke those words to me. He pushed a button and two servants entered carrying large, elaborate trays. They seated us at a table in front of the floor-to-ceiling picture window, and served dinner with expert care. The steak was delicious and the wine cool and dry. I couldn't take my eyes from his as he deftly consumed his food, sipped his wine, and talked about a picture he'd just made in Spain. I knew my reactions were those of a silly schoolgirl but I didn't care. It was just that simple—I didn't care.

The piano player arrived as we were starting on dessert. He apologized to Robert for being late and immediately sat down and tinkled familiar melodies on the grand piano in the corner. Imagine having your own piano player on call for last-minute dinner dates! You bet I was impressed.

We finished playing out the dinner scene from our script and proceeded to the next stage, the conquest.

Robert picked me up and carried me, like a bride, across the room to the biggest couch I'd ever seen. It ran at least twelve feet long, was easily five feet wide, and was covered with what seemed to be duck feathers, all soft and warm and fleecy. He placed me gently on the couch and slipped his hands under my sweater. It came off easily, and he unzipped my slacks. Soon, we were both on the couch nude. It's a funny thing to think of at a moment like that, but I noticed he didn't seem as husky and tan as he did on the silver screen. It was a disappointment, but a mild one. We made love there, smooth, satisfying love during which Robert whispered marvelous endearments.

Afterward we fell back exhausted. Then, like an explosion, a door flew open and someone started clapping with great gusto. "Bravo, bravo," a female voice yelled. I leaped up from the couch to see a young, shapely blonde coming toward the couch. Robert got up slowly and bowed to her from his naked waist.

He introduced us.

"Miss Baker, my wife, Marcia. Marcia, Trudy Baker."

"You've outdone yourself, Robert," his wife said as she looked me over from head to toe. "The whole scene was marvelous." Then she started to slip out of her tight shift. The piano player who had discreetly vanished a little earlier came back into the room.

"Wait a minute," I shrieked. "What's going on here?"

"She's sweet, Robert," Marcia said, now as nude as we were. "Hurry up, Louis," she scolded the piano player who was hanging his pants over the chair I'd sat in during dinner.

"Oh no," I said as I quickly got back into my bra, pants, sweater, and slacks. "I'm not the orgy type. Thanks for dinner."

I ran down the stairs, grabbed my bag, and raced along the winding drive. I must have walked for an hour before finding a cab to take me to the hotel.

I told the story to Rachel the next morning with great embarrassment.

"What are you upset about, hon?" she asked. "Chalk it up as something to tell your grandchildren."

I think my night with a leading man was the beginning of a new phase in my flying career. The yen for glamour seemed to be gone.

I had no further interest in actors after Robert and his troupe. Well, except Marlon Brando. I still wanted to meet him. You know how it is.

## ATHLETES

Most athletes like to sit and flex before dinner. We've all read about those college whiz kids who plow through the opposition on the gridiron every Saturday afternoon, and still breeze through advanced bacterial science with straight honor grades. Sorry, but we've never met one. All the athletes we've met have been rather slow and ponderous in their attempts to converse with us, unless they're complete pigs and just grab (linebackers tend toward this approach).

Of course, the nature of the sport they're engaged in determines somewhat their mental standing. Golf pros, tennis pros, swimming champs, and badminton winners tend to be a little more intelligent, at least in the way they present themselves to their stewardesses.

But no matter what sport the man is engaged in, one dominant and salient fact stands out: Athletes are the cheapest guys around.

Rachel dated a professional baseball player once. Their date consisted of one line of bowling, a game of skeet ball at the local penny arcade, and a shared pizza.

Never let it be said that stewardesses look only to a man for how much money he'll spend. That's not at all true. But when a guy is making forty thousand a year and starts reaching for a feel ten minutes after you've gotten into his car, he's got to come up with something better than skeet ball.

There is some advantage in dating an athlete if you're a sports fan yourself. He usually can come up with free tickets for you. He's sold most of his free ones to people like his sister, mother, and brother, but he should have a few left over. Naturally, these tickets always come with strings attached. For our money, or lack of it, we'd prefer to watch the game on TV with a date who just bought us dinner at "21."

# WRITERS

Most writers, even the very successful ones, never acquire a public name. Consequently, when you find out he's a writer, don't ask which novel he's written. He probably hasn't, but will say he's working on one.

Writers are the most quiet and reserved men on an airplane. They remain introspective and withdrawn, devoting most of their energy to obtaining an extra drink above the two-drink maximum.

The classic approach for a writer is to say he's researching a book or movie about stewardesses and would like to spend a few hours asking some questions. We usually accept, after convincing ourselves he really is a writer. Why not accept? You either become the underlying source of inspiration for a great novel or end up reading all your little idiosyncrasies in another best-seller, usually a very dirty one. Either way, you've become a lady of letters. The only possible trouble you can encounter is when you marry and your husband reads about all your little idiosyncrasies in someone else's book.

Stewardesses who majored in English in college are fair game for writers traveling on their flights. The writer can succeed with the girl as long as she envisions him writing the great American novel or Oscar-winning screenplay. As soon as she finds out he's only a junior editor of the *Montana Coal, Iron and Cobalt Quarterly,* she loses interest.

Between us, Rachel and I can count eleven different men who approached us with the line, "I'm writing a book on stewardesses and would love to be able to talk with you."

What we're planning on doing next is a book on millionaires. We intend to approach men of great wealth and say, "We're doing a book on millionaires and would love to be able to talk with you."

It's called reverse seduction.

# DOCTORS

Doctors are rich. Having so much money gives a doctor a sense of total power, except over those patients he's always dunning for a late bill. He also picks up a false sense of security in having to sound so cocksure in front of every patient, despite the fact he's never seen this disease before. We grow up thinking doctors can do no wrong. Then we discover how silly this is, especially when you're their patient—or stewardess.

The stewardess consensus is that doctors usually make their pitch via a note placed on their tray after dinner. Usually, it will contain something terribly clever like, "I am a doctor. I'm staying at the Mark Hopkins. My room number is 2030. Nine o'clock."

If you're pregnant, getting one of these notes could be construed as a good deal. If you're not, but maybe have a headache, it might also make sense to trudge up to his room. But remember— all doctors are married. You must have this firmly in mind before making any decision. And if you do decide to go, be on time. Doctors hate to be kept waiting.

# POLITICIANS

We feel sorry for politicians. They must, out of deference to their constituents, be at all times aboveboard and pure. They never are, of course, but they must make it look that way. Lately though, with the apparent acceptance of sin, misuse of funds, blackmail, and payoffs by our nation's leaders, politicians seem to be a little more relaxed, more pliable, and more willing to accept the fact they're the same as other men.

If a politician is about to make a play for you, he'll test you for signs of a loose tongue.

"Well, young lady, just what part of this fair nation of ours produced that charming accent?" he'll start.

"Texas, sir." Good answer.

"Well, how about that. You folks sure are going to benefit from that new dam. You know, I voted for it."

"What new dam?"

"Ho, ho, ho, got a sense of humor, too, huh?"

"Yes, sir."

"Well, no sense in a pretty young thing like you worrying about dams and things like that. That's for people like me to worry about, ho, ho, ho."

"That's certainly a lot to worry about."

"That's my job."

"Ho, ho, ho."

"By the way, young lady, you don't happen to know Sammy Jim Bowie, do you? Fine young Texas congressman."

"Sammy? I went to high school with Sammy. He sure was a creep. Guess he's changed."

That kills it. Had I extolled Sammy's virtues, or at least remained noncommittal about him, it might have gone further. But politicians hate to be talked about behind their backs. They do it too much themselves.

If the politician happens to be from your own home territory, there is no chance to play with him. Politicians always play far away from home and their voters. Puerto Rico or Alaska are safer than the local motel.

If you do become entwined with a politician, you can count on a secret, over-the-shoulder romance that must be carried on between votes on poverty programs and fund-raising appearances with his wife. It's better in the long run to stay away from politicians unless you figure they're going to lose in their next election and return to private life. When that happens, they're likely to divorce their wives for losing the election for them, and might even consider taking you on as a permanent addition to their new household and career.

## NEWSPAPERMEN

Newspapermen are usually traveling free, courtesy of your airline's public relations department. They're on your airplane with your airline's hope that someday, somehow, somewhere they'll say something nice about your airline. Before they board, they're fed, boozed up, and taken to the airport in a long, black Carey limousine. They're already drunk when they get on the plane, and you've been instructed by the airport public relations man to forget about the two-drink rule where this elite member of the press is concerned.

Obviously, newspapermen are spoiled by your public relations department. In fact, they're spoiled and drunk enough to think *you* come with booze, food, limousine, and free ticket.

Their approach is often direct, clumsy, distasteful, arrogant, lewd, and highly annoying.

All of this poses a dilemma for the stewardess. Just how much does she want to endear herself to her airline, its management, and stockholders? Do you go out of your way to be nice to the slob with the pencil behind his ear in 3B, or do you follow your natural inclinations and spill hot coffee on him? There is no answer, at least not in the manual.

## MILITARY MEN

Military men are generally polite in their advances to us. Whether this results from their rigid military training or is inborn is unanswered in our minds. But they'll approach us nicely, directly, and without great fuss.

Unfortunately, men in uniform assume a second-class paranoia because they're flying at half-fare. It's a shame they feel this way because we look at their half-fare status as something that should be done for our men in the armed services.

If a military man does make a pitch to a stewardess, and if she does accept, you can count on a pleasant evening with the best bars and restaurants included. Once a man gets away from the grim confines of his club at the military installation, he likes to enjoy the good life. And we do, too.

## ADVERTISING MEN

Advertising men are insecure. Their need to conform to every little whim of fashion indicates this. And because they're insecure, they approach us as they would a potential account, anxious to get all they can *now* because tomorrow we might sign up with another agency. Actually, their attitude in this respect is probably a realistic one.

But their insecurity poses even greater problems where a girl is concerned.

We know a stewardess who entered into a prolonged relationship with one of these three-button boys (they only button the top two on their jackets). He worked for one of the largest agencies in New York.

This stewardess, forgetting her loop or pill or whatever it was she was using, became pregnant by the Madison Avenue flash. She told him about her condition on a Friday night.

"Give me a few days to run this thing around the track, honey," he said thoughtfully. "Let's swish it around a little before we drink it."

She hadn't heard from him by Wednesday of the next week so tried to call him at the agency. She was told he no longer worked there but could be found at another agency.

She called the other agency and was told he had never started there because the account never materialized. But they thought he was with a pharmaceutical agency. She tried there and found he was out of town.

She tried him again the following week but he was no longer employed by the pharmaceutical agency. They didn't know where he was.

The gal had her condition taken care of, a course of action always under great debate when we get together, and finally ran into her ad hero at Friday's, a bar on First Avenue. She let him know just how furious she was.

"Well, sweetie, you know how it is. I wasn't running from you. This agency business is a tough sell, tough sell. Run all the time.

By the way, I just put in a new $597.95 amplifier in my pad. Let's go up and have a drink and talk about old times."

"Let's not rush into things," she replied. "Why not run some juice through your friggin' $597.95 amplifier and see if it blows up."

Assuming you don't misplace your loop, admen can be good for a fast night on the town. We find that admen make more pitches to us than any other group of men. They all have a strange attraction to stewardesses, which is part of their insecurity. An adman never dates just *a girl*. She has to have a handle, an image for him to date. That's why admen, when recounting past dates, will always say she was a stewardess, a model, an artist, a bunny, a writer, an actress, a director, or an heiress. It's kind of sad, really. A *girl* just won't do.

Their insecurity shows up in other ways, too. Everything they own has a price tag on it. They have a $597.95 amplifier, a $200 chair, a $107.25 watch, or a $210 suit. And until you get on to this dribble, you tend to be as impressed as they are. But then again, admen are impressed easily. So are their bosses and clients who prefer their underlings to look right rather than think right.

But there are worse dates.

## CIVIL SERVANTS

Asking a civil servant what he'd like to drink is like trying to get service from one when you're renewing your driver's license. He'll chitchat with his seat partner, look out the window, clean his nails, and light a cigar. After you've asked him for the fourth time, he'll look at you and say, "What do you want?"

Civil servants are a small part of our life. They aren't inclined to make a pitch and the few that do try fail mightily. But identifying them correctly helps build up our point score.

# LAWYERS

A stewardess usually takes the first step in her own seduction where a lawyer is concerned. Everyone in the world has a legal problem of one sort or another and wants free legal advice.

Consequently, all a lawyer need do is announce his profession at the earliest part of the flight. This takes him out of the running as far as the identification game is concerned, but puts him strongly in the running as far as the evening is concerned.

"I have a silly question and I'll bet you're tired of being asked silly questions but would you mind being asked another?" the stewardess will ask at an opportune moment.

"Go right ahead," replies the lawyer.

"Well, you see, three of us have this rent-controlled apartment in New York and the lease is up soon and we want to know whether the landlord can raise our rent now."

"Well, there are many factors to be considered here. This kind of a situation can be long and costly where the courts are concerned. That is to say, deeming your stand legal, in view of the validity of the elements heretofore contained in the lease instrument, might as well be construed as a de facto admission. See?"

"I think so."

"But I think it would be silly to spend all the legal fees required over this situation. Look, I'll call you when I come back to New York and we'll set a date when I can come up, look at the apartment, and check the lease."

"You have to actually look at the apartment?"

"Of course. That is to say, if, in fact, there is evidence of landlord neglect in certain vulnerable areas, we may be able to ascertain the validity of the entire clause in the lease instrument, as opposed to a part or portion thereof as might affect the entire agreement."

"Here's my number. And bless you."

# MUSICIANS

It's hard to tell a musician unless he's carrying a bass fiddle. When he does carry one, you're in for trouble.

Most airlines will sell a bass fiddle a seat at half the usual fare. This instrument is large and fragile, and its owner must carry his bass fiddle in this manner. Putting it in the cargo area of the plane would be certain disaster.

We had a jazz bass player on a flight to Los Angeles where he was to appear at the Monterey Jazz Festival. He carried his wooden seat companion, strapped it in with great care, and settled back for the flight. The fiddle caused no trouble until mealtime.

"Hey chick, where's the meat for my friend?" he asked.

"That's funny, sir. But obviously we can't give a meal to a bass fiddle."

"You're puttin' me on, chick. Like I bought a seat for my friend and he should get a meal, like."

"That is so funny. But we can't."

"Oh, like, I'm gonna flip baby all over this big eagle."

"All right. I'll get your friend a meal."

"Hey, wait a minute. Like, you forgot to serve him his juice, too."

"His juice."

"Yeh, like, his goon-water, you know. His *booze*."

"Absolutely not. Food, yes. But I know you're just going to drink his two drinks and that's against the rules."

"The rules? The rules? To be broken, baby, to be broken. One seat's worth two drinks, right?"

"I'll check with the captain."

"No, no, no, swinger. Don't upset our flyboy. I'm like shook enough already. Just bring my friend two gins on the rocks. No peel."

We were tempted to pour the drinks into the monster strapped next to the musician. But we didn't. Better a drunk bass fiddle than an upset musician.

Generally, musicians are good passengers. And their approach can always be counted on to be funny, different, and unobtrusive.

# TEACHERS

Teachers have managed to con the world for too long a time. The general conception we all have about teachers is that they represent purity of mind and body, a dedicated group of men and women interested only in educating the nation's youth.

But they're not that way. If you've been around at all, you know that female teachers rank among the world's greatest swingers. Put a knowledgeable guy in a bar loaded with women of different backgrounds and he'll head for the teacher. He knows.

The same goes for the masculine version of the teaching profession. Both sexes are weary of being looked at constantly by their boards of education for any violation of the highest code of personal conduct. Put them on an airplane where there isn't likely to be that scrutiny and you've got a man or woman on the prowl.

Married men working as teachers are even more prone to swing. They have both the school board and their wives on their back, and succeeding in accomplishing a little action on the side is as welcome as a pay increase.

The specific approach a teacher will make depends a great deal on what he teaches. If he teaches business law, he'll take the lawyer's tack. Math teachers will go after you à la engineer. And so on.

# SALESMEN

All the traveling salesmen jokes are true, at least based on what we've observed. The unique thing about a salesman is that he isn't at all concerned whether he scores with you or not. He has plenty of girls in the cities he visits, and his interest in you reflects his need to keep his stable fully stocked.

There is very little we can add to all the stories about salesmen. It seems the majority of our passengers are salesmen and, consequently, we're on the receiving end quite often. We suppose salesmen have become "old hat." Other men now have expense accounts and are good talkers. The day of the traveling salesman knocking over girls like bowling pins is gone.

Salesmen are generous to stewardesses. Very few flights go by on which we don't receive some sample from some salesman. His samples don't buy us but they're nice to receive.

## SUMMATION

Everyone has his own special pitch and to attempt to be all-inclusive in this chapter would be impossible. We'd end up covering such professions as undertakers, the clergy, mailmen, grape pickers, and male secretaries.

Despite the many bad thoughts we have about many men, we usually end up marrying one. That's the way it's supposed to go, and we wouldn't have it any other way.

Should we be asked to divulge what we consider the perfect pitch a man can make to us, we'd both agree that a courteous, reserved man with a sense of humor and a respect for the difficult job we perform would rank at the top of the list. Of course, climbing aboard our airplane with a copy of this book in hand will surely elicit some conversation from any stewardess. You might even end by checking the validity of what we've said.

# CHAPTER XX

# "Should We Strike?"

$\mathcal{W}$e belong to a union. It seems a good idea. As stewardesses, we're subject to an incredible number of company policies and rulings that can make life miserable. Our union tries to make our lives easier. It gives us the comfort of numbers, in a group with common problems and goals. Rachel and I have never been involved in a strike by our own stewardess union. But we've been affected by strikes by other unions within the airline.

We remember one strike when all the maintenance men walked out. They wanted their mother's birthday off or some such holiday. Naturally, without these people to fix the airplanes when they got sick, the airline couldn't operate. They immediately put all employees on half-pay, threatening that if the strike wasn't settled within fifteen days, we'd all go on no-pay. It wasn't a happy thought.

On the sixteenth day of the strike, money stopped coming. That meant a scramble for rent, food, and cosmetics funds. It was at this gray point in our lives that we realized the value of having a steady beau, preferably one with a well-paying job. The girls who did enjoy such a situation made out pretty well.

The strike also gave the hoarders the last laugh on those of us who had scorned them for their frugality. A fringe benefit of being a stewardess is the chance to walk off a flight occasionally with a couple of filets, a lobster tail or two, miniature packages of cigarettes, and whatever bottles of booze the first-class passengers didn't drink. Usually when we'd come home with an unusually good haul, we'd throw a party. Not so with the stockpilers. Their food would be carefully wrapped in foil, labeled with their name, and placed in the freezer for their own use. The miniature bottles would find a secure place in a locked drawer and the cigarettes would nestle alongside the bottles. Most of us think of this kind of Hooverism as distasteful and even antisocial. Except during a no-pay period.

We managed though, with the nurturing of the stew-bums who gladly seized this opportunity to further entrench themselves in our minds and hearts. Stew-bums have saved many a stewardess during a strike. There were rent parties, too, to which we invited everyone we knew. Each guest brought a bottle and five dollars for the cause—our cause. It was all marvelous fun and the take from such a party often far exceeded the rent needs.

In retrospect, some strikes were fun times. But others weren't, especially when the strikes were on other airlines. As soon as another airline that flies routes also served by our line goes on strike, we beef up service to those cities. This is all very neighborly. But it puts a severe strain on stews and crew to deliver the extra service.

Once in a true picture of management ingenuity, the airline brought back ex-stewardesses to fly during such a strike. Rachel spotted one of these rehired stewardesses in the terminal as we walked toward our flight.

"The uniform looks funny with the white hair," she commented casually.

I saw what she meant. "It's not white hair, Rachel. Just sort of gray."

"It's white, Trudy. She must be at least forty."

Rachel was right. The stewardess in question had obviously been away from the airline for more than just a few years. To our surprise, she was flying our trip with us. She was very pleasant, smiled a lot, and seemed willing to help.

We were off the ground and ready to bring the meals out of the galley when we realized our white-haired stewardess wasn't around. We looked for her in the cabin and found her chatting with a businessman.

"I used to be a stewardess, you know," she was telling him. "I'm married now and have four children. It's fun to be back helping."

If only she would help.

"I don't think I should actually serve meals, girls," she said. "I've been away too long and you two are expert at it. I'll keep everyone happy so you won't have to bother with that."

Today, in the jet era, the only way to keep passengers happy, to the extent they can be happy, is to give them what they're supposed to have, and give it fast. Our forty-year-old goodwill merchant went up and down the aisle smiling at everyone and telling them how much fun it was to be back flying and so on and so on. In the meantime, the two of us struggled to get the drinks and meals served, a chore that's hard enough to accomplish with three girls working at it.

We managed, despite our returning angel of the skies. Then she got sick. Fortunately, she made it to the lavatory.

Close to arrival time she came into the galley as we frantically tried to clean up. She said, "I know this may sound silly to you, but I'd love to make the PA announcement when we arrive. For old time's sake, you know. I think the people in the cabin would appreciate it, too. After all, they remember when I was flying the line."

"Why not?" Rachel answered.

We landed, and our *senior* stew got on the microphone.

"Ladies and gentlemen, this is . . . This is *Miss* Caleb. It wasn't so long ago that I was flying to cities such as this on a regular basis. In fact, many of you might even remember me. Well, anyway, coming back to serve aviation and everyone of you dear passengers is something I was most willing to do when asked by my airline's management."

Rachel shoved the standard arrival announcement sheet under her nose. She ignored it.

"Of course, all this new meal service has me a little befuddled. But the training we received in how to make a passenger feel comfortable in his flight never leaves one. A stewardess never forgets her dedication."

"Read this," Rachel said in a hard whisper, pointing to the announcement form.

"So, ladies and gentlemen, I say it is a vast pleasure to be back serving . . ."

Rachel cut the PA system, took the mike from our matronly partner, and gave the usual arrival pitch. The ex-stewardess seemed hurt, but smiled through it all.

We didn't even bother trying to say good-bye to the passengers as they deplaned. Our retread was right there shaking hands and laughing and cocking her head in humility at their words of encouragement. She came back to the galley after everyone had departed, fluffed her hair, and stated, "Imagine that. One of the gentlemen asked me for a date. Once a stewardess, always a stewardess, huh?"

"Sure," I said.

We flew with her again. She still managed not to do anything physical; we didn't allow her near the PA. After the strike we asked her why she'd called herself Miss on that one PA announcement she'd made.

"Well, I think the male passengers would prefer the illusion that we're all single. It makes them feel they might have a chance with *us,* silly boys." And this after passing around snapshots of her four children.

Want to know some of our gripes? Here they are:

*Thefts:* Our complaint is not about having things stolen from us. What does upset us is to have a supervisor grab us after a flight and say, "All right girls, empty your purse and coat pockets on the seat." She's come on the aircraft secure she'll find a filet in each pocket, a dozen miniature bottles of bourbon in the purse, and a frayed copy of *Field & Stream* under our girdle. The maddening thing is that these supervisors stole the airline blind during their flying days. Now, with a newfound sense of morality, they've turned private eye, their targets the girls who report to them.

*Being fired:* It was easy for a stewardess to be fired, until the union decided to show a little of its feminine muscle. There's no doubt, as many a seasoned traveler will testify, that a few girls do deserve to lose their jobs. What bothers us are the good stewardesses who, for one reason or another, make one small slip in performance or regulation, then receive a layoff or even the pink slip.

There was one rather famous case in which a girl was fired for being caught in the lap of the flight engineer. What had happened was this: the girl went to the flight deck to serve coffee and was pulled into the fellow's lap in a silly little gesture of playfulness. At the precise moment she landed, a supervisor, working the trip undetected, entered the cockpit. She immediately suspended the girl.

The union fought back. And won. The girl is still flying the line.

Certainly, there have been firings that appear warranted. Annual physicals will occasionally turn up a girl who is virtually blind. Or one who is pregnant. Also, certain girls will find themselves fed up with flying and, rather than resign, direct their change of attitude against any passenger who happens to be near.

*Bad letters:* It's appalling how many airline passengers write letters of complaint about stewardesses. Again, to indicate a rational view of this situation, we must admit that some letters are justified. But most really aren't.

*Drinking or smoking on the job:* Have you ever been on an airplane when the heating system decided to stop working? We have, and a quick shot of bourbon can do wonders for the human heating system of the stewardess. But we don't try it, even if our hands turn blue. It's against the rules. Same goes for smoking. We can't smoke when working a trip, even in the confines of the galley. Actually, the no drinking and smoking rules are sensible ones. But as with any rule, exceptions should be allowed when conditions warrant them.

*Weight:* Every airline watches its stewardesses with the eye of a carnival weight-guesser. They feel that even a pound over your listed weight is a pound to be lost. They make it easy for you to lose that pound. They suspend you. You sit home worrying about that pound and you eat to stave off the frustration. It's a losing battle. It's our belief that every girl can look attractive within a range of weights. Sure, some girls do become *fat,* and that shouldn't be allowed. But Rachel looks better when she's about five pounds over her listed weight. That's what should count.

*Age:* Every airline has its own rulings about when a girl becomes too old to fly. Never has a ruling caused so much controversy as with those airlines that retire girls at thirty-two. True, they ensure us ground jobs if we've stayed around that long. But most of us can't think of anything more distasteful than working as a stewardess supervisor. Of course, there's always the chance to teach at the stewardess college under the guidance of Big Momma. No thanks. If we haven't hooked a man before age thirty-two, we'd just as soon keep flying.

Many men believe a woman really isn't in her prime, both physically and emotionally, until she's in her thirties. But some airlines have decided we're over the hill at thirty. We're certainly not advocating white-haired stewardesses. We recognize the value to the airline of pretty young stewardesses. But thirty-two? Over the hill? Too old?

How about an age limit on stewardess supervisors? They all think young until they become supervisors. Then they adopt older ideas, believing their supervisor's role calls for a mother's approach to a daughter. OK. Let's have a minimum age for supervisors of sixty-two. That way they can justify their actions and stay out of trouble with vice presidents at the same time.

*Marriage:* Some airlines allow their girls to fly even after they're married. This seems reasonable, especially in light of their desire that we don't play around with the male passengers on our trips. Airlines that make you stop flying after marriage do it because they want men passengers to envision conquest after conquest when they travel. These airlines also say a married girl will find it difficult to make her marriage work without interfering with her stewardess schedule. That might be. Let us get married and when our performance slips, fire us. But let us get married—if we've found someone to ask us.

Anti-marriage rules force many girls to hide the fact they're married. This is a tricky feat to pull off and produces dialogue like this:

"You devil, you. I just found out you've moved and are married."

"I'm not married."

"But what about Harry, the man in your apartment?"

"Oh, Harry. I just live with him."

A stewardess who is married and hiding the fact must always have two telephones in the apartment so a man won't answer. A secretly married stewardess must also conceal the fact from her parents. This can be difficult when they come to visit. Hubby goes to the YMCA and is introduced as a friend.

"He seems very nice," says your mother. "He'd make a good husband, I bet."

"I don't know, Mom. He might turn out to be mean."

Of course, there's no way to continue the pretense when you become pregnant. They've got you there.

"It was quite a honeymoon," she says to her supervisor. "Got pregnant right away." The supervisor knows she was married long before and doesn't buy her story.

*Change of address notification:* We must notify the airline of any change of address within twenty-four hours of the change. Good rule. Makes sense. Except where Betty Elkin was concerned.

Betty came down with appendicitis one night and her roommate rushed her to the hospital. "Don't forget to call the airline and tell them," Betty said as they wheeled her to the operating room. Her roommate promised, but forgot. Betty was on a four-day break.

The roommate was out the next day when the airline called to ask Betty to come off her four-day and work a trip. There was no answer. So, they called the landlord of the two-family house where the two girls lived upstairs.

"Betty's not here," the owner informed the airline. "She's in the hospital."

A simple situation. It obviously was, except in the mind of Betty's supervisor, who promptly wrote her up for not notifying the airline of her *change of address*. The airline reviewed the case and didn't bring any punishment against Betty.

*Conduct unbecoming a stewardess:* Now here's a bit of vague, ill-defined, and questionable double-talk. Under this heading, we can be fired for almost anything. Naturally, the interpretation of this clause varies with the airline involved. Each airline chooses its girls for different reasons. Each airline likes a certain type of girl, and betraying her "type" would be construed as conduct unbecoming a stewardess.

American seems to prefer the all-American girl. They judge her conduct accordingly. It becomes difficult to ascertain what is an all-American girl. Hugh Hefner claims the girls in his centerfold are all-American girls, like the ones you find next door. We don't think American has this in mind.

TWA evidently interprets stewardess conduct as that of a Vassar or Wellesley graduate. TWA girls have that air about them, and to violate that vague, questionable image would not be prudent for a TWA hostess.

Braniff, from what we've observed, considers a large, full bosom necessary when judging stewardess conduct and appearance. Betty O'Riley's impressive overhang would not have violated the Braniff image. Her conduct is another matter.

United has average girls, in every sense of the word. This is good, because you can then apply average, middle-of-the-road criteria to a United girl's performance. Average usually has a negative meaning. Not so with United. It just means their girls aren't far out one way or the other, and usually wear medium-cup bras.

Why do National Airline stewardesses have that hard look? They're sexy, but it's a knowing look of sex, too knowing for most other airlines. Stew-bums say you almost expect a National girl to set an alarm clock next to her bed when entertaining a gentleman. We're sure that isn't true, but it is a graphic way of stating it.

PSA, that California airline, has what are probably the pick of American womanhood. Take everything good about all other stewardesses, lump it together in one package, and you have a PSA stewardess. Amazing for a smaller airline.

Air Canada naturally likes plump, British-looking girls. Their standards of stewardess conduct must be based on the British system, one that many men seem to prefer.

Eastern's girls are improving.

Delta's girls are Southern.

Pan Am's girls are primarily the snobby, jet-set type. Unfortunately, many of them only strive to be this way. They don't make it too much of the time.

Other airlines have their own standards. And as a stewardess you live up to those standards—or else.

One of the most exasperating jobs is that of a union leader in your city. We have a good friend who has held this job for over a year, and her life is a series of middle-of-the-night telephone calls from girls in trouble.

"I'm pregnant."

"They caught me stealing a lobster tail."

"I just got married."

"I've been raped."

"This VP is after me to go to bed with him. He says I'll lose my job. What should I do?"

"I told a passenger he was a pain in the you know what and I'm sure he's going to write."

"The captain's wife knows."

"My husband knows."

"The supervisor knows."

"I know."

And so on.

Also included in the union leader's life are the pleas for money by a broke stewardess, confessions of an alcoholic, dope runner, aborted mother, and just plain homesick gal. It's a tough job.

As a group, we're reasonably happy with our pay, even though it isn't great. Girls now start at about $345 a month. That sounds low, but the company pays for life insurance, medical bills, dry cleaning, and our hotels, meals, and cabs when we're away from home. Because we're home so little, we don't really need elaborate housing or a fancy car. Then there are the fringe benefits—the $40 weekends in Europe, the mere $312 to go around the world, the hotel passes, and all the other extras. How can we really complain?

# CHAPTER XXI

## "A Layover Is Not What You Think"

$\mathcal{E}$very job and every industry boasts its own peculiar set of terms and phrases. Being a stewardess for an airline is no different. We have our own jargon that we communicate with effectively. Some of it is as follows:

*Actual flying time:* The time from the moment the blocks are removed from the wheels of the aircraft at the point of departure to when they're replaced at point of arrival.

*ATC:* Air Travel Card. We give you credit for a little status when we know you have such a card. We credit you with similar status when you flash a membership card to an airline's VIP club. It doesn't always mean you deserve status. Some of our greatest disappointments are cardholders. But it's a reference point with which to begin.

*Belly:* Underneath the plane where the baggage is carried.

*Bid sheets:* Each month, every stewardess receives a bid sheet on which she bids for certain trips the following month. Naturally, the longer you've been flying, the more preference you're given. It takes at least a year before you've achieved enough seniority to get what you bid. This can fluctuate according to how rapidly the girls are finding men and leaving the job for marriage. In a good year, when romance is running wild, you can climb up the seniority ladder more quickly.

*Booze report:* How many bottles of liquor were served on any given flight? That question, and its answer, will determine how many bottles must be returned after the flight. It's all on the beverage report. By the way, we don't get away with as many bottles as the airline believes we do. It's not easy.

*Bumped:* We're going to Phoenix for a glorious weekend vacation. We're flying on a free pass. We get as far as Chicago and keep our fingers crossed. We're told it looks good—there are two open seats and we can have them. And then you come running down to catch that Phoenix flight at the last minute. You bump us off the trip. We spend the weekend drinking in Chicago to keep warm. Thanks.

*CAT:* This is not a term to describe a new counterespionage group. It stands for Clear Air Turbulence, that mysterious and undefinable rough air you hit when flying on a clear, beautiful day. It causes many problems, usually because seat belts are unfastened when we hit it. CAT never shows up on aircraft radar.

*Cattle car:* Tourist-class aircraft or the tourist section of a two-class airplane.

*Cockpit key:* Our government frowns on passengers entering the flight deck and hijacking the airplane. Thus, we have a federal regulation that dictates that the cockpit door will be closed and locked at all times. We each carry a key under our jacket.

*Credit time:* If any crew member is away from his home base for too long a time, the pay scale is adjusted accordingly to a higher rate. We then are paid for our credit time.

*Crew sched:* These are the men who schedule stewardess trips and check us in and out. They're located in operations and, for the most part, are pretty good guys.

*CTO agent:* City ticket agent who works behind the counter in the city.

*Deadhead:* It could mean you're dull. But more often it means a crew member is returning to his home base as a passenger. He or she has worked a trip to some city and must return home without a flight to work.

*Demo $O_2$ mask:* The oxygen mask we use to demonstrate procedure before takeoff. Black pepper in it is a marvelous way to reap revenge on a naughty girl.

*Ferry:* Bringing an aircraft or crew back from somewhere to another point. Passengers never fly on ferry flights.

*Flag stop:* A special stop to pick up passengers left stranded through the fault of the airline. Especially prevalent during bad weather in certain sections of the country or during strikes by other airlines.

*Flight deck:* Airline's fancy term for what you've always called the cockpit. This change in nomenclature is designed to dispense with the World War I image of pilot with silk scarf around neck and wind in face, goggles, etc. Call it what you will, but we must call it flight deck. OK?

*Flight pay log:* All crew members keep records of their flying time for pay purposes on this sheet, which is kept in the cockpit.

*FTO agent:* Field ticket agent who works behind the counter at the airport.

*Galley:* Where we cook up all the goodies you enjoy on your flight. Also called the buffet area, when someone wants to add class to the conversation. In reality, it's a kitchen, no cleaner or dirtier than yours at home and designed for the same functions. It's also the only solitary place on an airplane where a stewardess can retreat and lick her wounds. Please take note that we *hate* people to poke their heads in the galley when the drapes are closed.

*Jump seat:* An extra seat on an airplane where the stewardess sits on takeoff and landing.

*Layover:* Our moment of complete collapse. We lay over after working a trip to a destination away from home base. We stay there for a period of time and then return home on the return leg of the trip. If you're laying over somewhere too, and would like to "bump into" a stewardess, you might try the following hotels:

**New York**
> Lexington
> St. Moritz
> International Inn
> Commodore

**Miami**
> Skyways
> Miami International Inn

**Atlanta**
> Air Host Inn
> International Inn

Holiday Inn
Hilton Inn

## St. Louis
The Chase Hotel

## Chicago
Palmer House
Various airport motels

## Denver
Cosmopolitan

## Seattle
Olympia

## Washington, D.C.
Burlington
Shoreham
Conrad's
Mayflower

## Salt Lake City
Newhouse

## Boise
Boisean (Didn't know you could find a stewardess in Boise,
did you?)

## Dallas
Hilton Inn

## New Orleans
Hilton Inn

## Boston
Hilton Inn
Copley Square

## Los Angeles
International Inn
Airport Marina
Miramar
Santa Monica

## San Francisco
Hyatt House
Holiday Inn
Downtown Hilton

## Mexico City
Vista Hermosa
Maria Isabel

## Acapulco
Hotel Caleta

## Phoenix
Adams

## Newark
Robert Treat

## Toronto
Skyline

## Cleveland
Sheraton Cleveland

*Mechanical:* Trouble with the equipment on a flight that causes delay or cancellation.

*Milk run:* Those puddle-jumping flights that stop at many places before reaching their final destination. We just pray when working them that we won't develop aircraft trouble and be forced to spend the night in one of the intermediate cities.

*Mis-connect:* Our airline has booked you on the wrong flight or we were late and you missed your next trip. You're a mis-connect and we're sorry.

*OLP:* We call you this when you've made your reservation through one airline for passage on another. You're an off-line passenger.

*OSB:* Actually means Other Stations Boarding. You've made your reservations in one city but board in another. You're an OSB. Talk nasty to us and we shift the letters.

*Over-water pay:* Flying trips over water bring extra pay for stewardesses.

*PA check:* Our supervisor sneaks on board the plane before take-off and checks us for all necessary items. Gloves, flashlight, grease pencil, etc. Naturally, we're never 100 percent right, and as passengers, you should be happy supervisors conduct these PA checks. There's no telling what we'd forget without them.

*Pass rider:* An employee riding free on a pass. All such passengers fly space available, and are only there because the plane did not have a full load of paying passengers. Airline employees are instructed not to tell other passengers they're traveling free. There's no sense upsetting the guy next to you who has just paid $200 for his ticket.

*PSR:* Passenger service representative. His job with any airline is to try and soothe you when your feathers are ruffled. It's a very difficult job and you really can't blame any of these people for turning to the bottle later in their lives.

*Reserve:* When we're on reserve, it simply means we're on call to cover any trip that is short of a stewardess. Being on reserve is usually the plight of junior girls who can't win bids. You'll also find senior girls flying reserve because they didn't bother bidding for a particular month or turned their bid sheet in past the deadline. One thing is certain: Fostering a love interest is damned tough when you're on reserve.

*Seat chart:* The chart on which we record your names and destinations; that is, when we can spell your name. You might try helping us once in a while.

*Senior pay:* The senior stew on a trip receives extra pay for the paperwork she's responsible for.

# CHAPTER XXII

## "An Unhappy Landing"

$\mathcal{I}$ got on the 707 bound for San Francisco low in spirit. My gloomy mood was a combination of many things. I still had a bad taste in my mouth from my ugly experience with the Hollywood star. I couldn't get Sally Lu completely out of my mind. A kind of general lethargy had set in—I didn't have my old pep and zoom. I no longer bounced out of bed in the morning, eager to get on a plane, meet the day's passengers, wrestle with the flight's problems. The routine seemed monotonous. The problems were boring. I'd already met all the passengers. Clearly I was in the doldrums.

The Chuck situation bothered me, too. He was the greatest guy I'd ever met. Everything was marvelous between us. The fact that I didn't see him very often kept the level of excitement high. It was like a holiday when he turned up. He'd made it pretty clear that he might be interested in marrying me someday, some remotely future day when I'd gotten all the flying and the chasing after glamour out of my system. I was sick of flying as of right now. Did that mean I was ready to marry Chuck?

My thoughts sped round and round like little animals in a cage. I was really in a poisonous mood as I passed out the second round of drinks on the San Francisco flight. Suddenly I felt a tap on my fanny. I spun around. It was Mr. Shackwood in the last row of first-class seats. He was a man with one of those tight expressionless little faces and a hairline mustache. I never like that type. I waggled my index finger in front of his nose. "That's a no-no. Mustn't touch." That was my automatic answer to tappers and pinchers.

He beckoned me closer to him. "Lean over. I want to tell you something."

There was nothing to do but lean over and hope he wouldn't start crawling down the front of my blouse. "How about when we get to San Francisco," he said, "I buy you a dinner and then we go to my hotel and screw."

That was precisely the invitation I needed at that moment in my life. And from this vile little creep. "I guess you mean tonight," I snarled at him.

He grinned broadly, "That's right."

"That's what I thought." I walked away from him in utter disdain. Rachel was getting the dinner trays ready in the galley. "If Shackwood rings in the back of this section, you take him. I'm likely to toss him out a window."

"Sure, Trudy." He rang at that moment.

Rachel trotted off and was back a few minutes later.

"Trudy, did you know that one out of every ten girls will accept a direct pitch from a guy? Did you know that a magazine article suggested that a man simply stand on a street corner and say to the first ten girls who pass, 'How about going to bed with me?' The magazine says one out of the ten will accept. How about that?"

"I never heard of such a thing. It's ridiculous."

Rachel looked me squarely in the eye. She squinted a little and kept looking at me. Finally, she cleared her throat and said, "Well, Trudy, old friend and confidant, you'll be pleased to know that you're number ten."

"What are you talking about?"

"Shackwood back there. His theory. He told me all about it, and said he tried it on you. And he's bragging it worked. Tell me, did you accept a date with him tonight in San Fran? Did you agree to go to bed with him? Just like that?"

"Rachel, he's out of his nasty mind. I never agreed to any such thing."

"Did he pinch you?"

"He tapped me on the rear end."

"He tried with me, too. But they don't call me ol' swivel hips for nothing. Come on, Trudy, let's have it. What did you tell him?"

"Rachel, stop it. You know I never accepted anything from that . . . that cretin."

"Save your breath. It's him you'd better convince."

I avoided Shackwood as much as possible. Rachel took over

that side of the airplane. He sat there leering at me, his tongue going back and forth over his lips. He hissed at me a couple of times and tried to motion me over to him with his head. I looked the other way and served my passengers.

"Ladies and gentlemen, we now proudly present a feature-length motion picture for your enjoyment." Rachel was reading the standard announcement for show time on the 707. She went through the instructions about dialing the volume, tuning the music channels, and using the headphones. Everyone settled back to enjoy second drinks and the film. It was a brand-new Hollywood release, a grade-B thriller with go-go girls, good guys and bad guys, a sinister plot to steal sinister secret papers, wild chases in automobiles over sheer mountain cliffs, through sleepy little peasant towns and in airplanes that seemed to crash every twenty frames. All this frantic action completely captured the passengers, and I used the short lull to freshen up in one of the two vacant lavatories.

I latched the door behind me, drew a deep breath, and took a long look at myself in the mirror. I smiled at myself and myself smiled back. The smile took an effort. "Come out of it, girl," I scolded. "What's happened to the old Trudy?" I was reaching for the door latch when I heard knocking on the wall. It came from the next lavatory. I put my ear to the wall.

"Hi there," I heard faintly through the partition. It was Shackwood. "Clever, clever," he said. "Great way to be able to talk to me without anyone else listening. You're a clever one, sweetie pie. A-OK in my book. A-OK."

I should have pulled my ear away but I listened from sheer outrage.

"You know what, pumpkin? You've got great pectorals."

Suddenly I was back in Amarillo, and standing behind that wall in the next lavatory was Henry, my premed boyfriend with the Braille approach to necking. Two years of escape and this is how I ended up. I almost started to cry.

Shackwood laughed a deep, dirty laugh.

"Tits. Boobs. You've got great ones."

I opened the door and stepped out into the aisle. So did he. I tried to walk past him but he managed to say "Meet me in the one you just left in twenty minutes. A little quickie, huh?" He sat down with an air of conquest.

I debated whether to tell the captain. It hardly seemed worth the trouble. I was a veteran stewardess, not a green kid fresh out of school. I could handle an overbearing nut like Shackwood myself.

People were just finishing their molded kumquat dessert with whipped cream and almonds, the bad guy was about to run an ice pick through the head of the good guy, and Shackwood was dozing off when it happened.

POP! EEEEEAAAAAAAH!!! ZIP! ZIP! ZAP! S-T-T-T-T-T

Everyone leaped out of his seat at once. The dissonant, screeching sounds had rushed through all the earphones into everyone's inner ear. Passengers frantically tore the phones from their heads. The picture went black. And smoke started seeping from the entertainment control panel at the front of the aircraft.

Everyone started yelling at us at once.

"Something's wrong with the sound, miss."

"I was listening to a beautiful thing by Ravel when it happened. Terrible. Simply terrible."

"Man, they was just gettin' inta somethin' when everything like went to a minor chord."

"Boooooooooo," someone yelled from the couch section.

Rachel did a quick PA as I went forward to inform the captain of the problem. The flight engineer came back and opened the control panel. He touched a wire and sparks started flying.

"Goddamn it," he drawled, "I always said movies don't have any place on an airplane." He pulled a couple of wires loose and the smoke stopped.

"That's all I can do 'til we arrive. Better tell 'em they'll have to go to their local theater to see the end of the movie."

Rachel apologized on the PA and I started up the aisle to flash a stewardess smile at the disgruntled folks. I hadn't taken three steps when what never happens, happened. All together, in unison, all the oxygen masks dropped from their storage compartments above each seat. Down they came, orange face masks on white plastic tethers. They bobbed up and down in everyone's face. Most of the faces turned white. No one listens when the stewardess goes through the oxygen mask procedure prior to each flight. It's silly to worry about that. You'll never need them.

People started grabbing masks. Some, aware of the stated procedure, clamped them to their faces and started breathing quickly into them. Some yanked them right out of the ceiling slots. Five or six stood up, masks in hand, and yelled at Rachel and me for help. We showed them what to do. Then we grabbed our masks and started breathing.

It took us a few minutes before we began wondering why one of the cockpit crew hadn't come back to check on things. It was also strange we hadn't begun descending to a lower altitude. We continued to sit there breathing into the masks. Finally, the cockpit door opened and the first officer stepped into the passenger cabin. He looked around at the emergency scene, looked at us, and looked back again at the passengers.

"What the hell's going on here?" he asked Rachel.

She gingerly took the mask from her face and told him about the emergency situation in the cabin. "The masks dropped and that means cabin pressure has changed. You know that . . . sir."

"There's nothing wrong with the pressure in this plane."

"So why'd the masks drop . . . sir?"

"How do I know? Tell these people to get those damn masks off their faces. There's nothing wrong."

"Yes, sir."

We did a PA in which we said the problem had been corrected and that all was well. A few didn't believe us and kept on breathing into their masks. We almost had to pry the mask away from the woman who loved Ravel.

We walked up the aisle checking each passenger. No one seemed any worse for the experience, except Mr. Shackwood. Unfortunately, I'd forgotten about him and made the mistake of checking his side of the cabin.

He was sitting limply in his seat, his collar open, face white and wet. He rolled his eyes up at me and groaned.

"Are we going to die?" he asked weakly.

I couldn't resist it. "Yup."

His eyes really rolled now, and his lips quivered.

"Miss," he pleaded.

"Yes?"

"I'm sorry."

"For what?"

"For saying those things to you."

"You should be."

"If there was a priest here, I'd tell him that, too."

"I didn't know you were a religious man, Mr. Shackwood."

"Oh, yes. Eight kids, too. Forgive me."

"You're forgiven. Go in peace."

He looked relieved.

After much cockpit speculation about what had caused the masks to pop, it was decided that the short circuit in the entertainment system had also shorted out another circuit that controlled the masks.

"Do you know that more people are killed riding bicycles every year than on commercial airplanes, Trudy?" Rachel asked as we cleaned up the galley.

"I've been told."

"And that more people are killed at railroad crossings, too?"

"Those statistics must have come out before in-flight entertainment. I have the feeling this multimillion-dollar bird is about to fall out from under us."

"Let's not worry about it, Trudy. You're just generally jumpy anyway. You've been like a caged cat the past few weeks."

I tried not to worry anymore. I didn't have long not to worry because we had another mishap in five minutes. This time it was nothing as complicated as short circuits in the movies. It wasn't even as dramatic as the oxygen masks dropping by mistake. All it involved was Number Three engine quitting. You couldn't even see it, an obvious advantage a jet has over the easily observed prop engine. We didn't know it until our captain told us.

"Number Three quit," he said flatly.

"Figures," I mumbled.

"Huh?"

"I said it's good we have three more."

"Let's hope they don't quit."

"Could they?"

"Never know."

I smiled. "Two years is too long."

"What, Trudy?" The captain was in no mood for games.

"I said two years is too long. To be a stew. Don't you agree?"

"Oh, sure. Too long."

"That's what I said."

No one in the passenger cabin knew anything else had happened to the jet. And we weren't about to tell them, even though regulations state that passengers should be alerted to any malfunction that might possibly cause injury, no matter how remote the possibility. The loss of one engine was in no way a major threat to anyone's safety. But, if we went by the book, we'd tell them. We decided the book was for reading, not necessarily aloud. We skipped any announcement.

We started our letdown for the San Francisco approach when the cockpit signaled we were wanted up front.

"Small problem, girls."

My heart came up in my throat and stuck there. I swallowed it back down to where it belonged and listened as the captain explained the next foul-up in an already less-than-perfect trip.

"That little light says the gear won't go down. Doesn't mean it won't. But then again, you hate to turn your back on that little light. If it's right, no wheels. If it's wrong, wheels. That simple. Just like they told you in school." He laughed.

"We didn't tell them about the engine. We'd better tell them about this. What's procedure?"

"The usual. Crash position for everybody. Make sure they realize it might be just a foul-up in the bulb. But maybe not. You two have been around enough time. You know what to say."

"Two years."

"Oh yeh. I remember. Happy anniversary."

Rachel did the PA. I gave no sign of fear, although my heart was galloping. Shackwood flailed his arms around in the air for me to come.

"What's it feel like?" he asked with trembling lips.

"What's what feel like?"

"When you hit. You know, when you . . . hit. What's it like?"

"I haven't any idea. Don't worry. You'll be OK." I'd forgiven him. You can't bear a grudge in a plane with one engine out and maybe no landing gear.

A pass over the airport showed the wheels down in proper position. But that was no assurance they were locked in place. We dumped all excess fuel, had all passengers take the emergency position of head down between the knees, pillow on lap, eyeglasses off, high heels under seats, and seat belts securely fastened. We braced ourselves along with them as the big jet settled down onto the concrete ribbon at San Francisco. The wheels touched the ground, lost contact for a moment, touched again, and stayed there, firmly and securely locked under everyone.

I had just gotten out my deep sigh of very sincere relief when the captain's voice came over the PA. He had applied reverse thrust on the engines, the three of them that were functioning, and the plane was slowing down for the turnoff onto a taxi strip.

"Ah, ladies and gentlemen, a light in the flight deck indicates a fire condition somewhere on the aircraft. Please make ready for emergency evacuation through the emergency exits as marked. Please wait for your stewardesses to lead the way on the inflated chutes. This is purely a precaution in case fire is present."

Click. Off went his voice and a few shrieks came from the cabin. Rachel grabbed my arm and we blew out the emergency exits and popped the long, limp emergency chutes that dangled from the doorways to the concrete below. Fire vehicles were racing across the field, their sirens screaming loudly.

The chutes were supposed to inflate, providing a smooth trough for each passenger to slide down to the safety of the ground. But these chutes are famous for not fully inflating. Ours were no exception. They stiffened up halfway and quit.

Rachel helped the first passenger out the door, and we watched her bounce down, make it almost to the ground, and then roll off the edge. She landed with a resounding thud on the concrete. Rachel, realizing she should be down there to help clear the bottom, went next. She landed hard on her rear end, her skirt sliding up around her hips.

One little kid enjoyed the ride down. The Ravel lover refused at first. Then, after I insisted, she made the plunge. She went off the side almost immediately and landed on her shoulder, obviously hurt. Two ambulance attendants worked over her.

The cabin emptied out fast. Finally, only two people remained: Shackwood and me.

"No, no. After you." He'd suddenly gained some sense of courage and valor.

"*Now*, Mr. Shackwood."

"You first."

"Please, Mr. Shackwood. Quickly."

I wasn't about to argue with him. I grabbed the edges of the door and slid myself onto the chute. I no sooner touched the chute than I felt Shackwood jump on behind me, his legs hugging around my hips, his hands securely fastened on my chest.

"Wheeeee," he screamed as we slid down. We both went off the edge. Shackwood landed on top of me, his hands still holding onto my breasts as though they were handles.

I ached all over, but managed to scramble out from under his dead weight. "You . . . you . . . you dirty, filthy sex fiend," I screamed at him. Then I swung and my fist caught his jaw. It sent him back two or three steps.

Rachel grabbed me from behind and pulled me away. Shackwood started screaming to anyone who would listen about how he'd have me fired. I tried to go after him again but Rachel hung on tight. I finally just broke down and cried.

There had been no fire in the aircraft. It was just another one of those lousy little lights that decided to light up at the wrong time. Shackwood's complaint against me was dismissed after Rachel told my supervisor about his actions on board. Even with her testimony, the airline was a little reluctant to take the word of a stewardess over that of a paying customer, especially a religious family man with eight potential travelers for the future.

I was pretty well bruised, but nothing serious. I rubbed my

aches and pains for a week while on sick leave, and soon the black, blue, and purple spots disappeared. But the depression didn't.

Rachel tried everything, we dated every good-looking fellow we could entice. We partied, drank, told funny stories, saw funny movies, and kept every minute filled with some sort of gay activity. But it really wasn't very effective.

I told my supervisor about my feelings, and she appeared sympathetic—to a point.

"You know, Trudy, we can't have an unhappy, unsmiling stewardess serving our valued travelers, can we?"

That seemed logical.

"One must always remember, Trudy, that one paying to travel our airline expects the finest and most pleasant service from our girls."

"Yes."

"But one also knows that occasionally one becomes upset over certain situations."

"Yes."

"You've contributed two valuable years to service, Trudy. We recognize that. Now it's up to you. We can't have you flying the line in the frame of mind you obviously have developed recently. One can understand that, can't one?"

"Yes." Who was this One she kept talking about?

"I'd like to suggest a course of action, Trudy, that might prove valuable to you . . . and the airline. We can recommend a good psychiatrist who might help you become once again the happy, smiling stewardess you were. How do you feel about that?"

"Yes. I mean fine. Why not? One must do these things at times, mustn't one?"

"Guess what, Rachel?" I said with more enthusiasm than I'd been able to summon for weeks.

"Shackwood apologized, he's divorcing his wife, and you're marrying him."

"Right."

"Which goes to prove that one out of two girls will accept a marriage proposal from a perfect stranger."

"I'm going to a psychiatrist, Rachel."

"Why?"

"Our super thinks I should. And maybe she's right. Anyway, I kind of think it's that or stop flying. And I really don't want to quit."

"What doc are you going to?"

"She gave me a name. I think he's an old guy from Vienna with a beard."

"Take notes and tell me what he says," Rachel said "And I'll split the bill with you. That way he can shrink two heads for the price of one."

Remember, I told you way back at the beginning that we only had one head between us?

# CHAPTER XXIII

# "We'll Give It One More Year, Okay?"

$\mathcal{I}$t turned out the psychiatrist was a *young* man from Vienna with a beard.

"Take the chair by the window, Trudy. You'll be more comfortable." The doctor tactfully waved me away from the couch, a heavily tufted black leather monster that looked slippery and uninviting. He seated himself behind his desk and shuffled papers for a few minutes. I noticed he wasn't wearing a wedding ring, and my keen stewardess eyes could detect no pale, fleshy ring of a band hastily removed. An unmarried, I thought, and a doctor to boot. Unusual—very unusual.

"Now, Trudy, let's talk a bit. Let's see if we can't find out a few things about Trudy Baker."

"What's to find out? I feel rotten. Totally rotten."

"Totally?"

"Yes."

"Physically?"

"Headaches."

"That's all physically?"

"Yes."

He smiled and stroked his beard. "But I'm not a headache doctor, Trudy. You know that."

"But if my headache is psychosomatic, and I'm internalizing and reverting back to mother problems, my headache would certainly fall into your area of specialization. Wouldn't it?"

He sat up straight. I noticed for the first time a nervous tic in his left eye. If I didn't know better, I'd have thought he was winking at me.

He got up from behind his desk and walked to a table on the far side of the room. He poured a drink of water from a silver and teak executive pitcher and drank slowly.

"Could I have a drink, doctor?"

It startled him. "Oh, of course, Miss Baker." He couldn't find another glass and had to ring for his nurse. She brought one.

He sat down again behind the desk, his eye going at thirty winks a minute.

"Do you think you *do* have a mother problem, Trudy? Do you think you *are* internalizing?"

"How should I know? I just read a little before I came here. How should I know what's the matter with me? I just know I'm not the same Trudy everyone knows. I'm depressed and blue and itchy and jumpy. Thinking of climbing on another airplane gives me the creeps. And I want to keep on working as a stewardess."

He stroked his beard and said, "hmmmmummmm."

I felt a surge of vocal energy.

"You see, doctor, you fly long enough and you meet so many different people that sometimes you lose faith in the human race. Rachel says . . ."

"Who's Rachel?"

"Oh, she's my very best friend. We're very close."

"Hmmmmmmmmmmm."

"Why do you say hmmmmmmmmmmm, doctor?"

"Just how close are you and Rachel?"

"You couldn't get any closer."

"Hmmmmmmmmm. Has there ever been any intimacy between you?"

"Oh sure. We share the closest secrets. Why . . ." It dawned on me what he was getting at.

"Absolutely not, doctor. Rachel and I are normal, heterosexual young ladies."

He almost seemed disappointed. There was a long period of silence.

"Doctor, do you mind if I take notes?"

"Take notes? Why?"

"Oh, just for the fun of it."

"Well, I've never had this occur before with any patient. Do you always take notes?"

"I've never been to a headshrink . . . Ah, psychiatrist before."

He seemed to be searching back into his textbook past for a proper answer. His eye went faster.

"If taking notes will make you feel better, please feel free to take notes."

"Thank you." I pulled out a steno pad and pencil and sat poised in the chair. Neither of us spoke. The doctor kept his eyes on the desktop. I looked straight at him. He swiveled around in his chair and coughed and winked and cleared his throat.

"Now, Miss Baker, suppose we begin."

"OK."

Silence.

"Ah, let's see doctor. I was born in a small town and had a boyfriend named Henry."

"Henry, huh? Did you have a normal sexual relationship with this young man?"

"Well, we always did things in Braille."

"What?"

"Braille. He liked to touch me."

"I see. And you didn't like to be touched."

"Oh, no. I loved it. Especially my popliteal."

"What's that?"

I giggled. "I thought all psychiatrists had to become medical doctors before psychiatrists."

I think he got mad. He snorted.

"That's the back of the knee, doctor." I took note in my steno pad of his facial reaction. He didn't like being exposed as not knowing something.

"What did you just write there, Miss Baker?" he asked angrily.

"I wrote you got mad because I knew something you didn't know."

"I wasn't mad," he said with a mad voice. "You can't expect me to remember every term from medical school."

"Henry went to medical school. He's still going."

"Who's Henry?"

"My boyfriend. The one with the Braille."

"I think you're trying to make fun of me, Miss Baker."

I hadn't been really. And I felt sorry for the doctor feeling that way.

"Oh, don't feel that way, doctor. I wouldn't make fun of you. Honest."

He seemed slightly relieved.

"You have to realize, Miss Baker, that being a doctor on a retainer fee from a company places certain strains on that doctor. Most of my income is derived from the airline and I'd hate to think of you going back and making fun of me. It could cost me this job." He was sorry he'd said this. But I looked very understanding and tried to comfort him.

"Oh, doctor, I understand fully. It's very hard feeling secure these days in any company. I know." I took a few notes in my pad.

"What are you writing now?"

"That you're a nice guy."

"Oh, that's nice. Thank you."

"I guess being single is a problem for you, too." I couldn't help it. It just came out.

"Yes, a little bit . . . You see . . . Now wait a minute. We're getting off the track here."

"I sure don't want to do that."

"Good." Forty winks a minute now. "Let's talk about your recent experiences on the airplane that left you shaken."

I told him about Mr. Lippingdone and Mr. Shackwood. I told him about the drunks and pinchers and kids and captains. He said nothing. He just looked at his desktop and went "hmmmmm" a few times. I talked until I heard the tiny tinkle of an alarm bell ring from his desk drawer. It startled him more than it did me. He sat up straight and turned on a very large smile for me.

"I think we're getting somewhere now, Miss Baker. Or may I call you Trudy?"

"By all means."

"That ends our first hour together. See my secretary on the way out for an appointment next week."

I got up, stuffed my steno pad back in my purse, and walked to the door. He stopped me by saying, "This is just the beginning, Trudy. We have a long way to go. A long way. Perhaps in a few months I'll be able to recommend to the airline that you go back on the flying line. Of course, we'll continue to work together for at least a year. Maybe longer."

"Oh that'll be nice, doctor. And don't worry about a thing. I won't say anything that might upset the airline about you. In fact, I really like you."

He beamed. "That's good, Trudy. It's important for the patient to like his or her psychiatrist."

"In fact," I continued, "I know a great girl for you. Would you like me to fix you up?"

"O no, Oh, no, no, no, no, no. I'll just see you next week."

I nodded my head and left. I didn't make an appointment with the secretary. I just walked straight home, singing, happy, and gay for the first time in weeks. Rachel was at the apartment when I arrived.

"How was it?" she asked, never looking up from her copy of *The High and the Mighty*. (It was her tenth reading of it.)

"Great. He has problems. That's for sure. I think it might have something to do with his father never having taken him fishing. Or something like that."

"Idiot. He was supposed to help *you*. And me!"

"Who needs help? I feel the same as I always did . . ."

"Wow. This doc must be the best. What did he feed you? LSD?"

"He didn't feed me anything. I just feel better knowing someone else has more problems than I do. The blues have gone to someone else and I'm squared away."

"That's great, Trudy," Rachel said with much enthusiasm in her voice. "Great!"

I smiled.

"We'll give it one more year, OK? Then we'll both have found our respective knights on the white horses and we can move into houses next door to each other and write a book about it all over coffee."

"It's a deal, Rachel. One more year . . . By the way, do you think Betty Big Boobs would be interested in a young psychiatrist with a beard?"

We laughed.

We shook hands.

And had a mushroom pizza with extra cheese.

internal control region. On prolonged proteolysis the 30 kDa domain breaks down further generating metastable intermediates differing in size by a regular decrement of about 3 kDa. This result indicates that the 30 kDa domain itself is comprised of a set of periodically arranged smaller domains (Figure 3.7). A further crucial observation was the realization that each TFIIIA molecule contained 7–11 atoms of zinc, suggesting that each of these small domains might be stabilized by a single zinc atom. Analysis of the protein sequence showed that the amino-terminal three-quarters of the protein contained nine repeating units of structure, each of which was contained by the sequence ....C----C----------H---H.... In this structure, two closely spaced cysteine residues are separated by an average of 13 amino acids from two closely spaced histidine residues. The spacing of the cysteine and histidine residues in each repeating unit would allow a single zinc atom to co-ordinate with these four residues and so stabilize a 'finger' structure (Figure 3.8). Observed structural variations include the number of amino acids separating the co-ordinating cysteines and histidines and also the number of amino acids separating adjacent finger domains. Not only may the type of finger, but also the number of fingers, vary. Some proteins, such as the *Drosophila* 'tramtrack' protein, contain only two fingers while, at the other end of the scale, the Xfir protein from *Xenopus* contains 37 fingers.

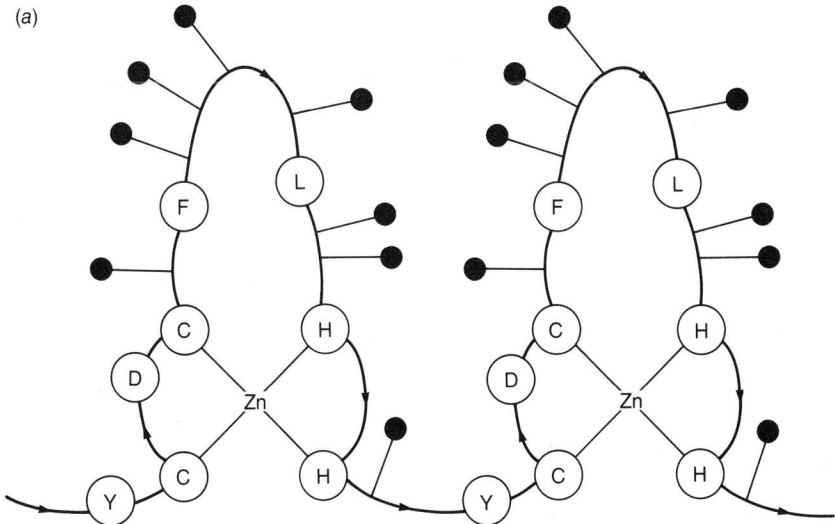

**Figure 3.8** (a) Positions of conserved residues in zinc fingers of the C–C....H–H type. The folding is centred on a tetrahedral arrangement of zinc ligands. The hydrophobic residues (Y, F, L) responsible for stabilizing the secondary structure are shown.

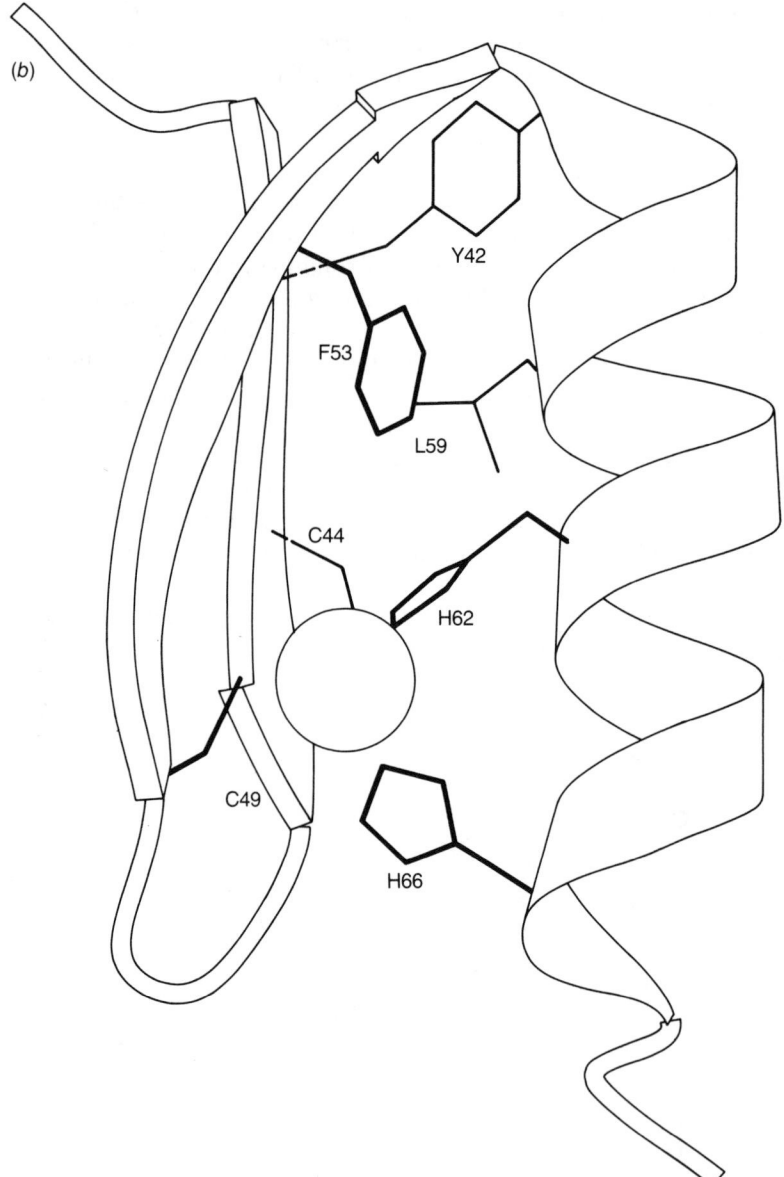

**Figure 3.8 (b)** The structure of finger 2 from the yeast SWI5 protein as determined by NMR.

The concept of the zinc finger as an independent protein domain has been established by the experimental demonstration that zinc is necessary for the correct folding of both classes of finger and that this correct folding is necessary for sequence specific recognition. The identity of the ligands in the folded structure has been confirmed by EXAFS measurements while the three-dimensional structure of a single TFIIIA type finger has been determined by nuclear magnetic resonance spectroscopy. In this structure (Figure 3.8) the polypeptide backbone fold consists of a well defined α-helix packed against two β-strands arranged in a hairpin structure. The length of the α-helix is dependent on the number of amino acids between the two histidines co-ordinated to the zinc atom. A three amino acid separation can accommodate this configuration whereas four and five amino acids cannot. (For some fingers an additional β-strand precedes this hairpin loop, creating a triple stranded structure. In examples of this type the third strand is necessary to stabilize the structure of the finger as a whole.) On the exposed face of the helix there is a high density of basic and polar amino acid side chains which are potentially involved in DNA binding. The finger structure is stabilized by both the tetrahedral co-ordination of zinc and by a hydrophobic pocket in the interior of the structure involving amino acids that are well conserved. Although the finger structure acts as an independent domain the linker sequences separating adjacent fingers also show conservation. These linkers between the last histidine of the proximal finger and the first cysteine of the distal finger are normally 7–8 amino acids long and in many examples contain the sequence TGEK-Y. Nevertheless, there is sufficient variation to suggest that the path followed by different linkers may vary substantially.

Since the identification of the zinc finger motif in TFIIIA many proteins containing this motif or related motifs stabilized by co-ordination with zinc ions have been characterized. These proteins contain three principal classes of domains which differ in the nature of the zinc ligands. In the TFIIIA type of finger, zinc is co-ordinated by two cysteines and two histidines, whereas in a second class, exemplified by the steroid receptors, cysteine residues are found in the position of the conserved histidine residues. In these latter structures the zinc is bound by four cysteine residues (Figure 3.9) but the path of the polypeptide backbone between the proximal and distal pairs of co-ordinating cysteines is distinct from that of the TFIIIA type of finger. A third class of zinc-containing recognition motif occurs in many yeast transcription factors and is exemplified by the GAL4 DNA-binding domain. This class of motif contains two zinc ions which are tetrahedrally co-ordinated by six cysteine residues, two of which ligate both metals (Figure 3.10).

The structures of the different classes of zinc finger also differ substantially in other details. In both the C–C....H–H and C–C....C–C classes the proximal cysteine residues reside in the β-sheet structures. By contrast, although the histidine residues involved in zinc co-ordination are often contained within the α-helix the corresponding distal cysteines are not. This difference is directly related to DNA binding. The DNA binding domains of the glucocorticoid and oestrogen receptors contain

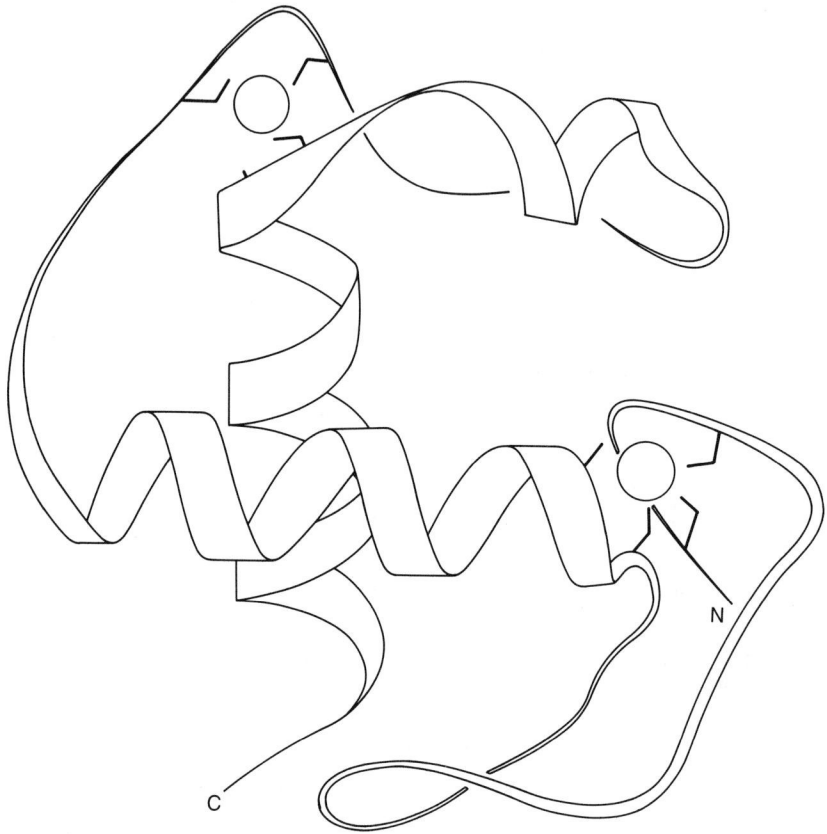

**Figure 3.9** The structure of the DNA-binding domain of the oestrogen receptor as determined by NMR. The zinc atoms are represented by small spheres.

two C–C....C–C co-ordination domains, the first of which is of similar extent to the TFIIIA fingers while the second is significantly shorter. Unlike the TFIIIA fingers both pairs of distal cysteines are immediately followed by an α-helical region. The second α-helix forms direct hydrophobic contacts with the first so that the two fingers and the two α-helices together form a single structural domain, the 'double-loop-zinc-helix'. This domain also includes a region that specifies the dimerization contacts. In the third type of zinc-containing DNA binding domain, typified by the GAL4 protein, the zinc stabilized structure is connected by a flexible region of polypeptide chain to a short amphipathic α-helix which forms hydrophobic contacts with another monomer in dimer formation.

The zinc finger is a structural protein domain that can be utilized for nucleic acid binding. However, it does not follow that all zinc stabilized

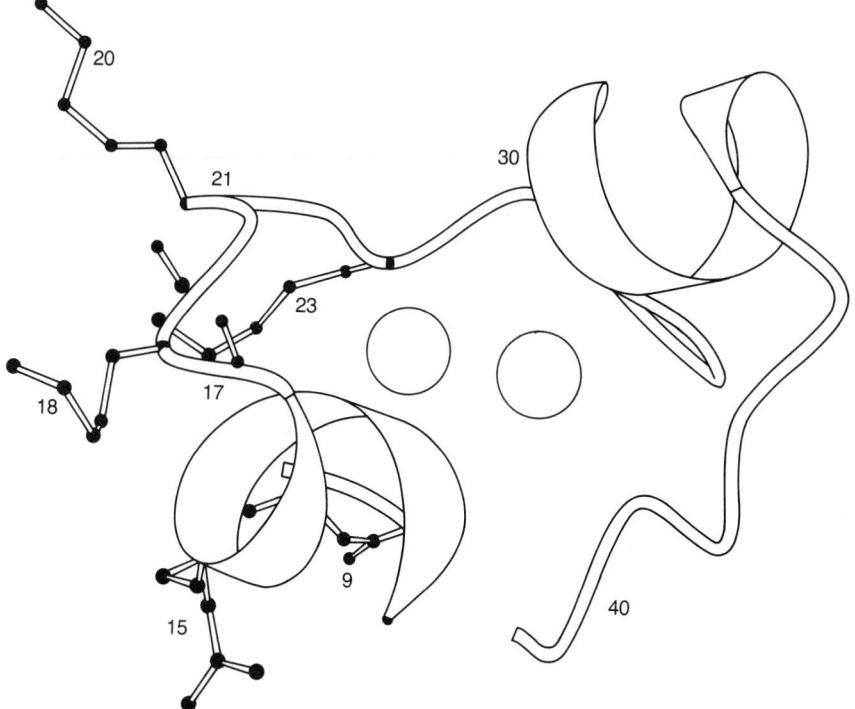

**Figure 3.10** The DNA-binding domain of the yeast GAL4 protein. Note the two adjacent zinc atoms, shown as spheres.

domains function in this way. For example, the T4 bacteriophage gene 32 protein, which binds co-operatively to single-stranded DNA, contains the sequence $C-X_2-C-X_7-\Psi-X_5-C-X_2-C$. This protein binds zinc but the metal ion is not required for interaction with DNA. Instead it affects the stability of the protein and enhances the co-operativity of binding to single stranded DNA by over a hundred-fold. In this case it has been inferred that the 'finger' structure is involved in protein–protein interactions.

*The interaction of zinc fingers with DNA*

The nine small domains of TFIIIA interact with 50 bp of the 5S RNA gene so that each domain of the protein could, on average, bind to about 5 bp of DNA. Indeed the repetitive character of the TFIIIA protein is also reflected in its binding site. Within this region the DNA exhibits a structural periodicity in which the sequence GG is repeated, on average, once every 5.5 bp. The DNA binding sites for other zinc finger proteins, notably the transcription factor Sp1, show a similar periodicity. More generally, the sequences in the binding sites for zinc finger proteins are asymmetrical.

What are the detailed interactions of a zinc finger with its DNA recognition site? All footprinting studies show that the principal base specific contacts made by the zinc finger domain itself lie in the major groove of DNA. Complementary experiments by finger-swop experiments (analogous to helix-swop experiments for the helix–loop–helix domain) show that each individual finger recognition unit spans three base pairs. For sequence specific recognition a minimum of two adjacent zinc fingers is usually required, so a crucial question arises of how adjacent fingers are oriented relative to each other along a DNA-binding site. One possibility is that successive fingers could track around the major groove with the linking region between fingers remaining contained within the groove (Figure 3.11). For one particular three-finger peptide, that contained within the Zif268 protein, a recent crystal structure shows that the three fingers adopt this configuration with each finger lying in the major groove. Each finger is positioned relative to its

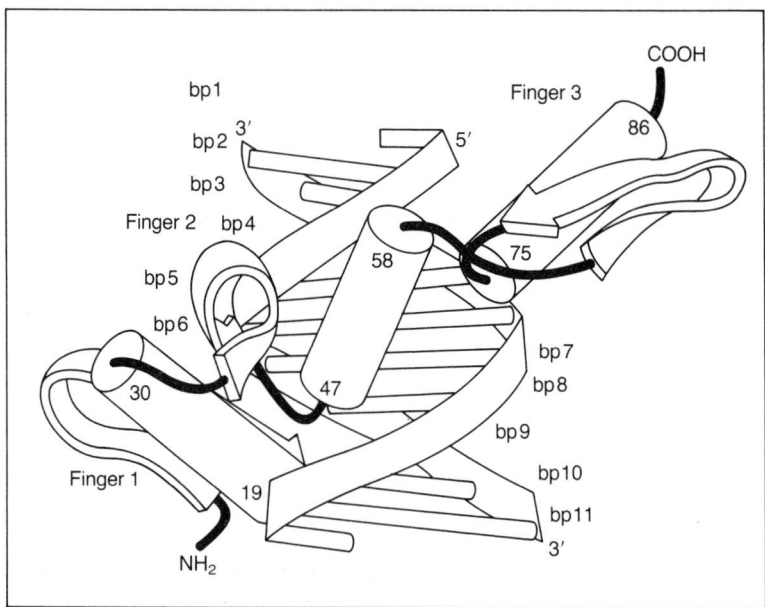

**Figure 3.11** (a) Sketch of the structure of the Zif268–DNA complex as determined by crystallography. Successive fingers lie in the major groove.

neighbour so that one could be superimposed on the other by a screw-like motion involving a rotation of 96° and a translation of about 10 Å. The base specific contacts are made by the proximal end of the α-helical region which covers three base pairs. The sugar–phosphate backbone is contacted by one of the zinc co-ordinated histidine residues, an interaction which is assumed to orient the finger with respect to the bases. An unusual feature of this structure is that the three fingers contact almost entirely a single strand of the DNA duplex. The linkers between the fingers are set above the major groove and are not directly involved in DNA contacts. One consequence of this arrangement is that each zinc finger acts as a distinct modular unit for sequence recognition.

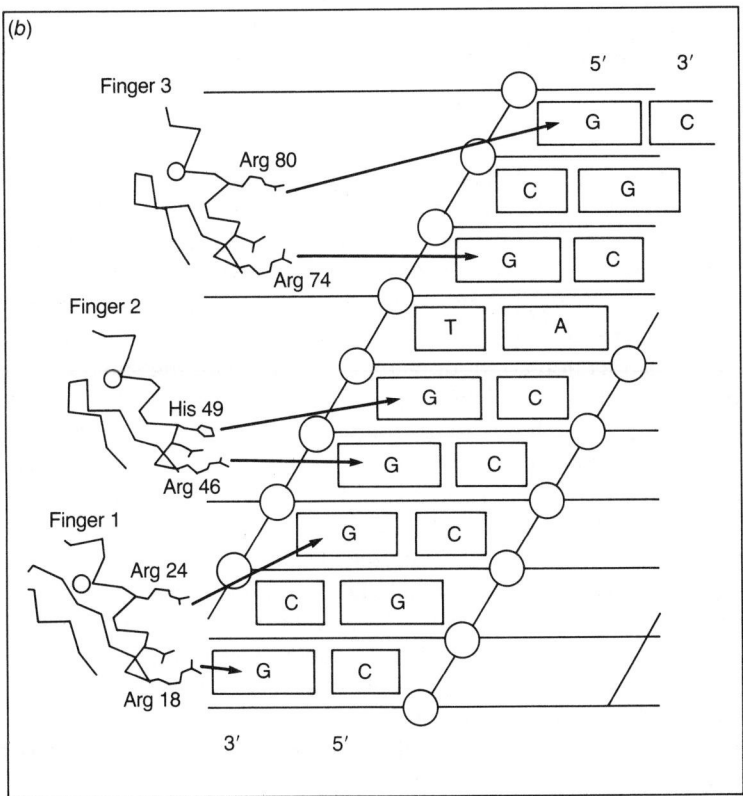

**Figure 3.11 (b)** Summary of the base contacts made by the Zif268 zinc finger domain. The DNA is represented in a cylindrical projection.

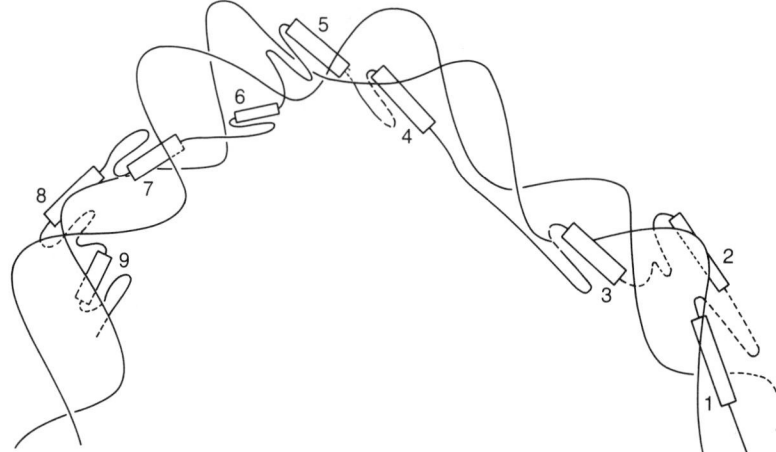

**Figure 3.12** A model for the binding of the TFIIIA protein to the internal control region. The nine fingers are arranged to contact short sequences modules within a 50 bp region.

However, given the differences in the linker sequences between fingers, it seems highly likely that the relative spatial disposition of adjacent fingers may differ in different proteins such that, for example, a linker sequence may cross a minor groove. For TFIIIA, although there is a periodicity in the recognition sequence, most evidence now suggests that the nine fingers are grouped in units of up to three fingers which recognize distinct non-contiguous regions of the binding site (Figure 3.12).

Although the binding of the Zif268 fingers to DNA is probably typical of all fingers of this class, other fingers can form additional contacts. Examples are provided by the N-terminal fingers of the yeast SWI5 and the *Drosophila* 'tramtrack' proteins. In both these cases, additional amino acids N-terminal to the normal boundary of the domain are required for binding. In these fingers the additional amino acids form a third β-strand, which is assumed to be the opposite DNA strand across the major groove from that contacted by the α-helical region of the finger (Figure 3.13).

As with the archetypal zinc finger, the recognition specificity for the other zinc-binding domains is largely confined to regions of the α-helix. For the DNA-binding domain found in steroid hormone receptors the determinants for sequence specific recognition lie within the α-helix immediately distal to the first cysteine tetrad (Figure 3.14). Mutation of three critical amino acids within this helix can effect an alteration of the binding specificity from that of the oestrogen to that of the progesterone receptor. However, the α-helix is not the sole determinant of specificity. For each receptor the DNA recognition domains bind as dimers to a palindromic sequence containing three conserved bases on each side. But

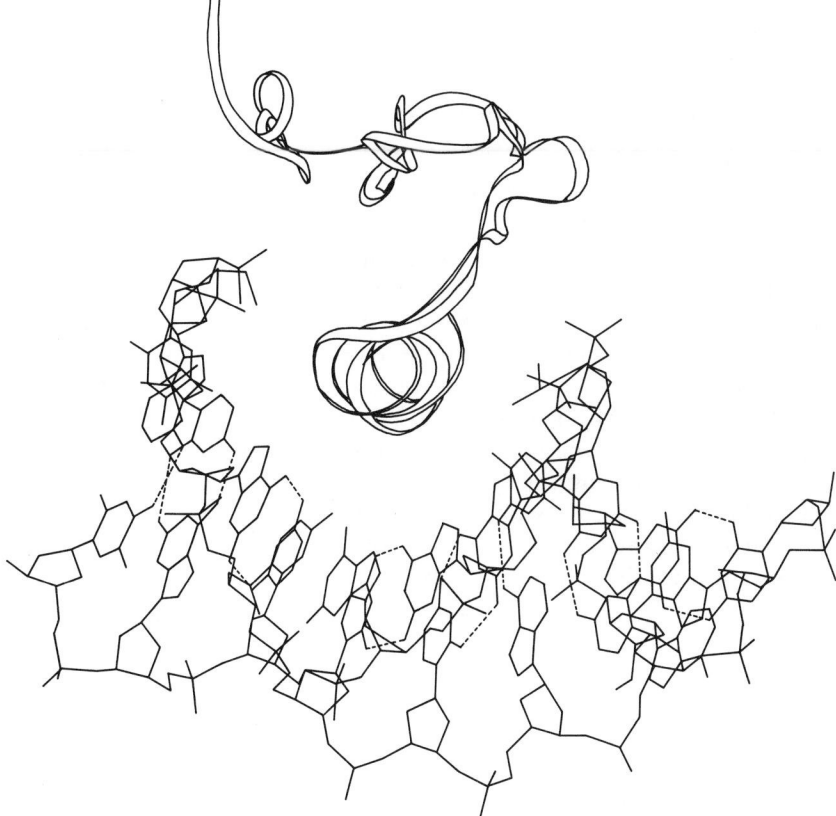

**Figure 3.13** A zinc finger with three antiparallel $\beta$-strands can make an additional contact with the sugar-phosphate backbone across the major groove.

the separation between the conserved trimers differs for different receptors. This means the rotational orientation of the individual components of the dimer must also be different and be determined by the position of the dimerization contacts relative to the $\alpha$-helix responsible for sequence recognition.

In GAL4, as with other zinc-containing motifs, direct contact with the bases is mediated in the major groove by amino acids contained within a short $\alpha$-helical region. However, most of the contacts to the sugar–phosphate backbone are effected by amino acids in the more extended chain (Figure 3.15). The GAL4 protein, like the steroid hormone receptors, binds to its DNA recognition site as a dimer with the two monomeric units being held together by a short-coiled coil of two parallel $\alpha$-helices. A feature of particular interest is that the arginine residues at the base of each of these $\alpha$-helices make contact with the sugar–phosphate backbone across the minor groove at the centre of the binding site and impose a narrowing upon it.

### 3.2.3 Other DNA-binding structures

The helix–turn–helix and zinc finger motifs are the best characterized DNA-binding domains that confer sequence specific binding. Several other structures clearly exist. The restriction enzyme *Eco*RI specifically binds to and cleaves the sequence d(GAATTC) in double stranded DNA. The protein is a dimer of 31 000 Da subunits which select the recognition site through amino acid side chains located at the end of a pair of parallel α-helices inserted into the major groove (Figure 3.16). This selectivity is achieved by the formation of specific hydrogen bonds between either arginine or glutamic acid residues and the DNA bases. A second important feature of the interaction is the distortion of the structure of the DNA in the binding site. At the central ApT base step the twist of the double helix is reduced by about 25°, that is, the DNA is unwound. The consequence of this unwinding is to rotate one half of the recognition site relative to the other and also to widen the major groove by

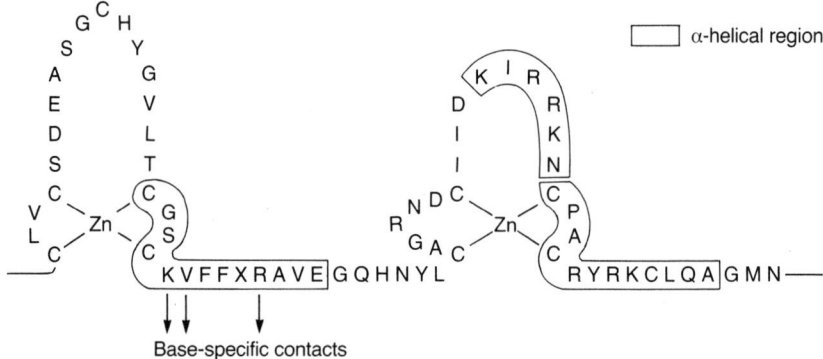

**Figure 3.14** Amino acids responsible for sequence specific recognition in the glucocorticoid receptor.

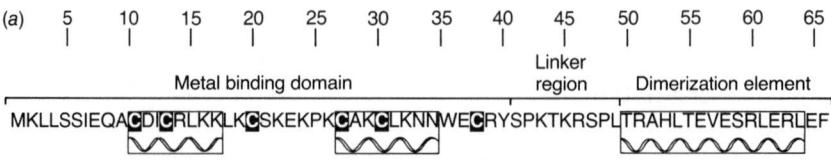

**Figure 3.15** (a) Sequence organization of the DNA-binding domain of the yeast GAL4 protein.

(b)

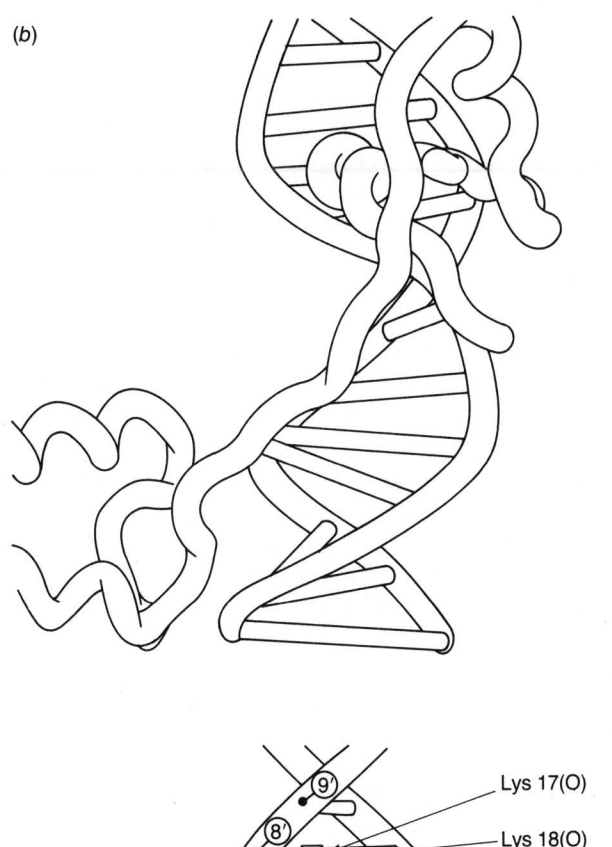

(c)

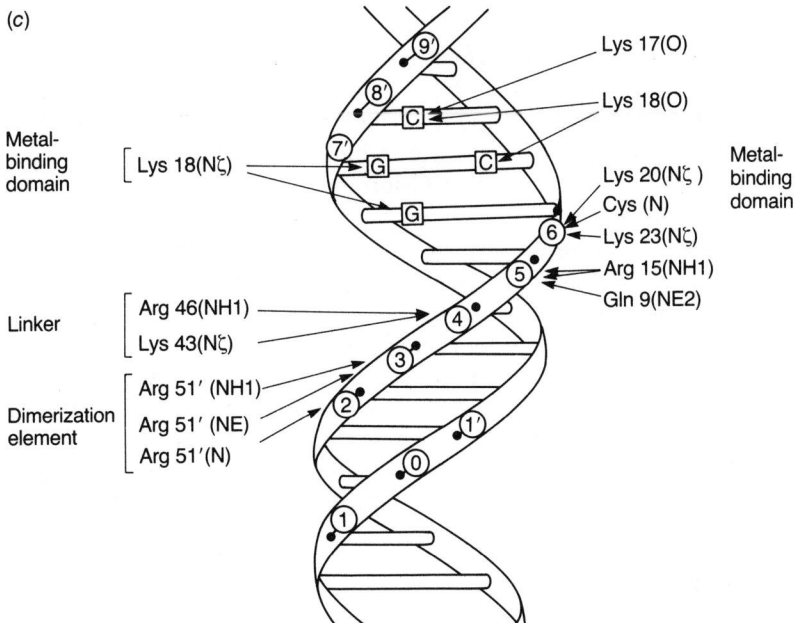

**Figure 3.15 (b)** Schematic diagram of the disposition of the GAL4 protein when bound to DNA. (c) Summary of the base contacts made by the GAL4 protein.

approximately 3.5 Å. These features allow the two recognition helices to fit into the groove and at the same time realign the base pairs to provide a surface for hydrogen bonding with the protein that is not present in the undistorted DNA. In addition to the unwinding the DNA is also bent by a roll into the minor groove at the extremities of the recognition site.

The *Eco*RI restriction enzyme utilizes α-helices for recognition in a different manner to the helix–turn–helix motif proteins. β-structures can however also be employed for this purpose. The *E. coli met* repressor (MetJ) represses transcription, both of its own gene and of those required for methionine and S-adenosyl methionine synthesis. This latter compound acts as a co-repressor, binding to repressor protein itself. The MetJ protein is a dimer of 12 000 molecular weight subunits whose polypeptide chains are highly intertwined with each other. The protein binds to a palindromic tetranucleotide sequence, the 'Met box', reminiscent of the *trp* operator. However, the mode of interaction with the binding site is completely different from that of the *trp* repressor. Instead of a helix–turn–helix motif a β-strand from each subunit is intertwined to form a two-stranded antiparallel β-sheet which fits into the major groove of DNA (Figure 3.17). Interestingly, many of the contacts with the sugar–phosphate backbone are made by amide groups in the peptide linkage. A similar structure of antiparallel β-strands has been proposed for sequence specific recognition by IHF, with the important distinction that, in this case, the structure fits into the minor rather than the major groove of DNA.

Another structural motif which has the capability of binding specific sequences by minor groove recognition is the HMG box. This motif consists of a conserved sequence of 80 amino acids which was first identified in certain abundant non-histone chromosomal proteins, HMG1 and HMG2 (HMG = High Mobility Group, so-called because of high electrophoretic mobility in starch gels) but which has subsequently been found in a large variety of eukaryotic transcription factors and proteins concerned with DNA replication. Although little is known about the structure of the recognition domain the motif can often occur in tandem in the same polypeptide chain and, in such cases, the protein has the capacity both to bend and wrap the bound DNA. A feature of particular interest is the preferred binding of the abundant HMG proteins to DNA structures which differ from the canonical double helix. Notably, HMG1 binds to cruciform structures as well as to bent doubled helices formed on reaction with *cis*-platinum.

### 3.2.4 Heterodimer formation

Many DNA binding proteins, especially those containing a helix–turn–helix motif, act as homodimers with two identical sequence

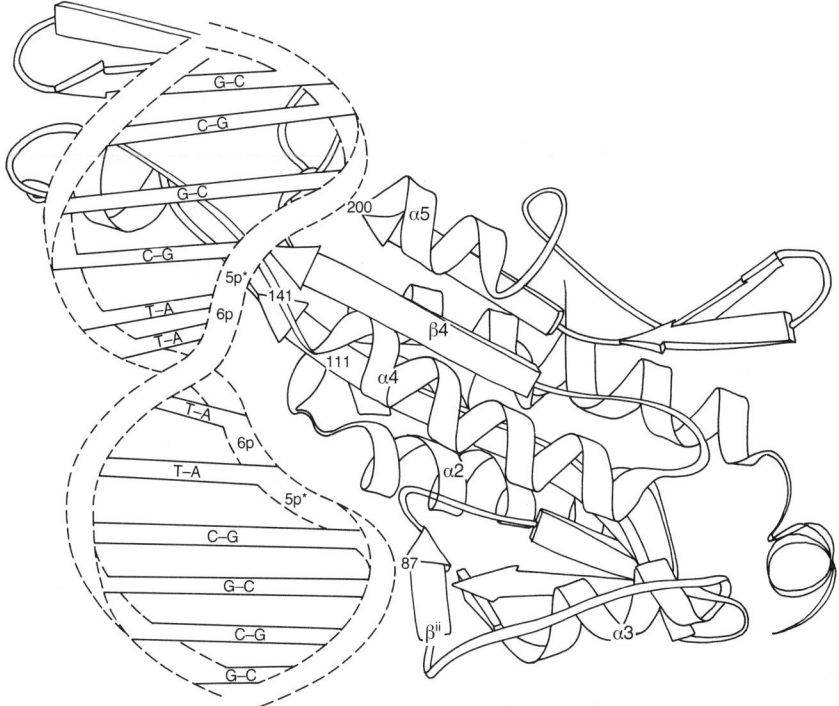

**Figure 3.16** Structure of the *Eco*R1 restriction endonuclease as determined by crystallography.

recognition domains. For such proteins the optimal DNA-binding site is of necessity palindromic. However, additional flexibility in sequence recognition can be conferred by the formation of heterodimers between similar proteins with different binding specificities. In eukaryotes, two classes of such proteins have so far been characterized. These are the 'leucine zipper' proteins and the 'helix–loop–helix' proteins. The essential feature of each of the monomer units of these proteins is that they contain an α-helical region containing leucine or similar side chains repeated in the primary sequence in an alternating pattern of three and four residues. This arrangement places these hydrophobic side chains on the same face of the helical surface in each helical turn (Figure 3.18). Such an α-helix has the potential to bind tightly by interactions between these hydrophobic residues to a similar α-helix in a parallel orientation, thereby allowing the formation of dimers between either identical or non-identical polypeptides. In these proteins the dimerization domain is, in general, in close proximity to a basic DNA-binding region. In these

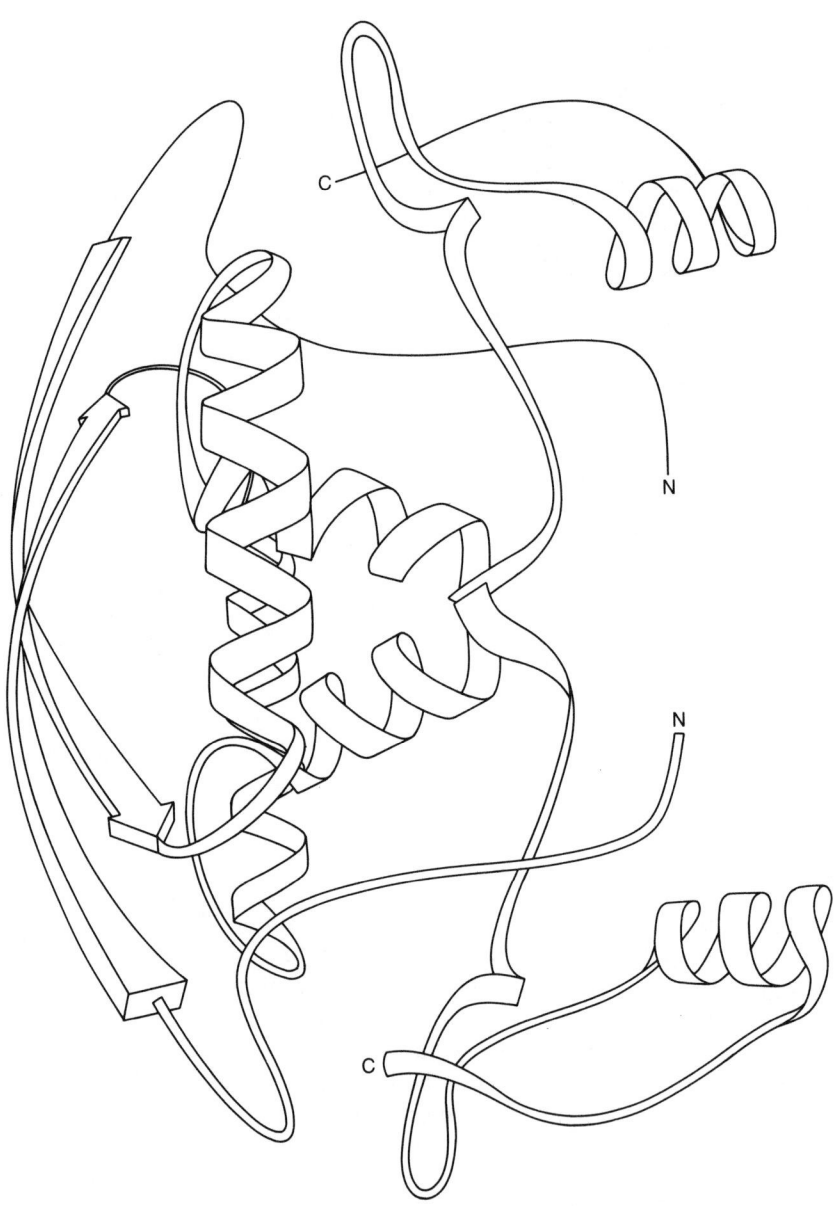

**Figure 3.17** The structure of the MetJ repressor dimer as determined by crystallography. The principal contacts to DNA are mediated by the β-strands at the left of the figure.

proteins the structure of this region is largely α-helical. Directly established and sequence specific recognition appears to be mediated by interactions in the major groove (Figure 3.19).

The leucine zipper on Bzip class of proteins is widely distributed. In yeast a homodimer of the GCN4 protein activates transcription of the *his3* gene. In mammalian cells recognition of a similar sequence is effected by a heterodimer of the Fos and Jun proteins, both of which are intimately involved in the regulation of the cell cycle. For these latter two proteins homodimer formation also occurs but the affinity for the binding site is much reduced. A similar principle is also apparent for the 'helix–loop–helix' proteins. In both *Drosophila* and in mammals this class of proteins includes regulators that are necessary for the development of a particular cell type. A good example are two proteins of this class, daughterless and scute, required for the development of the nervous system of the *Drosophila* larva. Daughterless protein is expressed in most cells of the embryo while the expression of scute is restricted to the presumptive neuroblasts. In the absence of either

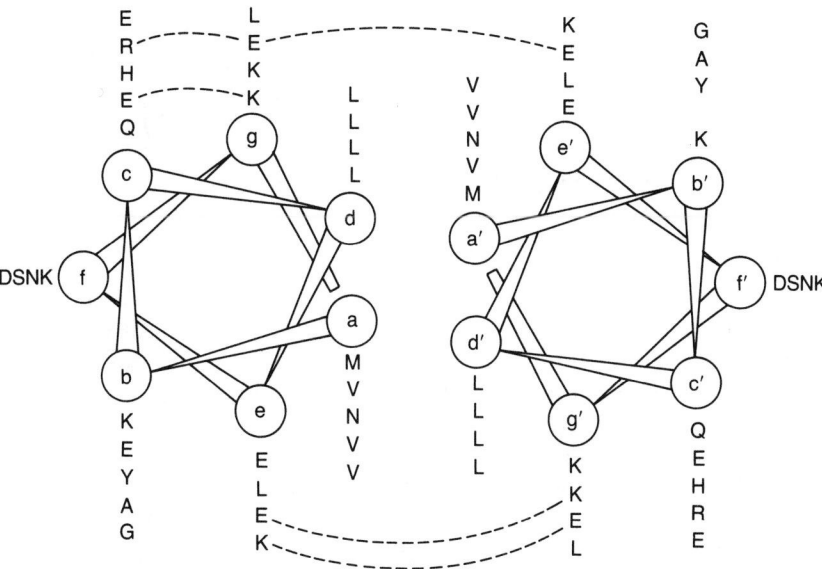

**Figure 3.18** Leucine 'zippers'. Dimerization between two parallel α-helices mediated by hydrophobic residues (predominantly leucine and valine) occurring every 3–4 amino acids apart.

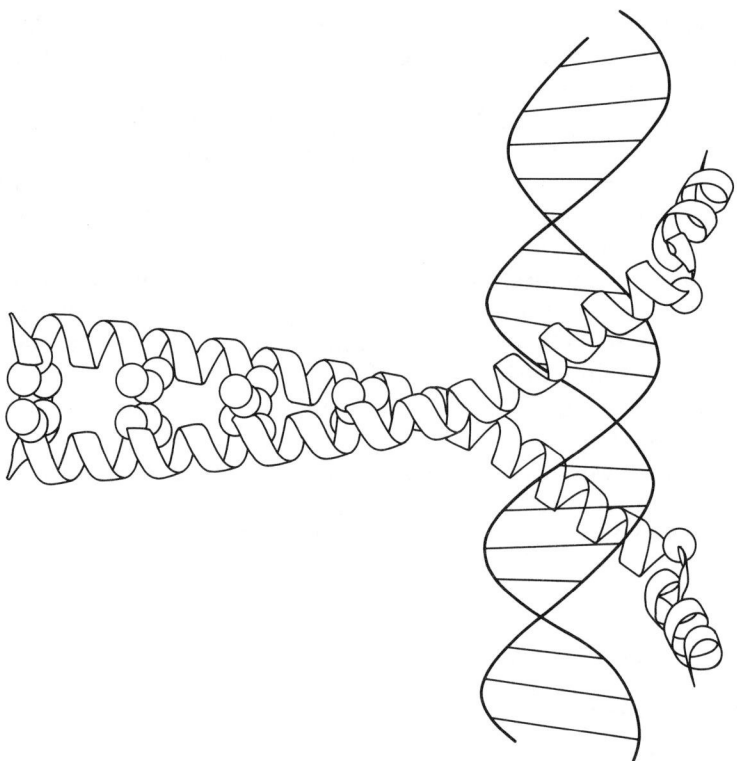

**Figure 3.19** The binding of a B-zip dimer to DNA.

protein the nervous system fails to develop properly. When mixed these two proteins form a heterodimer which binds tightly to sites within the regulatory regions of genes expressed in the nervous system. Homodimers are unable to do this efficiently. The specificity of binding is therefore conferred by heterodimer formation while the specificity of activation is conferred by the spatial localization of the scute proteins to the presumptive neuroblast cells. The daughterless protein thus appears to act as a general regulator which is only functional in conjunction with another protein. The eponymous phenotype of certain mutants of the daughterless gene indicates that the daughterless protein has a function in other tissues which is independent of scute.

### 3.3 CO-OPERATIVE BINDING TO DNA

The leucine zipper and helix–loop–helix heterodimers act as single DNA-binding entities; that is, heterodimer formation precedes DNA binding.

There are, however, many cases where the binding of proteins to contiguous sites on the DNA is enhanced by protein–protein interactions between the bound proteins. One effect of such interactions is to increase the affinity of both components for the DNA-binding sites and thus to extend the effective binding site for the protein–DNA complex.

Such co-operative interactions are exhibited by dimers of the λ $C_I$ repressor which have the potential to form tetrameric complexes via their C-terminal domains. The organization of the tripartite leftward and rightward operators of phage λ allows such interactions between dimers bound to two adjacent sites. However, once such co-operative binding has occurred, the binding of a repressor dimer to the third element of the operator site is then independent of the other repressor dimers. For the rightward operator the initial binding of the repressor occurs at $O_R1$. This interaction facilitates binding to $O_R2$, which is a slightly weaker site. Although $O_R2$ is weaker, initial occupancy will occur at a significant frequency at this site and will facilitate binding to $O_R1$, thereby increasing the probability of occupancy of both $O_R1$ and $O_R2$. By contrast, the affinity of a repressor dimer for an isolated $O_R3$ site is 25-fold less than that for $O_R1$, and consequently occupancy of $O_R3$ only occurs at high repressor concentrations in the wild type operator. If, however, the affinity of $O_R1$ for repressor is reduced by mutation, then co-operative interactions can take place between repressor molecules bound at $O_R2$ and $O_R3$.

Since the occupancy of adjacent binding sites by repressor dimers is dependent on an interaction between two protein molecules, the concentration dependence of occupancy is no longer hyperbolic, as it would be for independent binding, but instead is sigmoidal (Figure 3.20). An important consequence of this dependency is that occupancy increases rapidly over a small range of repressor concentration and attains a level of >99% at concentrations significantly lower than those required for the same level of independent binding. It is consequently a property of this system, and of other co-operative protein–DNA binding, that any modification of the protein–protein interactions required for co-operativity will result in a substantial change in occupancy. In the life cycle of phage λ the modification that occurs is the proteolytic cleavage by RecA protein of the $C_I$ repressor between the N-terminal and C-terminal domains on induction of the prophage. The result of this cleavage is that co-operative interaction between bound dimers can no longer occur and therefore the effective concentration of the repressor is reduced to a level at which the occupancy of both operator sites is very low. Repression is thus relieved and transcription can proceed from both $P_R$ and $P_L$. This mode of regulating co-operative interactions is peculiar to the biology of the phage. In principle such regulation could also be mediated by a reversible covalent modification, for example phosphorylation, or by an allosteric effector.

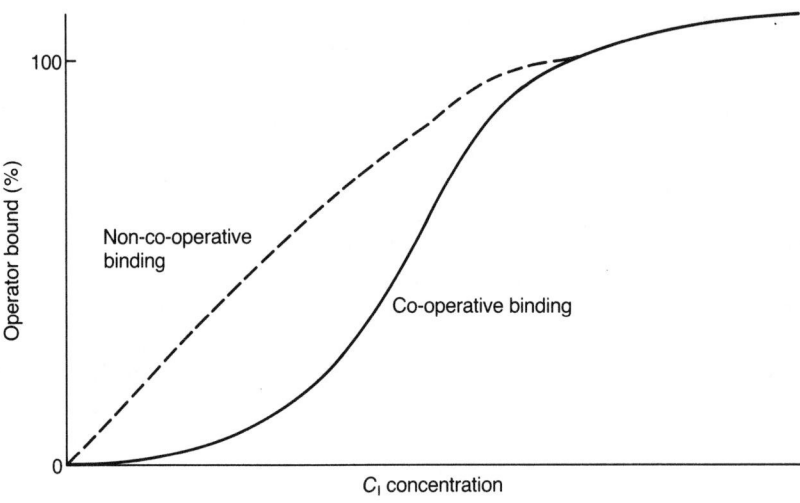

**Figure 3.20** The concentration dependence of co-operative versus non-co-operative binding of a protein to DNA. The specific example of the $\lambda$ $C_I$ protein is shown.

## 3.4 CO-OPERATIVITY AT A DISTANCE: DNA LOOPING

In principle, co-operative interactions between DNA-binding proteins are not restricted to proteins bound at contiguous binding sites. All that is required is that the local concentrations of the interacting protein molecules be sufficiently high, since the binding energies consequent on the protein–protein interactions themselves are relatively low. This can be achieved by tethering the second protein molecule to the DNA, either at an adjacent or at a distant site, or simply by increasing the concentration of the unbound protein. This latter method, although effective in artificial situations, has not been shown to be adopted in biological systems. There are, however, now many examples of long-range interactions between DNA-bound proteins. In such complexes, the intervening DNA is looped between the constituent proteins and the ability to form a loop is determined by the properties of the DNA domain. In general, the formation of looped complexes requires that the interacting proteins be in the correct angular orientation relative to each other. This means that, for loops of less than about 500 bp, the distance between double helical binding sites can only vary by integral multiples of double helical turns. This is because, in this range of DNA length, the torsional flexibility of DNA is insufficient to stabilize bending between two protein binding sites that are not in the appropriate angular register. This restriction, the so-called 'face-of-the-helix' effect, has been experimentally observed in several cases. The classic example of this effect is that required for the repression of the *E. coli ara*BAD operon. Transcription of this operon is controlled by the AraC protein. This protein binds to two operator sites, the I or induction site (formerly termed $O_1$), immediately adjacent to the promoter, and $O_2$, about 270 bp upstream of the startpoint. To maintain the repression of the operon in the absence of arabinose both the $O_2$ and I sites are necessary, while induction requires only an intact I site. A set of classic experiments is indicative of a direct interaction between $O_2$ and I. When the distance between I and $O_2$ is increased or decreased by multiples of $n + \frac{1}{2}$ helical turns, constitutive expression is observed, that is, the promoter behaves as if only the I element is present and that any interaction between I and $O_2$ has been abolished. However, when the distance is altered by an integral multiple of helical turns, repression is retained. This quantized effect is observed over a range of at least 300 bp and is fully consistent with the formation of a DNA loop between AraC molecules bound at I and $O_2$. Loop formation has been directly demonstrated *in vitro* with an AraC dimer binding simultaneously to both sites in the absence of arabinose, thus preventing access of the RNA polymerase to the *ara*BAD promoter region. On induction by addition of arabinose the topology of AraC binding changes (Figure 3.21). The binding of one of the monomers to the $O_2$ site is disrupted and instead the AraC dimer binds to two adjacent sites within the I element. In this position the protein can now activate transcription. This change in the occupancy of the AraC binding sites implies that arabinose, by binding to the AraC protein, induces or permits substantial structural changes in the protein which allow a different dimerization geometry.

The principle of looping has also been directly demonstrated in an artificial system using $\lambda$ $C_I$ operator sites. The experiments of Hochshild and Ptashne show that, when the separation between two operator sites is increased to four, five or six double helical turns, co-operative binding between the sites is maintained and the DNA between the binding sites is significantly distorted (Figure 3.22). By contrast, no co-operative binding is observed when the separation is $4\frac{1}{2}$ or $5\frac{1}{2}$ helical turns. If this loss of co-operativity were indeed a consequence of the torsional rigidity of the DNA between the binding sites, co-operativity should be restored by allowing free rotation of the DNA, even if the separation were otherwise unfavourable. The introduction of a gap into the construct with a $5\frac{1}{2}$ turn separation achieved this restoration.

Another natural system in which a functional role for loop formation has been directly demonstrated is the repression of the *lac* operon. In addition to the principal operator site within the promoter region of this operon there are two additional weak binding sites, the 'pseudo-operators', situated 92 bp upstream and 401 bp downstream respectively of the primary site. *In vivo* maximal repression of transcription requires

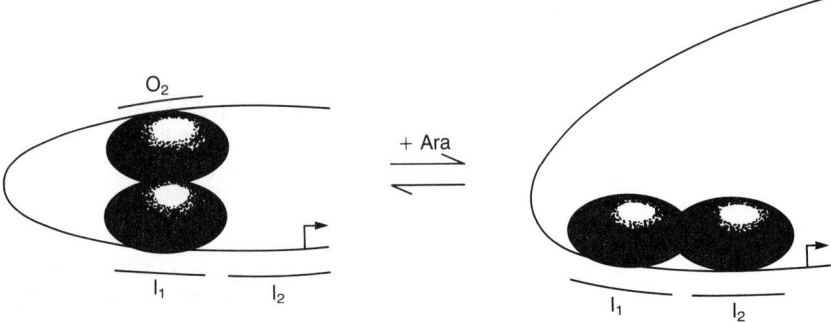

**Figure 3.21** The regulation of the *ara*BAD promoter by AraC protein. In the absence of arabinose, AraC subunits bind to $O_2$ and $I_1$ and thereby promote looping. With arabinose present the subunits bind to two adjacent sites $I_1$ and $I_2$ and drive the transition to the unlooped state.

the presence of both these sites. Thus, deletion of the downstream pseudo-operator results in a 20-fold rise in the basal level of transcription. Such observations suggest that the full repression of the *lac* operon requires the simultaneous binding of one repressor tetramer to both the operator and a pseudo-operator to form a DNA loop which further impedes access of RNA polymerase to the promoter site. Indeed, *in vitro*, when mixed with DNA containing separated operator sites, the *lac* repressor forms loops when the DNA concentration is low, or at high DNA concentrations forms 'sandwiches' in which one repressor molecule simultaneously binds to operator sites on two different DNA molecules.

The *lac* repressor mediates co-operative interactions between distant DNA binding sites by virtue of the strong protein–protein interactions which maintain the tetramer as a distinct stable entity. This contrasts with, for example, the assumed interactions between CAP and RNA polymerase, which are dependent on a high local concentration achieved by tethering the proteins. The *lac* repressor tetramer is also an example of a bivalent DNA-binding protein: that is, it has two functional, and in this case, equivalent, DNA binding surfaces. In other bivalent proteins, for example the integrase of phage λ, the two binding surfaces may not be equivalent. For such proteins, and also for homologous, but weak, interactions between proteins bound at separated sites, loop formation may only occur efficiently if the bending of DNA between the two binding sites is facilitated either by the intrinsic curvature of DNA or by a further protein whose function is to bend the DNA. Such facilitated looping, which does not require protein–protein interactions between the bending protein and the other proteins involved in the complex, is apparent in the activation of certain promoters for bacterial nitrogen

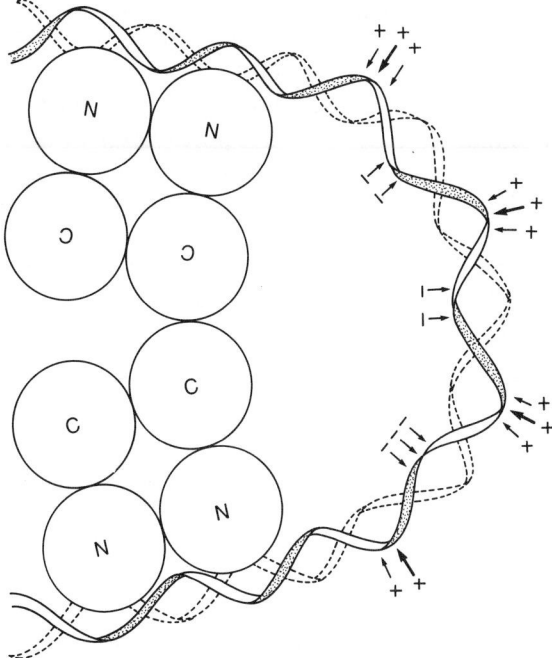

**Figure 3.22** The looping of DNA induced by the co-operative interactions of the λ C$_I$ protein. The DNA in the induced loop is hypersensitive (+) to DNase I cleavage where the minor groove is on the outside of the loop and is protected (–) where the minor groove is on the inside of the loop.

fixation genes and in several recombinogenic nucleoprotein complexes. Mechanistically there is no formal distinction between complexes where the loops are small, as in the complex of λ integrase and IHF at *attP*, or where they are larger, as for the nitrogen fixation genes.

## 3.5 PROTEIN FLEXIBILITY IN DNA–PROTEIN COMPLEXES

Changes in protein structure on DNA binding can also be an important component in the formation of a DNA–protein complex. For example, the proximity of the DNA ligand can induce a coil to helix transition in the amphipathic AK regions characteristic of the C-terminal tails of histone H1 and also in the DNA-binding domain of proteins of the Bzip class. A similar stabilization of an α-helix on DNA binding has been described for the DNA-binding domain of the glucocorticoid receptor. Another functionally significant transition is the encirclement of the DNA substrate by the EcoRV restriction endonuclease. Such ligand dependent transitions allow the establishment of structures which could not be attained by a simple docking procedure. By contrast the structure of DNase I is essentially the same when crystallized as the free protein or as a complex with its substrate. Again the structure of zinc fingers of the C–C....H–H (TFIIIA) class in solution as determined by NMR is, on average, very similar to that when bound to DNA in the Zif268–DNA cocrystal. By contrast, in solution, zinc fingers in tandem act as structurally independent modules with the intervening linker being highly flexible. It is precisely this flexibility that allows the fingers to be positioned in a structurally determined manner relative to each other when bound to DNA. In this context the flexible linker is simply a passive connector.

## REFERENCES

Aggarwal, A K., Rodgers, D W., Drottar, M. *et al.* (1988) Recognition of a DNA operator by the repressor of phage 434: a view at high resolution. *Science*, **242**, 899–907.

Dunn, T.M., Hahn, S., Ogden, S. *et al.* (1984) An operator at –280 base pairs that is required for the repression of the *ara*BAD operator: addition of helical turns between the operator and promoter cyclically hinders repression. *Proceedings of the National Academy of Sciences of the USA*, **81**, 5017–20.

Harrison, S.C. (1991) A structural taxonomy of DNA-binding domains. *Nature*, **353**, 715–19.

Hochshild, A. and Ptashne, M. (1986) Co-operative binding of λ repressors to sites separated by integral turns of the double helix. *Cell*, **44**, 681–7.

Johnson, A. *et al.* (1979) Interactions between DNA-bound repressors govern regulation by the λ phage repressor. *Proceedings of the National Academy of Sciences of the USA*, **76**, 5061–5.

Lobell, R.B. and Schleif, R.F. (1990) DNA looping and unlooping by AraC protein. *Science*, **251**, 528–32.

Marmorstein, R. Carey, R., Ptashne, M. and Harrison, S.C. (1992) DNA recognition by GAL4: structure of a protein–DNA complex. *Nature*, **356**, 408–14.

Miller, J., McLachlan, A.D. and Klug, A. (1985) Repetitive zinc-binding domains in the protein transcription factor TFIIIA from *Xenopus* oocytes.

Oehler, S., Eismann, E.R., Krämer, H. and Müller-Hill, B. (1990) The three operators of the *lac* operon co-operate in repression. *EMBO Journal*, **9**, 973–9.

Pavletich, N. and Pabo, S.C. (1991) Zinc finger – DNA recognition. Crystal structure of a Zif-268-DNA complex. *Science*, **252**, 809–17.

Rhodes, D. and Klug, A. (1993) Zinc finger structure. *Scientific American*, **268**, 32–9.

Schultz, S.C. *et al.* (1991) Crystal structure of a CAP–DNA complex: the DNA is bent by 90°. *Science*, **253**, 1001–7.

# 4

# The mechanism of RNA chain initiation

The initiation of the transcription of an RNA molecule from a DNA template requires the manipulation of the DNA by the transcribing enzyme, RNA polymerase. This enzyme must first recognize its binding site, which is specified directly, or indirectly, by a specific DNA sequence. Then, strand separation of a limited region of the DNA duplex, usually about one double helical turn, precedes the actual initiation of the RNA chain. Mechanistically this process is analogous to other biological processes in which DNA unwinding occurs, such as the initiation of DNA replication and site specific recombination. In these latter processes the unwinding or melting of the duplex is often preceded by the tight wrapping of the DNA on the surface of a large protein complex.

## 4.1 THE PROMOTER

The DNA sequences which specify the site for the initiation of transcription comprise the promoter region. As originally defined genetically, the promoter contains all those sequences which are required for the optimum expression of a transcription unit. Strictly this definition would include those sequences that are required both for optimum initiation and for optimum elongation. In this book, the term promoter is restricted to only those DNA sequences in the former class.

In enterobacteria the promoter site minimally specifies a binding site for RNA polymerase. For most transcription units, however, this polymerase binding site is insufficient for maximal rates of transcription, and additional DNA sequences specify binding sites for other DNA binding proteins; these can interact, either directly or indirectly, with the polymerase to activate transcription. These auxiliary binding sites are, in bacteria, normally situated adjacent to, or overlapping with, the RNA polymerase binding site, but in certain cases they may be as many as

1000–2000 bp distant from the initiation startpoint. These distant activating sites are termed 'enhancers'.

In eukaryotes the structure of promoter sites is largely similar, with the notable difference that the promoter sequences do not directly specify an RNA polymerase binding site. Instead, the sequences within the promoter site specify sites for DNA-binding proteins which, when bound to their target sites, themselves constitute a binding site for the RNA polymerase enzyme. The essential difference between the eubacterial and eukaryotic systems is thus that in eubacteria the polymerase locates a promoter site by protein–DNA interactions, whereas in eukaryotes the dominant mode of recognition involves protein–protein interactions. In eukaryotes the binding sites for auxiliary activating proteins can again be several kilobases from the transcription startpoint, either in 5' or in a 3' direction. In addition, particularly with genes encoding small RNA species transcribed by RNA polymerase III, these auxiliary proteins may bind within the transcription unit itself. Finally, it should be stressed that sequences which are defined genetically as necessary for optimal transcription may not themselves directly interact with the transcription apparatus. Particularly in eukaryotes, sequence specific DNA-binding proteins may be involved in modulating chromatin structure and thus the accessibility of binding sites for other proteins more directly involved in transcription initiation.

## 4.2 RNA POLYMERASES

In both prokaryotes and the eukaryotic nucleus the transcribing enzymes are large multi-subunit protein complexes with molecular weights of approximately 500 000 Da. Bacteria, including both the eubacteria and archaebacteria, contain only one type of DNA dependent RNA polymerase which is responsible for the synthesis of all RNA species. By contrast, in the eukaryotic nucleus three different RNA polymerases participate in RNA synthesis: RNA polymerase I synthesizes predominantly ribosomal RNA (rRNA), RNA polymerase II synthesizes mRNA precursors and certain small RNA species, and RNA polymerase III is responsible for the synthesis of transfer RNA species (tRNA), 5S rRNA and other small RNA molecules. All these types of polymerase, both bacterial and eukaryotic, contain regions of sequence homology, particularly in the larger subunits, suggesting a common evolutionary origin. In the eukaryotic cell, however, RNA polymerases are not confined to the nucleus. They also occur in chloroplasts and mitochondria. In the former organelles the polymerase closely resembles the eubacterial enzyme in structure and function, whereas in mitochondria the enzyme has a relatively simple structure containing only two subunits of molecular weight of about 50 k Da each. In addition, the DNA of certain bacteriophages may encode a phage specific RNA polymerase. For both coliphages T7 (or T3) and N4 the RNA polymerase is a single polypeptide with molecular weights of 100 k Da and 350 k Da respectively.

In the enterobacterium *Escherichia coli* the RNA polymerase comprises two principal components, the core enzyme, which is required for both the initiation and the elongation of an RNA chain, and auxiliary polypeptides which bind directly to the core component and which are necessary for either accurate initiation or for the termination of RNA synthesis. The core enzyme itself is composed of three types of subunit, $\alpha$, $\beta$ and $\beta'$, present in the proportions of 2:1:1. $\beta'$ and $\beta$ have molecular weights of 145 k and 140 k respectively, while the $\alpha$ subunits are much smaller, having a molecular weight of 37 k Da each.

To locate a promoter site on the DNA the core polymerase must be associated with an additional polypeptide, termed a $\sigma$ factor. This polypeptide confers the ability to recognize a specific DNA sequence. Typically eubacteria contain several $\sigma$ factors, each of which allows the polymerase to recognize and bind to a different class of promoter site. In *E. coli* the most abundant of these is the vegetative $\sigma$ factor, $\sigma^{70}$, which directs the enzyme to the promoters for most transcription units expressed during normal vegetative growth. In addition, there are other less abundant factors which are required for the transcription of genes required for nitrogen utilization and also for genes expressed when bacteria are subjected to a sudden temperature shift or another similar metabolic insult.

Although the $\sigma$ factors do not by themselves bind strongly to specific DNA sequences, when bound to the core enzyme they confer promoter selectivity on the core–sigma complex. The vegetative $\sigma$ factor targets the polymerase to two conserved hexameric sequences in the vegetative promoter, the –10 and –35 regions which are defined by the consensus sequences TATAAT and TTGACA respectively (Figure 4.1). Other sigma factors, such as the heat shock sigma, $\sigma^{32}$, target the enzyme to different –10 and –35 regions (Table 4.1), while others, such as that required for the expression of the nitrogen utilization genes, target the polymerase to sequences located 25 and 12 bp upstream of the transcription startpoint. Yet another sigma factor, that required for the expression of the late

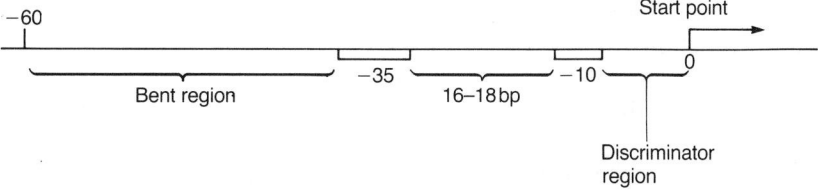

**Figure 4.1** Sequence organization of $\sigma^{70}$ bacterial promoters.

**Table 4.1** Consensus promoter sequences for recognition by different *E.coli* sigma factors

| Sigma factor | −35 | −25 | −10 | Spacer |
|---|---|---|---|---|
| $\sigma^{70}$ (rpoD) | TTGACA | | TATAAT | 16–18bp |
| $\sigma^{32}$ (rpoH) | CTTGAA | | CCCCATtTa | |
| E | GAACTT | | TCTGA | |
| $\sigma^{54}$(rpoN) | | CTGGcA | TTGCA | 6bp |
| $\sigma^{S}$(rpoS/katF) | GTTAAGC | | CGTCC | |
| flagellar genes | TAAA | | GCCGATAA | |
| T4 gp55 | none | | TATAAATA | |

**Figure 4.2** Structural organization of bacterial sigma factors (hth = helix-turn-helix).

genes of bacteriophage T4, restricts sequence specific recogition to a heptameric −10 sequence.

The different sigma factors contain homologous structural regions as shown in Figure 4.2. At the carboxy-terminal end of the polypeptide are found one or two helix–turn–helix motifs while close to the amino-terminus is a second conserved region. This latter region is believed to define the contact site with the core enzyme while the helix–turn–helix motifs are responsible for the sequence specific recognition of the −35 and −10 regions. Mutation in either of these motifs can alter the promoter selectivity conferred by the sigma factor.

## 4.3 THE KINETICS OF TRANSCRIPTION INITIATION

The process of transcription initiation is a dynamic multi-step process in which the rate of initiation is determined by the slowest step in the reaction. For initiation at eubacterial promoters the polymerase must first locate a functional binding site at which it forms a loosely bound initial complex. This initial binding is followed by a set of conformational adjustments in the polymerase–promoter complex, which ultimately result in the melting of one turn of the DNA duplex at the transcription startpoint. This second defined complex is termed the 'open' complex and is poised to initiate the synthesis of an RNA molecule. The last steps in the process are this initiation itself and, finally, the clearance of the promoter site by the transcribing enzyme, thus leaving it accessible for interaction with another polymerase molecule. Depending on the type of promoter, any of these steps may limit the overall rate of initiation.

When analysed experimentally the reaction is usually simplified to a two-stage reaction:

$$E + p \rightleftharpoons (Ep)_i \rightleftharpoons (Ep)_o$$
$$\quad\quad K_B \quad\quad k_f$$

where $K_B$ is the initial binding constant of the polymerase to the promoter site and $k_f$ is the forward rate of formation of the open complex. In general, the overall activity of the promoter is fairly accurately described by the expression $K_B k_f$.

## 4.4 THE MOLECULAR INTERACTIONS OF RNA POLYMERASE WITH A PROMOTER SITE

How does RNA polymerase locate promoter DNA from amongst a huge variety of other sequences? In common with many other DNA-binding proteins the rate of location is about two orders of magnitude greater than would be expected from random three-dimensional diffusion. The simplest explanation is that RNA polymerase is always in close proximity to a DNA molecule by virtue of a non-specific electrostatic attraction and consequently, for most of the time, diffuses rapidly along this DNA molecule and only rarely diffuses to another DNA molecule (Figure 4.3). Once diffusing in this mode the polymerase must distinguish promoter DNA sequences from other sequences. In principle this might be accomplished by rapid conformational oscillations in the protein so that it alternated between a non-specific and a sequence specific binding mode. A second possibility is that the overall configuration of promoter DNA differs from that of non-promoter DNA and the polymerase recognizes this particular structural feature in an analogous manner to that of a metabolic enzyme identifying its substrate. Within the polymerase–promoter complex itself the DNA clearly assumes a distinct configuration: promoter DNA contains phased bending sequences and the polymerase–promoter DNA complex itself behaves anomalously when electrophoresed through polyacrylamide gels. More direct evidence that the configuration of promoter DNA is a significant determinant of promoter location is the observation that intrinsically bent DNA sequences can, by themselves, act as promoter sites, even though such sequences contain only a very limited homology to the consensus promoter sequence. Indeed, in many promoters the naturally occurring DNA upstream of the −35 region is often intrinsically bent. More importantly, the activity of a promoter is exquisitely sensitive to the direction of curvature in this region. Shifting the phase of the bending by half a double helical turn from the natural configuration, which is equivalent to

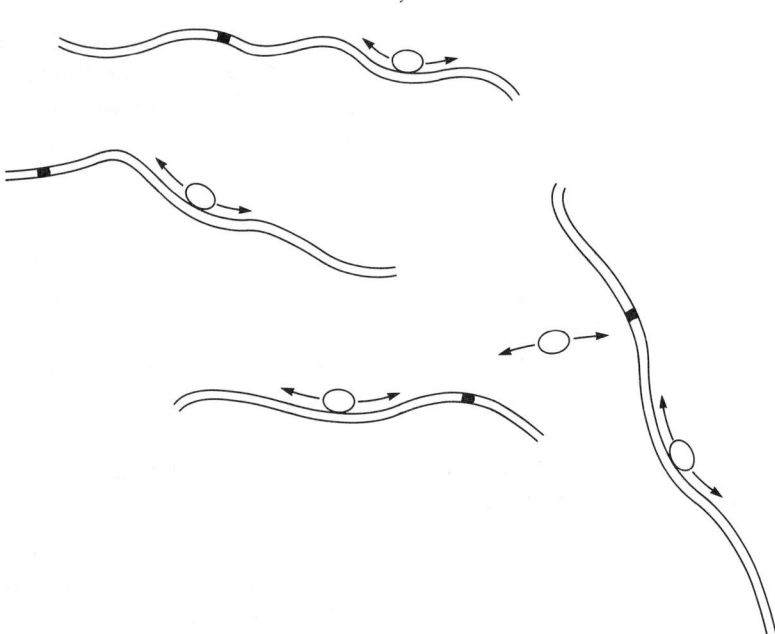

**Figure 4.3** Location of binding sites by DNA-binding proteins. The protein can diffuse along the DNA (one-dimensional diffusion) or can diffuse in solution between different DNA molecules.

altering the direction of bending by 180°, results in a substantial drop in promoter activity, which is restored by a further shift of 180°. Unexpectedly, when correctly phased bent DNA is placed 60–90 bp upstream of the transcription startpoint, beyond the previously observed limit of binding for a single polymerase molecule, transcriptional activity is conserved. This observation suggests either that the curved DNA serves simply to direct the polymerase to the promoter region or that the curve allows the DNA to bend back to make additional contacts with the enzyme.

Once the polymerase has located the promoter, the contacts in the initial complex, as probed by nucleases, extend from about 50–60 bp upstream of the transcription startpoint to approximately position –4 (Figure 4.5). However, the transition to the open complex is accompanied by a change in the extent of DNA interacting with the enzyme. In this complex the upstream boundary of the polymerase protein remains the same while the other boundary is now about 20 bp downstream of the startpoint. This transition thus involves an effective extension of the polymerase protein relative to the promoter DNA and, consequently, a conformational change in the enzyme. At the same time the conformation of the DNA itself also

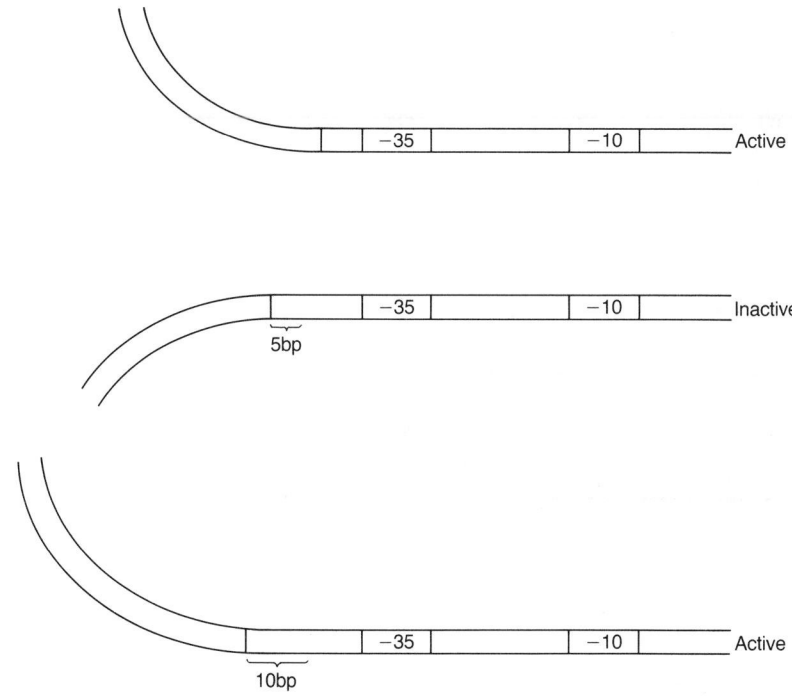

**Figure 4.4** The direction of intrinsic bending upstream of a promoter can influence promoter activity.

changes. In the closed complex there is no evidence for any major distortions of the native DNA double helix. By contrast, in the open complex the region of about 11 bp around the startpoint of transcription becomes accessible to methylation by dimethylsulphate on the 1-position of adenine bases and on cytosine. Both these reactions can only proceed when the DNA is no longer base-paired, indicating that, in the open complex, strand separation occurs over one turn of DNA at the transcription startpoint. However, with other reagents, conformational transitions in the DNA are detectable prior to strand separation. On binding of the promoter DNA by RNA polymerase many bases become more accessible to reaction with singlet oxygen, a reagent which is a sensitive probe of distorted DNA regions. These distortions can be either tight bends or local unwound regions. With a second reagent, copper-*o*-phenanthroline, which preferentially reacts with unwound, but not necessarily strand separated DNA, it is observed that at an early stage in the formation of the polymerase–promoter complex, the DNA in the distal part of the –10 region becomes sensitive to the reagent. As open complex formation proceeds this patch of sensitivity migrates toward the

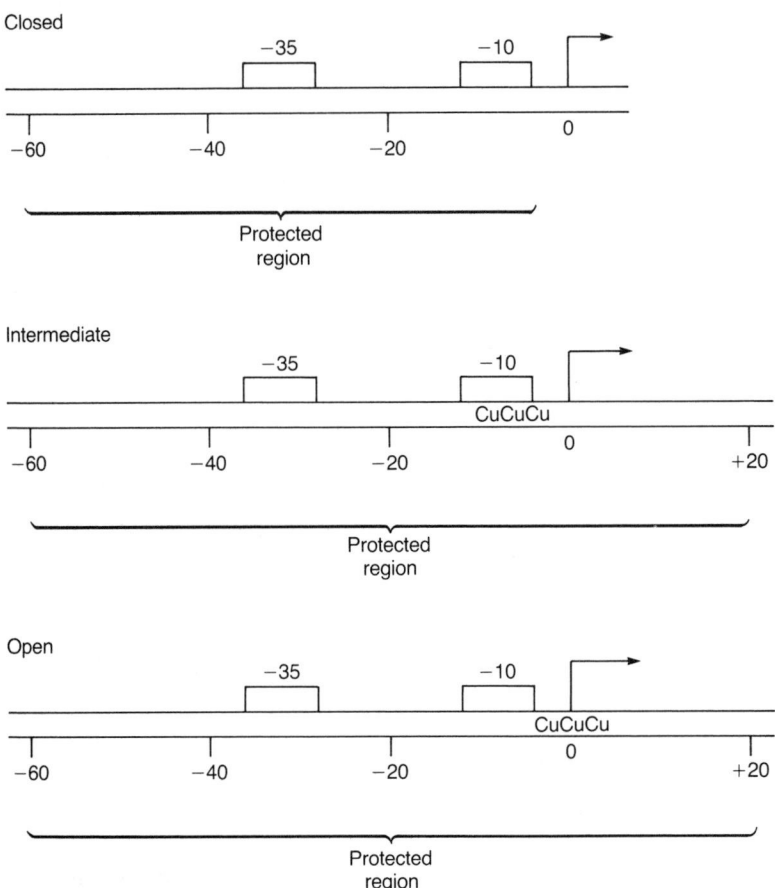

**Figure 4.5** Variation in the extent of protection of promoter DNA by *E. coli* RNA polymerase and in the accessibility to copper-*o*-phenanthroline (Cu) during the transition from the closed to the open initiation complexes.

transcription startpoint. This pattern of changes suggests that the unwinding of DNA by RNA polymerase is nucleated in the –10 region and only subsequently becomes localized at the transcription startpoint. The overall picture is thus of substantial changes in the conformation of both the RNA polymerase and the promoter DNA in the transition from the closed to the open complex.

Once the synthesis of the RNA molecule has been initiated the RNA chain is extended by the stepwise addition of nucleotides complementary to the transcribed template strand of the DNA. However, after the synthesis of a short length of RNA, usually about 5–12 nucleotides long, the sigma factor is released from the transcribing complex and becomes available for association with another core polymerase molecule to form a functional holoenzyme. Meanwhile another *E. coli* protein, NusA, binds to the elongating RNA polymerase. This protein has several functions; it can increase the length of time the transcribing enzyme pauses at particular sites and is also involved in normal transcription termination. In addition, it can couple to the polymerase proteins which act as antiterminators, which suppress RNA chain termination at most terminator sites. Since NusA competes with sigma for binding to the core polymerase, it must dissociate from the enzyme to regenerate free core polymerase following transcription termination (Figure 4.6).

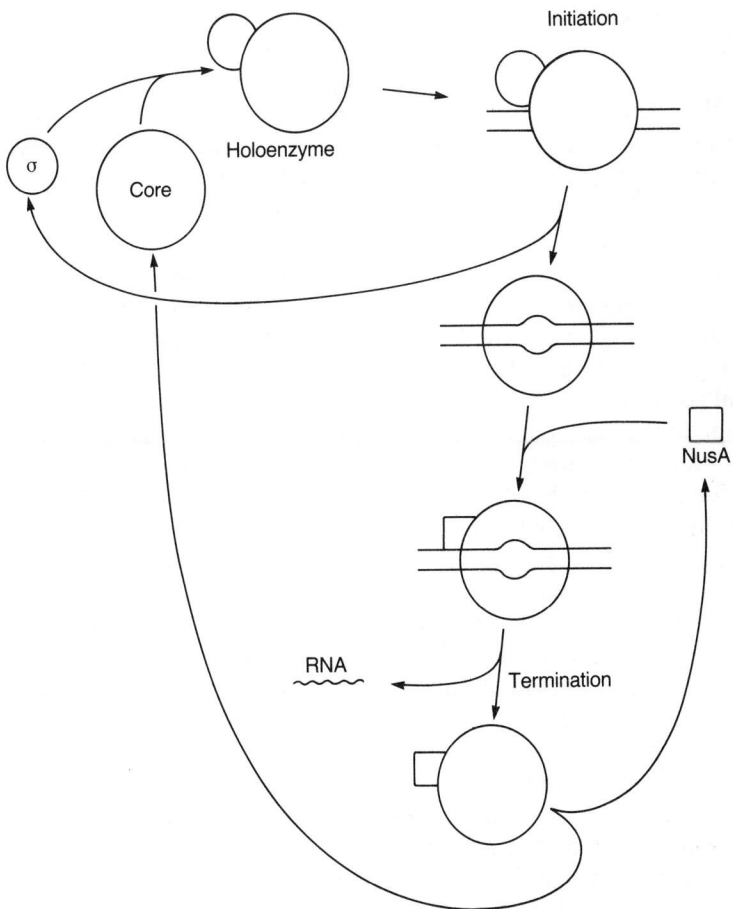

**Figure 4.6** The cycling of initiation and elongation (NusA) factors during bacterial transcription.

## 4.5 THE TOPOLOGICAL CONSEQUENCES OF TRANSCRIPTION

The manipulation of DNA by RNA polymerase has two principal topological consequences, one resulting from the binding of the enzyme to a promoter site and the second from the movement of the polymerase during transcription. The melting of approximately one turn of DNA during open complex formation means that this process is accompanied by a change in linking number of ~−1. However the measured values of the topological change can attain 560–610°, equivalent to a value of $\Delta L$ of 1.6–1.7. This suggests that not all of the topological change can be accounted for by this melting. However, a change in $\Delta L = ~−1$ is observed at an early stage in the establishment of the polymerase–promoter complex, prior to any detectable changes in the conformation of promoter DNA. The interpretation of this observation is that this topological change is a consequence of the polymerase constraining the DNA in a form in which the topological change is principally, and possibly, wholly writhe. On conversion to the open complex this writhing of the DNA molecule would be transformed into an untwisting with little change in linking number. In other words, to achieve strand separation the polymerase must rotate relative to the promoter DNA, and thus apply a left-handed torque.

When an RNA polymerase molecule progresses along the DNA template during transcription, the enzyme and the DNA molecule must, because the DNA is helical, rotate relative to each other. If the polymerase were to rotate around the DNA there would be no topological consequences, with respect to the DNA, resulting simply from the passage of the enzyme. If, however, this rotation of the polymerase were impeded or prevented, then the DNA molecule must itself rotate (Figure 4.7). For a DNA molecule with free ends this rotation would eventually be dissipated as a rotation of the double helix. However, for a closed circular DNA molecule, or for a DNA domain with anchored ends, this option is not available. Instead, the rotation of the DNA will be reflected in local alterations in the superhelical density. Since the relative motion of the polymerase to the DNA is in a right-handed sense, the DNA ahead of the advancing enzyme will, in principle, be overwound by one right-handed turn for every double helical turn transcribed by the polymerase. Similarly, the DNA behind the polymerase will be underwound by one left-handed turn for the same progression. The consequence of this process is a region of positively supercoiled DNA preceding the enzyme and a region of negatively supercoiled DNA behind it. The positively supercoiled region can be relaxed by DNA gyrase (in eubacteria) and the negatively supercoiled region by topoisomerase I. However, if the rate at which the topoisomerases can relieve the torsional stress is less than the rate at which it is generated by transcription, there will be local changes in the conformation of flanking DNA generated by the passage of the polymerase.

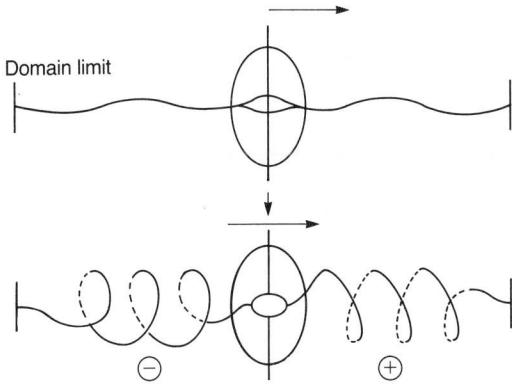

**Figure 4.7** The twin domain model for the generation of superhelicity. A transcribing fixed polymerase produces positive supercoils ahead and negative supercoils behind in a constrained DNA domain.

Evidence that transcription can by itself induce topological changes in the DNA template has been inferred by inhibiting the activity of the topoisomerases. In particular, when DNA gyrase is inhibited by specific drugs, plasmid DNA extracted from bacteria is often positively super-coiled. The occurrence of this positive supercoiling requires transcription and is thought to be generated by the motion of polymerases along divergent transcription units. In this situation the transcribing poly-merases effectively divide the plasmid DNA into two topological do-mains, one 5' to both genes and the second 3' to both genes (Figure 4.8). The DNA in the former domain will be negatively supercoiled and in the latter positively supercoiled. When gyrase activity is inhibited positive superhelicity will accumulate in the 3' domain while the excess negative superhelicity in the 5' domain will be removed by topoisomerase I. The net result is a positively supercoiled plasmid DNA molecule.

The local superhelicity generated by a transcribing polymerase molecule should be clearly distinguished from the unwinding that occurs during the initiation process itself. Whereas the net topological change resulting from the motion of the polymerase is zero, because the positive and negative supercoiling cancel each other, the unwinding resulting from strand separation is a net unwinding of the DNA template at the site of polymerase attachment, which is only removed when the transcribing enzyme terminates transcription. For a closed circular DNA this unwinding would, in the absence of compensating reactions, add one positive topological turn to the remainder of the DNA domain for each transcribing enzyme.

The existence of transcription induced superhelicity implies that the rotation of the polymerase around the DNA is impeded and that changes in the conformation of the template DNA are energetically preferred. In

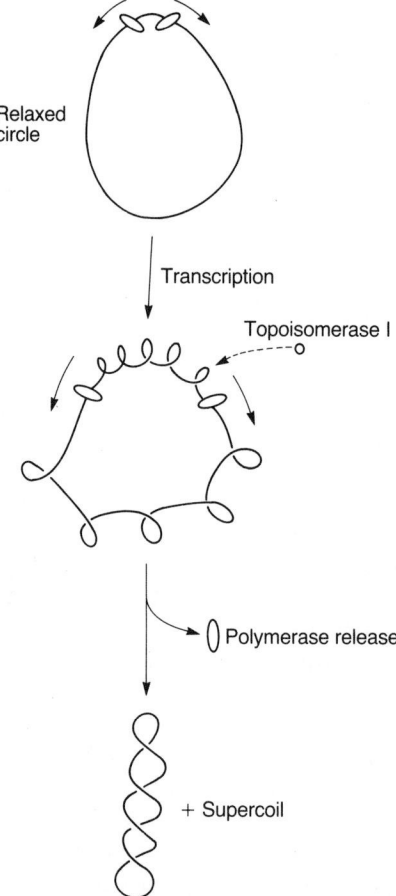

**Figure 4.8** The generation of positively supercoiled DNA by transcription in a bacterium or a test tube lacking DNA gyrase.

addition the production of local changes in superhelical density means that DNA may assume local densities that are substantially different from the average superhelical density (usually negative in bacteria) and consequently the DNA may undergo conformational transitions, such as the assumption of Z-DNA conformation which would not normally occur at average superhelical densities. A second implication is that changes in the local DNA structure generated by transcription from one promoter could influence the superhelicity, and hence the activity, of an adjacent promoter.

## 4.6 TRANSCRIPTIONAL ACTIVATORS

In contrast to many $\sigma^{70}$ dependent promoters on bacteriophages T5 and T4, optimal transcription from a majority of bacterial promoters requires the intercession of an additional ancillary DNA binding protein(s) which acts to increase the rate of transcription initiation. The step in the initiation process which is affected by such proteins can be different in different promoters and is dependent on which step is rate-limiting in the absence of the activator. Nor is a particular transcriptional activator restricted to a single mechanistic mode of activation. Thus the catabolite-activator protein (CAP or CRP) increases transcription at the *lac* promoter by increasing $K_B$ but not $k_2$, at the *gal*$P_1$ promoter by increasing $K_B$ and $k_2$ and at the *mal*T promoter by increasing the rate of escape from the initiation complex.

How do such activator proteins work at the molecular level? Consider first the positive control of the *lac* promoter. The binding site for the dimeric CAP molecule is centred at position −61.5 from the transcription startpoint in helical phase with the DNA bound to RNA polymerase. This site is only occupied when CAP is activated by binding cAMP, which itself accumulates in the bacterial cell as a consequence of glucose starvation. When CAP is bound, both the activator protein and RNA polymerase have higher affinities for the regulatory region, showing that the binding of the two proteins is co-operative. After the transition to the open state of the promoter two further features of the nucleoprotein complex are apparent. First, the DNA bound to CAP is more distorted, as judged by its reactivity to singlet oxygen, than the same DNA bound to CAP in the absence of RNA polymerase. Secondly, the DNA upstream of the CAP binding site extending to position approximately −90 is also unusually reactive to singlet oxygen. A further surprising feature of ternary complexes of CAP and RNA polymerase bound at a promoter site is that the protein interactions extend upstream beyond the established binding sites for either protein alone. The inference from this and related observations is that the DNA bend induced by CAP allows the polymerase to contact a second region of DNA, thus delimiting a loop (Figure 4.9). At the same time the existence of mutations in CAP that abolish positive activation, but are unaffected in DNA binding, suggest that CAP directly contacts RNA polymerase. The amino acids that are implicated in positive control are in close spatial proximity to two DNA sequences, located one, and one and a half turns respectively from the mid-point of the CAP binding site, where DNA distortion is evident in the ternary complex. Since these same sequences are also inherently bendable, a role for CAP induced DNA bending in the determination of the local topography of the complex is apparent.

The CAP induced activation of the *lac* promoter is an example of a control system in which the affinity of the regulatory protein for its DNA binding site is modulated in response to a metabolic signal. For some other promoters activation is constitutive; that is, the affinity of the regulator for DNA is essentially invariant and the occupation of its binding site is dependent solely on its concentration. One promoter which is activated in this way, and has similarities to the *lac* promoter, is the $P_L$ promoter of bacteriophage λ. For optimum activity this promoter requires sequences upstream of the normal polymerase binding site. Within this region are two binding sites for the integration host factor

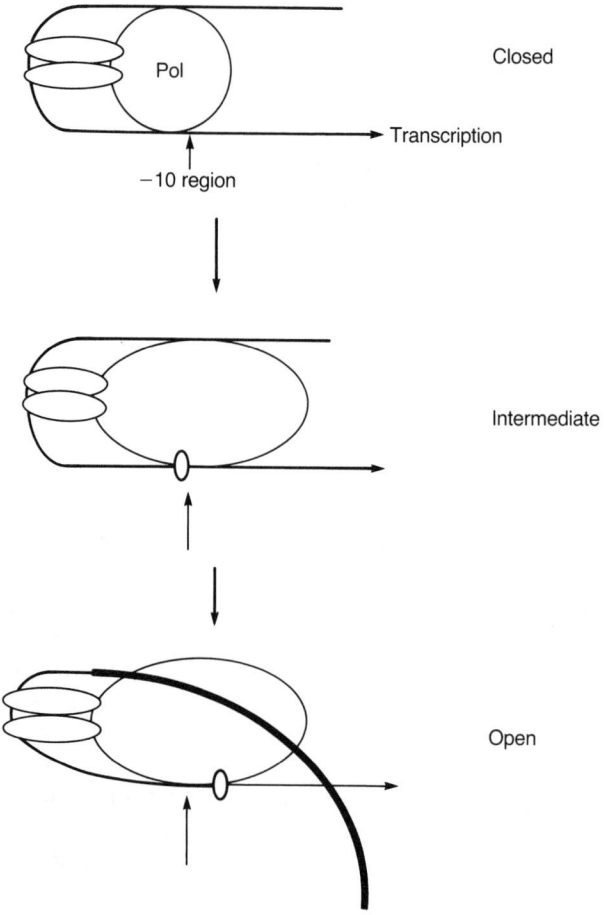

**Figure 4.9** Topological changes in promoter DNA in the ternary CAP–RNA polymerase–DNA complex during the transition from the closed to the open complex. It is assumed that the DNA makes a second contact to RNA polymerase upstream of the CAP binding site.

(IHF) centred at positions $-90$ and $-180$. This protein, like CAP, has the ability to bend DNA significantly. Both *in vitro* and *in vivo* removal of the IHF binding sites reduce the activity of the promoter by about four-fold. The function of IHF is to increase the $K_B$ for polymerase binding. Again, there are two ways in which this might be accomplished. There could either be direct contact between the activator protein and the polymerase or, alternatively, IHF might act simply by bending the DNA to a sufficient extent so that the polymerase can make additional contacts.

In addition to acting as a transcriptional activator IHF can also function as a repressor. In particular the $\lambda$ *cin* promoter contains a binding site for IHF in the vicinity of the $-35$ hexamer. When IHF occupies this site, either *in vitro* or *in vivo*, transcription is blocked. In this promoter the centre of the IHF binding site is positioned so that the protein will bind to the opposite face of the DNA to RNA polymerase; or, put another way, the centre of the binding site is displaced by half a double helical turn relative to the position of the CAP binding site in the $galP_1$ promoter. This means that, when bound at the *cin* promoter, IHF will bend the DNA in the opposite direction to that required for wrapping the DNA around the polymerase protein, and thus could by this means directly prevent stable binding of the polymerase to the promoter DNA (Figure 4.10).

In the examples of the *lac* and $\lambda$ $P_L$ promoters, both CAP and IHF facilitate the initial binding of the polymerase to the promoter site. However, in the $galP_1$ promoter, CAP facilitates both the initial binding and the closed to open complex transition. In this promoter the CAP binding site is centred at position $-41.5$, two double helical turns away from the position of the corresponding binding site in the *lac* promoter. For this promoter the requirement for CAP for *in vivo* activation can be overcome by replacing the CAP binding site by curved DNA. As in the similar case of the intasome, the function of the resulting polymerase–promoter complex is crucially dependent on the orientation of the inserted curve to the extent that a change of approximately $180°$ in the direction of bending moves the transcription startpoint half a double helical turn upstream, from the $galP_1$ start to the $galP_2$ start. This result emphasizes that it is the direction of DNA curvature which is important in establishing the appropriate polymerase–promoter contacts, and further suggests that one aspect of the activation of the *gal* promoter by CAP is the insertion of a bend in the DNA (Figure 4.11).

An activator protein that increases the rate of initiation by affecting solely $k_2$ is the MerR protein, which is required for the expression of the *mer*T regulon encoding proteins which are necessary for the detoxification of mercury. The *mer*T promoter is unusual in that the separation between the $-10$ and $-35$ hexamers is 19 bp in contrast to the usual 16–18. Despite this suboptimal structure, the polymerase by itself readily forms

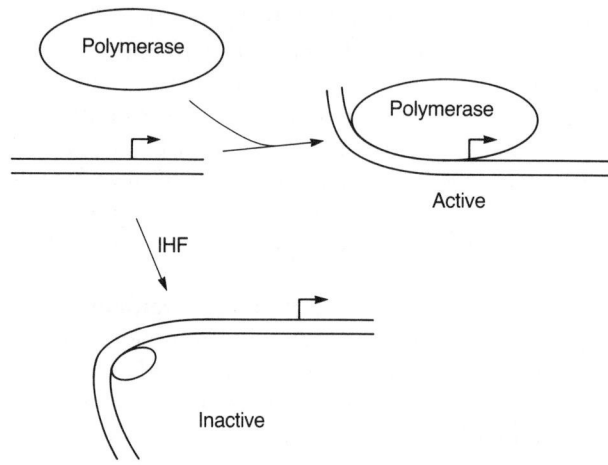

**Figure 4.10** IHF can repress transcription by bending DNA in an inappropriate direction.

a closed complex but is blocked in the transition to the open complex. The MerR protein binds as a dimer at a site centred at position −27 (Figure 4.12). In the absence of mercury both MerR and polymerase bind to the promoter region and the polymerase remains locked in a closed complex. However, in the presence of mercury the metal ion binds to the MerR protein and the initiation complex is immediately converted to the open state. This transition, as in the case of the *lac* promoter, is accompanied by a substantial distortion of local conformation of DNA at positions −26 and −27. Interestingly, the induction of this distortion, which by itself involves an unwinding of the DNA about 30°, is a property of MerR itself and does not require RNA polymerase. This implies that one function of MerR is to alter the structure of the DNA to accommodate the structural changes that normally accompany the transition from the closed to the open complex. In this context it should be noted that the unusually long spacing between the −10 and −35 regions might act to provide an energetic barrier to a premature activation of the promoter. At the same time the ability of the RNA polymerase to form a relatively stable closed complex at this promoter ensures that the enzyme is poised to provide a very rapid response to minimize the toxic effects of mercury ions.

Although the *mer*T promoter activation is illuminating in terms of promoter function it is not typical of mechanisms which increase the rate of conversion of closed to open complexes. The classical example of this type of activation is mediated by $\lambda\,C_I$ protein which facilitates initiation at the $\lambda\,P_{RM}$ promoter. In this example the regulatory protein binds at a

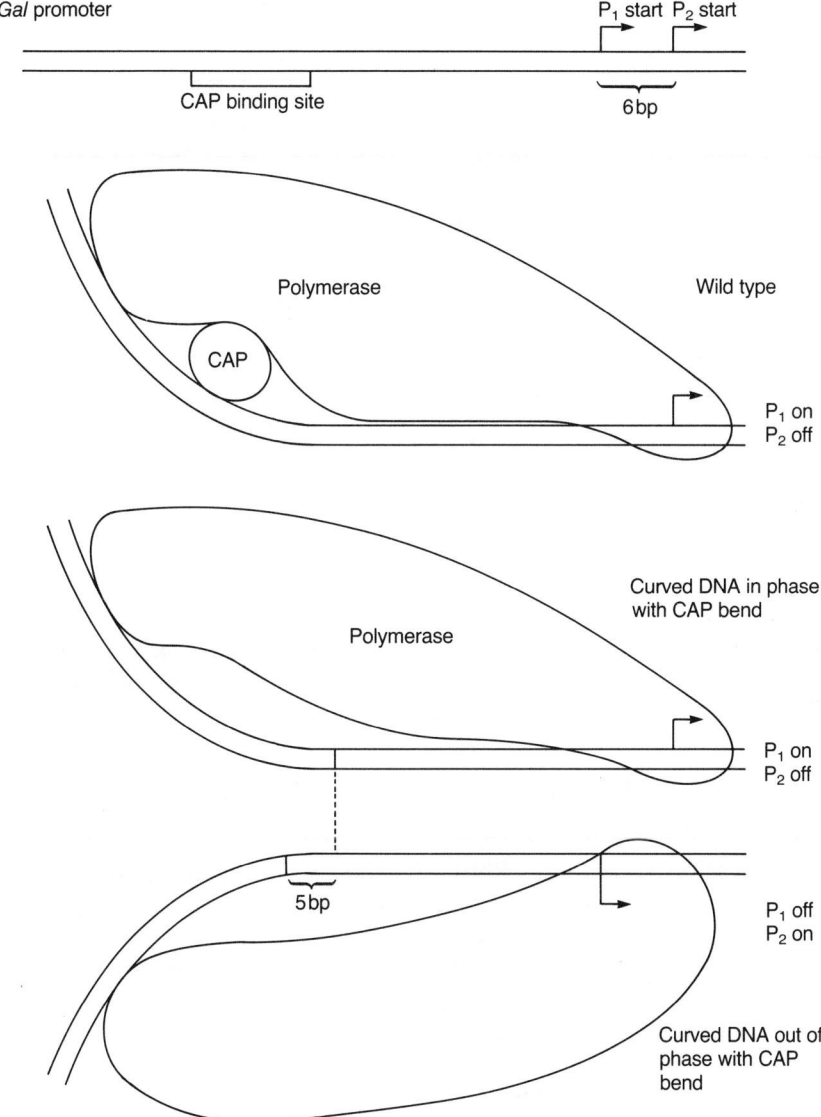

**Figure 4.11** Transcription startpoint selection in the *gal* promoter can be determined by the direction of DNA bending upstream.

similar relative position to that occupied by MerT but it does not by itself induce any detectable distortion in the promoter DNA. Instead, it appears to directly contact the bound RNA polymerase. Its probable role is thus to promote the conformational transition in the transcribing enzyme

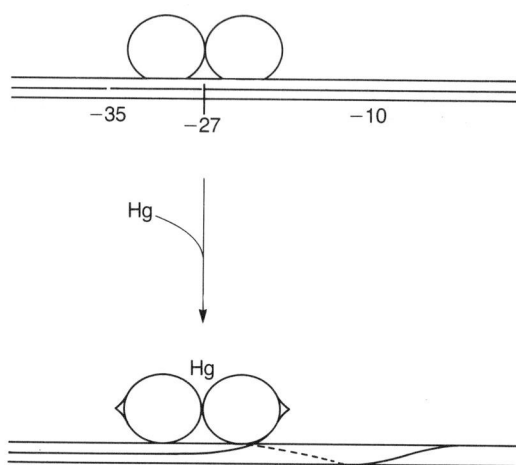

**Figure 4.12** The MerR protein alters the relative orientation of the −10 and −35 regions by untwisting the DNA in the vicinity of position −27.

itself that accompanies the opening of the promoter rather than directly affecting the structure of the DNA. (Note that it is not excluded that MerT may also perform this additional role.)

## 4.7 TRANSCRIPTIONAL ACTIVATION BY NEGATIVE SUPERHELICITY

The initiation of a single RNA molecule requires the unwinding of approximately one double helical turn of DNA. It would therefore be expected that this process would be facilitated by negative superhelicity. For many promoters this is indeed the case, the rate of transcription initiation being increased by up to a hundred-fold on a negatively supercoiled template. However, the mode of activation is dependent on the nature of the particular promoter. In the majority of cases so far studied RNA polymerase binds with approximately the same affinity to relaxed and supercoiled templates, but its rate of isomerization, $k_f$, from the closed to the open complex is much greater on supercoiled DNA. This is fully consistent with the notion that the energy available from supercoiling is utilized directly to unwind the DNA. Nevertheless, for some promoters negative superhelicity has little or no effect on the isomerization rate but instead increases the initial affinity of RNA polymerase for the promoter site. In one such example, that of an *ada* promoter with a mutation which increases the apparent curvature of the promoter DNA around −60, $K_B$ is increased by supercoiling by nearly one order of magnitude. However, this effect is only observed over a very limited range of superhelical density. This suggests that activation requires that an appropriate writhe be imposed on the DNA and that precise orientation of this writhe relative to the protein is critical.

Negative superhelicity not only affects the activity of RNA polymerase by itself, it can also influence the regulation of promoter function by transcriptional activators. For example, on relaxed DNA, CAP activates transcription at the *lac*P$_1$ promoter by increasing $K_B$. However, with negatively supercoiled DNA as a template, both $K_B$ and $k_2$ are increased by CAP. How might this be accomplished? One possibility is, as discussed above, that in the triple complex of CAP, polymerase and promoter DNA the DNA is looped by CAP in a negative writhe to form additional contacts on the backside of the polymerase (Figure 4.9), and consequently the formation of such a triple complex would be favoured by negative superhelical strain.

## 4.8 HOW DOES RNA POLYMERASE MELT PROMOTER DNA?

The fundamental question of the mechanism of transcription initiation is how the diverse protein–DNA and protein–protein contacts in the transcription initiation complex can be utilized to effect the melting of approximately one turn of promoter DNA. Consider first two possible extreme solutions to this problem which have been proposed. First, an initial left-handed wrapping of DNA in the complex could be converted to a local untwisting by a simple extension of the polymerase–promoter complex (Figure 4.13). Alternatively, the polymerase could function as a torque-wrench defining a micro-domain of DNA by tight contacts. A relative rotation of one of these contacts would then induce local unstacking at a sensitive site within the domain (Figure 4.14). The first model requires both that the promoter DNA in the unmelted state be wrapped in at least one left-handed superhelical turn to account for the topological change consequent upon promoter opening, and also that the extent of wrapping in the open complex be less than in the initial complex. Although intuitively attractive, this model is not consistent with the available evidence. The DNA that is sufficient for promoter function for the $\sigma^{70}$ holoenzyme extends from approximately 42–45 bp upstream to 20 bp downstream of the transcription startpoint. To accommodate one superhelical turn of DNA within this region implies a substantial distortion of the structure of the bound DNA, which is not observed in the initial complex. To the contrary, the transition to the open complex is accompanied by an increased distortion of the bound DNA upstream of the −10 hexamer. More strikingly, the length of sequence required for the $\sigma^{54}$-containing polymerase is even shorter, as is that which specifies the late promoters of bacteriophage T4. Similarly,

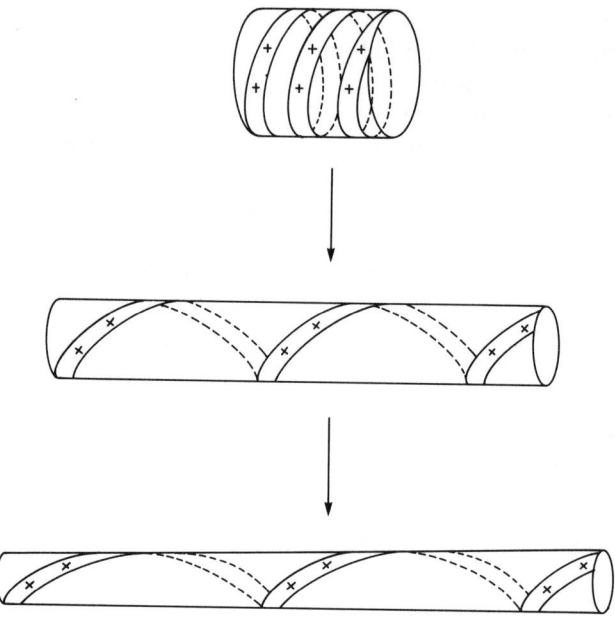

**Figure 4.13** How DNA, represented as a ribbon, can be distorted by altering the pitch of the superhelix.

the sequence bound by the unrelated RNA polymerase encoded by bacteriophage T7 extends for only about 25 bp. In promoters of this type the melting of the DNA must be contained and eventually stabilized within a defined micro-domain.

A major problem in the unwinding process is how unstacking is nucleated. A possible mechanism which has been proposed for both RNA polymerase and for the Tn3 resolvase is that unstacking is initiated by the protein sharply bending the DNA so that a kink is introduced at a specific site. A kink by definition requires the unstacking of adjacent base pairs and thus constitutes a weak point in the double helix. In the polymerase–promoter complex the proposed kink would be positioned approximately 16–18 bp upstream of the transcription startpoint, a location where the minor groove of DNA is orientated away from the protein surface. Once a kink has been formed in the closed complex, additional unwinding would be produced by a change in conformation of the protein, leading to the formation of the intermediate complex. One possible change would be an extension of the superhelically wrapped DNA (the Indian rope trick) resulting in an alteration in the intrinsic twist of the bound DNA, although other topologically equivalent changes in shape are clearly also possible. The distortion of the DNA in

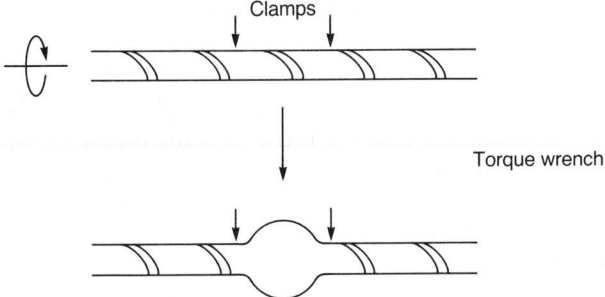

**Figure 4.14** The 'torque-wrench' model for DNA unwinding. Torsional stress is applied between the clamps, resulting in the unwinding of DNA in a limited region.

the region of position –26 in the open complex would also be fully consistent with such a process, since the accessibility of the DNA to osmium tetroxide at this position strongly suggests that the DNA must unwind to a limited extent at this position.

How does the untwisting of promoter DNA correlate with the observed unwinding? The formation of the open polymerase–promoter complex on closed circular DNA is accompanied by an average change in linking number of approximately –1.7 to –1.8. while in the closed complex this change is calculated to be approximately –1.2. This latter value is very similar to the change expected from the total untwisting of 12 bp at the transcription startpoint. However, within the closed complex there is no evidence for any substantial untwisting of the DNA. The inference is that, in the closed complex, the topological unwinding is present as writhe although the precise configuration remains undefined. The transition to the open complex can thus be thought of as a conversion of writhe to twist. Nevertheless, in the open complex there is an additional unwinding of approximately half a turn. How can this be accounted for? Two observations are relevant. First, open polymerase–promoter complexes are preferentially located at the apices of the interwound form of superhelical DNA, an observation which is consistent with the polymerase making a second contact with the DNA upstream in addition to its primary contact with the promoter site. By binding to two separated sites on the DNA the polymerase molecule delimits a DNA domain. Secondly, the transition from the closed to the open complex formed at the *lac* promoter in the presence of CAP is accompanied by a substantial increase in the overall bend in the DNA around the complex, which would be consistent with a value of > 180°; that is, the structure would be similar to an apex. A change in the direction of the DNA bend implies, in this case, a change in writhe. The magnitude of such a writhe would be sufficient to explain the missing half turn, which would then imply that toroidal wrapping of the DNA around the enzyme makes little or no contribution to the topology of the open complex. What is the origin of this writhe? The untwisting of the DNA in the promoter is thought to be initiated in the –10 region and the untwisted region then migrates to the transcription startpoint. Such a migration would generate negative superhelicity immediately upstream of the enzyme. Since this region constitutes a closed domain the superhelical strain would be confined and be manifest as a writhe (Figure 4.9). Since this process further unwinds topologically the DNA in the polymerase–promoter complex it will be driven by negative superhelicity. There is one further implication of this mechanism. It is established that the change in linking number associated with the polymerase–DNA complex is maintained during the subsequent initiation and elongation of the RNA molecule, suggesting that the overall topology of the complex is also maintained. In this context the generation of the additional writhe could function to apply a torque to the enzyme and so drive the unwinding of the DNA during the extension of the RNA molecule. Because of the generation of negative superhelicity behind the enzyme during this relative motion the writhe would be self maintaining.

## REFERENCES

Ansari, A.Z., Chael, M.L. and O'Halloran, T.V. (1992) Allosteric underwinding of DNA is a critical step in positive control of transcription by Hg-MerR. *Nature*, **355**, 89–7.

Bracco, L., Kotlartz, P., Kolb, A. *et al.* (1989) Synthetic curved DNA sequences can act as transcriptional activators in *Escherichia coli*. *EMBO Journal*, **8**, 4289–96.

Buc, H. and McClure, W.R. (1985) Kinetics of open complex formation between *E. coli* RNA polymerase and the *lac* UV$_5$ promoter. *Biochemistry*, **24**, 2712–23.

Buckle M., Buc, H. and Travers, A.A. (1992) DNA deformation in nucleoprotein complexes between RNA polymerase, cAMP receptor protein and the *lac* UV$_5$ promoter probed by singlet oxygen. *EMBO Journal* (In press).

Liu, L.P. and Wang, J.C. (1987) Supercoiling of the DNA template during transcription. *Proceedings of the National Academy of Sciences of the USA*, **84**, 7024–7.

Zinkel, S.S. and Crothers, D.M. (1991) Catabolite activator protein-induced bending in transcription initiation. *Journal of Molecular Biology*, **219**, 201–15.

# 5

# The regulation of promoter selectivity in eubacteria

## 5.1 CONTROL OF STABLE RNA SYNTHESIS

Broadly speaking, bacterial genes can be divided into two main classes. The first class, which includes the majority of genes in the chromosome, codes directly for protein products. These genes are transcribed into mRNA which are short-lived molecules with typical half-lives of 2–5 minutes. The transcription of genes in this class is in general regulated by DNA-binding proteins in addition to RNA polymerase, acting either to repress or activate transcription initiation. By contrast, the second class of genes does not code for proteins, but rather for RNA products, such as ribosomal and transfer RNA species, that play structural and functional roles in translation. Unlike mRNA, the tRNA and rRNA species are metabolically stable and have very long half-lives. These products are also extremely abundant, such that during exponential growth these RNA molecules account for roughly 97% of the total RNA content of the cell. At maximum growth rates a bacterium such as *Escherichia coli* divides every 20 minutes. Each bacterium contains approximately 10 000 ribosomes and hence the same number of copies of each rRNA molecule. Thus each cell must synthesize this number of rRNA molecules in every generation, a process that requires a high rate of transcription. To meet this requirement most bacteria contain multiple copies of the rRNA genes; in *E. coli* there are seven. Even with this number of gene copies, at maximum growth rates an RNA molecule must be initiated at the rate of one every second on each rRNA transcription unit. At such high growth rates at least 50% of the actively transcribing RNA polymerase molecules in the bacterial cell are engaged in the transcription of stable RNA genes. In addition to this high transcription rate the stable RNA genes are also subject to at least two forms of regulation, known as stringent and growth rate control.

In a rapidly growing bacterium a major proportion of the available energy is required for the synthesis of ribosomes which themselves are necessary to maintain the capability for protein synthesis in the progeny bacteria. In this environment any perturbation which diminishes the efficiency of the translation process usually results in an abrupt cessation of the accumulation of both ribosomal and transfer RNA. The classic example of this phenomenon is the so-called 'stringent' response. When a bacterial culture is effectively starved of a required amino acid the cells accumulate two unusual guanosine nucleotides, guanosine 5′-diphosphate 3′-diphosphate (ppGpp or guanosine tetraphosphate) and guanine 5′-triphosphate 3′-diphosphate (pppGpp or guanosine pentaphosphate), the former to millimolar levels (Figure 5.1). This rapid increase is correlated with the cessation of stable RNA production. This cessation of production results from a reduction in the rate of transcription initiation by about 90% coupled with an increase in the rate of breakdown of the nascent RNA.

In general, during the exponential phase of growth, there is an excellent, but not absolute, correlation between the level of ppGpp and the rate of accumulation of stable RNA. Mutant bacteria which fail to synthesize guanine polyphosphates when starved of an amino acid also continue to accumulate stable RNA. Such bacteria are said to be relaxed. However, in addition to mutations which directly affect the level of ppGpp, the *in vivo* response of stable RNA synthesis to amino acid limitation can also be altered by mutations in the genes encoding subunits of RNA polymerase. In particular, mutations in both *rpo*B and *rpo*D alter the correlation between stable RNA production and ppGpp levels. These two classes of mutation strongly suggest that the ultimate target of ppGpp is RNA polymerase itself.

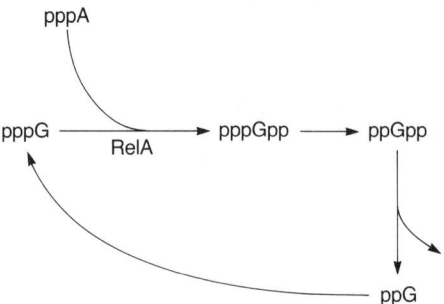

**Figure 5.1** The generation of ppGpp on amino acid starvation.

The second mode of control of the transcription of stable RNA genes is growth rate control. In different media bacteria grow at different rates. However, in general the rate of transcription of stable RNA genes is tightly coupled to the rate of growth such that no more ribosomes and tRNA molecules are produced than are required to maintain that growth rate. This means that, as the growth rate increases, so does the rate of stable RNA production. This tight coupling of stable RNA production with growth rate is largely, but not entirely, exerted at the level of transcription initiation. The synthesis of many other RNA species, for example *lac* mRNA, does not however respond to growth rate variation in the same manner. In such cases the rate of RNA production fails to increase, and in some cases may even fall as the growth rate increases.

## 5.2 STABLE RNA PROMOTERS

Stable RNA promoters must, *in vivo*, meet two requirements: they must support an extremely high rate of transcription initiation at rapid growth rates and they must also possess the capability to be regulated by stringent and growth rate control mechanisms. In structure these promoters are homologous to other $\sigma^{70}$ promoters, although in general the sequence of the −35 region is not optimal. In addition they also contain two other characteristic features (Figure 5.2). First, the optimal activity of the promoter depends not only on the core promoter region but also requires upstream sequences, which in some examples may extend for more than 100 bp proximal to the transcription startpoint. The function of these upstream sequences is dependent on the growth phase of the bacterial cell. In the early exponential phase of growth the whole upstream region is required, but in stationary phase the upstream sequences do not modulate the activity of the promoter and are dispensable for optimum activity. Secondly, a highly conserved G-C rich sequence, the 'discriminator', is located immediately downstream of the −10 region in stable

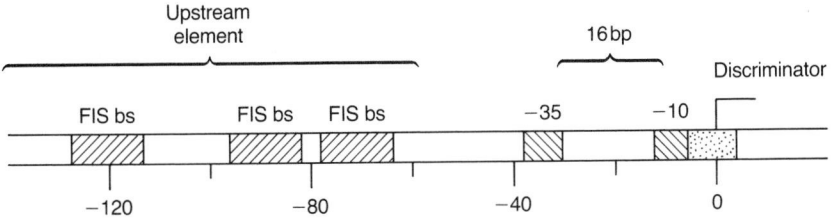

**Figure 5.2** The organization of stable RNA promoters in *E. coli*.

RNA promoters from *E. coli* but not from *Bacillus subtilis*. For the two *E. coli* promoters so far tested, *tyr*T and *Fis*, this sequence is necessary for stringent control, whereas, by contrast, the upstream element can be deleted without altering the pattern of regulation. For example, when the *tyr*T discriminator is mutated from GCGCCCCGC to GCTTAAGGC, expression of the *tyr*T gene becomes relaxed. Similarly, this same mutation alters the response of the promoter to growth rate such that instead of behaving like a stable RNA promoter the modulation of RNA production is more similar to that from the *lac* promoter. Thus, whereas stringent control appears to be dependent primarily on the nature of the discriminator sequence, growth rate control is dependent on both the discriminator and the upstream element (Figure 5.3).

What is the mechanism for the regulation of promoter activity at the molecular level? To understand this mechanism fully it is first necessary to discuss the properties of the *E. coli* RNA polymerase holoenzyme. *In vitro* this enzyme will initiate from stable RNA promoters lacking an upstream element on both relaxed and negatively supercoiled DNA. The presence of the upstream element does, however, increase the rate of transcription, notably from supercoiled templates by increasing the

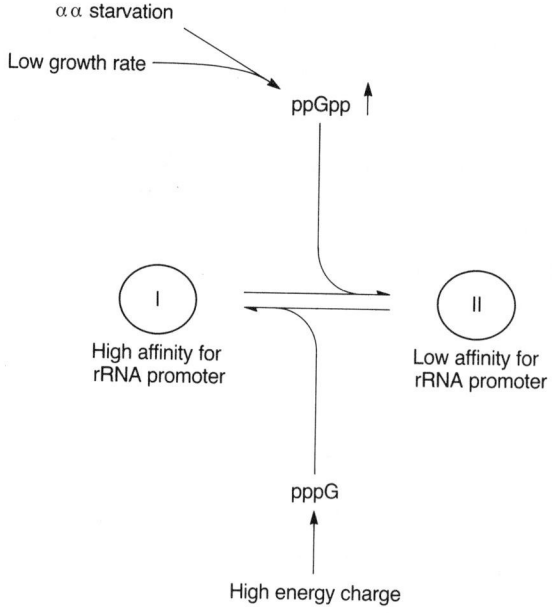

**Figure 5.3** The physiological role of promoter elements for stable RNA transcription.

initial affinity of the polymerase for the promoter site. Importantly, the limiting step in the initiation process at these promoters is the initial binding of the transcribing enzyme. This process is regulated *in vitro*, transcription from both relaxed and supercoiled DNA being inhibited by physiological concentrations of ppGpp, although that from relaxed DNA has only a limited sensitivity. Nevertheless, in both cases the inhibition is dependent on the nature of the discriminator sequence. This phenomenon is consistent with the notion that the natural target of ppGpp is RNA polymerase itself. Further evidence that this is correct is the observation that ppGpp alters the physical properties of the holoenzyme, reducing its sedimentation coefficient from 14 S to around 12.5 S without changing the subunit composition. This reduction implies a substantial change in the overall shape of the enzyme, suggesting that the nucleotide has the potential to alter its conformational state. Fortuitously, two functionally distinct states of the *E. coli* holoenzyme can be distinguished and partially separated by zone sedimentation. The slower sedimenting form preferentially utilizes negatively supercoiled DNA as a template, whereas the faster sedimenting form is equally active on supercoiled and relaxed DNA. These forms also differ in two other respects. First, the 'fast' form is active at low salt concentrations and the 'slow' form at high salt concentrations. Secondly, the mode of regulation of activity differs. For the 'fast' form, initiation at stable RNA promoters is inhibited by ppGpp and enhanced by GTP. In other words, the enzyme senses the concentration ratio of these two nucleotides. By contrast, for the 'fast' form such initiation is inhibited by ADP and activated by ATP. The important point is that only one form of the enzyme is sensitive to ppGpp. This sensitivity can be conferred *in vitro* by the ω subunit. However, this result is in conflict with the genetic demonstration that a null mutation in the *rpo*Z gene encoding ω does not affect the stringent response *in vivo*.

When RNA polymerase binds to a stable RNA promoter *in vitro* it protects DNA sequences extending 60–70 bp upstream of the transcription startpoint, yet the polymerase dissociates very rapidly from the promoter site and the resulting rate of initiation is slow. This implies that additional components are required for the high rates of transcription observed *in vitro*. Such high rates require sequences in the upstream region. How do these sequences function? The *tyr*T, *tuf*B and *rrn*B P1 upstream regions contain three binding sites for the FIS (factor for inversion stimulation) protein. FIS was initially characterized as a protein which promotes the inversion of certain segments of DNA but is dispensable for growth in laboratory conditions. It is a small dimeric protein which tightly bends DNA but possesses only very limited sequence selectivity. For some stable RNA genes FIS functions *in vivo* as a necessary transcriptional activator. *In vitro* FIS protein, when bound to the upstream region, will similarly stimulate transcription, but only from a supercoiled DNA template. The extent to which FIS increases the rate of transcription *in vivo* is strongly dependent on the intrinsic strength of the promoter. In general, as for the CAP protein, any mutations which decrease affinity of RNA polymerase for the promoter, for example, down point mutations in the –10 region, result in an increased dependence of transcription on FIS function. This same phenomenon is also observed *in vitro*. Not only does FIS preferentially stimulate transcription from weak promoters but also this protein will override the impairment of promoter function by ppGpp.

A second protein which binds to similar sequences is a small basic protein known variously as H1 or H-NS. This protein is again not essential for viability but mutations in the cognate gene are characterized by a variety of phenotypes which together indicate that the active protein functions as a repressor of transcription. The genetic evidence therefore suggests that, for at least some stable RNA genes, transcription is activated by FIS and repressed by H1 binding to the upstream element.

What is the function of the upstream element and how is it affected by FIS and H1 function? The DNA of the upstream elements of stable RNA transcription units is either bendable or intrinsically bent. In a supercoiled DNA molecule such a region would be expected to be located at the apex of the interwound form of DNA and could then make widely separated contacts with the polymerase (Figure 5.4). The property of curvature is inherent to such regions. If the polymerase had a sufficiently high affinity for the promoter site the enzyme could by itself stabilize the loop and would not then require ancillary proteins such as FIS to increase the rate of transcription initiation. If, however, the polymerase were effectively limiting, either as a consequence of promoter mutations or of a low concentration of the enzyme itself, FIS would function to bend the DNA into the appropriate configuration and thereby stabilize a loop. The three FIS-binding sites in the upstream regions of the characterized stable RNA promoters are organized in double helical phase such that full occupancy would form a DNA bend of 180–270°, that is effectively equivalent to an apical loop. IHF would act in an analogous manner at the $\lambda\ P_L$ promoter. H1, by binding to similar sequences, would antagonize the action of FIS and also prevent any thermally induced random bending activating transcription. In other words, H1 would act to prevent the assumption of the active DNA configuration.

Two conclusions may be drawn from this pattern of regulation. First, both FIS and H1 are relatively promiscuous DNA-binding proteins and are involved in processes involving the manipulation of DNA other than transcription. Both, however, have a strong predilection for bendable sequences. They are not specific regulators in the sense of the *lac* repressor and indeed both are dispensable. Secondly, the complexity of

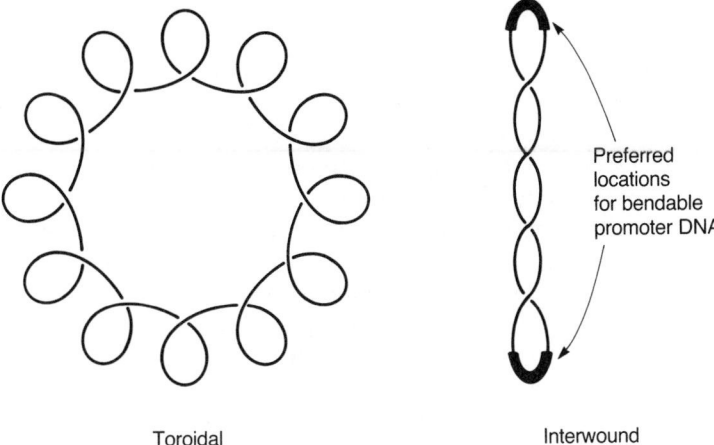

Toroidal

Interwound

Preferred
locations
for bendable
promoter DNA

**Figure 5.4** A model for the regulation of transcription initiation by the *E. coli* DNA-bending protein FIS.

the pattern of proteins binding to the stable RNA promoter regions implies that there may be other, as yet functionally uncharacterized, DNA binding proteins that regulate their activity.

## 5.3 THE TRANSITION FROM EXPONENTIAL GROWTH TO STATIONARY PHASE AND VICE VERSA

How does the pattern of regulation of stable RNA transcription reflect the physiology of the *E. coli* cell? The transitions from an exponential phase of growth to stationary phase and vice versa represent an enormous shift in the quantitative patterns of gene expression. In the exponential phase the cell utilizes the available energy to increase the capacity for protein synthesis. In the stationary phase the cell operates on a replacement economy and functions to conserve the available capacity.

How are these switches accomplished? One crucial factor appears to be the availability of the FIS and H1 proteins. The intracellular concentration of FIS increases rapidly immediately before entry into the exponential phase and thereafter falls steadily. By contrast, H1 attains its highest concentration at the onset of the stationary phase at a time when the concentration of FIS is very low. Other components of the transcription machinery, notably RNA polymerase itself, do not exhibit such substantial fluctuations in availability. The hypothesis is therefore that the ancillary DNA-binding proteins are important regulators of stable RNA transcription during growth phase transitions. The intracellular level of FIS is subject to both autoregulation and to stringent control, but it is not yet known how the level in H1 is regulated.

The growth phase transitions may also be associated with other significant changes in the intracellular milieu. One of the first events in the transition to the exponential phase of growth is a rapid increase in the intracellular concentration of $K^+$ to about 200–300 mmol. Thereafter, in addition the intracellular salt concentration may vary substantially. At the onset of the exponential phase of growth the intracellular concentration of $K^+$ is in the region of 200 mmol and, in the absence of buffering of the medium, this concentration falls steadily to attain a concentration of some 30–50 mmol by the stationary phase. To a certain, but limited, extent this fall may be offset by a rise in the concentration in intracellular $Na^+$. Nevertheless, the overall result is a substantial net fall in the intracellular ionic strength. Associated with these changes, but not necessarily causally related, are alterations in the both the energy charge (the ATP/ADP ratio), and the negative superhelicity of the DNA. Entry into the exponential phase is accompanied by a sharp increase in energy charge and a short transient increase in negative supercoiling, while in the stationary phase the level of negative supercoiling is significantly lower than in the mid-exponential phase.

What is the biological role of FIS in the transition from stationary to exponential phase? Entry into exponential growth is characterized by a short transient burst in stable RNA transcription. The paradox is that, under laboratory conditions, FIS is present in high concentrations, yet, for the most active stable RNA promoters, has little effect on maximal activity even though the upstream elements of these promoters contain multiple strong binding sites for the bending protein. One difference apparent in the absence of FIS is a slight delay in the appearance of the initial burst of transcription. The inference is that FIS acts to kickstart cells into exponential growth and so would confer a selective advantage on *fis*⁺ cells. From our knowledge of the biological properties of FIS and from the high conservation of the positions of the FIS binding sites in the upstream regions of stable RNA promoters, this kickstart would operate principally under conditions of effective polymerase limitation, which, under natural conditions, could conceivably be induced by prolonged nutrient deprivation. Functionally the protein would act to stabilize the configuration of DNA that is necessary for optimal initiation. The rapid changes in superhelicity at the onset of exponential growth would be accompanied by alterations in both the twist and writhe of DNA. Because the twist changes, the phasing of intrinsic bends in the DNA relative to the helical repeat would also change, with the consequence that, over approximately 100 bp of DNA, the direction of the overall bend would change. In other words, an appropriate direction of bending of free DNA might only be attained efficiently at certain superhelical densities. By stabilizing the required configuration at a suboptimal density, FIS could increase the efficiency of initiation at a crucial time.

In this context the biological relevance of the pattern of regulation of RNA polymerase also becomes apparent. The conditions which favour the activity of the 'slow' form (high ionic strength and a negatively supercoiled DNA template) are those which predominate at the onset of the exponential phase. By contrast, the conditions which favour the activity of the 'fast' form (low ionic strength and a low superhelical density) are those which are found during the stationary phase. The regulation of the promoter selectivity of RNA polymerase by nucleotides is also consistent with this pattern. During the exponential phase of growth the bacterial cell is geared to the production of the machinery for protein synthesis, with a relatively assured constant energy supply whose level will depend on the nature of the carbon source. However, under such conditions the supply of amino acids, and therefore the efficiency of the translation process, may be less assured. This latter parameter is reflected in the relative levels of GTP and ppGpp which are monitored by the 'slow' form of RNA polymerase. It is thus this form of the enzyme which has the potential both to mediate the stringent response and to modulate the rate of transcription initiation of stable RNA genes as a function of the carbon source dependent variations in ppGpp levels. The regulation of the 'fast' form of the polymerase by an ATP-ADP couple is also fully consistent with the physiology of the stationary phase of growth induced by acidification of the growth medium. In this state the potential for growth of the culture is limited, not primarily by the availability of amino acids, but by the ability to generate ATP. By monitoring the energy charge in the cell the RNA polymerase adjusts the rate of transcription of the stable RNA genes to the available energy supply.

In the stationary phase, the morphology of an *E. coli* cell is clearly distinguishable from that of a cell in the exponential phase of growth. The bacterium is rounded instead of elongated and the DNA content is reduced to one genome per cell. In this respect the growth phase transition may be regarded as a simple form of differentiation analogous to the sporulation of *Bacillus subtilis*. Some housekeeping genes, including the stable RNA genes, are expressed both during the exponential and stationary phases of growth, albeit at quantitatively different levels. There is, however, a certain class of about 50 genes in *E. coli* which are only involved in the assumption of the changed morphology and are expressed during the stationary phase. The mechanism of transcriptional regulation of these genes is entirely different. The promoter structure of these genes differs from those normally expressed during exponential growth, containing the conserved $-10$ and $-35$ sequences C/TTGCAA and CGGCT/AAGTA respectively. The regulatory gene that is required

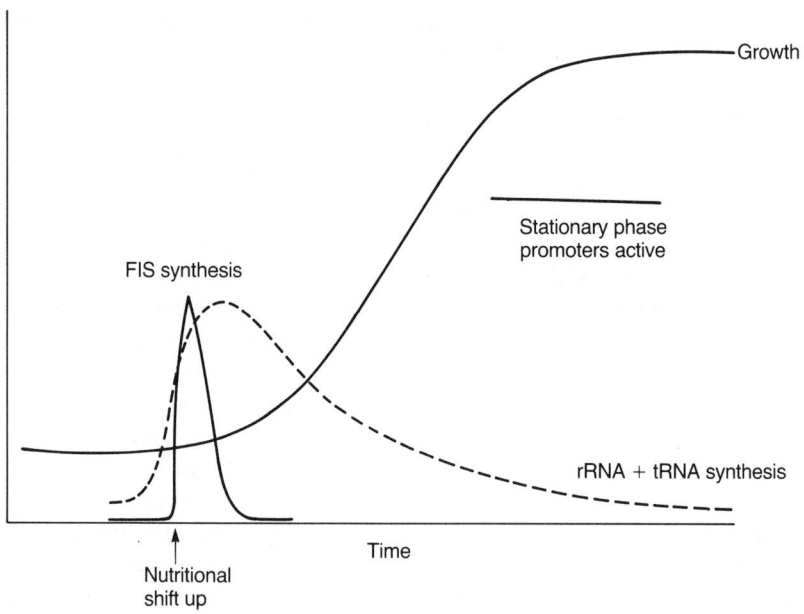

**Figure 5.5** Changes in the transcription apparatus during the growth cycle of *E. coli.*

for the expression of this class of genes is homologous to the $\sigma^{70}$ subunit of RNA polymerase, and consequently it has been inferred that the transition in growth phase requires not only a change in the regulatory properties of the $\sigma^{70}$ containing holoenzyme but also the activation of an independent set of genes for which the core polymerase is complexed with a different sigma factor (Figure 5.5).

## 5.4 SIGMA FACTORS AND PROMOTER RECOGNITION

The regulation of stable RNA synthesis by purine nucleotides is in essence a quantitative modulation of the interaction of RNA polymerase with its promoter site. Although this mode of control may alter the extent of the binding site with which the enzyme interacts, there is no indication that it affects the primary recognition of the promoter site; that is, the –35 and –10 hexamer sequences utilized by the polymerase remain unchanged. However the recognition specificity of the polymerase can be changed by substituting the sigma factor associated with the core polymerase. In *E. coli* and closely related bacteria, such alternate specificities are associated with the transcription of small sets of genes required for the heat shock response, for nitrogen fixation, and for the production of flagella. The sequential substitution of sigma factors is also a feature of programmed transcription in bacteria in situations where the expression of successive sets of genes is required for a transition to a different cell state. The simplest example of such a transition is the progression from an exponential to a stationary phase cell in *E. coli*. More complex programmes are characteristic of sporulation in *Bacillus subtilis* and of growth transitions in *Streptomyces* species. Similarly, the development of certain bacterial viruses of *E. coli* and of *B. subtilis* is dependent on phage-encoded sigma factors.

## 5.5 THE HEAT SHOCK RESPONSE

The heat shock response is a ubiquitous phenomenon in both prokaryotes and eukaryotes. It is characterized by the rapid induction of a small set of proteins on exposure of cells to any environmental insult that results in the denaturation or unfolding of proteins. The classic mode of induction is a heat shock, a significant, but non-lethal, increase in temperature. The response may also be induced by, for example, exposure to heavy metal ions, ethanol or amino acid analogues. In the latter two cases the structure of some nascent proteins is disrupted in such a way as to prevent normal folding. Predominant among the induced heat shock proteins are the 'chaperonins' which permit the reassumption of the correct tertiary structure by unfolded proteins. In addition, the heat shock proteins include proteins required for the solubilization of denatured aggregated proteins and also proteases. Synthesis of the vegetative sigma factor itself is also increased in concert. A further notable feature of the temperature dependent response is a concomitant and substantial reduction in the rate of transcription of stable RNA. Under conditions of mild heat shock the transcriptional induction is transient, and normal patterns of gene expression are restored, provided the products of the heat shock regulon are functional.

The expression of the genes of the heat shock regulon is normally dependent on the product of a single gene, *rpo*H (previously known as *hin* or *htp*R). The product of this gene is a 32 kDa protein, $\sigma^{32}$, which contains two regions of homology to $\sigma^{70}$; $\sigma^{32}$ associates with the core polymerase, and directs binding to the promoters of the heat shock regulon. *In vivo* the heat shock sigma factor and the vegetative factor appear to compete for the core polymerase; enhanced levels of the vegetative factor result in a reduced expression of the heat shock genes while decreased levels result in an enhanced response. The induction of the heat shock regulon is correlated *in vivo* with a rapid increase in the intracellular concentration of $\sigma^{32}$. Under normal growth conditions this protein is present at low concentrations and is necessary for the transcription of the chaperonin genes. This low level is in part a consequence of the short half-life of the protein. However, in heat shock, not only is the protein itself stabilized, but also the efficiency of translation of its mRNA is increased. As with the response itself the resulting increase in the levels of the factor is transient, the maximum concentration being attained within a few minutes of the initial rise in temperature. Although the increase in $\sigma^{32}$ levels is sufficient to account for the induction of the heat shock genes it does not adequately explain the shutting off of the transcription of stable RNA genes, since the absolute levels of $\sigma^{32}$ remain below those of the vegetative factor. Simple competition between the two sigma proteins can not therefore be the sole determinant of the transcriptional switch. A possible explanation is that free $\sigma^{70}$ requires one of the chaperonins to maintain it in the active state. Heat shock would result in the sequestration of the chaperonins by unfolded proteins, with a consequent inactivation of $\sigma^{70}$. Such a mechanism would explain why the *rpo*D gene encoding $\sigma^{70}$ is under the control of a $\sigma^{32}$ directed promoter. Thus, on induction of the heat shock regulon, the replacement of $\sigma^{70}$ would be co-ordinated with that of the chaperonins (Figure 5.6).

The transience of the heat shock response is no longer observed if the internal milieu of the cell remains inimical to the normal structural stability of proteins. This occurs either when one of the chaperonins is no longer functional or when the destabilizing condition is sufficiently strong, for example, if the temperature is too high (50 °C) or in the continuous presence of high concentrations of ethanol. The continued and virtually exclusive expression of the heat shock genes at temperatures that are too high for viability requires that the intracellular level of $\sigma^{32}$ be maintained. However rpoH itself is not part of the heat shock regulon. The regulatory region of this gene contains three promoters; two of these are recognized by the vegetative holoenzyme, but the sequence of the third does not correspond to promoters of the $\sigma^{70}$ or the $\sigma^{32}$ classes. Instead it is inferred that this third promoter is responsible for the transcription of the gene at very high temperatures and that its recognition requires an additional minor sigma factor (Figure 5.6).

## 5.6 $\sigma^{54}$: A TARGET FOR TRANSCRIPTIONAL ENHANCERS

The spatial arrangement of the recognition sequences for $\sigma^{70}$ and $\sigma^{32}$ are very similar, with the centres of the two recognition elements separated by approximately two double helical turns. However, there are several diverse sets of genes in different bacteria in which the two conserved elements in the promoters are separated by only a single double helical turn. These sets include those for nitrogen assimilation in *E. coli* and *Salmonella*, those for nitrogen fixation in the closely related bacterium,

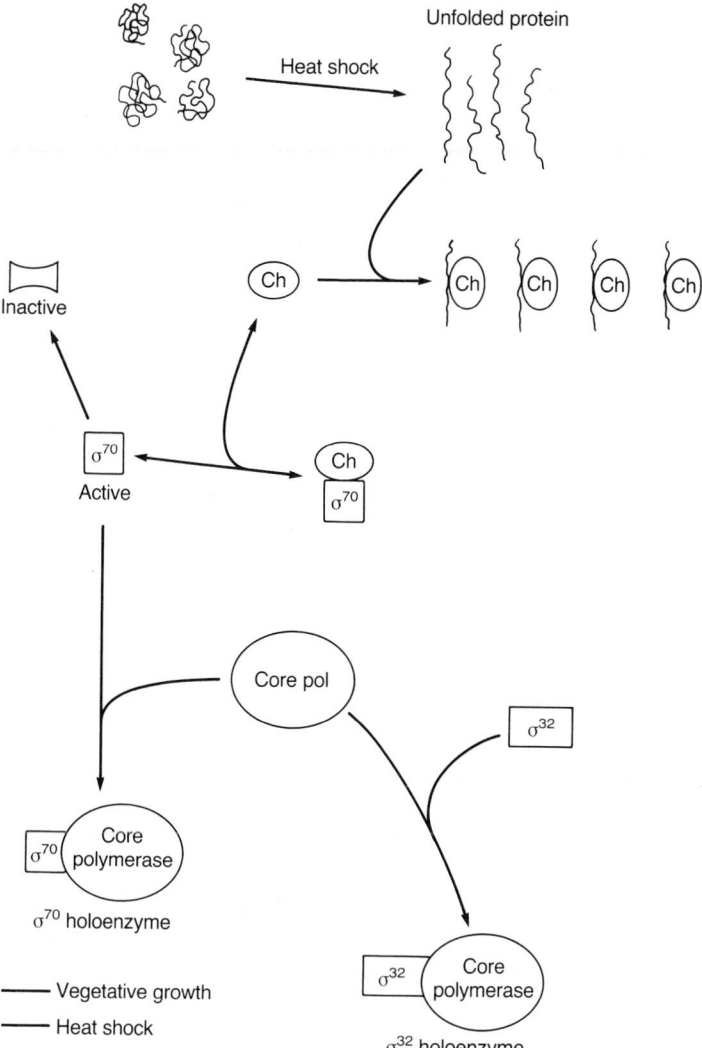

**Figure 5.6** The regulation of RNA synthesis during the heat shock response.

*Klebsiella*, those for flagella production in *Caulobacter*, and those for the metabolism of xylitol and related compounds in *Pseudomonas*. For all these gene sets the promoter sequences are closely related, suggesting that a common regulatory mechanism has been adapted to different purposes in different bacteria.

The best understood of these regulons are those for nitrogen assimilation and nitrogen fixation. For these regulons, not only is the promoter structure common, but also the other genes required for transcriptional regulation. The activity of any promoter in these sets is dependent on three genes, *rpo*N (also known as *ntr*A or *gln*F) which encodes a sigma factor, *ntr*C (*gln*G) or *nif*A which encode DNA-binding transcriptional activators, and *ntr*B(*gln*L) which encodes a protein kinase/phosphatase responsible for the regulation of NtrC activity.

How do these proteins regulate the activity of the target promoters? The initial signal for the activation of these promoters is the depletion of available ammonia. The intracellular concentration of the rpoN product, $\sigma^{54}$, remains relatively constant under these conditions. On association with the core polymerase the enzyme forms a closed initiation complex but is unable to proceed to the open complex. This implies that, in the cell, the promoters for these regulons are occupied by polymerase. The transition to the open complex requires a direct protein–protein interaction between the polymerase holoenzyme and one or other of the transcriptional activators. The interaction between RNA polymerase and NifA or NtrC possesses two unusual features. Either of these activator proteins can effect activation in an orientation independent fashion when placed at considerable distances (up to 1–2 kb) from the polymerase binding site. This activation at a distance is dependent on the rotational orientation of the binding site with respect to the double helix, a characteristic that is indicative of DNA looping between the activator protein and the polymerase and which is also formally analogous to the phenomenon of transcriptional enhancement observed in eukaryotic systems. Indeed, DNA loops between the two bound proteins can be directly visualized by electron microscopy. However, once the RNA polymerase is allowed to transcribe the DNA, the looped structures disappear. The looping model is also supported by other aspects of NifA responsive promoters. For example, in the *nif*HDK regulatory region, between a NifA binding site centred at −132 and the polymerase binding site, is a binding site for IHF centred at −56. Since IHF is known to induce bends in DNA a plausible role for this protein would be to facilitate loop formation. The second feature of the NtrC and NifA transcriptional activators is their requirement for ATP. These DNA-binding proteins, in common with all others that regulate $\sigma^{54}$ dependent promoters, possess an ATPase activity that is dependent on both binding to the target site and phosphorylation of the protein. This activity is required absolutely for driving the transition from the closed to the open initiation complex.

A crucial property of transcriptional enhancement by the NifA and NtrC proteins is the selection of the target promoter. Transcription of glutamine synthetase operon, glnAG, is driven by two contiguous promoters, one of which is dependent on $\sigma^{70}$ and the other on $\sigma^{54}$. Only the $\sigma^{54}$ promoter is activated by NtrC. Thus, even though the enhancer proteins can act over relatively large distances, activation is restricted to a particular set of promoters. This contrasts with eukaryotic systems in which the promoter selectivity of enhancer protein binding sites is conferred as a consequence of their position within the same DNA domain as the target promoters. The target of the bacterial enhancer proteins is thus the $\sigma^{54}$-containing holoenzyme itself. It has been proposed that a highly conserved glutamine rich amino-terminal domain of the sigma factor itself is required for the protein–protein contacts necessary for enhancement to occur. Such domains in eukaryotic transcription factors have this precise property.

A further question is why the $\sigma^{54}$-containing holoenzyme should be utilized for the expression of such diverse functions in different bacteria. The assumption is that, in all cases, this sigma factor confers the ability to respond to an enhancer protein and this ability allows the rapid activation of polymerase molecules already bound to a particular small class of promoter sites.

The mechanism by which $\sigma^{54}$-dependent promoters function begs the question of how this response is coupled to the appropriate environmental signal. The primary signal for the activation of the nitrogen assimilation promoters is ammonia depletion, since glutamine synthetase is the only enzyme that can convert ammonia at low concentrations to an organic form. Cells grown in the presence of high ammonia concentrations contain about five molecules of NtrC protein, sufficient only to bind to the regulatory region of the $\sigma^{54}$ dependent promoter of the glutamine synthetase operon. This region contains multiple NtrC binding sites with a high affinity for the protein. In high ammonia concentrations NtrC cannot activate transcription, but on ammonia depletion its phosphorylation by NtrB protein allows activation to occur. Expression of glnAG raises the intracellular concentration of NtrC(GlnG) to about 70 molecules per cell, at which level the protein can bind to other NtrC dependent promoter regions, amongst which are those for the nitrogen fixation genes. On re-addition of ammonia the reverse process occurs. NtrC is dephosphorylated by NtrB as a consequence of the association of the latter protein with a third component $P_{II}$. The activity of $P_{II}$ is also dependent on ammonia levels; in high ammonia concentrations the protein is unmodified, whereas in limiting ammonia concentrations it is uridylylated, so that it can no longer interact with NtrB. This modification cycle parallels that of glutamine synthetase itself. The activity of this enzyme is regulated by a reversible adenylylation, the less active form being adenylylated.

This modification is catalysed in both directions by an adenyl transferase whose regulatory subunit itself undergoes a reversible uridylylation. When uridylylated, the transferase catalyses the deadenylylation of the synthetase, whereas the unmodified transferase adenylates the synthetase. This uridylylation, as for the $P_{II}$ protein, is a response to low glutamine levels, or limiting ammonia (Figure 5.7).

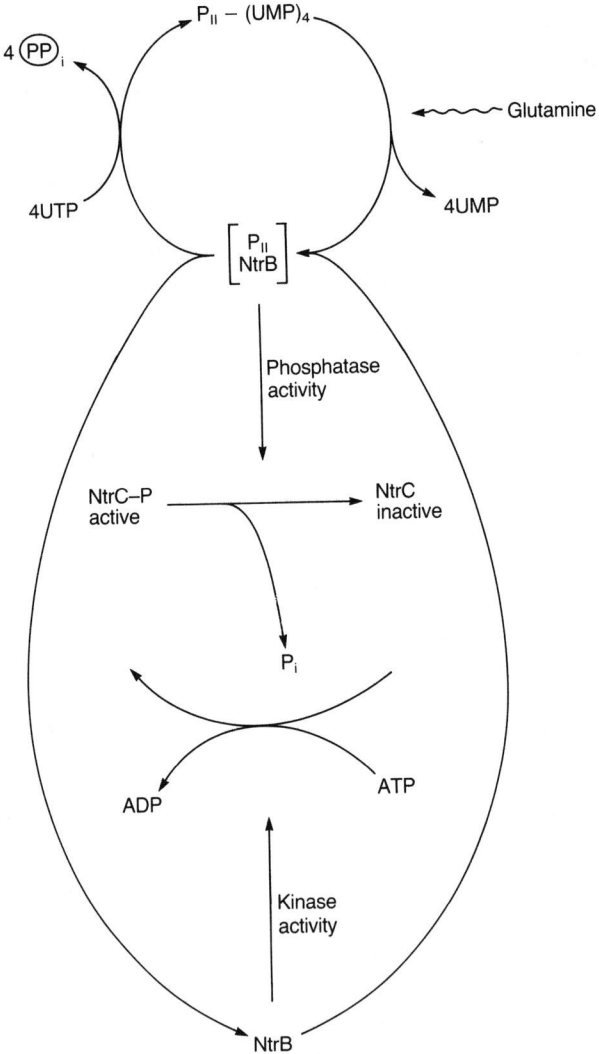

**Figure 5.7** The regulatory cascades for the activation and inactivation of the NtrB protein.

## 5.7 THE TRANSCRIPTIONAL PROGRAMMES OF BACTERIAL VIRUSES

The multiplication of viruses in their host cells is often characterized by a complex temporal pattern of gene expression in which different classes of RNA transcripts are synthesized sequentially. A classic example of this mode of transcriptional regulation is bacteriophage T4 (Figure 5.8). Immediately after infection transcription of one strand, the l-strand, of T4 DNA proceeds from a number of promoter sites on the T4 genome to produce early RNA. This RNA synthesis occurs even in the presence of

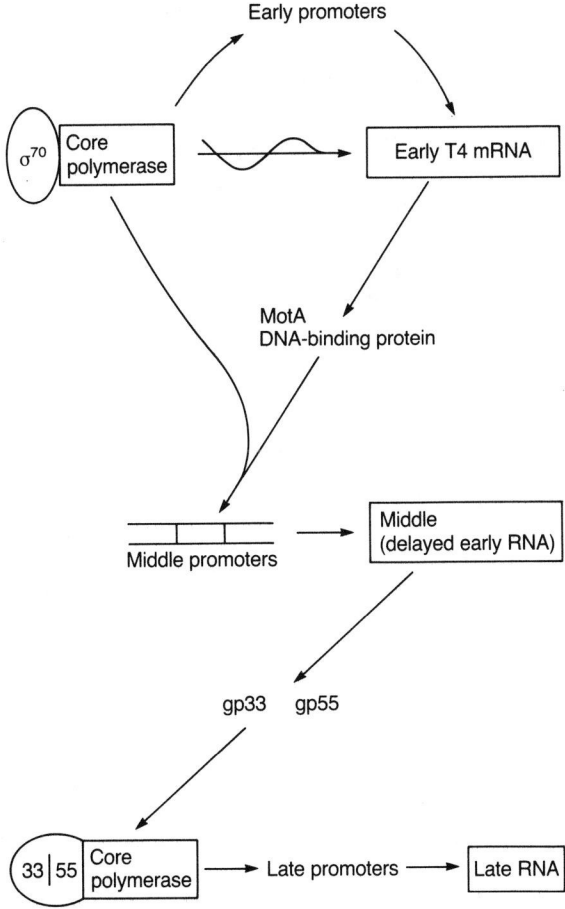

**Figure 5.8** The temporal control of transcription during the life cycle of bacteriophage T4.

inhibitors of protein synthesis, such as chloramphenicol, and is not dependent on the function of any T4 genes in a previous infection cycle. *In vitro*, these same promoters are utilized efficiently by the polymerase holoenzyme containing $\sigma^{70}$, although their consensus sequence does not correspond well with that of the homologous bacterial promoters. Following the transcription of the early class of RNA transcripts a second set of transcripts, termed 'middle' RNA, appears 2–4 minutes after infection at 37 °C, again synthesized predominantly from the l-strand. The production of this RNA requires the function of the phage *mot*A gene. Finally a third set of transcripts, the 'late' RNA, is synthesized principally from the r-strand of DNA. The onset of this transcription correlates with that of DNA replication on which, in a normal infection, it is absolutely dependent. In addition to this requirement late RNA synthesis requires the expression of phage genes 55, 45 and 33. Throughout this entire transcriptional programme all phage RNA synthesis retains the rifampicin sensitivity of the host RNA polymerase indicating that at least the β-subunit of the enzyme is necessary for the production of all classes of phage RNA.

In addition to the demonstrable dependence of the transcriptional switches on the function of specific genes the host RNA polymerase is itself successively modified throughout the infection cycle. Thus, shortly after infection, the subunits of the polymerase are altered by the covalent addition of ADP-ribose, a function that is dependent on the non-essential mod and alt genes. A second modification is the binding on the phage-encoded RbpA protein which is retained by the core polymerase throughout the synthesis of RNA. The function of this latter modification is so far unknown. A further factor that may influence the transcription of the T4 genome is the substantial, but transient, reduction in the intracellular ionic strength consequent upon leakage from the cell immediately after infection.

How is this complex pattern of transcription and polymerase modifications co-ordinated at the molecular level? The switch from early to middle RNA requires the recognition of a distinct class of promoter sequences which lack the –35 hexamer characteristic of early promoters. Instead, centred at about –30, the middle promoters contain the recognition sequence for the DNA-binding MotA protein. MotA functions as a positive regulator, possibly analogous to the $C_I$ repressor, and potentiates initiation by the $\sigma^{70}$ containing polymerase holoenzyme. An additional complication of this phase of the transcriptional programme is that certain genes normally transcribed from MotA dependent promoters are also transcribed by polymerases initiating at early promoters as a consequence of a failure of the RNA polymerase to terminate at ρ dependent terminators that are functional *in vitro*.

The regulation of late RNA synthesis belies the apparent simplicity of late promoters. These consist only of a highly conserved TATAAATA located approximately 10 bp upstream of transcription start sites, although they contain in addition 'flexible' DNA sequences positioned at –25/–26 as in bacterial $\sigma^{70}$ dependent promoters. *In vitro* late promoter recognition can be accomplished by the complex of gp55 with the core polymerase. In such complexes gp55 acts as a sigma factor, although this protein is not homologous with other sigma factors. However, as with $\sigma^{54}$–polymerase–promoter complexes, such complexes at late promoters remain in the closed state.

How then is the transition to the open complex effected? *In vivo*, the regulation of late RNA synthesis is complex. T4 late gene expression requires the function of two T4 genes, genes 33 and 45, in addition to gene 55. The protein products of all of these genes bind to RNA polymerase. Gp45, which binds least tightly, is also a component of the machinery for DNA replication; a crucial feature of late T4 gene expression is their dependence on DNA replication. The transcription of these genes is not turned on unless the replication of viral DNA is initiated; if this replication is blocked, this transcription is substantially reduced. Nevertheless, it is possible to at least partially uncouple late transcription from replication by the introduction of breaks into the viral DNA *in vivo*.

How is this coupling of transcription and replication accomplished at the molecular level? Two components of the T4 replication machinery, in addition to gp45, are necessary for coupling to occur. These are the products of genes 44 and 62. *In vitro*, these proteins, in the presence of gp55 and gp33, are sufficient to stimulate initiation at late T4 promoters. Their function in DNA replication is to serve as a 'sliding clamp' for the DNA polymerase by binding to the junction of the DNA primer and template. These proteins have the property that they can bind to a simple break in the DNA template: a nick in a single strand. Once bound at such a site these accessory proteins can activate late transcription at a promoter site that can be located at a considerable distance either upstream or downstream from the nick. In other words, the nick acts as an enhancer element. The difference between this element and classical enhancers is that *in vivo* the binding sites for the accessory proteins are likely to be the DNA replication forks and thus be mobile (Figure 5.9).

The remaining question is how the link between the replicating complex and the RNA polymerase is accomplished. The target of transcriptional enhancement by the replication proteins is the gp55 containing RNA polymerase. Neither the core polymerase nor the $\sigma^{70}$ containing enzyme is capable of enhancement. *In vitro* gp33 is sufficient to mediate the coupling between the replication complex and RNA

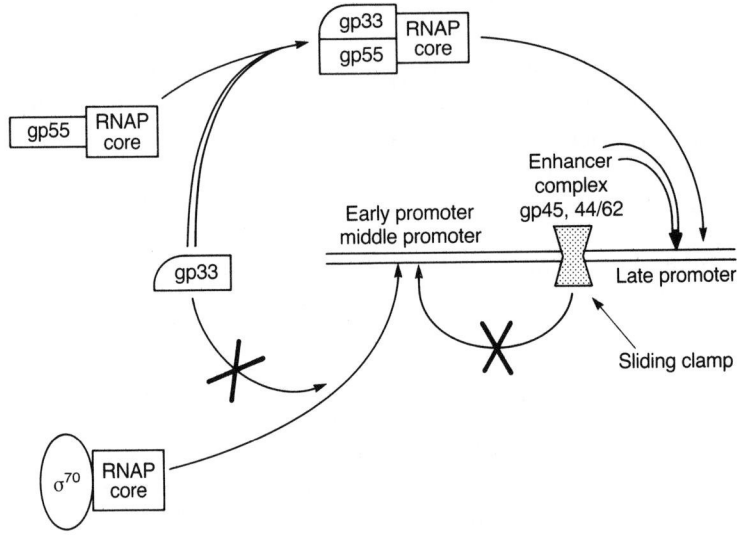

**Figure 5.9** The coupling of T4 late transcription is mediated by the gene 33 product connected to the replicating complex.

polymerase. Not only does this protein promote enhancement by increasing the rate of isomerization to the open complex, a reaction that requires ATP as for $\sigma^{54}$ dependent promoters, it also suppresses any low levels of unenhanced late transcription; nor is there any absolute requirement for any T4 induced modifications for enhancement to occur.

These experiments show that enhancement depends on two distinct functions: promoter recognition, which is dependent on gp55, and communication between the enhancer site and the promoter. For phage T4 late transcription, this latter function is dependent on gp33 and requires protein–protein interactions with both the RNA polymerase and the proteins of the replication complex. The other important aspect of transcriptional enhancement is that it is promoter specific. This selectivity is presumably a consequence of the inability of gp33 to interact with the $\sigma^{70}$ containing polymerase and is thus conferred by the potential for protein–protein interactions (Figure 5.9).

REFERENCES

Cashel, M. and Gallant, J. (1969) Two compounds implicated in the function of the RC gene of *Escherichia coli*. *Nature*, **221**, 838–41.
Herendeen, D.R., Williams, K.D., Kassavetis, G.A. and Geiduschek, E.P. (1990) An RNA polymerase-binding protein that is required for communication between an enhancer and a promoter. *Science*, **248**, 573–8.

Hoover, T.R., Santero, E., Porter, S. and Kustu, S. (1990) The integration host factor stimulates interaction of RNA polymerase with NifA. *Cell*, **63**, 11–22.

Lamond, A.I. and Travers, A.A. (1983) Requirement for an upstream element for optimal transcription of a bacterial tRNA gene. *Nature*, **305**, 248–50.

Lamond, A.I. and Travers, A.A. (1985) Genetically separable functional elements mediate the optimal expression and stringent regulation of a bacterial tRNA gene. *Cell*, **40**, 319–26.

# 6

# The mechanism of eukaryotic transcription

Unlike the situation in prokaryotes, transcription in eukaryotic nuclei is partitioned between three distinguishable RNA polymerases, each of which produces a particular class of RNA species. Each of these polymerases requires auxiliary proteins to facilitate RNA chain initiation since, in contrast to the prokaryotic enzyme, the nuclear polymerases are unable to initiate at promoter sites by themselves.

The polymerase responsible for the synthesis of most messenger RNA precursors is RNA polymerase II. The promoters utilized by this enzyme in higher eukaryotes usually contain a conserved sequence, TATAAAT (otherwise known as the 'TATA' box), located about 30 bp upstream of the startpoint. In addition, a more weakly conserved sequence, the initiator, in the immediate vicinity of the startpoint itself also potentiates transcription (Figure 6.1). The binding sites for transcriptional activators are located both at short distances upstream (the 'upstream elements'), but also may be found several kilobases distant from the startpoint, either upstream or downstream. These sites are termed 'enhancers'. This organization, although typical, is not found in all polymerase II promoters. In particular the promoters for 'housekeeping' genes normally lack a TATA box. In fungi the promoter organization is generally similar except that the distance of the TATA box from the startpoint is not as precisely defined as in higher eukaryotes and may be found up to 100 bp from the startpoint.

The *trans*-acting factors necessary for transcription are of two types: first, the general transcription factors which are necessary and can, at least *in vitro*, be sufficient for transcription from the TATA box and thus are not generally promoter specific, and secondly, the factors that are required for transcription activation at only a limited class of promoters.

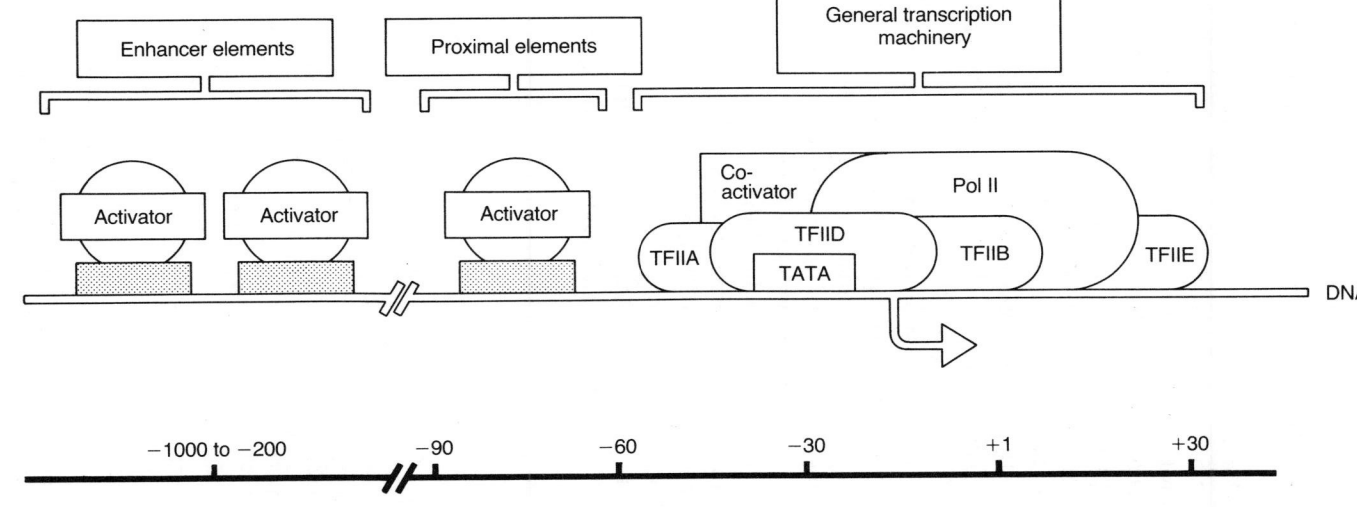

**Figure 6.1** Organization of an RNA polymerase II dependent promoter.

The general factors include RNA polymerase II itself, and a number of other proteins designated TFIIA-F. *In vitro*, the initiation complex is formed by sequential assembly. The first event is the specific binding of the highly conserved protein TFIID to the TATA box. This binding is accompanied by the introduction of a sharp bend in the DNA which is maintained in the fully assembled initiation complex. Although only a relatively small protein, TFIID alters the path of the double helix by up to 180°, with the TATA box at the apex of the turn. One consequence of this distortion is that proteins binding upstream of the box are brought into close spatial proximity to the transcription startpoint (Figure 6.2). In this configuration they have the potential to interact with either RNA polymerase II or with other transcription factors during the process of transcription initiation. The binding of TFIID is followed by TFIIB and finally by TFIIE/F and RNA polymerase II.

The mechanism of initiation at promoters which lack a TATA box follows a different pathway. The principal difference is that the initial binding event is directed by the initiator element whose precise function is promoter specific. The initiator in the adenovirus IVa2 promoter is recognized weakly by RNA polymerase II itself, as is also that in the adenovirus major late promoter, which does contain a TATA box. However, whereas at the major late promoter, the factors TFIID, -B, and -A will bind together in the absence of polymerase, all complexes formed at the initiator contain the polymerase. Initiator sequences in other promoters contain a site for specific DNA-binding proteins. A further difference between TATA dependent and TATA independent promoters is

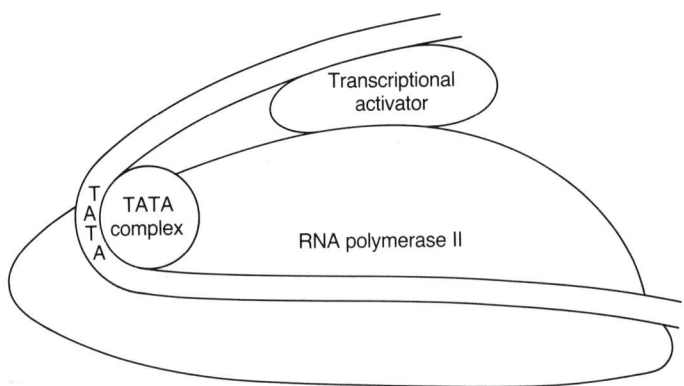

**Figure 6.2** Bending of DNA by TFIID in the TATA complex could bring transcriptional activators bound to USEs into close spatial proximity to RNA polymerase.

that the former initiate at a precise point while the startpoints for the latter are heterogeneous.

At most promoters the assembly of the initiation complex and the subsequent initiation by RNA polymerase II require promoter specific transcription factors. Such factors facilitate the extension of the polymerase beyond the transcription startpoint. Transcription initiation is also dependent on ATP hydrolysis additional to the requirement for ATP as a substrate for RNA synthesis.

## 6.1 EUKARYOTIC TRANSCRIPTIONAL REGULATORY ELEMENTS

As with prokaryotic DNA-binding proteins, eukaryotic transcription factors can act as both positive and negative regulators of transcription. The mode of control can depend both on the nature of the protein and on the disposition of the binding site relative to the startpoint of transcription. For promoters utilized by RNA polymerase II, two classes of DNA elements required for optimal activity can be distinguished: upstream elements and enhancers. The former specify in general the binding sites for transcriptional activators and are usually located within a region 100–200 bp upstream of the TATA box. By contrast, the latter may be found up to several kilobases proximal or distal to the transcriptional startpoint. These enhancer elements are probably functionally heterogeneous. Some may directly mediate activation of transcription from the initiation complex itself or through factors bound to the upstream elements, whilst others may function to specify the chromatin structure that is necessary for the access of other transcription factors (Chapter 7). Latterly it has become apparent that the mechanism of activation from the former type of enhancer element can be, in principle, similar to that from upstream elements. What differs is the extent of protein–protein interactions that are necessary to establish activation at a distance as opposed to that mediated by an upstream element.

How is activation at a distance mediated? Three types of mechanism have been considered (Figure 6.3): direct protein–protein contact between factors bound at an enhancer and those in the transcription initiation complex, the transmission of an altered DNA structure between a protein bound at the enhancer and the initiation complex, and, finally, the induction of the co-operative binding of transcription factors by the enhancer bound factor so that the DNA between the enhancer and the initiation complex is covered (the 'oozing' model). The latter two models require that the enhancer element be exclusively *cis*-acting, while the second model has the additional requirement that the enhancer and the initiation region be in the same topological domain. However, experimentally an enhancer has been shown to retain its function when, although on the same DNA molecule as the TATA box, it

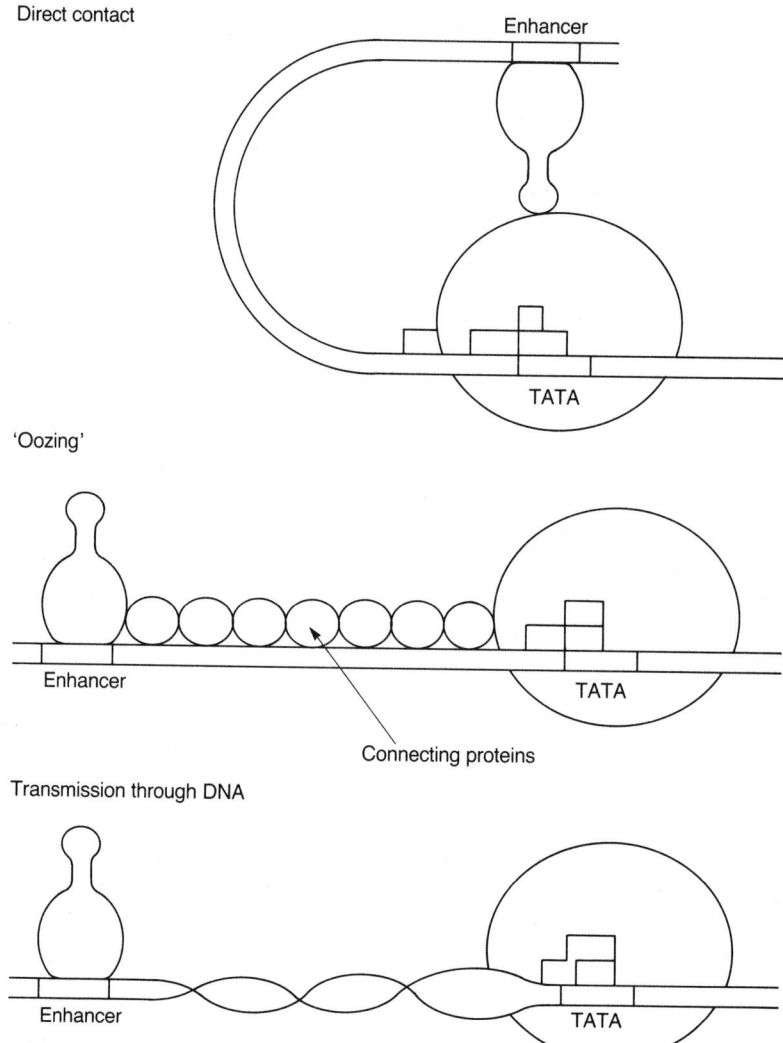

**Figure 6.3** Proposed mechanisms of enhancer action.

is topologically uncoupled by allowing free rotation of the double helix between the two points (Figure 6.4). This elegant experiment is complemented by other observations which demonstrate that, in certain circumstances, enhancer elements can act in *trans* provided that contact be mediated between the enhancer site and the initiation site. Such a requirement can be fulfilled by two catenated DNA molecules, one of

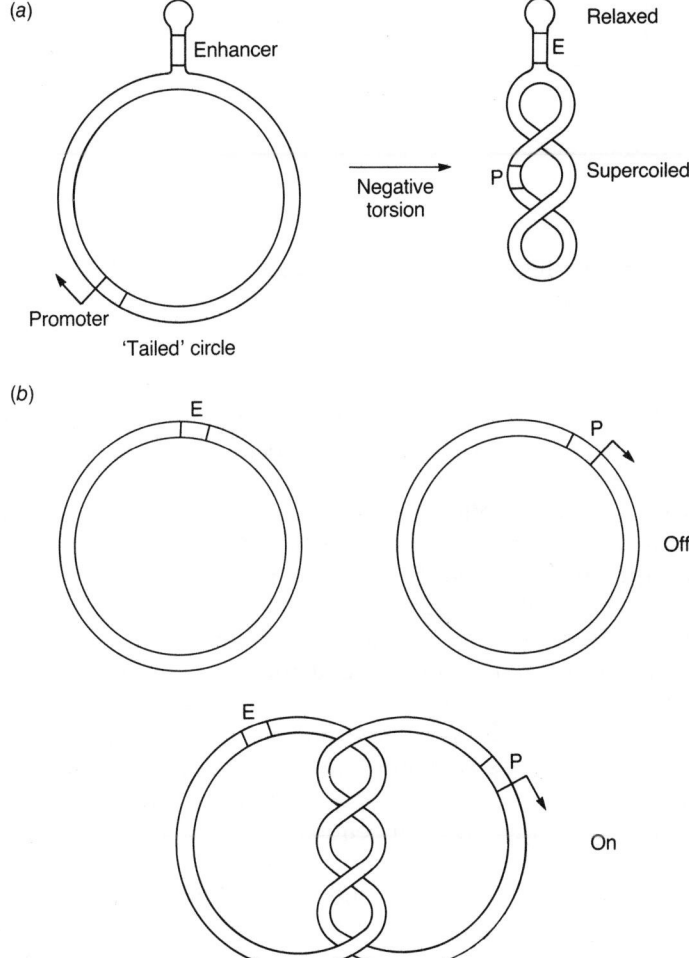

**Figure 6.4** (a) Topological separation of enhancer (E) and promoter (P) in a 'tailed' circle. (b) Catenation of DNA circles allows an enhancer on one circle to activate a promoter on the other.

which contains the enhancer element while the second contains the initiation elements. This mode of action is also incompatible with the oozing model. A further characteristic of enhancer elements is that they usually contain multiple binding sites for the activator proteins and, in general, the more such sites are present the more potent the enhancer activity of the element. This effect could be a consequence of increasing the occupancy by co-operative binding and thereby increasing the

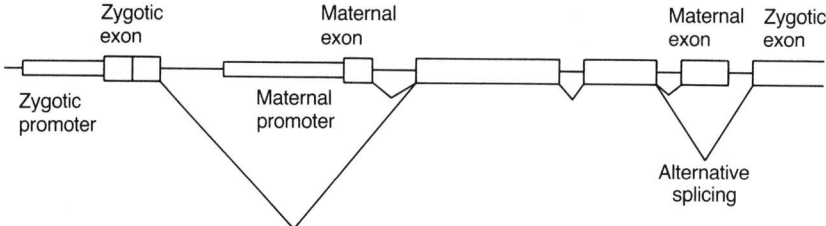

**Figure 6.5** Organization of a gene whose expression is directed by two promoters and exhibits differential splicing.

probability of making direct contact with the initiation complex, or it allows the possibility of multiple contacts between the proteins bound in the different regions.

Typically the transcription of class II genes is regulated in a variety of different ways. For example, in multicellular organisms the gene product may be required in different tissues at different stages of development, or within a single cell type a particular gene may be required to respond to a variety of physiological stimuli. In terms of gene organization, diverse patterns of transcriptional regulation can, in general, be accommodated in two ways. Thus, a gene may contain more than one promoter, independently regulated but which direct the synthesis of messenger RNA species containing the same coding sequence. In such cases the different messenger species are generated by appropriate splicing and generally differ in sequence in at least the untranslated regions (Figure 6.5). In the early embryo of *Drosophila* the maternal and zygotic transcripts often arise in this way. Alternatively, a gene may contain a single transcription startpoint whose utilization is determined by a number of different regulatory elements which function independently. The promoter thus has a modular structure. One gene of this type is the *fushi tarazu* regulatory gene of *Drosophila* which is expressed in three distinct phases during early embryogenesis. Initially the gene is transcribed zygotically in the blastoderm stage in a pattern of seven stripes. Subsequently, after gastrulation, its expression is confined to a subset of cells in the developing central nervous system (Figure 6.6). At least the first two phases of expression are controlled by different, but overlapping, regions of the sequences specifying transcriptional regulation (Figure 6.6).

## 6.2 EUKARYOTIC TRANSCRIPTIONAL REGULATORS: STRUCTURE

In general, proteins which act as transcriptional activators, and some that act as repressors, have a modular structure. An activator typically

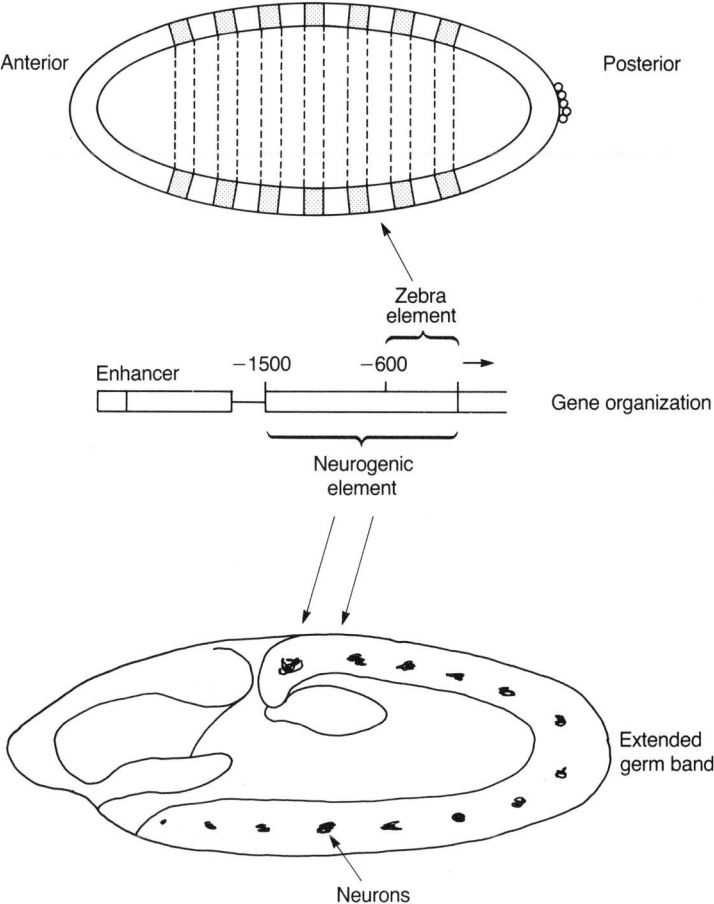

**Figure 6.6** Embryonic expression of the *Drosophila* pair-rule gene *fushi-tarazu* in (top) cellular blastoderm and (bottom) extended germ band stages.

contains a sequence specific DNA-binding domain and a separable activation domain. More complex factors may also contain other domains which regulate the overall structure and thus the activity of the factor.

The independent nature of the modules of transcriptional activators was first demonstrated by domain swap experiments using the yeast activator GAL4. In these experiments the protein sequences in GAL4 required for activation were fused to the DNA-binding domain of the bacterial repressor LexA. The resulting fusion protein was then able to activate transcription *in vivo*, directed from a LexA binding site (Figure 6.7) showing that the activation domain is functionally independent of the

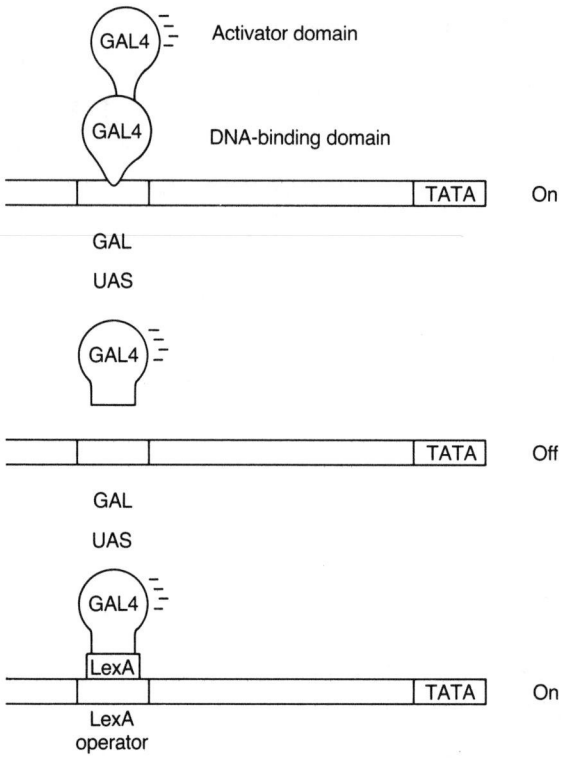

**Figure 6.7** Transcriptional activation requires the activator to contain both a DNA-binding and an activation domain. In this example the LexA DNA-binding domain can substitute for the GAL4 DNA-binding domain.

DNA-binding domain. In other examples the separation of the functional components of the factor is more extensive. Thus, in the case of the glucocorticocoid and oestrogen receptors the specificities for activation, for DNA-binding and for ligand binding can be switched by the interchange of the corresponding modules. Even within a particular functional domain the protein may be structurally modular, that is, consist of independent regions of highly ordered conformation. The most notable form of this type of organization occurs in the DNA-binding domains of proteins containing multiple zinc fingers of the C—C....H—H type. Here the individual fingers have the potential to act as independent structural units.

The modular nature of transcription factors is also apparent in the organization of their genes. In the gene encoding TFIIIA the zinc fingers are encoded by individual exons. Another example includes the *broad* and *tramtrack* genes in *Drosophila* which encode multiple zinc finger

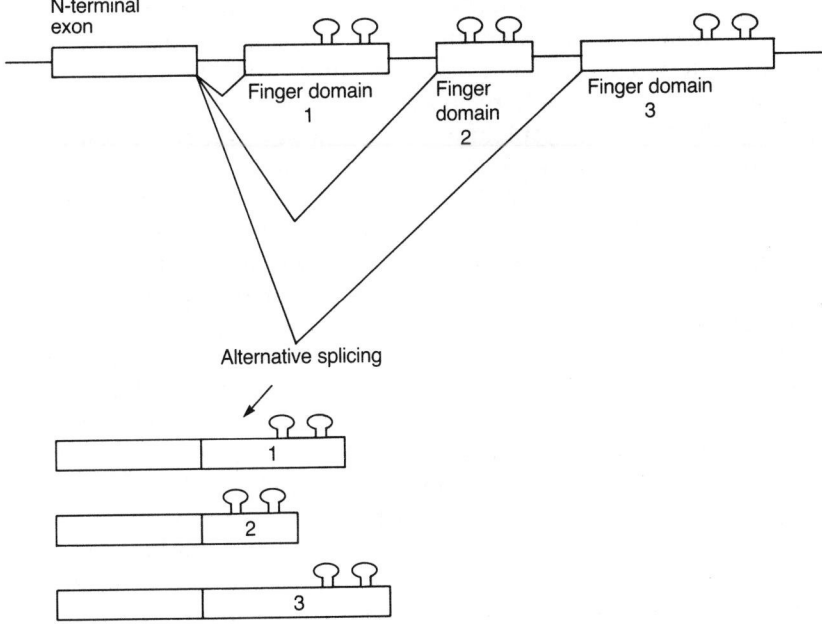

**Figure 6.8** Alternative splicing of mRNAs from the *Drosophila* 'broad' complex generates proteins with different zinc finger domains and different binding specificities.

DNA-binding proteins, which in the latter case are believed to function as repressors. In each locus these proteins contain a common N-terminal domain (part of which is highly conserved between the two loci) which is spliced to different nucleic acid-binding domains, each of which contains two zinc fingers (Figure 6.8). For *tramtrack* the different proteins have the same temporal, but a different spatial, pattern of expression during embryonic development, suggesting that the selective expression of one particular protein is determined by tissue specific regulation of splicing and not at the level of transcription.

The existence of independent functional modules in transcription factors has important implications for their protein structure. In simple terms a factor can be considered to consist of structurally determined domains separated by flexible regions. These flexible regions can serve at least two functions: first, to orient the functional domains to contact either other proteins or other domains within the same protein, and secondly, to serve as targets for the regulation of the activity of the factor. It should be emphasized that this separation into structural modules is a general property of proteins and is also found in prokaryotic DNA-binding proteins. An example of the latter is the $\lambda$ $C_1$ repressor in which the N-terminal DNA-binding domain is separated from the C-terminal oligomerization domain by a flexible region of poly-peptide chain. This flexible region is the target for proteolytic cleavage mediated by the RecA protein on induction of a lysogen. Similarly, in 'tramtrack' the conserved N-terminal domain and the DNA-binding domain are separated by a 'PEST' sequence which again serves as a target for proteolytic cleavage. Although, in principle, the functional modules have the potential to fold into determined structures, this potential may only be realized in the presence of an appropriate ligand. A particularly apposite example of the latter phenomenon is provided by the basic DNA-binding region of leucine zipper proteins. In solution these basic regions are only partially structured but on binding to DNA they are induced to form an $\alpha$-helical structure which then mediates sequence specific recognition. Similarly the C-terminal arms of histone H1 have the potential to form alanine–lysine rich $\alpha$-helices. In solution these domains are again relatively unstructured, presumably due to the repulsion between lysine residues. However, on binding to DNA these regions assume an $\alpha$-helical structure which in this case is believed to stabilize the configuration of the DNA in condensed chromatin.

## 6.3 SPECIFICITY AND SELECTIVITY OF EUKARYOTIC TRANSCRIPTION FACTORS

In prokaryotes the induction or repression of transcription is a rapid and precise process which is normally mediated either by a single protein or at most a small number of proteins. Rapidity and precision imply that the DNA-binding proteins involved must bind to their target sites with both high specificity and affinity. A classic example of such a protein is the *lac* repressor which binds to specific operator sites with a dissociation constant as low as $10^{-13}$ m. This binding is about $10^6$ times tighter than that when bound to non-specific DNA sites. Since the number of mole-cules of the *lac* repressor in the bacterial cell is normally very low (~10) this high specificity and affinity is necessary to achieve high occupancy and consequently maximal repression. Although the *lac* repressor is an extreme example, other bacterial DNA binding proteins such as the $\lambda$ $C_1$ repressor possess similar characteristics.

By contrast, the specificity and affinity of many eukaryotic transcrip-tion factors is often much lower. The heat shock factor is a notable exception to this generalization, with an association constant in the range of $10^{12}$–$10^{13}$ $m^{-1}$ for specific binding sites. Thus the steroid receptors bind to their specific binding sites with association constants close to $10^9$ $M^{-1}$, a value that is only a 100-fold greater than that for non-specific sites.

Similarly, the association constant of the polymerase III transcription factor TFIIIA for its site on the 5S RNA gene is approximately $5 \times 10^9 \, \text{m}^{-1}$. At first sight these values are paradoxical. The concentration and absolute amounts of DNA in the eukaryotic nucleus are always greater than, and often vastly in excess of, the corresponding parameters in the bacterial nucleoid. The simple expectation would therefore be that eukaryotic DNA-binding proteins, including transcription factors, should possess a higher affinity and/or selectivity than their bacterial counterparts. There would, however, be a price to pay for such a solution. A higher affinity, while maintaining selectivity, would mean that a protein would remain bound to a non-specific site for a substantially longer time. Since the relative proportion and number of non-specific sites for an average DNA-binding protein in the eukaryotic genome are very much higher than in the prokaryotes, the location of the correct sites would take much longer at the same protein concentration. This dilemma is well illustrated by a prokaryotic example. A mutation in the *lac* repressor increases its affinity for both specific and non-specific sites by about 100-fold; that is, its selectivity is maintained. The consequence of this mutation is that the repressor no longer fully represses *lac* transcription in the absence of inducer. Instead, as the inducer concentration increases so also does the extent of repression. This trend is only reversed at high inducer concentrations when full derepression is observed. The explanation is that, in the absence of inducer, the repressor is sequestered by non-specific binding sites to the extent that the *lac* operator, at least in some cells, is not occupied. When the inducer concentration is raised the occupancy of the operator, and hence the degree of repression, is increased. Only when the affinity for the operator is reduced sufficiently by high concentrations of inducer is derepression achieved. There is a further price for high affinity, or strong, binding. Regulation by inducer binding or by phosphorylation typically changes association constants by $10^3$. A change of this magnitude for a protein binding with high affinity would mean that the bound protein would only dissociate slowly with a consequent lag in response.

For eukaryotic transcription factors precision of binding and response is often achieved, not by high affinity or selectivity, but by the cumulative effect of multiple weak interactions between several components. One consequence of these properties is the acquisition of flexibility and more utilization of combinatorial control mechanisms. For example, while a single component of a heterodimer may not specify a binding site with sufficient accuracy, this may be achieved in the heterodimer both by the specificity of the resulting DNA–protein contacts and by protein–protein contacts. The possibility of a single protein forming heterodimers with different proteins increases the range of available specificities and also allows the dimerization step itself to be regulated.

## 6.4 Sp1 TRANSCRIPTION FACTOR

This protein was initially characterized as a mammalian transcriptional activator that binds to the 21 bp repeats of the SV40 early promoter. The factor has a molecular mass of some 110 kDa and contains three zinc fingers which constitute its specific DNA-binding domain. The activation domain consists of two adjacent glutamine rich regions which are bounded by sequences enriched in serine and threonine residues. Although on SV40 DNA the protein binds to an upstream element, in other systems Sp1 binding sites can act as enhancers provided there is an additional Sp1 site closely distal to the TATA box. This latter site can be activated, not only by an Sp1 element acting as an enhancer, but also by the overproduction of a mutant Sp1 protein that lacks a functional DNA binding domain. The clear implication is that the activation of transcription by Sp1 in this situation requires the interaction of at least two Sp1 protein molecules. A direct demonstration that two Sp1 molecules can interact in this way has been elegantly shown by an experiment in which two Sp1 binding sites were placed at opposite poles of a circular DNA molecule. When Sp1 binds to this DNA the two Sp1 molecules interact so that the intervening DNA is looped between forming a figure-of-eight (Figure 6.9). Similar interactions take place even when Sp1 is bound to short DNA fragments. In this situation what is normally observed is an aggregate in which many Sp1 molecules with their bound DNA participate. However, when one of the two glutamine rich sequences is deleted only two Sp1 molecules are observed in the complex, suggesting that these sequences are necessary for protein–protein contacts.

The ability of Sp1 to induce the formation of DNA loops explains how distant Sp1 binding sites can act as enhancers but does not explain the activation process. The enhancer element in this situation acts by increasing the probability of contact between Sp1 molecules, an event which is necessary for activation. Once contact has occurred a DNA-bound Sp1 molecule can be phosphorylated by a protein kinase whose activity in turn requires double stranded DNA. One possibility is that the process of activation may generate, as in the case of other polymerase II transcription factors, a negatively charged region which can then facilitate the initiation of transcription.

## 6.5 HEAT SHOCK TRANSCRIPTION FACTOR (HSF)

In all eukaryotes, as in prokaryotes, a sub-lethal temperature shock induces the expression of a small set of genes. This induction is rapid and does not require protein synthesis. At the same time the expression of a substantial number of other genes is turned off. The former class of genes, the so-called 'heat shock' genes, is also induced by a variety of

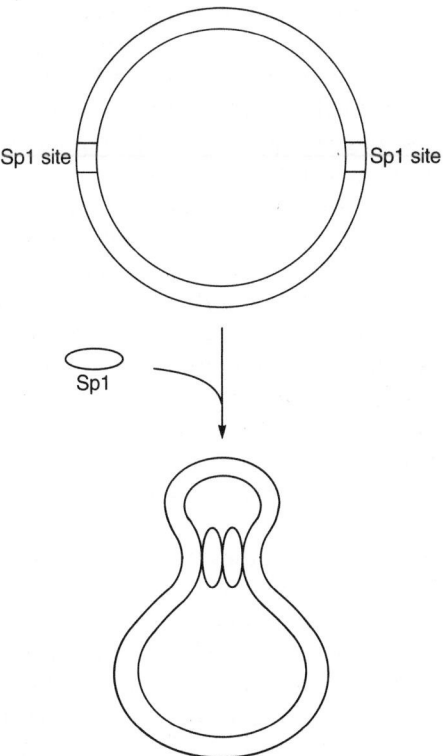

**Figure 6.9** The transcription factor Sp1 forms dimers with a second molecule bound far from the first site.

other environmental insults, including, for example, the presence of amino acid analogues and the presence of moderate concentrations of ethanol or of heavy metal ions. All these environmental inducers can be related to the appearance of unfolded proteins in the cell. Both heat *per se* and heavy metals denature protein structures while both amino acid analogues and ethanol result in the misincorporation of amino acids into nascent proteins, with a consequent failure of these proteins to fold correctly. The function of the major heat shock proteins, which include hsp70 and hsp100, is to act as protein chaperones. In other words, they act to maintain the tertiary structure of proteins by catalysing their folding into an appropriate conformation. Although the major heat shock proteins are produced in large amounts when induced by the relevant stimuli, some at least are also continuously present in cells. Others are specifically required at different stages of development. Among proteins of this type are the small heat shock proteins of *Drosophila*. Their transcription, like that of hsp70, is induced by heat shock, but in addition they are also expressed at high levels on entry into pupation. This phase of synthesis is not accompanied by hsp70 induction. Although there is one mode of transcriptional regulation that is common to all these genes, individual genes also have the potential to be regulated independently in a different manner. How is this independent regulation effected? In the small heat shock genes the transcriptional regulatory element can be dissected into two principal regulatory elements additional to the TATA box. Close to this element is a region that is required for the heat shock response, while further upstream, often 800 or more base pairs distant from the startpoint, are additional activating elements which are necessary for the expression prior to pupation. These elements are functional in the absence of those required for heat shock and contain binding sites for the receptor for the steroid hormone ecdysone, which is present at high levels at the time of the independent induction of the small heat shock genes. The regulatory region of these heat shock genes has a simple modular organization.

What is the molecular basis of the classic heat shock response? The *cis*-acting elements that determine the transcriptional induction occur as contiguous arrays of variable numbers of the 5 bp sequence nGAAn arranged in alternating orientation. These arrays of heat shock elements (HSEs) may be located relatively close to the TATA box, as in the *Drosophila* hsp70 and hsp84 genes, or may be more than 300 bp distant in other natural regulatory sequences. Large arrays are also functional in synthetic constructs where they are placed several kilobases upstream or downstream of the TATA. In these positions the elements act as enhancers.

The HSEs constitute the binding site for a transcriptional activator, the heat shock factor (HSF). The structure of this protein is highly conserved throughout eukaryotes. In solution *in vitro* it exists principally as a trimer of three identical monomeric units. Each subunit of the HSF is believed to bind to a single 5 bp HSE such that the binding to contiguous elements is highly co-operative. However, there is an apparent paradox in the symmetries of the structure of the binding site and of the protein. Whereas the binding site is inherently two-fold symmetrical, the protein is inherently three-fold symmetrical (Figure 6.10). Association of the two would thus require a flexible structure in the protein which would enable the binding of the protein to binding sites with elements in different orientations. This flexibility could be provided by the coiled coil structure through which the monomeric units are believed to associate.

Not only is the binding to individual arrays of HSEs co-operative but so also are the interactions between adjacent arrays. One example of this phenomenon occurs in the *Drosophila* hsp70 gene. Here two arrays

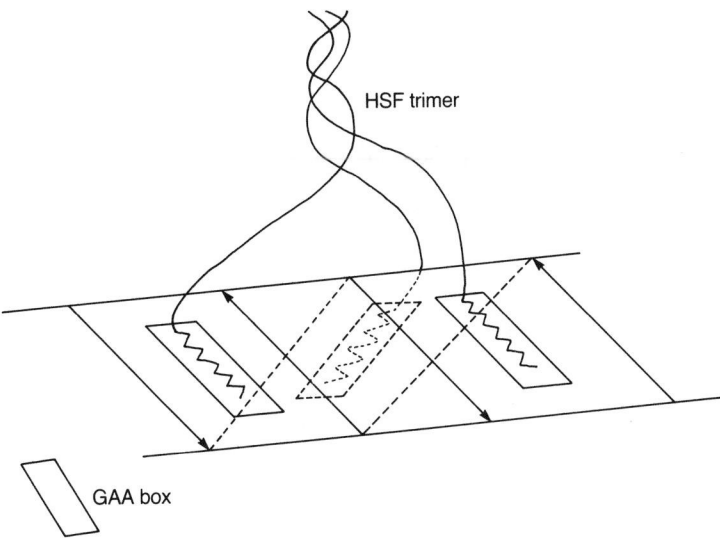

**Figure 6.10** Model for the binding of the trimeric heat shock factor (HSF) to DNA.

are present, located approximately 60 and 85 bp upstream of the startpoint respectively. *In vivo* the extent of transcriptional induction on heat shock is 100 times greater with both arrays than with only one (either proximal or distal). *In vitro* the co-operativity can reduce the rate of dissociation of the factor from adjacent arrays by at least 1000-fold. In general the major heat shock genes, that is those which are both expressed at high levels and are highly induced, contain multiple arrays.

The details of the principles of the transcriptional regulation of the heat shock genes differ in different organisms. In the yeast *Saccharomyces cerevisiae* the HSF is not only necessary for transcriptional activation on heat shock, it is also an essential protein that is required throughout the life cycle of the organism to maintain sufficient levels of the heat shock proteins. This dual function is reflected in the continued occupancy of the HSE both before and during heat shock. Although the factor is always bound to DNA *in vivo*, increased transcription of the heat shock genes is correlated with increased phosphorylation of the factor, with the greatest extent of phosphorylation being observed on heat shock itself. By contrast in other organisms, the fission yeast, *Schizosaccharomyces pombe*, *Drosophila* and man, the HSF binds to DNA *in vivo* only after heat shock. In this situation induction enables the factor to bind DNA and thereby activate transcription. Again, the induction is accompanied by

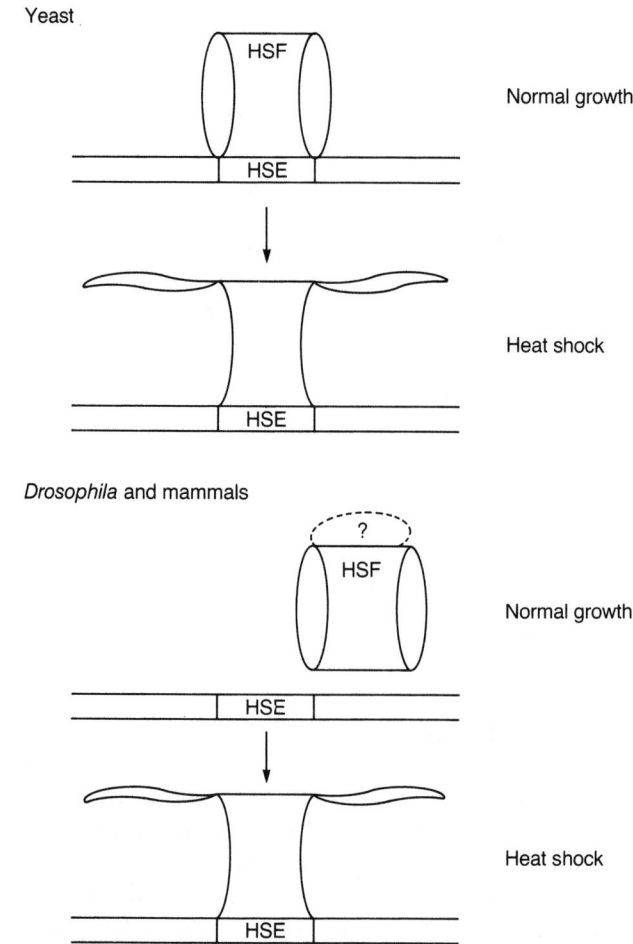

**Figure 6.11** Different mechanisms for the activation of the heat shock factor (HSF) in yeast, *Drosophila* and mammals, (HSE = heat shock element.)

substantial phosphorylation of the protein. How is this change in occupancy effected? The purified factor binds with high affinity to HSEs, independent of its state of phosphorylation. This suggests that *in vivo* the binding activity may be regulated by a second protein. Possible candidates for such regulators are the major heat shock proteins themselves. One hypothesis proposes that the heat shock proteins bind to HSF and thereby block its binding capacity, either sterically, by inducing a conformational change, or alternatively by preventing oligomerization. On heat shock, or any other inducing stimulus, the concentration of unfolded proteins in the cell would rise and sequester the heat shock proteins bound to the factor. The factor would then be free to bind to DNA. Such a mechanism would be consistent with the transient nature of the heat shock response. Once unfolded proteins are refolded or eliminated by protease activity and a new equilibrium attained, the intracellular concentration of heat shock proteins would rise and they would again be available to bind to HSF molecules (Figure 6.12). Although there is no direct evidence supporting this feedback mechanism there is a precedent in mammalian cells for the association of a heat shock protein with a transcription factor. Here the glucocorticoid receptor in uninduced

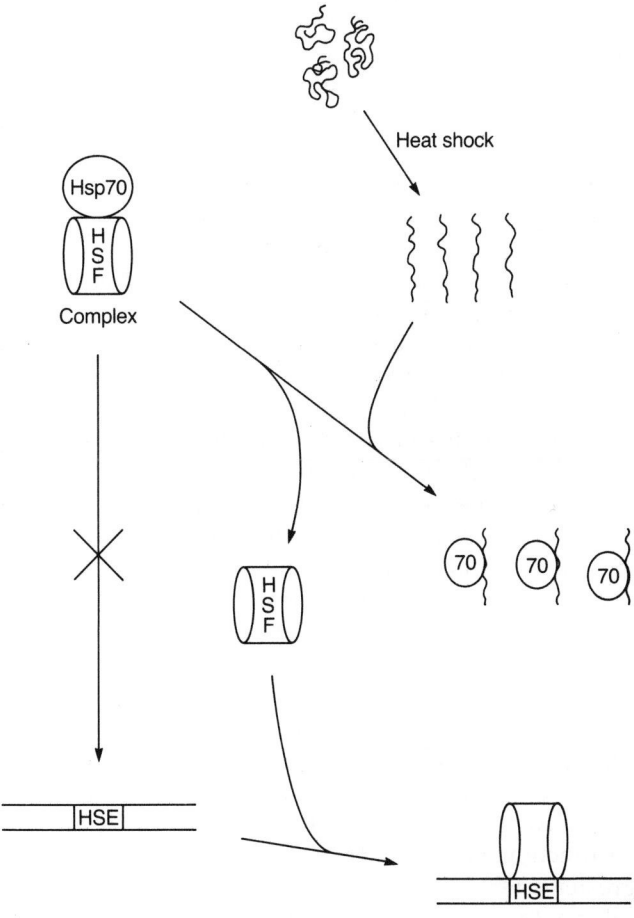

**Figure 6.12** Model for the induction of the heat shock response in *Drosophila* and mammals. Heat shocks results in the unfolding of some proteins which then sequester hsp70 bound to the HSF.

cells is normally associated with hsp90 and in this form does not bind to its target site. On induction hsp90 dissociates and the receptor binds. Although the most characteristic feature of the heat shock response is the transcriptional induction of the heat shock genes themselves, the expression of a substantial number of other genes is substantially reduced. The finding that the *Drosophila* factor binds to at least 100 chromosomal loci other than those encoding the heat shock proteins is consistent with the notion that the factor can act as a repressor as well as an activator.

## 6.6  HOW DO TRANSCRIPTIONAL ACTIVATORS WORK?

A crucial question for the regulation of transcription is how proteins bound at regulatory sites communicate with the general transcription factors and RNA polymerase II bound at the TATA box region. The activation domains of different positively activating factors have diverse structures. In some cases the activation domain is strongly acidic, in others glutamine or proline rich sequences predominate. The problem is how such different structures can elicit the similar responses from the general transcription apparatus. There is, however, some evidence that different types of activator are mechanistically distinct. For example, Sp1, but not acidic activators, can stimulate transcription from promoters lacking a TATA box, although Sp1 also activates TATA containing promoters. Similarly, acidic activators cannot work synergistically with either Sp1 or the proline rich activator NF1.

How is an activating domain constructed? Studies with acidic activators show that for this class both the net negative charge and its disposition are important. Many transcription factors contain acidic activating domains. One such is the yeast GAL4 protein. In this protein, replacement of the acidic region with other naturally occurring activators or with designed acidic regions retains activation function. Notable among the designed activators is an amphipathic α-helix with negative charges confined to one face. This structure functions as an activator, but when the sequence is scrambled so that the overall charge is retained but its distribution in the helical configuration is no longer restricted to one face, activator function is sharply diminished (Figure 6.13). The net negative charge on such a helix is small and its activator function is only moderate. Provided the disposition of the negative charges is appropriate an increase in charge is usually accompanied by an enhancement of activator function. Such an increased charge either activates transcription to a greater extent when the activating protein is bound in a constant position relative to the startpoint, or confers the ability to activate from a greater distance. One of the most potent natural activators, found in the particle of certain herpesviruses, is VP16. This protein, when fused to a DNA-binding domain, can activate transcription from sites several

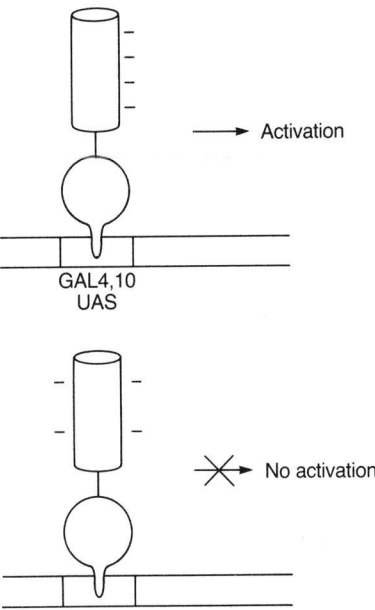

**Figure 6.13** Activation of transcription by an amphipathic $\alpha$-helix.

kilobases distant from the transcription startpoint. Such proteins can additionally, if present in the cell in high enough concentration, activate transcription from a promoter that lacks upstream activating elements. Concomitantly, activity from other promoters is reduced, producing a 'squelching' effect which is attributed to the sequestering of an essential transcription factor(s). The ability to activate without being tethered to DNA suggests that the primary function of an activator region is to affect the structure, and possibly function, of the initiation complex and not to provide a looped DNA structure with a functional topology in a similar manner to prokaryotic activators such as CAP. More crucially, the activation function of the unbound activator implies that the efficacy of acidic activators can be directly related to the effective activator concentration. This will depend both on the charge of the domain and its location relative to the initiation point. The more distant an activating element is from the startpoint the lower will be its effective concentration in the absence of other constraints. To understand this we make the simplified assumptions that the startpoint is fixed in space and that the DNA between the startpoint and the site of the bound activator is free to assume any configuration (Figure 6.14). In this situation, the activator can occupy any point within a sphere whose radius is determined solely

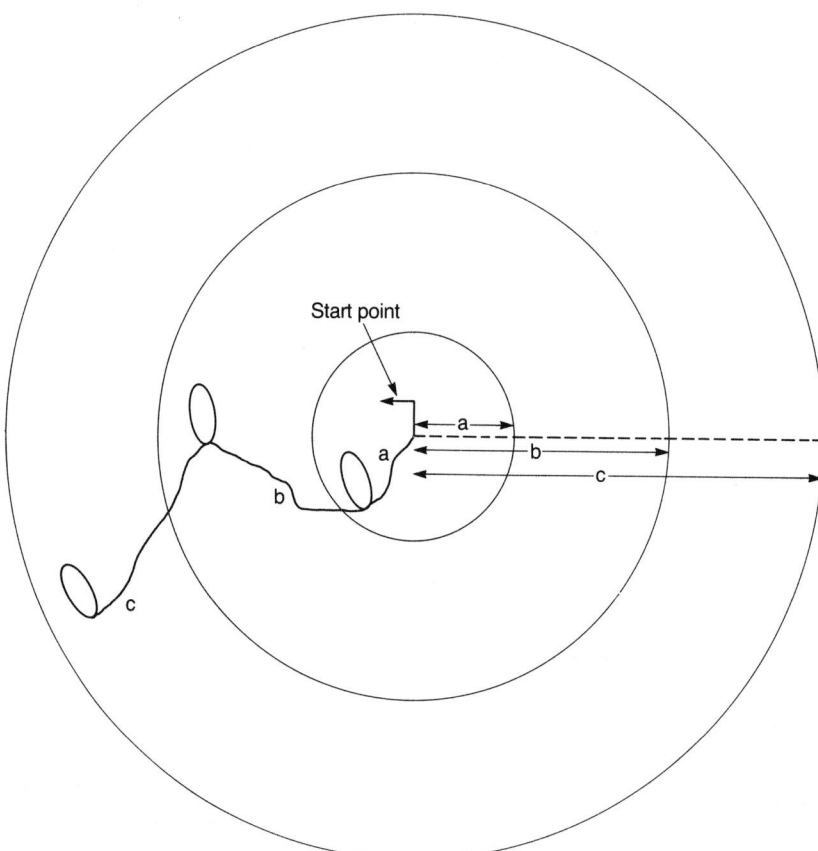

**Figure 6.14** The dependence of activation of a promoter by an enhancer. The enhancer can be located anywhere in a sphere whose radius is the greatest distance of the enhancer from the transcription startpoint.

by the length, when fully extended, of the DNA between the startpoint and the activator element. The effective concentration of the activator would in these circumstances be proportional to the cube of the distance between the two points. This argument still holds if the degree of condensation of the chromatin between the two points is, on average, constant. Clearly a greater distance can be counteracted by an increase in the charge on the activator. Another mechanism by which the effect of distance can be ameliorated is to form an ordered structure in which the activator is constrained in close spatial proximity to the startpoint. A potential example of this type of mechanism is found in one of the heat

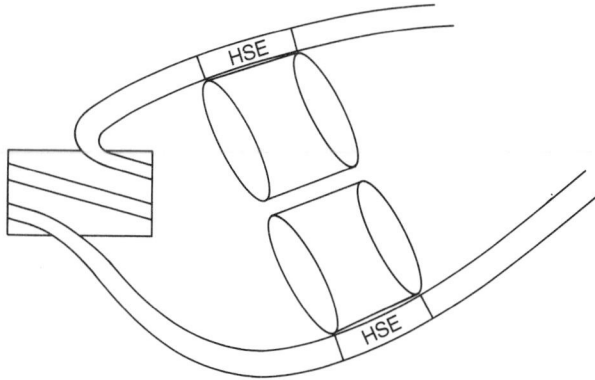

**Figure 6.15** Two HSF molecules brought into close spatial proximity by an intervening nucleosome.

shock genes, hsp26, in *Drosophila*. In this promoter the heat shock elements are located approximately 60 and 300 bp upstream of the start-point (Figure 6.15). *In vivo* these sites are separated by a tightly positioned nucleosome. The wrapping of the DNA in this particle would have the effect of bringing the two elements close to each other in space and would thus facilitate any contacts between bound heat shock factors.

The existence of activator domains whose function is to make protein–protein contacts with other proteins implies that the activity of such domains will be directly regulated to ensure that activation only occurs in the cell at the appropriate time and place. Regulation of activator concentration is simply achieved by regulating DNA binding and, provided the nuclear concentration is sufficiently low, such a mechanism may be sufficient. However, the activator domains would still be free to bind other proteins under these circumstances. Another mode of regulation is to mask the activator domain either with a second protein or by altering the tertiary or quaternary structure of the transcription factor itself. An example of masking is the regulating of GAL4 activation function by the GAL80 protein (Figure 6.16). GAL4 activates genes in yeast that are required for the utilization of exogeneous galactose, yet the upstream activating element is constitutively occupied. Control is achieved by GAL80 which, in the presence of galactose, binds to the activating domain of GAL4 and thereby blocks contacts with the initiation complex. The unfolding of a multi-domain factor to expose the activating surface is probably an integral part of the mechanism of activation by the heat shock factor. In budding yeasts deletion of several

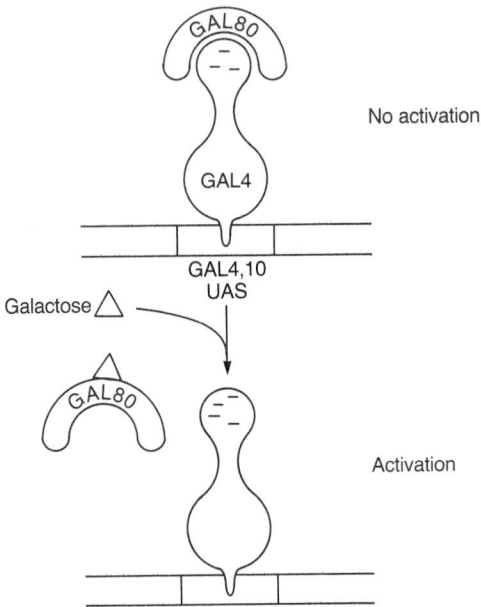

**Figure 6.16** Unmasking of the activation domain of the GAL4 protein.

regions of the factor results in constitutive activation to a greater or lesser extent. By itself this observation implies that activation is negatively regulated; deletions could disrupt either intramolecular contacts which maintain the inactive state or intermolecular contacts with negative regulators. *In vitro* the factor can be activated by heat alone, suggesting that a change in configuration is an integral part of the activation process. Such changes could be modulated both by phosphorylation and by interaction with other proteins.

What is the target of activation domains? By default it has been assumed that activation is mediated by direct contact between proteins. One general transcription factor which is necessary for activation to occur is TFIID. This protein has been characterized in yeast, *Drosophila* and mammalian cells and shown to be a small polypeptide of 23–37 kDa. It consists of two identified sequence domains, a highly conserved basic domain at the C-terminus (which is required for selective binding to the TATA box sequence itself), while at the N-terminus there is a short divergent sequence which, in the eukaryotic forms, is rich in glutamine residues. By contrast the yeast N-terminal sequence is much shorter, highly charged and lacks a glutamine rich region. Transcriptional activation by both acidic activators and by glutamine rich sequences requires the N-terminal domain of the eukaryotic TFIID. However, there is suggestive evidence that this N-terminal domain is not the direct target of the activator domains of specific transcription factors. By itself the TFIID polypeptide fails to support an Sp1 dependent activation of transcription in a reconstituted *in vitro* system. Nevertheless, this protein can replace functionally inactivated TFIID in a crude extract. In addition, the TFIID activity purified from nuclear extracts is physically and functionally distinguishable from the cloned protein. The inference is that the TATA box-binding polypeptide, TFIID, is insufficient by itself to mediate transcriptional activation, but instead requires additional postulated 'coactivator' proteins which transmit the activation signal from the specific transcription factor to the transcription machinery common to all promoters of this class. On this hypothesis, different types of activator domain would use different coactivators for transmission.

There is, however, one example where the direct target of a transcriptional activator is known. This is the synthetic activator in which the DNA-binding domain of GAL4 is fused to an acidic α-helix. This protein acts *in vitro* to recruit TFIIB during the formation of the pre-initiation complex and can be directly crosslinked to the general transcription factor. Whether this activity is representative of all acidic transcription activators remains to be established.

## 6.7 TRANSCRIPTION BY RNA POLYMERASE III

*In vivo* transcription initiation by RNA polymerase II requires the formation of a nucleoprotein complex containing many disparate components. This also appears to be true for the two other RNA polymerases in the eukaryotic nucleus. Of these, RNA polymerase III is dedicated to the synthesis of short RNA species, for example 5S ribosomal RNA, transfer RNAs and a miscellany of other RNA species, while polymerase I is nucleolar and is dedicated to the synthesis of the major ribosomal RNA species.

A distinguishing feature of most polymerase III promoters is the presence of an activating element downstream of the transcription startpoint. The archetypal example of such an element is the TFIIIA binding site in the 5S RNA genes which spans a region from 45 to 90 base pairs downstream of the initiation site. This protein is not sufficient by itself to direct RNA synthesis by polymerase III. Two other proteins, TFIIIB and TFIIIC, are also necessary. The formation of the initiation complex requires the initial binding of TFIIIA which is then followed by the sequential accretion of TFIIIC and TFIIIB, and finally by the polymerase itself. The resulting nucleoprotein complex is then competent for transcription. Interestingly, the structural integrity of the complex is maintained during the transcription process. This means that TFIIIA remains associated with the complex during the relative motion of the polymerase and the DNA and must therefore be able to accommodate the melted region at the point of elongation. One mechanism by which this might be accomplished would be for the factor to partially dissociate from the DNA to allow the passage of the melted region. It could, for example, be envisaged that one or two, but not all, of the three principal points of contact of the transcription factor on the DNA could dissociate at any one time and then re-form (Figure 6.17).

Although well studied, the 5S RNA genes are in certain respects atypical of class III genes. tRNA genes again contain an internal control region but in this case it constitutes a binding site for TFIIIC. This binding site is bipartite such that its two components can be separated by variable lengths of DNA which, if long, form loops extending from the transcribing complex. This bipartite organization allows introns within the gene to be accommodated and could also serve the same function as the multiple attachment sites for TFIIIA. A further feature of tRNA genes and other class III genes is the presence of a conserved TATA box located upstream in approximately the same position as that in class II promoters. Additionally some other polymerase III genes contain upstream activating elements which act as binding sites for more specific transcription factors.

## 6.8 THE ESTABLISHMENT OF REPRESSION

In prokaryotes the classical method of repression is a direct steric occlusion of either RNA polymerase itself or a required activator protein by a DNA-binding repressor. While such mechanisms must also operate in certain cases in eukaryotes there are some examples where the binding of a genetically characterized repressor to its target site is insufficient to mediate repression of the regulated gene. One such set of genes is those coding for functions specific to the **a** cell type of yeast. In the opposite cell type, α, these genes are marked for repression by the co-operative binding of the α2 and MCM1 proteins to a conserved operator. Although these two DNA-binding proteins are required for repression their occupancy of the operator site does not by itself turn off transcription. Instead at least two other proteins SSN6 and Tup1 are necessary (Figure 6.18). If the SSN6 protein is fused to the DNA-binding domain of the bacterial LexA protein repressor an operator for LexA will direct repression in the absence of a functional α2-MCM1 operator. This result suggests that the function of the α2 and the MCM1 proteins is to recruit, by protein–protein contacts, SSN6 and TUP1 to the regulatory region so that these latter proteins can then act to repress transcription. One consequence of this type of mechanism,

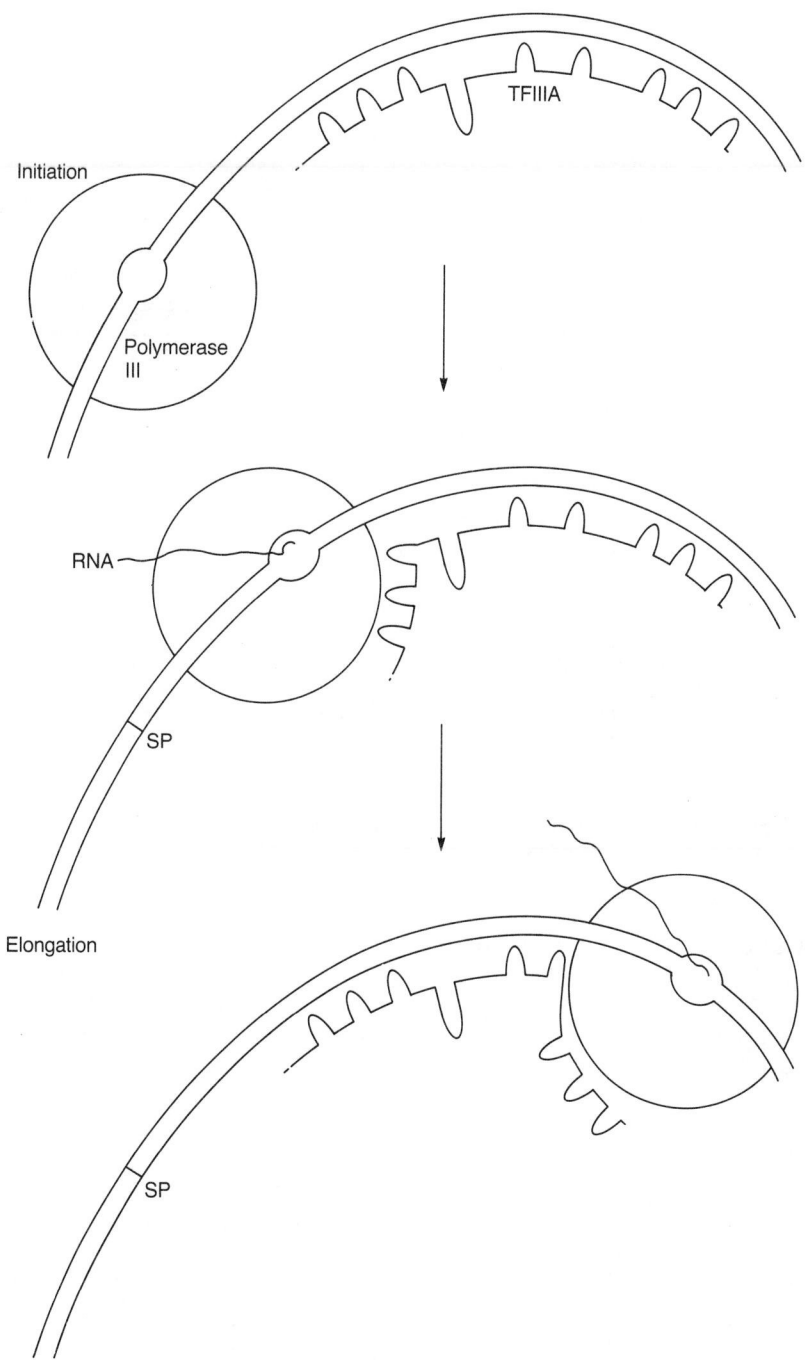

**Figure 6.17** Passage of RNA polymerase III through bound TFIIIA.

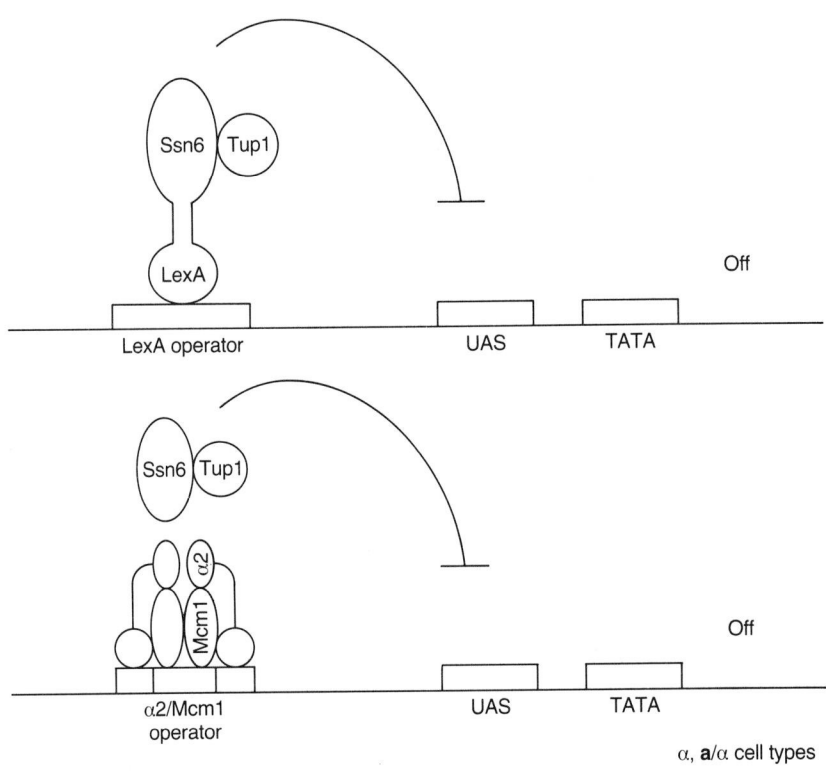

**Figure 6.18** Establishment of transcriptional repression by the Tup1 protein.

where the actual repression is mediated by proteins that do not themselves bind to DNA, is that these proteins can regulate genes of different classes; they are general repressors. The specificity for the establishment of repression is then provided by gene specific DNA-binding proteins.

## REFERENCES

Horikoshi, M., Bertolucci, C., Takada, R. *et al.* (1992) Transcription factor TFIID induces DNA bending upon binding to the TATA element. *Proceedings of the National Academy of Science of the USA*, **89**, 1060–4.

Keleher, C.A., Redd, M.J., Schultz, J. *et al.* (1992) Ssn6-Tup1 is a general repressor of transcription in yeast. *Cell*, **68**, 709–19.

Mitchell, P.J. and Tjian, R. (1989) Transcriptional regulation in mammalian cells by sequence-specific DNA binding proteins. *Science*, **245**, 371–8.

Ptashne, M. and Gann, A.A.F. (1990) Activators and targets. *Nature*, **346**, 329–31.

Pugh, B.F. and Tjian, R. (1991) Mechanism of transcriptional activation by Sp1: evidence for co-activators. *Cell*, **61**, 1187–97.

Sharp, P.A. (1992) TATA-binding protein is a classless factor. *Cell*, **68**, 819–21.

Sorger, P.K. (1991) Heat shock factor and the heat shock response. *Cell*, **65**, 363–6.

# 7

# Chromatin and transcription

In the eukaryotic nucleus the template for transcription is chromatin, not naked DNA. The action of transcription factors and the transcription assemblies should be viewed in the context of a situation in which the accessibility of the DNA to these proteins is determined by the gross structure of the chromatin. The ability to regulate chromatin structure is consequently a major component of transcriptional regulation. Such control can occur either at a local level, affecting perhaps up to a kilobase of DNA, or alternatively more generally affecting the structure and activity of a whole domain comprising many kilobases, or ultimately a whole chromosome.

## 7.1 LOCAL CONTROL OF CHROMATIN STRUCTURE

The fundamental structural unit of chromatin is the core nucleosome particle, which consists of an octameric assembly of the four core histones, H3, H4, H2A and H2B, complexed with 145 bp of DNA. In the presence of a fifth histone, H1, this assembly can condense to form a higher order structure in which each nucleosome is now associated with 168 bp or two full superhelical turns of DNA whose extremities are 'sealed' by contacts with H1. This condensed structure may take the form of a 'solenoid' (Figure 7.1). Certain variants of histone H1, notably those found in the sperm of invertebrates, can further condense chromatin by forming a bridge between adjacent solenoidal structures. H1 is also an essential determinant of the average spacing between histone octamers, a parameter which varies between different organisms and between different tissues in the same organism.

Within a chromosome the degree of condensation is variable. In general, regions of chromatin which are transcriptionally competent, although not necessarily transcriptionally active, are more accessible to digestion by endonucleases such as DNase I than are the 'closed' regions which are not available for transcription. Within the generally accessible

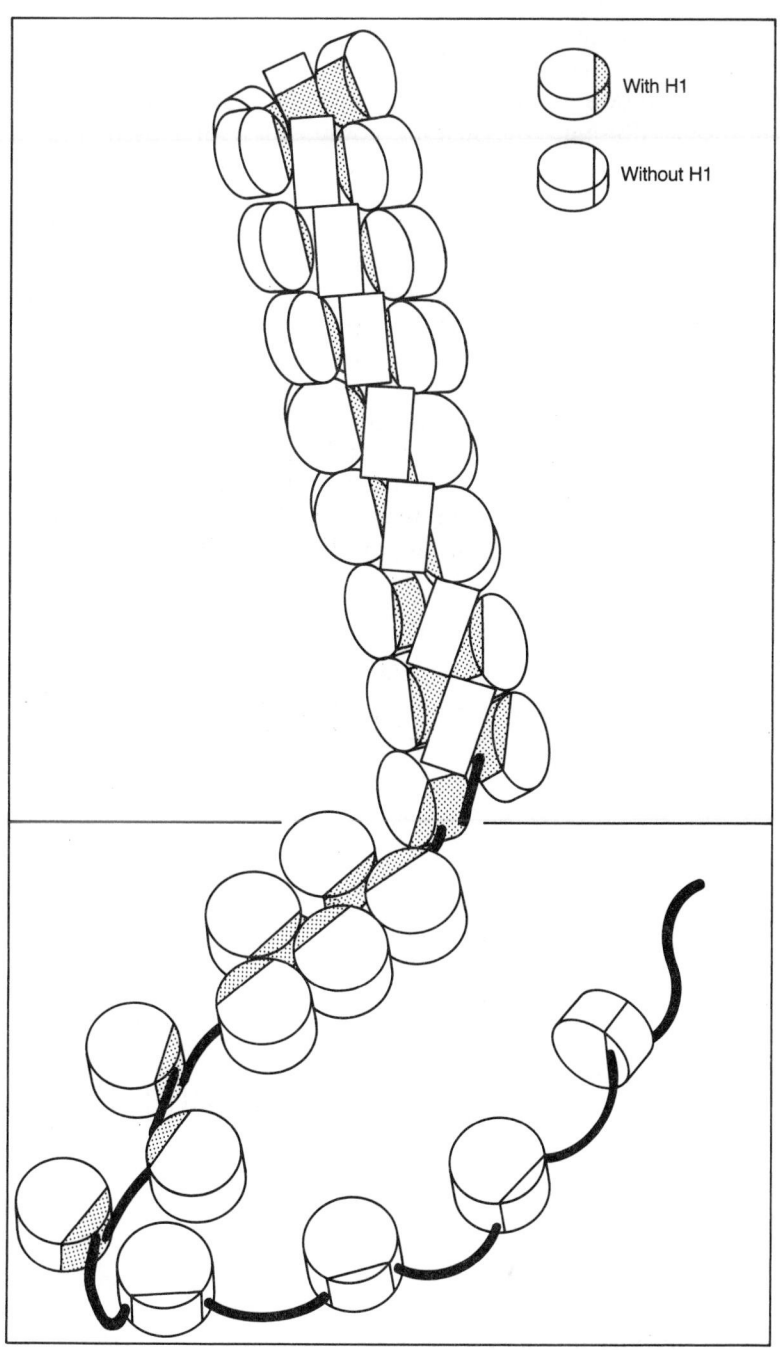

**Figure 7.1** Different levels of organization of chromatin.

or 'open' regions there are short stretches of DNA, normally up to 200–300 bp in extent, which are extremely sensitive to nuclease cleavage. These hypersensitive sites are usually correlated with the target sites for other DNA-binding proteins involved in transcription or DNA replication. Although the histone composition of closed and open chromatin does not differ substantially (both, for example, contain histone H1), the global structure of the chromatin in these two regions must differ, and consequently the nature of the association of H1 with the DNA and other histones is presumed to change during transitions between the open and closed states. It is the regulation of these transitions that is one determinant of transcriptional competence.

One example of a battery of genes whose transcriptional competence changes during development are those encoding the oocyte specific variant of the 5S RNA genes. These genes are transcriptionally active in the oocyte and initially in embryonic development, but are switched off at an early stage. By contrast, the activity of the somatic 5S RNA genes is maintained throughout development in actively dividing tissues. The repression of the oocyte specific genes correlates with the accumulation

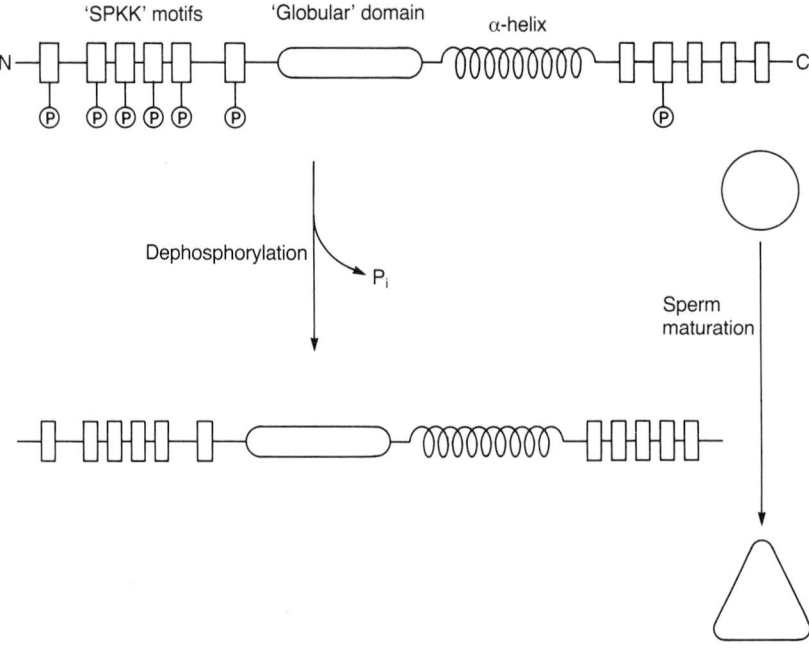

**Figure 7.2** Structural organization of sea-urchin sperm histone H1 and changes in covalent modification during sperm maturation.

of the somatic H1 histone and with a reduced accessibility of the oocyte 5S DNA in chromatin to RNA polymerase III. This effect can also be mimicked *in vitro* by the addition of purified somatic H1 histone to H1 depleted chromatin, but the precise molecular basis remains to be established.

Transitions between different states of condensation of chromatin are associated both with the replacement of particular histones by others in a homologous class and with the covalent modification of the proteins themselves. In transcriptionally active chromatin the core histones are often, but not invariably, highly acetylated. A notable case is that of histone H4, where the principal sites of acetylation are basic residues situated at the N-terminus of the protein. The disposition of these residues is such that they lie on one face of a putative α-helix. Another type of covalent modification is phosphorylation. In histones this normally occurs at serine or threonine residues in the sequence S(T)PXX, a motif which occurs frequently in the N- and C-terminal regions of histones H1 and H2B. Phosphorylation of tandem repeats of this sequence at the N-terminus of histone H1 of sea-urchin sperm reduces the affinity of H1 for DNA and is correlated with a partial decondensation of chromatin (Figure 7.2). Substitution of one histone for another is again often associated with changes in transcriptional competence during development. For example, in the chicken erythrocyte the transition to the transcriptionally inactive nucleus in the ultimate developmental step is accompanied by the substitution of histone H5, a homologue of histone H1, for the normal H1A and H1B variants. Conversely, the transcriptional activation of sea-urchin sperm chromatin after fertilization is correlated with the loss of the sperm specific H1.

Classically histones have been regarded as repressors of gene transcription. Direct evidence that histones can act in this way has been obtained from genetic experiments in yeast. In this organism the nucleosome content can be depleted by the restriction of histone H2B or H4 synthesis. One consequence of such depletion, which reduces the nucleosome content by up to 50%, is a substantial transcriptional activation of certain, but not all, inducible genes. This activation is independent of the function of the upstream activating element. By contrast, the constitutive transcription of rRNA, tRNA and 5S RNA is unaffected by such depletion.

How might such activation be effected? A mammalian example of this mode of control is the control of the polymerase II dependent promoter in the LTR of mouse mammary tumour virus. The activity of this promoter is dependent on induction by steroid hormones which potentiate DNA binding by the glucocorticoid receptor. In the uninduced state the MMTV LTR promoter is occupied by an array of about eight positioned nucleosome, one of which, centred about 150 bp upstream from the transcription startpoint contains the three DNA-binding sites for the receptor (Figure 7.3). On induction this nucleosome loses its characteristic position signature, that is, it no longer protects the DNA from nuclease digestion. At the same time a second transcription factor, the abundant NF-1, binds to a sequence situated at the downstream border of the same nucleosome, and is believed to directly activate transcription initiation. Whether the glucocorticoid receptor remains bound in these circumstances is an open question.

How is this change in chromatin organization effected? Two of the glucocorticoid response elements (GREs) bound in the nucleosome are oriented so that the recognition sequences in the major groove face away from the protein surface and are therefore accessible to the receptor. It is assumed that *in vivo* receptor binding to the nucleosome-bound DNA results in a disruption of the structure of the nucleosome that removes the steric block to NF-1 binding and also increases the accessibility of the DNA to nucleases. However, this change in structure probably does not involve complete dissociation of the histones; induction results in a partial loss of histone H1 from the promoter DNA but not the core

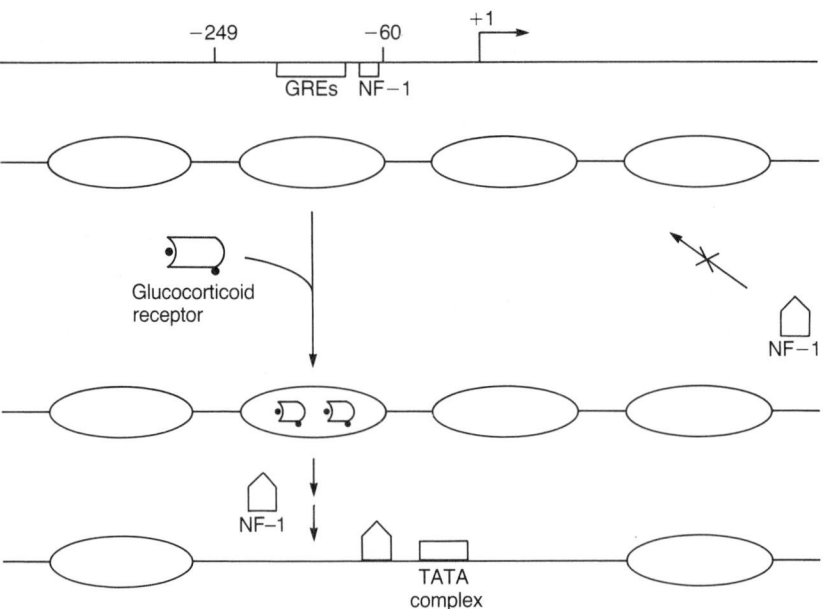

**Figure 7.3** Activation of the MMTV LTR promoter by nucleosome displacement induced by the glucocorticoid receptor.

histones. A further question is the role of the glucocorticoid receptor. *In vitro* the binding of the receptor and NF-1 to promoter DNA are mutually exclusive, while *in vivo* the binding of the receptor to the induced promoter is not detectable. One possibility is therefore that the function of the receptor is to act transiently to prime activation by NF-1.

A change in chromatin organization is a necessary prequisite for activation of the MMTV LTR promoter. A similar phenomenon occurs in yeast at the promoter for the PHO5 gene encoding an acid phosphatase. Transcription of this gene is induced by low exogenous levels of inorganic phosphate. Again, the regulatory region of this gene is occupied by an array of positioned nucleosomes (Figure 7.4). However, in this case there is a short gap in the array which contains a binding site for a positive regulator, the PHO4 protein. On induction PHO4 is functionally activated by relief of the inhibition by PHO80 protein, with a resulting change in the structure of the two nucleosomes bordering the PHO4 binding site. This transition allows additional binding to a previously masked second PHO4 binding site, with consequent full activation of the promoter. Its occurrence is, however, completely

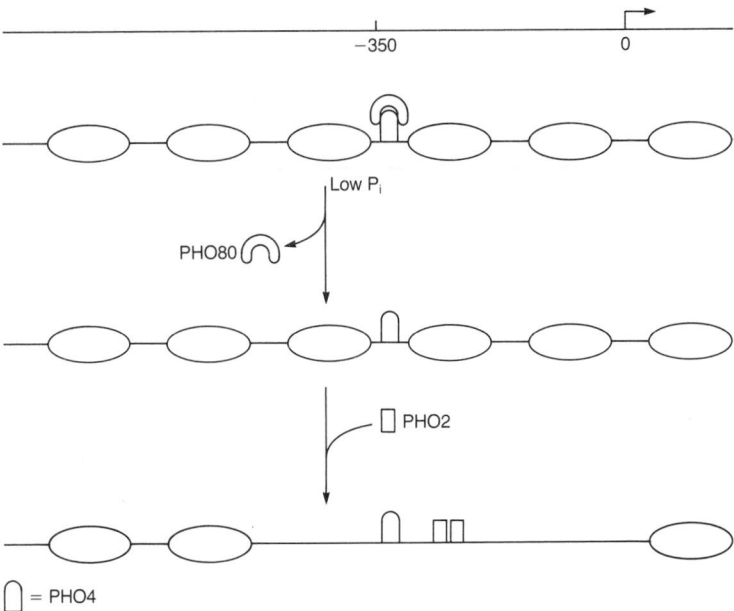

**Figure 7.4** Activation of the PHO5 promoter involves changes in chromatin organization.

dependent on the presence of the exposed PHO4 binding site. Thus for both the PHO5 and MMTV LTR promoters one function of the transcriptional activator is to alter the local chromatin environment.

The activation of some inducible genes in yeast, for example those which are involved in the metabolism of galactose and are regulated by the GAL4 protein, is also dependent on histone function. This effect is distinct from activation by histone depletion which may be regarded simply as a consequence of lower occupancy of the DNA by nucleosomes. In particular, deletions within the N-terminal region of histone H4 result in failure to induce the genes to their full extent. The molecular reason for this failure is not clear but one possibility is that, since the N-terminal sequence is a target for acetylation, a failure to acetylate might result in a loss of efficiency in the disruption of nucleosome arrays. Another possibility, which is not exclusive to the first, would be that the N-terminal tails of histone H4 participate actively in the opening of the chromatin structure associated with transcriptional activation, possibly by direct interaction with other proteins. In this context it should be noted that acetylation of histone H4 is not a general characteristic of inducible systems, since in the MMTV promoter the nucleosome that is disrupted on activation by steroids is not acetylated on this histone.

Likewise, repression can also be effected in *cis* by organizing nucleosome positioning within a restricted region. The α2 protein of yeast acts to repress the expression of a set of genes in α but not in a strains of yeast. One gene regulated in this way is the STE6 gene which contains an α2 binding site situated 200 bp upstream of the transcription startpoint (Figure 7.5). In **a** cells the regulatory region is open and the TATA sequence is free of nucleosomes. However, in α cells, the DNA between the α2 binding site (now occupied by the repressor) and the startpoint contains an array of positioned nucleosomes, one of which now covers the TATA sequence. This precise array can be disrupted by mutations in the N-terminus of histone H4, in the same region that influences transcriptional induction. These mutations, which are not lethal, result in depression of the STE6 locus. The inference is that the α2 repressor directs the positioning of nucleosomes, either by direct contact or through the intermediary of another component. It is the positioning itself that represses STE6 expression and thus, in this context, the α2 protein represses by proxy.

Although there are many examples of genes where transcriptional induction results in a change in chromatin organization, it is also true that, for other inducible genes, the structure of the chromatin in the regulatory region is essentially independent of transcriptional activity as such. In these examples the local organization modulates transcriptional competence by determining the accessibility of binding sites for

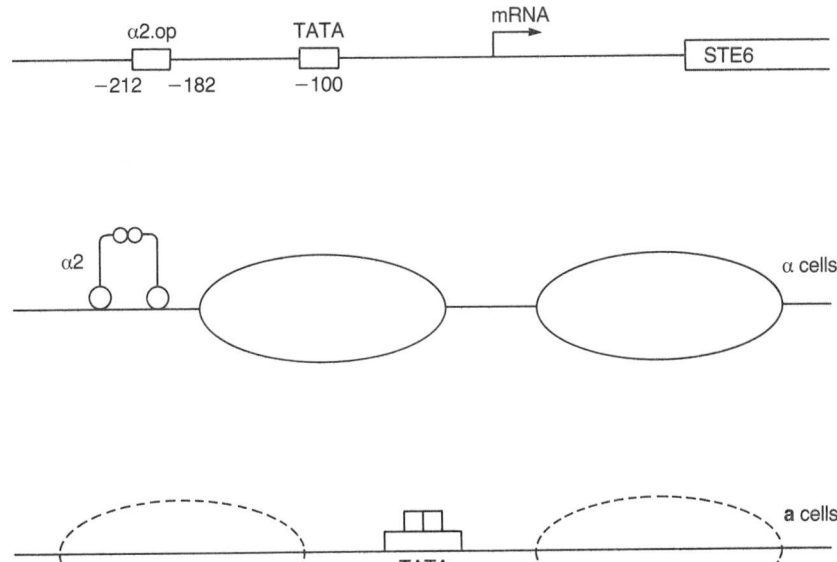

**Figure 7.5** The α2 repressor positions nucleosomes over the regulatory region of the STE6 promoter and thereby represses transcription by proxy.

regulatory proteins. Once such proteins are bound to an accessible site they are free to act without any subsequent linear reorganization of the chromatin. The question is then how such accessible sites (the DNase I hypersensitive sites) are kept free of nucleosomes. Although it is possible in some cases that the DNA sequences within such regions may constitute poor binding sites for histone octamers (they may, for example, contain long (dA).(dT) tracts), it seems unlikely that such sequences would be sufficient by themselves to exclude nucleosomes since the difference in binding energies between good and bad binding sites for nucleosomes would be expected to be relatively small compared to the total binding energy. Nevertheless, it remains conceivable that such effects could influence competition for a particular site. It is much more likely that the local organization of chromatin in these regions is established by an active process. If this is the case, what are the necessary components? One important component is probably the transcription factor TFIID. *In vitro* the establishment of accurate and regulated transcription from polymerase II promoters assembled into chromatin requires at least the initial presence of this factor. Such assembled templates with inducible promoters, for example that for a *Drosophila* hsp70 gene, have an important property. The basal transcription in the absence of the specific transcriptional activator is very low in contrast to the naked template, whereas the induced level of transcription is relatively unaffected. This effect is thus analogous to histone depletion in yeast where loss of histones raises the basal level of transcription of some inducible genes. *In vivo* there is also evidence that for the same gene an active TATA box is important, but not necessarily essential, for the establishment of a DNase I hypersensitive region. However, *in vivo* the TATA box is not sufficient. In addition, two other regions have been defined as contributing. One is the binding site for a transcriptional activator, the GAGA protein, so-called because it binds to a sequence of alternating A and G residues; the second determinant is an ill-defined region downstream of the transcription startpoint. In general, only two of the three determinants need to be present for accessibility to be established, although clearly, for transcriptional activity, an active TATA box is necessary.

Another possibly significant consequence of the local organization of nucleosomes in control regions is an alteration in the spatial disposition of regulatory sites. In the hsp26 promoter of *Drosophila* a single positioned nucleosome separates the binding site for the heat shock transcription factor (HSF) from the TATA box. A nucleosome in this position would bring the factor into close proximity to the TATA box and thus could, in principle, facilitate the induction process (Figure 6.15).

## 7.2 THE STRUCTURAL ORGANIZATION OF CHROMATIN

The fundamental functional unit of chromatin is a domain which can be defined as a region of a chromosome which is insulated from adjoining regions by a boundary which delimits both transcription and replication functions. A domain may contain one or more transcription units and is thought to correspond to the loops of chromosomal DNA which have been observed in the lampbrush chromosomes of the newt *Triturus*. Within a domain there are regulatory sites which act as dominant regulators of the whole region. These sites, variously termed 'locus control regions' (LCRs) or 'domain control regions' (DCRs), are, in principle, necessary for the activity of all the transcriptional units enclosed within the boundaries but do not necessarily by themselves define the boundaries. The initial identification of these *cis*-acting elements, then termed LARs or 'locus activating regions', was based on their property of making the expression of associated genes or gene clusters independent of their position within the genome. One consequence of this property is that this expression is dosage dependent, that is, it is proportional to the number of copies in the nucleus following transfection of cells or the creation of transgenic animals.

## 7.2.1 Chromosomal superstructure

A crucial element of the domain concept is the nature of the structures that define the boundaries of the domain. It is generally assumed that the DNA that ultimately defines a boundary contains binding sites for specific proteins. These proteins are either part of, or are physically attached to, rigid elements within the chromosome. These elements are variously termed the 'scaffold' or 'matrix', and the DNA regions which define the attachment sites are known as scaffold or matrix attachment regions (SARs or MARs). Operationally SARs are defined as DNA sequences which will bind to isolated scaffold or matrix preparations *in vitro*. Their sequences are generally A-T rich and they bind both histone H1 and topoisomerase II with high affinity. An important question is whether the SARs as defined by the *in vitro* assay correspond to the DNA associated with boundaries *in vivo*. Consistent with this possibility is the observation that topoisomerase II is concentrated in the central region of chromosomes and is relatively absent from the loops. The association of an enzyme of this type with SARs reinforces the idea that boundaries delimit functional units within which the topological state of the DNA is regulated independently of neighbouring domains.

Genetic elements which functionally define the boundaries of a chromosomal region have been described for the major hsp70 locus in *Drosophila*. This locus, mapping at position 87A7, contains two divergently transcribed hsp70 genes which are separated by a segment of DNA having the properties of a SAR. Flanking this locus are a pair of sites, termed scs (specialized chromatin structure) and scs', situated 5 and 3 kb respectively downstream of the two transcription units. The scs elements are characterized biochemically as sites of topoisomerase II action. Genetically, when linked to a different transcription unit, the *white* gene, whose function can be readily screened, they confer position independent expression within the bounded region. By themselves however they are unable to activate a transcriptionally disabled gene lacking appropriate regulatory sequences. These properties imply that the scs elements act as insulators preventing the bounded gene from coming under the influence of other regulatory sequences outside the bounds. Consistent with this role is the observation that an scs element placed between an enhancer and its target promoter will block the activating effect of the enhancer. Similarly, scs elements limit the border of puffed regions of the chromosome characteristic of high transcriptional activity. In the presence of the bounding elements the limits of a puff are sharply defined; without them a puff in the same region is more diffuse and covers a more extensive region.

How do boundaries operate at the biochemical level? Both scs elements possess SAR activity but it is clear that this property by itself is not sufficient to confer boundary function, since the putative SAR element between the hsp70 genes at 87A7 does not block enhancer function. Nevertheless, by analogy to the lampbrush chromosomes, it seems likely that attachment to a chromosomal matrix or scaffold may be necessary to form boundaries. Nevertheless, in the case of the yeast silent mating type locus, HMLα, it has been possible to travel full circle. The repressed state of this locus is dependent on the activity of 'silencer' elements at the extemities of the regulated region. One of the proteins that binds to such elements is RAP1 (repressor–activator binding protein, also known as TUF and GRF-1). This protein, together with other proteins that are normally associated with the chromosomal scaffold, allows the formation of DNA loops between its target sites. Repression of the silent mating type loci also requires the function of additional specific genes, notably the SIR genes and the direct involvement of nucleosome arrays. The same mutations in the N-terminus of histone H4 that relieve repression by α2 protein also derepress HMRα by a factor of up to $10^6$. Certain point mutations in this region of H4 can be suppressed by mutations in the SIR3 gene, suggesting that a nucleosome array is directed and maintained by SIR3 function and that this array is necessary for repression. In addition to directing the repression of the silent mating type loci, RAP1 also binds to the terminal telomeric regions of yeast chromosomes. In these locations it also acts in conjunction with SIR gene function to silence the transcriptional activity of neighbouring genes (Figure 7.6).

Within a domain delimited by boundaries, the particular temporal and spatial pattern of regulation is determined by the locus or domain control region(s). These are normally apparent as DNase I hypersensitive sites which contain multiple binding sites for transcriptional regulatory proteins and function as enhancer elements. In the chicken lysozyme gene there is a single such site situated 6.1 kb upstream of the transcription startpoint. By contrast, in the chicken and human globin gene clusters there are multiple sites which are required for the activity of the whole domain (Figure 7.7). (The chicken cluster also contains an isolated hypersensitive site in a different position, which is not found in the human cluster.) These LCRs contain several target sites for the GATA protein, which also binds to the globin equivalent of the TATA box. It is hypothesized that these enhancer elements act immediately after replication to activate one of the globin genes. A high local concentration of GATA target sites within the enhancer element would allow the transcription factor to compete effectively with histones. Once bound to the enhancer the GATA proteins could facilitate the binding of another GATA molecule to the promoter region of a newly replicated globin gene, again allowing effective competition with histones (Figure 7.8).

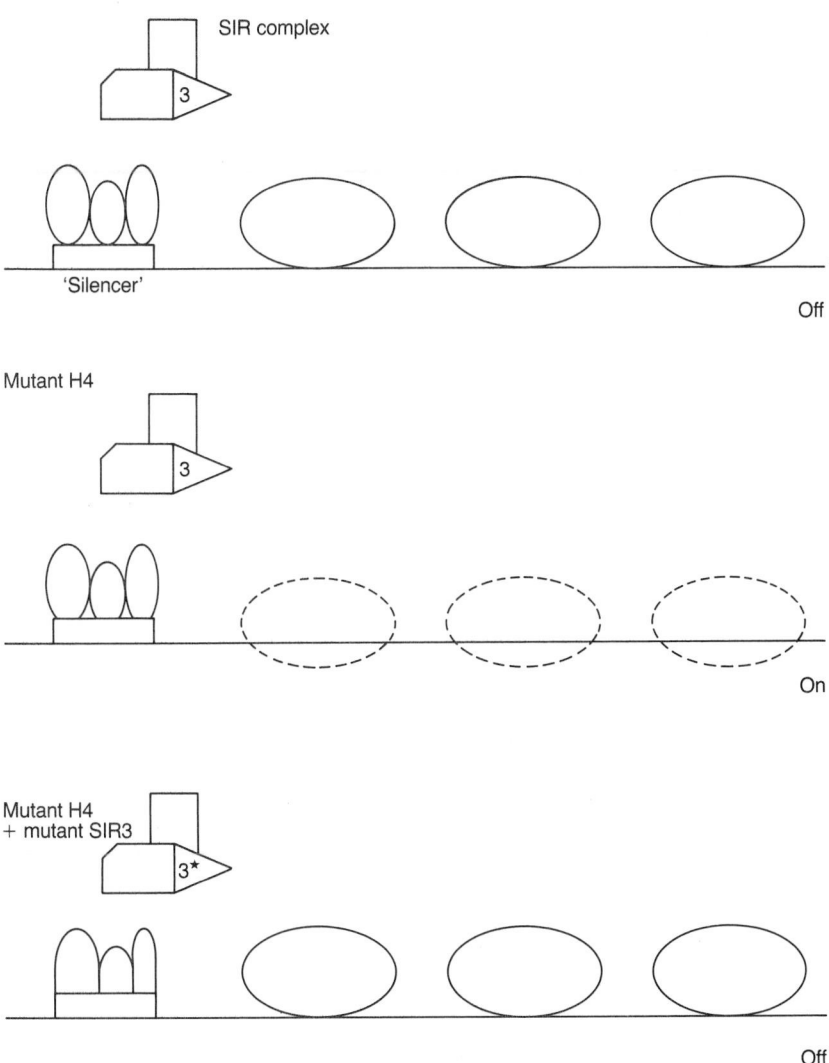

**Figure 7.6** Histone H4 and SIR 3 proteins interact to 'silence' transcription.

A remaining question is how a particular globin gene is selected for activation. In the human globin gene cluster there are four globin genes which are expressed at different times during development. These genes are separated by several kilobases of DNA. They are organized on the chromosome in the same order as that of their temporal expression *in vivo*, with the earliest expressed gene, the globin, closest to the LCR. A simple model to explain the progressive activation of these genes is to assume

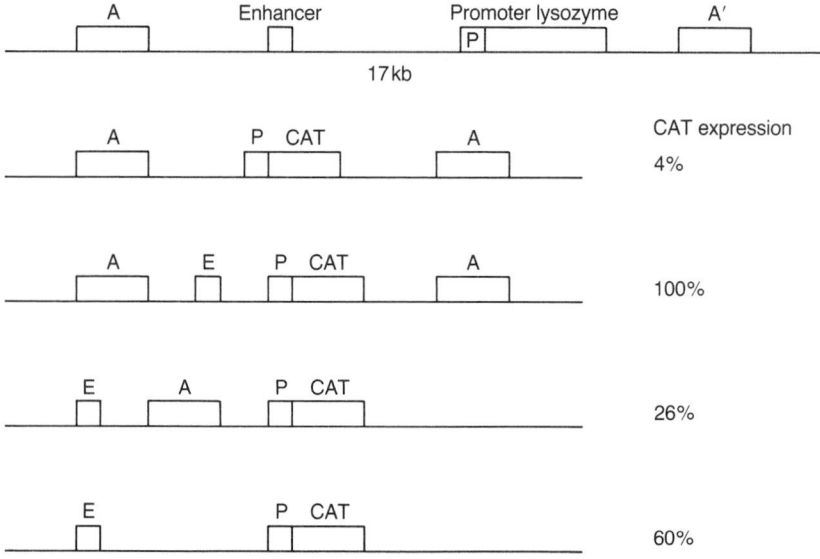

**Figure 7.7** The boundary elements, A and A', are required for optimal expression of the chicken lysozyme gene but do not themselves activate transcription.

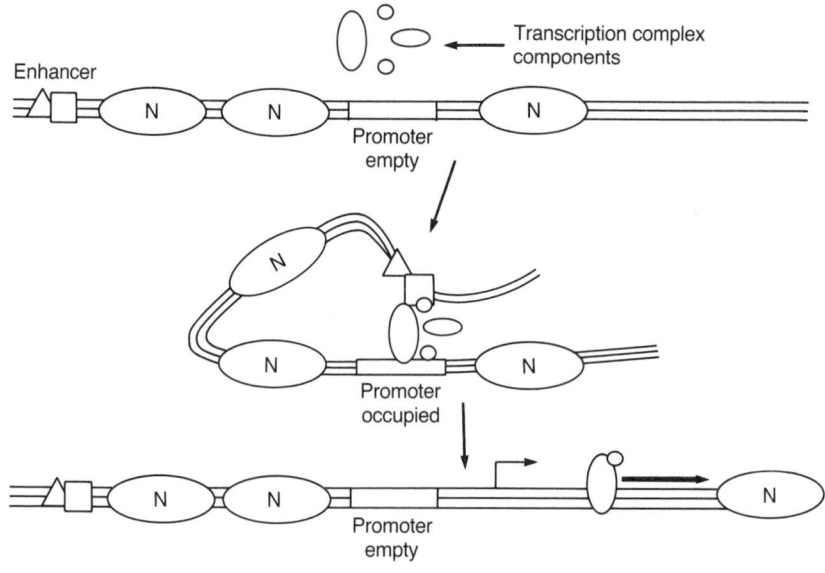

**Figure 7.8** LCRs could act to maintain the activated state after DNA replication.

that, at the earliest stage of globin expression, all the globin genes are, in principle, accessible to the enhancing action of the LCR. However, the closest gene to the LCR will be one with the highest probability of activation precisely because of its proximity. For the next gene in the series to be activated with high probability it is necessary for the accessibility of the first gene to GATA protein to be blocked so that an active transcription complex cannot be established. In both chickens and mice, repressor proteins with this putative function have been identified.

## 7.3 HETEROCHROMATIN

A further aspect of the global regulation of chromatin structure is the condensation and consequent repression of particular genes or, in extreme cases, of whole chromosomes. Examples of the latter phenomenon include the inactivation of the X chromosome in mammals and of the entire paternal complement of chromosomes in the somatic tissues of the male mealy bug. Chromatin in this state is termed heterochromatin; in most nuclei it is typically confined to short regions of chromosomes. In general the establishment of heterochromatin at specific loci takes place early during embryonic development and is then maintained throughout subsequent nuclear divisions. This process can thus be regarded as an epigenetic phenomenon.

In the salivary gland nuclei of *Drosophila melanogaster* the four chromosomes are connected by a heterochromatic region, termed the chromocentre. Characteristically, a gene in the immediate vicinity of this region is subject to variable repression which depends on the availability of the proteins required for heterochromatin formation. A particularly striking example of this phenomenon is 'position-effect variegation' in which one copy of the *white* gene whose function is required for the development of eye pigment is close to the chromocentre. Irradiation of such flies results in eyes which contain segments lacking the red pigment as a consequence of the repression of the *white* locus. This effect can be either suppressed or enhanced by mutations in other genes. One such suppressor locus in *Drosophila* is that encoding the HP-1 protein. This protein is associated with heterochromatic regions and contains a peptide sequence, the chromobox, which is also contained in other chromatin associated proteins. HP-1 by itself does not bind to DNA and therefore its association with specific regions of chromatin is presumed to be mediated either directly or indirectly by specific DNA-binding proteins. At least two proteins in this category have been identified in *Drosophila*. Both are zinc finger proteins and mutation of either encoding gene suppresses position-effect variegation. Conversely, there are other loci whose mutation enhances the observed variegation. The lack of these gene products thus allows the extension of the heterochromatic region in the same way as multiple gene copies of HP-1. The establishment of heterochromatin in the vicinity of the chromocentre is consequently assumed to depend on a balance between different classes of chromatin associated proteins with opposing functions. This phenomenon is reminiscent of the silencing mediated by yeast RAP1 located at telomeres.

## 7.4 THE REGULATION OF TRANSCRIPTIONAL COMPETENCE

The functional state of any independent transcriptional unit is correlated with the overall chromatin structure. The precept that in biological systems nothing (as far as possible) is left to chance requires that the chromatin structure, and hence transcriptional competence, will be actively regulated in both a positive and a negative manner. Although many details of this mode of regulation remain to be established the general pattern is that a functional domain is targeted by a specific DNA-binding protein which can then direct the assembly of a multi-protein complex composed of proteins which by themselves possess only limited selectivity. According to the nature of the proteins in the complex the domain will then be either repressed or activated.

A notable example of this type of regulation is provided by the HO gene of the yeast *Saccharomyces cerevisiae*. This gene encodes an endonuclease which is necessary for the initiation of the mating-type switch and is consequently only expressed early in the cell cycle. Genetic studies have identified a number of genes, termed SWI1–SWI6 (SWI = switch), SNF5 and SNF6, that are required for the transcriptional activation of HO. Of these only one, SWI5, is known to be a sequence specific DNA-binding protein with a target site within the regulatory region of HO. Three others, SWI1, SWI2 and SWI3, however, are required for the expression of a large set of genes in addition to HO but do not themselves bind to DNA. SWI2, for example, is identical to the SNF2 gene which is known to be necessary for the transcription of genes involved in sucrose metabolism. The biochemical functions of SWI1 and SWI3 are not known but the protein sequence of SWI2 is highly homologous to other proteins known to function as DNA and RNA helicases. The similarity of the phenotypes of this class of genes required for transcriptional activation has led to the suggestion that all these proteins are assembled into a single large complex.

The requirement for helicase homology in proteins involved in transcriptional activation is a general phenomenon in eukaryotes. A second example is the *brahma* gene from *Drosophila*. This gene is necessary for the activation of multiple homeotic genes and is homologous to SWI2, particularly within the region that is common to helicases. Finally another gene with putative helicase function that increases the rate of transcription is the product of the *maleless* gene in

*Drosophila*. This gene is one of the four known regulatory loci required for the increased transcription of X-linked genes in males. This phenomenon, termed 'dosage compensation', ensures that these genes are transcribed to the same extent in males, which have only a single copy of the X chromosome, as in females, which have two copies. The *maleless* protein is, however, more homologous to known RNA, rather than DNA helicases, and consequently it remains possible that this helicase affects transcriptional activity by interacting with the nascent RNA.

How might proteins such as brahma and SWI2 act? A crucial experiment is the demonstration that a chimeric protein formed by fusing SWI2(SNF2) to the DNA-binding domain of the LexA protein activates the transcription of a gene under the control of a *lex*A operator. This result implies that the multi-protein complex, with its associated helicase activity, resides at the operator site. A second set of observations relates SWI gene activity to chromatin structure. In particular the dependence of HO gene transcription on SWI1-SWI3 can be relieved by mutations in genes encoding histone H3 and a protein related to HMG1. A similar effect is achieved by deletion of one of the two copies of genes encoding histones H2A and H2B. These findings suggest the possibility that the SWI gene complex acts, directly or indirectly, to open up the chromatin structure and so regulates the accessibility of binding sites for other proteins that act directly as transcriptional activators. In such a context what would be the function of a helicase? A simple model is that helicase activity would result in a disruption of higher order chromatin structure by altering the local topology of the DNA. In the nuclei of multicellular eukaryotes this disruption could involve the displacement of histone H1 followed by a co-operative disassembly of the structural order in chromatin. (Figure 7.9).

There remains the issue of how these proteins are targeted. The evidence here remains circumstantial. However, candidates for such targeting proteins are SWI5 for the HO gene and the product of the *trithorax* gene for the action of the *brahma* locus on the activity of homeotic genes.

A corollary to the existence of systems for establishing transcriptional competence would be systems for the maintenance of the repressed state. One such regulator is encoded by the homeotic gene *Polycomb* (*Pc*), which is one of a number of genes that act to repress specific groups of homeotic genes in *Drosophila*. Polycomb protein accumulates at the chromosomal locations of its regulatory targets but does not itself bind DNA. However, it contains a chromobox sequence homologous to that found in the heterochromatin protein HP-1. A possible inference is that *PC* maintains the chromatin of its target genes in a repressed state, structurally similar to that found in heterochromatin and that this

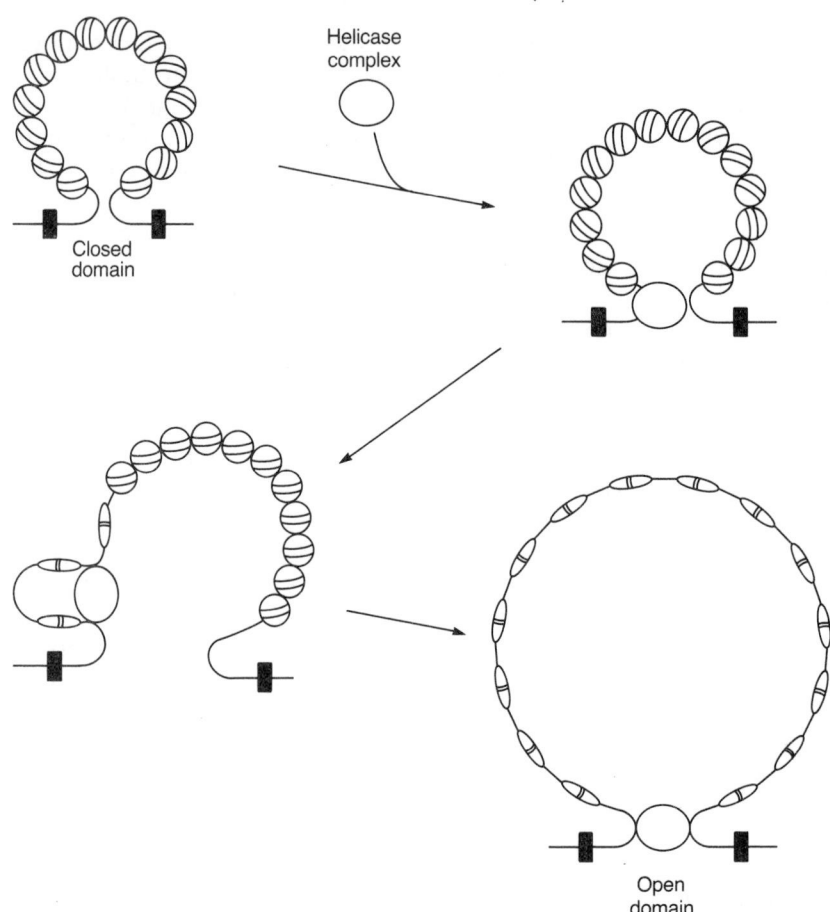

**Figure 7.9** How a DNA helicase might affect chromatin structure.

repression can be counteracted by genes including *trithorax*. Consistent with this idea is the observation that mutations in *Pc*, which relieve repression and result in ectopic expression of certain homeotic genes, are suppressed by mutations in *brahma*.

Again, the maintenance of repression requires that repressing proteins be targeted to the appropriate genes. As yet there is no indication of which DNA-binding protein can interact directly with *Pc*. However, the formation of heterochromatin requires the function of a zinc finger protein as well as HP-1. In this case it seems possible that the establishment of the repressed state involves a multi-protein complex, nucleated by sequence specific DNA binding, with subsequent accretion mediated by protein–protein contacts. A necessary prelude to the establishment of the repressed state is the removal of activator proteins. Again, the possibility exists that, as for the acquisition of transcriptional competence, a processive DNA helicase could actively evict these proteins, thereby allowing a co-operative loss of competence.

## REFERENCES

Almer, A., Rudolph, H., Hinnen, A. and Hörz, W. (1986) Removal of positioned nucleosomes from the yeast PHO5 promoter on PHO5 induction *EMBO Journal* **5**, 2681–7.

Felsenfeld, G. (1992) Chromatin as an essential part of the transcriptional mechanism. *Nature*, **355**, 219–24.

Grunstein, M. (1990) Chromatin and transcription. *Annual Review of Cell Biology*, 643–78.

Peterson, C.L. and Herskowitz, I. Yeast SWI1, SWI2 and SWI3 genes as global activators of transcription. *Cell*, **68**, 573–83.

Richard-Foy, H. and Hager, G.L. (1987) Sequence-specific positioning of nucleosomes over the MMTV promoter. *EMBO Journal*, **6**, 2321–8.

Tamkun, *et al.* (1992) *Brahma*: a regulator of *Drosophila* homeotic genes. *Cell*, **68**, 561–72.

Travers, A.A. (1992) The reprogramming of transcriptional competence. *Cell*, **69**, 573–5.

# Index